*"A well-plotted, multilayered story. . . .
Legal investigator Sara Townley's ingenuity and
resourcefulness shine through."*

—Linda O. Johnston, author of the
Kendra Ballantyne, Pet-Sitter mystery series

Meeting the Informant

Who did this guy think he was, Deep Throat?

"Hello?" Adrenaline made my scalp tingle as I
wrapped my hand more tightly around the keys. Sane
people did not wander down dark alleys at midnight.
I didn't even have a damned flashlight. . . .

"Hello?" I took two steps into the gray alley, away
from the security of the streetlight. My good angel
was whispering, *Don't be a fool—get out.* My bad
angel yelled, *Chicken!* Keeping my back against the
wall, I edged down the alley. I reached the Dumpster,
carefully skirting its hulking mass.

"Is anybody there?"

Two more steps . . . I nearly stepped on him. *Him.*

CATNAPPED

An Animal Instinct Mystery

Gabriella Herkert

AN OBSIDIAN MYSTERY

OBSIDIAN
Published by New American Library, a division of
Penguin Group (USA) Inc., 375 Hudson Street,
New York, New York 10014, USA
Penguin Group (Canada), 90 Eglinton Avenue East, Suite 700, Toronto,
Ontario M4P 2Y3, Canada (a division of Pearson Penguin Canada Inc.)
Penguin Books Ltd., 80 Strand, London WC2R 0RL, England
Penguin Ireland, 25 St. Stephen's Green, Dublin 2,
Ireland (a division of Penguin Books Ltd.)
Penguin Group (Australia), 250 Camberwell Road, Camberwell, Victoria 3124,
Australia (a division of Pearson Australia Group Pty. Ltd.)
Penguin Books India Pvt. Ltd., 11 Community Centre, Panchsheel Park,
New Delhi - 110 017, India
Penguin Group (NZ), 67 Apollo Drive, Rosedale, North Shore 0745,
Auckland, New Zealand (a division of Pearson New Zealand Ltd.)
Penguin Books (South Africa) (Pty.) Ltd., 24 Sturdee Avenue,
Rosebank, Johannesburg 2196, South Africa

Penguin Books Ltd., Registered Offices:
80 Strand, London WC2R 0RL, England

First published by Obsidian, an imprint of New American Library,
a division of Penguin Group (USA) Inc.

First Printing, September 2007
10 9 8 7 6 5 4 3 2 1

Copyright © Gabriella Herkert, 2007
All rights reserved

OBSIDIAN and logo are trademarks of Penguin Group (USA) Inc.

Printed in the United States of America

To my parental units, Christ and Beverly Wendling—
as usual, it's all your fault.

To Ed and Joe—
I was normal until I met you.

To Rolph and Kristen—
you were normal until you met me. Bummer.

To Marschel, Sherry, Teresa, Greg, and Polly—
I'm hoping for a group rate at the home.

And for Ker—
I miss you.

Chapter One

"**D**o I appear to be kidding, Sara?"

Well, he had me there. Senior partners at big Seattle law firms did not kid. They intimidated with pinstripes and Picassos. I'd be more likely to spot a grin on one of the presidents on Mount Rushmore and, in the case of my boss, Morris Allensworth Hamilton IV, more life in the eyes.

"No, sir."

"I expect immediate results."

"Yes, sir."

With a regal nod I was dismissed. I stomped down the three floors to my cubicle near the storage room. As the investigator for the law firm of Abercroft, Hamilton, and Sterns, I didn't expect an invitation to the executive dining room, but for one wild moment I'd actually thought this missing millionaire was my ticket to the big time.

I dropped into my desk chair and pulled my laptop closer, opening a new file.

Name: Flash Millinfield. Age: 10 years. Description: Gray hair, brown eyes, 10 pounds, approximately 12 inches tall. Last known location: Masterson Estate, Mercer Island, Washington. Occupation: Cat. Resources: Sole beneficiary of $2 million trust left by his owner, Millicent Millinfield. Family: None. Reasons for fleeing: See occupation.

After two hours of tedious phone work, my digits ached and I wasn't any closer to finding my missing cat. I flipped through the thin file my boss's secretary, widely known as Elizabeth the Evil, had deigned to let me copy. In it was a photo of my missing client lounging casually in a backyard hammock. If my life were to progress to lounging, I wouldn't be missing. I took a Snickers bar from my desk, unwrapped the candy and took a bite, letting the chocolate and caramel swirl on my tongue as consolation for my frustrated professional ambitions.

"I'd love one, thanks." Joe Nelson said from the opening to my cubicle. He slouched across the room and slumped into my visitor's chair.

I tossed him a candy bar.

"Joe, you're going to have to stop sleeping in your clothes. You're a Harvard graduate shar-pei." He leaned back in the chair, closing his eyes. His perpetual associate pallor was an unhealthy compliment to eye circles that rivaled Spuds MacKenzie's.

"Mmm."

"And you might consider real food once in a while."

"I'm on that." His eyes suddenly blinked open, a flash of navy blue. "What did the big boss want?"

"He gave me an important new case."

If I was going to lie, I'd tell whoppers.

"A personal audience?"

"Yeah. It's a pretty big deal. Missing, uh, heir. Millionaire. In fact, I'd better get back to it." I made a show of shifting papers on my desk.

"Sure." He pushed himself up and started to shuffle away. "If I were you," he threw over his shoulder, "I'd start with the local cathouse."

"If you knew, why the heck did you ask?" I called to him.

"I was making polite conversation." He grabbed the top of the cubicle wall to peer over, his eyes dancing. "I consider it the cost of the candy bar."

He dropped out of view.

"I hope you enjoyed it, because it's your last, buddy."

His laugh floated to me. He was right, of course. My missing-cat case was a dog. Typical of my boss's commitment to my career growth, but a blow to my ego nonetheless. Still, a visit to the pet-sitter would get me out of the office on a sunny day so my life didn't seem so much like life imprisonment without parole.

The drive to Mercer Island took two hours, but the house was worth it. It was magnificent; a gabled antebellum fantasy. The front door opened and a tall, silverhaired man stepped out. He was dressed in crisp white walking shorts and a purple short-sleeved shirt. Sort of a yuppie Weight Watchers Santa.

"Ms. Townley? I'm Jeff Randall. Thank you for coming." His smile warmed blue eyes. "Please come in." He led the way into the house. I took off my sunglasses, blinking as my eyes adjusted. Okay, so I wasn't in Kansas anymore. Heavy carved furniture, plush carpets, gilded mirrors. I'd seen more user-friendly museums. All they needed were red ropes and KEEP OFF THE FURNITURE signs.

Jeff gestured to a chair with spindly legs and brocade silk coverings.

"Thanks, no. I know you've already searched, but I'd like a quick look around, if that's okay."

He smiled warmly. "You're a woman after my own heart. Straight to work it is. Shall we start in the kitchen?"

"Great." I followed him into a restaurant-sized kitchen. "When was the last time you saw the cat?"

"Monday night." He leaned against the counter, arms folded across his chest as I wandered around the room. I gestured toward one cabinet and he nodded.

I circled the room, opening cabinets without any idea what I was looking for. Paw prints? Ransom note demanding catnip from a neighborhood tom with a bad reputation?

"Does the cat have the run of the house?" I followed Jeff into a pantry, looking behind boxes and a bag of specialty cat food that leaned against the wall, a few morsels spilling onto the white linoleum. Must be the maid's day off.

"The doors upstairs are kept closed, although I've checked all the rooms since I realized he was missing. Other than that, he's free to go wherever he chooses."

Returning to the living room, I checked behind drapes and couches, resisting the urge to trill, "Here, kitty, kitty."

"Has he ever gone missing before?" I asked.

"He's a cat." Jeff shrugged. "I am, however oddly, responsible for his well-being. It feels like that should include finding out where he's going; then I remember he's a cat. Anyway, I felt I should inform someone, and here you are."

"Any chance he got out? An open door or window?" We moved to a sitting room decorated in the same heavy oak style of the living room.

"The house has been vacant. The owner, Stuart Masterson, is away on business. None of the help lives in. Millicent Millinfield did while she was alive, but her position hasn't been filled since her death. The cleaning girl only comes on Friday." Jeff stood behind a hideous green armchair.

"How did she die?"

"Millicent?"

"Yes."

"She was involved in one of those multiple-car pileups that inevitably make the ten-o'clock news."

"I'm sorry."

"I appreciate that, but I barely knew her and I'm sure it was quick."

"So, Millicent died and the cat stayed? That's kind of funny."

"I never really thought about it, but I suppose it is. Millicent had lived in before her death. I guess being personal assistant to a billionaire requires around-the-clock attention. It must pay well, too. The trust was quite a surprise. Who leaves millions to a pet? The cat was hers, and . . . well, no one actually said anything about the cat, one way or another. I was already staying in the guesthouse. The trust company contacted me to take care of the cat."

"And Stuart Masterson didn't object to the cat staying in the house without Millicent?"

"No one said anything to me. Maybe Stuart Masterson is a cat person. Maybe he let the cat stay because they shared a banker."

"That's a good deal."

"For me as well."

"What's Stuart Masterson like?"

"I haven't actually met him." Jeff shrugged. "It's too bad, because from everything I've read, he's quite a character."

"What do you mean?" I poked my head into a little library with beautiful first editions behind heavy leaded-glass bookshelves.

" 'Eccentric' is charitable, I suppose. He's mercurial. He has been reported to disappear and reappear in dramatic fashion. The magazines say he's made fortunes and lost them over his career, making headlines along the way."

"You said you haven't met him?" I asked, reading spines. There was probably a fortune in this room alone.

Jeff ran a finger along a Chinese vase sitting on a small table. "I suppose anyone can be a little starstruck." He gestured toward the door and I preceded him.

"I won't tell," I whispered.

He winked. "I appreciate that."

"What about other people? Has anyone else been in the house recently?"

"Perhaps I shouldn't speak out of school, but . . ."

I waited. People always talked if you waited. I'd seen it on *CSI*. Ten seconds of silence and nuns confessed. Still, Jeff seemed pretty casual. No fidgeting or eye twitching. Then again, he was a guy dedicated to finding a cat. Not exactly on *America's Most Wanted*.

"Mr. Masterson's children have been here. His business partner's been here as well."

"Is that unusual?" I peered into a small closet.

"I don't believe Stuart's on good terms with either his children or his partner." After checking a guest bathroom bigger than my living room, where a full cat dish and litter box appeared untouched, we climbed a marble staircase. Marble, for Pete's sake. We walked the length of the hallway without opening the doors.

"Why?"

"The children—grown men, actually—have . . . well, problems."

"What sort of problems?"

"Drugs, I believe. Flowing from that, money problems. I believe Mr. Masterson has adopted a tough-love approach that has caused a rift in the relationship."

"Cut them off, huh?"

Jeff smiled. "Perhaps."

I followed him into a small sitting room. How many rooms did this mausoleum have, anyway?

"And the business partner?"

"Former business partner, recently disengaged from employment and resorting to that all-American sport, litigation."

That was a very classy way to say *fired*. He had style. I swallowed a laugh.

"What does Masterson Enterprises do, exactly?" I asked.

"Don't quote me on this, but I believe it's an IP trolling firm."

I stared.

"They purchase or invent intellectual property. Patents, that sort of thing. Then they license them to different companies all over the world that actually incorporate the designs and products in their own products."

"So Masterson Enterprises doesn't actually make anything?"

"No."

"Which is why Stuart Masterson can run the thing out of his house, I suppose."

"Well, there are a couple hundred employees all over the world, of course. Inventors in their garages. Lawyers in fancy downtown offices. Accountants in home-office cubbyholes. But, yes, the main business is actually run from here on a virtual basis."

"Do any of these people have keys?"

"Not the regular employees, certainly. The others, I don't know. Henry Jepsen might. He's the partner. Stuart and Sterling, the heirs apparent, have always struck me more as the unauthorized-entry types." Surprised, I stopped, turning to look at him. His lips were pursed, his eyebrows raised. We laughed. "Of course, I'll deny that if you repeat it."

I moved my fingers to my lips, turning an invisible key. Okay, it was a stupid case, but he was a nice guy and I should really just get on with it.

"Have you checked with the neighbors? If he did get out, maybe someone's seen him."

"I posted his picture and knocked on a few doors. No luck." We left the house and stood on the wide porch, a faint breeze stirring the too-warm August air.

"Do you mind if I see the picture?"

"Certainly. This way."

I followed Jeff to the guesthouse. I waited at my car while he disappeared inside, returning a minute later with a color picture in a silver frame, and a black-and-white handbill. He gave me both.

I looked at the picture first. It showed a too-blond middle-aged woman in a stylish suit holding a limp gray-and-white cat, dangling over one arm. Feline civil protestor carted off by the police.

"I take it this is the infamous Flash?"

Jeff smiled. "The limp gray one, yes."

I smiled back. "And his esteemed benefactress?"

"Millicent, yes."

I handed the frame back to Jeff and looked at the paper. He'd used the photo to make the flyer, adding REWARD on top and a phone number at the bottom.

"You get many calls on this?"

"A few. Most of them seemed . . . how shall I put it . . . challenged? Or perhaps they were just kids." He sighed. "What will you do next?"

"I'd like to check around some more. Call the shelters. You might want to leave food and water on the porch. He might show up if he's hungry."

"I simply cannot believe I've spent two whole days in pursuit of a recalcitrant cat." He shook his head, his hands on his hips. "It's not a very dignified activity for a reasonably intelligent adult. Two adults, now that you've joined the search party."

I pulled open my car door, reaching inside for a business card and pen. Quickly, I scratched my home number on the back of the card and handed it to him.

"Give me a call if he turns up. Otherwise, you'll be hearing from me tomorrow."

"Despite the circumstances, I'm delighted to meet you, Sara Townley." He offered his hand and we shook. He really was very charming. I suppose if I had to have a stupid case, it helped to know that the client wasn't laughing at me; he was laughing with me.

Yeah, right.

Chapter Two

I went home to self-medicate with kung pao chicken. So, my career was going nowhere and hell was five degrees cooler than my apartment. I had a fan and a fortune cookie. Things could be worse. There were probably hundreds, tens, or at least one other thirty-four-year-old cat detective without MSG. Somewhere.

I reached the heavy glass security door and fumbled for my keys. My peripheral vision caught a flash inside the door just before it opened to reveal my best friend, Russ.

"Today is your lucky day." Russ's melodious tenor was pitched to its seductive best, dripping drama. I refused to ask, knowing it would drive him crazy. At six-one, with a swimmer's broad shoulders, narrow hips, and the grace of a dancer, Russ wasn't often ignored. His chocolate eyes and leering grin told me he didn't expect me to end his streak.

"If it's Ed McMahon, I prefer cash." I flashed him a smile and kissed his cheek.

"Aren't you going to ask?" He took my take-out bag and opened it for a better look.

"I know how you feel about gossip. I wouldn't want to compromise you. Besides, aren't your love-struck fans waiting for your radio show to start?" I stopped long enough to wrestle envelopes from my narrow mailbox.

"I've got a couple of minutes before I have to be at

work." Russ followed me into the elevator, rocking back on his heels as I closed the gate and pushed the button for the fourth floor.

"I can't stand it. Why can't you just ask like a normal person?"

"And spoil your fun?"

He moved to face me, glaring. "I'm only telling you to save you the embarrassment of walking into your place with that hair." He rolled his eyes and I smoothed my hair reflexively. "You've got company. Tall. Blond. Gorgeous." He raised one eyebrow suggestively. "Married."

The elevator's grinding gears echoed loudly in the tiny space.

"You've been holding out on me." He grinned. "You never said anything about emerald eyes. And I definitely would have remembered you mentioning that butt."

"He's here? How do you know?" I croaked. I swayed a little, my mind refusing to process the information. The elevator came to a shuddering stop, but I was frozen in place. Russ peered at me for a moment before reaching past me to open the gate. He pushed me into the hall.

"I bumped into him in the elevator. We introduced ourselves like civilized people. He's been here since noon. And you won't need the moo shu. He's cooking."

"Cooking? Cooking where?" Barely whispering, I stared toward my apartment.

"Your place, of course." Russ's expression clouded. "Sit down. Put your head between your knees. Take deep breaths." He nudged me toward a heavy armchair opposite the elevator doors.

"You let him in?" I was appalled, gaping at him before dropping my head down and gasping for air.

"Of course not. He was already in. I assumed he had a key. He is, after all, your husband. I had been thinking you'd made the whole story up, since I wasn't invited to the wedding." He pouted a little. "Then again, he seemed pretty real this afternoon."

I lifted my head. "What am I going to do? What am I supposed to say?"

"Gee, I don't know. How about, 'Hi, honey, what's for dinner?' Maybe Miss Manners has a chapter on renewing acquaintance with disappearing husbands. I mean, there must be thousands of women who meet a guy in Vegas, spend a week doing God knows what, and then get married, only to have the guy disappear for four months with no explanation."

"I'm gonna be sick." I put my head back between my knees.

"For someone constitutionally incapable of being disconcerted, you're doing a pretty good impression of a damsel with the vapors. Unfortunately, there's no time to do anything about the clothes. My advice is to get naked as soon as possible. Maybe he won't notice."

Russ grabbed my hand and dragged me to my apartment door. I dug my heels in.

"There isn't anything you aren't telling me, right?" Russ asked, suddenly serious.

"Like?"

"I don't know. He's a wife beater. A loan shark. A Republican. Whatever kept you from telling your best friend all the details."

I swallowed hard. What was I going to say? I hadn't told Russ. I couldn't even explain why. It was the only thing he didn't know. My childhood. Foster care. My maybe-dead-but-more-likely-lying-in-wait drunk of a father. Bankruptcy and what I'd done to make ends meet. He'd held my hand and kicked my butt and cried for me. Then there was Connor, and he was beautiful and scary and out of control, and I couldn't share it with anyone. Russ knew everything about me except my husband, and my husband didn't know me at all.

"Nothing like that," I whispered.

Russ stared straight into my eyes. He tugged a curl and patted my shoulder. Then he nodded.

"History favors the brave," Russ soothed in my ear. He reached past me, turned the knob, and pushed hard. I stumbled forward. Leaning close, he whispered, "I'll want details," and left on a wave of egg roll perfume.

I stood absolutely still. He was moving around. Closing things. Cooking . . . onions. It smelled like onions. In my kitchen. The one he'd never seen. Never even asked to see. A quickie wedding, four months of near silence, and then . . . well, invasion.

I brought my left hand up, searching for the small scar on my ring finger. I probably should have told him I was allergic to metal before he'd given me the ring. Two hours and a visit to the emergency room later and my finger had been branded for life. The scar was the only tangible proof that I'd been married. Until onions.

"Are you coming in?"

I flinched. Running would be stupid. It was my apartment. Attack didn't seem that great an idea either. His silhouette was bigger than I'd remembered. When in doubt, pretend nothing's wrong.

"Hi, honey, what's for dinner?" A little too Doris Day but not bad, all things considered.

"Burritos." He shifted and I could suddenly see him clearly. Asthetically pleasing. Cowboy fit. Emerald eyes. Military haircut. Tight black T-shirt and faded blue jeans. Man, when I went nuts I did it for a good cause. He was beautiful. Sexy. Barefoot. Okay, so he made himself at home.

"Dinner's ready. You coming?" He turned and strolled into the kitchen. The jeans were good from this angle, too. It didn't absolve his sneak-attack tactics, but it wasn't half-bad.

I followed him into my tiny kitchen. He moved to the stove while I stared at the narrow wicker bistro table. It held filled juice glasses and navy blue place mats I'd never seen before. A water glass full of colorful flowers sat next to the wall. Maybe the navy was just a cover he used. Maybe he was from one of those commando home-makeover programs. Either way, I'd just keep my cool and act natural.

"Why are you here, Connor?" I blurted.

He never looked up. "Because you're here."

He turned with a plate in either hand heaped with the

biggest burritos I'd ever seen. After staring me down for a full ten seconds, he placed the plates on the table and came over to pull my chair out for me. Automatically I sat down.

"Eat before it gets cold."

I pulled the napkin from its place under the silverware and placed it on my lap. The food smelled delicious. No word for four months; then we're sitting down to dinner like an old married couple. It was totally weird. Why was he here? What did he want? Divorce. He must want a divorce. Dinner was just a way to keep things amicable. The smell of burritos was a sedative to the senses. It was the only thing that made sense. I set my fork down, my appetite vanishing.

"It's fine with me," I told him. "It's the right thing. The only thing, really. It won't be a problem."

"You're not eating. Don't you like it?"

"No. I mean, yes. Sure. Whatever," I took a bite. Damn, he could cook, too. That was a shame. "I'll take care of it."

"Take care of what?"

"The divorce."

"What divorce?" Connor continued to eat so calmly I wanted to scream. He could at least pretend to be a little sorry we were breaking up.

"Our divorce." Belligerence bled into my voice.

"We're not getting a divorce."

"We're not?" The squeak in my voice infuriated me.

"No, we're not."

"I think we should."

"No."

"It's not just up to you, Connor. And I think we should get a divorce."

"No. Do you want more salsa?"

I glared at him but he just kept eating, his eyes steady on mine, his face expressionless. He never looked at his plate and he didn't drop a bite. It wasn't human. I tried a new tack.

"Impulsive Vegas marriages don't last. We need to face facts."

"Don't generalize. Our marriage wasn't impulsive; it was instinctive. There's a difference."

"Do tell."

"An impulse is a spontaneous urge. Instinct is the accumulation of learning, adaptation, and evolution. It's much more reliable."

"No one evolves that much in a week." I pushed my plate away.

"Obviously I did."

"Connor—"

"No divorce. Which I believe I mentioned at the time."

"You can't hold me accountable for things you said to me when you weren't wearing clothes."

He laughed and I felt my face heat.

"I'll remember that. You see, we've already resolved one issue."

"So, let me get this straight. We get married. I'm still not too sure how that happened, but let's forget about that for a second. Four months pass with random, impersonal contact, and I'm on the verge of putting your face on a milk carton when you turn up and we're suddenly a regular married couple."

Connor finally put down his fork, his smile fading.

" 'Regular' might not be accurate. As for the rest, 'restricted exercise' means limited outside contact. When I could, I wrote or called. You could really use a cell phone, by the way. The second I was wheels-down I came here. It's not a great answer, but it's what we have. All we need is to spend some time together. And I didn't hit you over the head with the details the second you got home because you were already thinking about running." He rested his arms on the table, one hand covering the other above his empty plate.

"I don't run."

"The Roadrunner has nothing on you. Hell, you spent five minutes trying to convince yourself to leave the entryway."

"I was surprised; that's all."

"Shocked is more like it. I told you I'd come."

I jumped up from the table, stepping to the sink and pushing my uneaten burrito into the disposal before rinsing the plate.

"My job will take a little while to get used to, honey. That's all." He raised his voice above the gushing spray.

That's all. Understatement of the year. I turned the faucet to hot, nearly scalding my hands. Jumping back, I gripped the edge of the sink. Connor reached past me and turned the water off before taking me by the shoulders and turning me toward him. I stared at his hand holding my shoulder. Geez, the guy even had beautiful hands. I swallowed hard, my eyes focusing on the weave of his T-shirt as it strained across his chest. I could see the cotton flex with each breath he took. Slow, deep breaths.

"Sara?"

I didn't dare meet his eyes.

"Sara?" His hands moved to tangle with mine, interlacing our fingers.

Our hands looked . . . married. *Oh, my God.* For the first time it felt real. Really real. Like I hadn't imagined it. I couldn't breathe. A husband. My husband.

I looked up. The rush went all the way to my toes. *Wow.*

"Yeah, um, what?" That Marilyn Monroe breathiness couldn't possibly be me.

"We're agreed then."

I couldn't say anything. I couldn't think anything. And I really wished he would just shut up and kiss me. He was leaning down so close. Maybe if I just stood on my tiptoes . . .

Suddenly we were kissing. Not hello-how're-you-doing-cousin kind of kissing either. Honest-to-God-I-remember-seeing-you-naked kissing. He broke contact, holding my upper arms and creating an inch of space between our bodies.

"Connor?"

"I'm not starting my honeymoon in the damn kitchen."

It took a moment for my mind to translate his words

into comprehensible English. Honeymoon. Kitchen. We were still in the kitchen. Linoleum had never seemed romantic to me before then. I gulped back a giggle. He might have created physical space between our bodies, but his eyes were moving over me with the touch of a fevered caress. His lips were parted and his breath came in harsh little gasps. Power made me giddy.

"That's okay, since, as part of my move-in special, my landlord threw in a bedroom."

I took his hand, leading him out of the kitchen and through the living room into the bedroom. I stopped inches from the bed and turned. Connor, backlit from the living room, stripped off his T-shirt and dropped it to the floor. I reached forward and slid my hands from his shoulders to his flat belly, feeling the breath he raked in and held, noting the fine tension in the muscles that flexed beneath his warm skin. I leaned forward and planted an openmouthed kiss just above where his dog tags lay suspended from a chain. His hand cradled my chin and tipped my head up, and then we were kissing. Mouths open and exploring. Hands touching and stroking. His lips were against my cheek, my ear, my neck. His fingers fumbled between us, tugging at my blouse. Connor lifted his head and took a half step backward, peering down at the delicate silk.

His hands grasped the gaping edges of the blouse and jerked it open, a sharp ripping sound filling the air as the buttons popped off. Direct was good. I could handle direct. Connor proved much more adroit at the removal of my bra. Bare from the waist up, I threw my arms around him and held him close, shuddering at the friction of his chest against mine.

"You've got about five seconds to get naked, Sara." I lifted one foot, dispatching a shoe while holding on to Connor for balance. By the time I had rid myself of the second shoe, Connor had my trousers unfastened and was sliding them down my legs, taking my panties and my socks with them. I reached for the buttons on his jeans and yanked, but only the top button came free. I pulled a second and then a third time.

"You know, all things considered, Connor, button-fly jeans might not be the right answer for someone in your, um, situation. For future reference, I mean."

He reached down and tore the jeans free, shucking them down his legs and off in one motion. We fell together onto the bed, scooting toward the center.

"The jeans seemed like a good safety valve."

"That Levi Strauss had no sense of brotherhood."

"External impulse control. It seemed like a good idea, since my body has known since this morning that I was coming."

I couldn't help myself. I laughed.

"I meant here. Coming here, Sara."

I laughed harder at his aggrieved tone. Then he kissed me and I didn't laugh any more.

We spooned for a long time afterward. A Navy SEAL cuddler. Go figure. Unused to sharing my bed with anyone, I was uncomfortable with his arm beneath me, and I really wanted to switch pillows with him. I always slept on the same pillow. Always. I'd just have to wait until he fell asleep, then take my pillow back.

"I hadn't planned it quite like this," Connor murmured into my ear.

"You were thinking dominoes?" I lifted onto an elbow, twisting so I could share my disbelief with a look.

Gold-tipped lashes fluttered over twinkling green eyes. A small, self-deprecating smile touched his lips.

"Well, I'd meant to talk about things before we ended up in bed."

Suddenly wary, I lay back down, turning my back and pulling myself toward the edge of the bed. Leave it to me to hook up with the only macho guy on the planet who wanted to talk about things. He snuggled closer.

"We did talk. We're not getting a divorce. Then we went to bed. It's not exactly world peace we're negotiating."

He sighed against the back of my neck. I could feel him sitting up before he reached across me to turn on the bedside light. I reached for the discarded sheet, keeping my back to him and my eyes closed.

"Sit up and talk to me, Sara."

"Let's talk in the morning." Whatever happened to rolling over and going to sleep? Didn't he read the guy guide?

"Let's talk now. We should have talked it out before we made love."

His hands touched my shoulders, tugging gently, pulling me toward the center of the bed and into a semireclining position. Grudgingly, I abandoned my possum pose, opening my eyes, leaning forward, and propping myself up with the ill-favored pillow, careful to keep the sheet tucked under my arms. Connor exhibited no such modesty. Distracted, I pulled at the sheet, flipping the extra material over his lap. He grabbed my wrist.

"What?" I asked.

"What does marriage mean to you, Sara?"

Curveball. Was he looking for Webster or Dr. Phil? I sat up straighter.

"I don't know, Connor."

His zero-to-sixty change of direction was scaring me. I hated being scared. I pulled my arm away and he let go. I tried to figure out a way to get some clothes on without either walking naked across the room or stripping the sheet from Connor so he'd be back to his birthday suit. Naked seemed . . . well, really naked right then.

"To me, marriage means commitment," Connor said.

I turned to find him staring at me. I stared back.

"Commitment. That sounds right." I searched his face, but I didn't have a clue about where he was going. "Are you talking about moving? Living together? Is that possible with your job? You're not going to give up the SEALs, are you? You love the navy."

"It's not about my job."

I was confused for a moment before panic set in.

"You're not expecting me to move, are you? I've got

a whole life here, Connor. Friends, a job, a Starbucks on every corner." The thought of leaving everything I had in Seattle settled into my stomach like a stone.

"It's not about any damn job," Connor said. He flung back the sheet and strode across the room. He paced to the bathroom door, then back. He ran his hands through his hair, completely oblivious to his own nakedness. I wouldn't be that oblivious if the building fell down. I twined the sheet around me and went to the dresser, turning my back on Connor as I pulled a T-shirt, underwear, and shorts from the drawer. I gritted my teeth and dropped my cloth shield. Slowed by fumbling fingers, I dressed before turning back to him.

He seemed . . . calm. Not frustrated or even mildly irritated anymore. Left behind was a determined expression and controlled patience. I'd rather have him explode than humor me. Finally he pulled his jeans on, without bothering to button them. I did my best not to let my eyes trace the pattern of hair as it disappeared beneath denim. What was wrong with me? *Focus, Sara.*

"Are you committed to me, Sara? To our marriage?"

"Yes." I braced myself against the dresser. "We can work it out, Connor. Lots of people do the long-distance thing." Even I was surprised to hear me say it. Great sex had me addled. "We can work something out." His silent regard unnerved me. I was starting to sweat, my heart hammering so loudly I was sure he could hear it across the room.

"Forget logistics. We'll figure them out later. Right now let's stick to the basics."

"Basics?"

He walked slowly across the room to stand directly in front of me. My hands tightened their grip on the dresser before he reached out and touched my arms, sliding his hands down and tugging until his hands were holding mine tightly. His emerald eyes bored into me. "Where is your wedding ring?"

"My, um, wedding ring?" When had I gone stupid?

"You know, the symbol of our love and fidelity."

"I'm allergic." I pulled my hands free, stooping to pick up the discarded sheet and moving back toward the bed.

"You're allergic?"

I threw the sheet across the bed, smoothing it into place before tucking it in.

"Yeah. Pretty much to all metal. Well, maybe I wouldn't be to the really good stuff." Mortified, I kept my eyes fixed on the pattern of the sheet. "I'm not implying my ring wasn't good or anything. I just meant . . . Oh, Christ, I can't really wear jewelry; that's all." I moved to the other side of the bed, smoothing nonexistent creases.

"And that's all?"

"Of course that's all. What did you think?" I did look at him then.

"You seem a little unsure, Sara. And I clearly came as a surprise to your friend Russ. I guess I'm just wondering if you're not wearing your ring because our marriage is some sort of secret you're keeping from the people close to you." Connor stood quietly, his face composed.

"I haven't been scouted by the CIA. If I'd tried to keep a white dress and afterglow to myself, my head would have exploded. And I did tell Russ. Well, sort of."

"What did you sort of tell him?" A red heat showed itself along Connor's cheekbones.

"Well, um." There was a right answer here but I doubted *I was overwhelmed by lust* was it. I couldn't say that. I'd sound like a slut.

The phone rang.

Chapter Three

After taking the phone call and tossing a vague explanation about a break in an important case in Connor's direction, I raced out of the apartment as if fleeing Alcatraz. I definitely need to work on my casual act. Mr. No Divorce didn't break a sweat.

Connor hadn't tried to stop me. He hadn't yelled or sulked or any of the things any normal human being would have done. Wasn't he mad? He'd been . . . I don't know . . . calm. Controlled. Creeping me out.

Jeff Randall opened his front door as I stepped from my car. "I didn't really expect you to come out here this late."

"It's no problem, Jeff." *And you've got really good timing.*

"Please, come in."

I followed him to the living room, sitting on the couch while Jeff dropped into an armchair.

"So what's up?" My mind was still on Connor. Guilt at my own cowardice chewed at my conscience. Life had suddenly gotten very complicated.

"Sara?"

I shook my head, bringing my attention back to Jeff. "I'm sorry. What did you say?"

"I just wanted to tell you about a phone call I got earlier. He said he had information about Flash, but if this is a bad time . . ." There was definite puzzlement in his blue gaze.

"No. It's nothing. Did this man give you a name?" I reached for my notebook before realizing I'd come out of the house in just my T-shirt and jeans.

"No. He just said he knew something about Flash and that we should get together to discuss it." Jeff crossed his legs, letting his hands rest along the arms of the chair.

"And did you agree to go?"

"He wanted to meet in Pioneer Square at midnight. It seemed rather odd to me." He shrugged. "Still, if he knows something, I didn't want to just dismiss it. I called you to ask your advice. Actually, I thought I'd be able to tell you all of this over the phone, but you didn't really give me a chance."

I tucked my hair behind my ear, feeling my face heat with embarrassment. I could hardly say I'd needed a reason to get out of my own place. I crossed my legs.

"Yes, um, well, where exactly were you supposed to meet this guy?"

"Pioneer Square. An alley on the south side of the square, off Yesler."

"Did the caller ask for money?"

"He said we could come to an arrangement, but he didn't mention any figure."

"Okay. I appreciate the call, Jeff." I stood up and he did, too, following me to the front door.

"Are you going to this meeting?"

"I'm just going to go and have a look."

"It's a rough neighborhood. Maybe you should reconsider. It's probably a wild-goose chase, anyway. Someone looking for a reward because of the flyers."

"You're probably right." I patted him on the upper arm. "Don't worry. I'll be fine. Like I said, I'm just going to have a quick look." *And put off going home for a little while longer.*

"You're the expert. Be careful, Sara."

"I always am."

*   *   *

I parked under a streetlight across from the alley in Pioneer Square, the windows rolled three-quarters of the way up despite the still-stifling temperature. What could this guy possibly have to say that required meeting in an alley in the dead of night? Still, if I solved this case in a day, even Morris would be impressed. Then maybe I'd finally get some real casework instead of all this stupid paper-trail stuff. And it beat the heck out of going home to explain my sexual addictions to Connor. Carefully surveying my surroundings, I took note of the only other person in the square, lying on a bench not three feet away, one fist wrapped around the leg of a shopping cart. Another five minutes; then I'd go. As anxious as I was to find the cat, I wasn't going to sit out here with a bull's-eye on my back, even if it did mean I wasn't at home explaining myself to Connor. Geez, what a mess.

A knock on the window and I screamed, nearly hitting my head on the roof. After a quick look, I rolled the window down.

"Do not scare me like that."

"You?" Russ scoffed. "That scream nearly gave me a heart attack. Besides, you called me, remember?"

"Get in."

Russ went to the other side of the car and I reached over to unlock it. He slid into the passenger seat.

"Where'd you park?"

"Right behind you, Marlowe. I switched off the headlights a block back, just like you asked. For which you owe me combat pay, which I will forgo only in favor of lurid details of your marital reconciliation."

I slapped him on the leg.

"Why are we here when you could be there? Discord already?"

"I'm working a case."

"So why did you need me, Tonto? Wouldn't the navy have been a smarter call?"

"The navy . . . well, don't go there. Besides, haven't we always done the real crazy stuff together? For the last eight years, anyway? You wouldn't want me to hurt your feelings by excluding you from situations where bail might prove necessary. You'd do the boo-boo-lip thing, and you know I can't take that."

"You're babbling."

He was right. I was babbling. Nerves or marriage. Probably both.

"As entertaining as I am finding it," Russ said, "I have to be back to the station in fifteen minutes or that idiot engineer will start playing 'Feelings.' I'm pretty sure he's on Prozac."

"You're Tonto. I'm the Lone Ranger." I went back to scanning the street.

"Keep dreaming, kemo sabe."

"Right. Anyway, I just need you to watch my back if this guy shows up."

"What guy?"

"I'm not sure."

"Well, he picked a really nice place to pick up women."

I stared at him. "It's . . . atmospheric."

"So was the Bates Motel. This is a stupid idea, Sara."

"It's not a big deal. I'm just going to talk to him."

"Is he just going to talk to you?"

I sighed. Russ was right. This was universally stupid. I wouldn't even have considered it if I hadn't been so eager to get out the door before the heart-to-heart got ugly. I was not good with the Hallmark moments.

"You're right," I told Russ.

"Oh, my God. You didn't just say—dare I believe it— 'You are right, O magnificent one.' "

"Good thing you were sitting down," I said dryly.

"Absolutely. I could have bruised myself with a swoon."

I laughed. He would swoon, too. "Okay, buddy, we're calling it a day."

"Thank goodness. The FCC has really been cracking down on felony Muzak." Russ reached for the door and hesitated. "Seriously, everything okay at home?"

"It's a work in progress, I guess."

"You okay?"

"Sure. I'm tough."

"Yeah. You and the Stay Puft Marshmallow Man. I'm on the air until six a.m. Call me if you need me."

"You're a pal."

"Love you."

"Love you, too."

Russ got out. I reached across and locked his door, watching him get into his car. He pulled around me and tooted his horn. I watched him go. I had to go home. Eventually. What the hell was I going to say?

My peripheral vision caught a faint red glow. A cigarette, maybe? I leaned forward, arms resting on the steering wheel, trying to pick it out of the darkness. Was that him? Jeff had said the alley, and I'd assumed he meant out in the open. Maybe this guy really was the shy type. I looked for Russ's taillights but he was already gone. Stupid. This was really dumb. Of course, it did put off going home for another few minutes. It would take ten seconds. And I was already here.

I checked the sleeping homeless man, then the street. Only the glow of the cigarette disturbed the night. I got out, carefully relocking the car. The quiet click reassured me as much as the hard press of my keys as I laced them between my fingers. I crossed the street, angling toward the alley opening. I caught the faint, acrid smell of a cigar as I neared the alley, hesitating for a moment before stepping under the streetlight. A dim bulb glowed above a hulking Dumpster halfway down the alley. Who did this guy think he was, Deep Throat?

"Hello?" Adrenaline made my scalp tingle as I wrapped my hand more tightly around the keys. Sane people did not wander down dark alleys at midnight. I didn't even have a damned flashlight. I made a deal with myself: I'd go as far as the lightbulb I could see halfway down the alley. If I didn't find the guy, I'd do the sane thing and get the hell out of Dodge.

"Hello?" I took two steps into the gray of the alley, away from the security of the streetlight. Another drift of cigar smoke assaulted my senses, mingling with the smell of rotting garbage. My good angel was whispering, *Don't be a fool—get out.* My bad angel yelled, *Chicken.* Keeping my back against the wall, I edged down the alley. I reached the Dumpster, carefully skirting its hulking mass.

"Is anybody there?"

Two more steps and I reached the end of the trash container, stepping into the weak light provided by the bulb. I nearly stepped on him. *Him. Holy shit.*

The tepid light barely managed to illuminate the circle at my feet beyond the fuzzy gray of ashes. The man was behind the trash container, out of view from the street. He was faced away from me, lying on his side, one arm stretched in front of him, the other hidden from view. Nausea rose in me. I brought my hands up, covering my mouth, my keys digging deeply into my left hand. I bolted upright at a sudden scurrying beneath the trash can. I shuddered at the thought of rats. It took all my will to sidle closer to the man. A trail of sweat rolled between my breasts, chilling my entire body. Despite the lingering heat, I shivered. I should help him. He could be drunk or sick or injured, needing help. I should do something.

I straightened, peering around the Dumpster toward the streetlight, moving a step closer to the body. Without taking my eyes from the alley in front of me, I reached out with the toe of my new running shoes and touched him. He was stiff. *Oh, God.* What the hell was I doing here? I forced myself to look at the man; then I couldn't look away. My feet remained frozen, refusing to move, to help me escape. Queasiness came in waves, and my hands began to sweat. I took another small step before kneeling behind him, tugging at the silken cloth of his shoulder, turning him toward me. Dark purple made a bold statement against his white shirt. The underlying coppery scent cloyed at my throat. It was the genetic equivalent of the inkblot test.

My scream echoed in the alley as a new fear struck:

The killer could still be out there. Waiting for me. I stayed low, frantically searching the deep shadows. A crash erupted behind me. My feet finally received the message from my sluggish brain and I was running for my life. I didn't look around. My blood pounded in my ears. My legs churned. I glanced over my shoulder and the lights went out.

Chapter Four

I woke up with the worst hangover of my entire life. In that first instant I couldn't remember having had anything to drink. Then my surroundings started to sink in. I was lying on my back in the middle of the cold street. Three distorted faces peered down at me as if I had been dropped down a well. Emergency vehicles were parked in a scatter pattern, their headlights creating the illusion of daylight. The raging sirens and strobing red lights made me my stomach heave, and I closed my eyes as I fought the need to be sick.

"Hey, try to stay with us now," a calm male voice said as a hand lightly patted my cheek. "Stay awake. I'm a paramedic. You've hit your head. Can you open your eyes?" The voice and hands prodded simultaneously.

I blinked up at him, then squinted to avoid the flashlight the sadist shone in my eyes.

"Okay, can you tell me your name?"

"Sara."

"What's your last name, Sara?"

"Townley."

"Where do you live?"

"Seattle. Downtown."

"When were you born?"

"None of your business."

"That's fair." His inflection never changed. "You were unconscious for a couple of minutes, Sara. That means a probable concussion. We're going to put you into the ambulance and ride you downtown so the doc can have a look. Is that okay with you, Sara?" Without waiting for a reply, he continued, "On my count, one, two, three."

The chatty paramedic and a silent companion slid me onto a gurney, covered me with a sheet, and pushed me to the back of the waiting ambulance. Another man appeared, grabbing at the arm of the first paramedic.

"I need to talk to her."

"At the hospital. After the ER checks her out." The medics lifted me into the back of the ambulance.

"What about Bridges?"

"Chipped tooth, split lip, and a foul mood. We're not even going to take him in."

"Meet you there after I finish with the crime scene unit."

"Right."

The paramedic climbed in beside me and slammed the door, muffling the blare of the siren. I moved my head from side to side, trying to clear it.

"The guy. The one in the alley. He's dead, isn't he?" I asked, dreading the answer. I turned to look at the paramedic, who'd perched himself next to me. "Do you know who he was? What he was doing there?"

"The police are going to come by the ER and talk to you after they finish downtown."

Police. Oh, holy mother. The police. Of course. A dead body meant the police. They probably thought I killed him. Maybe they were going to arrest me. I'd lose my job. Morris would probably fire me personally. I'd have mug shots worse than Nick Nolte's. My head pounded.

"Sara. Hey. Open your eyes. You can't sleep now." The paramedic spoke into my ear.

I flinched, the pounding in my head picking up speed.

"Tell you what, Sara. How about if we do a little paperwork on the way? Fill in some forms. Keep you alert."

"Sounds great." Why not? I was only on my way to

jail and the unemployment line. What did I care if the last thing I did as a free woman was answer insurance questions? It would make my final minutes pass slower.

The emergency room was deserted as the paramedic and the driver wheeled me past the admitting desk and into a curtained examination area. They transferred me to a bed and told me to wait for the doctor. After they left I sat up, gently swung my legs over the side of the bed, and eased my feet to the floor. I held tightly to the edge of the bed, steadying myself. When the blackness didn't return, I stepped across to a plastic chair and sat down just as the curtain was whisked back and a kid dressed in surgical scrubs and tennis shoes sauntered in. I assessed him carefully. I diagnosed acute bedhead, terminal freckles, and a chronic need for identification if he hoped to pass as an adult. He glanced at a chart in his hand.

"Miss Townley, I'm Dr. Keller." James Brown's baritone in the body of Howdy Doody came as a complete surprise. "I understand you hit your head." Howdy was a consummate professional. Even without the blow to the head, it would have been like watching a Japanese movie dubbed into English. He checked my blood pressure and heart rate, jotting notes on the chart. He reached out and repeated the flashlight-in-the-eyes trick before placing a hand on either side of my face and turning it first one way and then the other.

"Does that cause any discomfort?"

"No."

"Could you look at the curtain behind me and read the top line of the label for me?"

" 'Made in the USA.' "

"Good. Any headache, blurriness, double vision, nausea?"

"All of the above."

"On a scale of one to ten?"

"Four."

"Any other pain?"

"No."

"Well, it looks like you suffered a mild concussion. Without additional symptoms we don't really need a CAT scan, but I want to keep you under observation for the next twenty-four hours to make sure nothing else is going on. If you have someone available to look after you at home, I'll release you. If you don't, I can admit you overnight. Preference?"

"Home." *Oh, no.* Connor. He was going to expect some sort of explanation. I heard husbands were like that. Even erstwhile ones. My mind began to race at the idea of a heart-to-heart with Connor on the first day we actually spent together as a married couple. I could start with, "I've got a great story we can tell the grandkids one day. Fifty years from now, when it starts to seem remotely funny."

"Okay. A nurse will be in shortly with some paperwork and then she'll call someone to come get you. In the meantime, the police want to talk to you. Are you up for that?"

Please, please, can I?

"Sure. No problem."

Chapter Five

I was waiting for the cops. That couldn't be good. I had a killer headache, no pun intended, an adolescent doctor, and a dead body I couldn't explain. Behind door number two, there was the soon-to-be-guilt-ridden best friend—totally not his fault—and the bound-to-have questions husband I didn't know what to do with. Orange jumpsuits and three squares a day won hands down.

A man walked into my cubicle, and I could tell with a glance that he was a cop. He was in his midfifties with steel gray hair, thick glasses, and a rumpled blue suit several years out of style. All he needed was a trench coat and an unlit cigar to pass for Colombo.

"I'm Sergeant Thomas Wesley, Ms. Townley." He flipped his identification open and waited while I peered at it through blurry eyes. I recognized his raspy baritone from the alley.

He looked around before leaning against the bed while holding a crumpled notebook and pencil stub he had pulled from one tattered pocket. His air of readiness jump-started my flagging energy. It didn't help my headache.

"How are you feeling? That was a bad blow you took."

"I'm blessed with an amazingly hard head."

He smiled at me but it never reached the cold gray of his eyes. I sat up a little straighter.

"If you're feeling up to it, I'd like to ask a few questions about what happened tonight."

"I didn't kill him." Clearly I had to hope I was never taken prisoner of war.

"I thought we might start with some background." He flipped pages in his notebook nonchalantly. "What's your full name?" He seemed unfazed by my protestation of innocence. He probably heard the same thing all the time.

"Sara Townley."

"Address?"

"One-oh-eight Virginia. Seattle. I didn't even know him." The verbal diarrhea continued. This might be my first corpse, but I'd seen enough movies to know that blabbermouths always ended up in the big house. Unfortunately, the events of the evening hadn't left me at the top of my game.

"Phone number?"

"I recited it."

"Why were you in the alley?"

"I was meeting someone."

"Who?"

"I don't know his name."

"It was a man you were meeting?"

"I guess."

"You don't know?"

"Not exactly."

"Well, maybe you could explain the purpose of the meeting?"

"Aren't you supposed to read me my rights?"

"I'm just trying to get a better idea of what happened tonight. But I'll read you your rights, if that'll make you feel better."

"It would." He did. It didn't.

"Would you care to make a statement at this time?"

"Do I need a lawyer?" A picture of Morris posting my bail flashed through my mind. I'd rather do life.

"Why would you need a lawyer?"

"I was in an alley with a dead guy."

"True."

"I'm no coroner, but bleeding through a particular spot in his chest didn't really strike me as a natural cause of death."

"When did you realize he was dead?"

"When I rolled him over."

It finally registered. This cop didn't think I killed the guy in the alley. He was way too cool. Then again, maybe that was his shtick. Maybe he was lulling me into a false sense of security and he was just waiting to slap the cuffs on. That didn't make any sense. He'd asked when I knew the dead guy was dead, not when I killed him. And he hadn't said anything about the guy I'd hit. Or maybe he'd hit me. I took a deep breath, relieved. Calling Morris no longer seemed inevitable. As long as I didn't breach any attorney–client—or attorney–cat—confidences, cooperation was probably a good thing. I might not even get fired.

"How do you know I didn't kill him?" Now that I didn't think I was going to be doing twenty-to-life, I was a little miffed I wasn't perp material.

"I don't."

"If I'd killed him, I wouldn't have run screaming from the alley. And I'd know how he died. How did he die, anyway?"

"I'm just trying to find out what you saw and heard, Ms. Townley." He was very professional. How annoying.

"No. You have some reason for thinking I didn't kill him."

"When you rolled him over, did you see any type of weapon?"

"I don't think so." I closed my eyes, trying to remember exactly. I swallowed hard as my mind replayed the scene in vivid detail. "No. He was facing away from me. I pulled his shoulder and he sort of flopped onto his back. I saw the blood and then I got out of there."

"Did you scream?"

"Like a teenager in a slasher flick. Why?"

He ignored me. "Did you touch the body anywhere else?"

"We didn't know each other that well." What kind of people was this guy used to dealing with?

"Did you recognize him?"

Once again, I struggled to replay the scene in my mind. I saw blood and pinstripes but no face.

"I don't think so." I wasn't really sure. If I'd known him, I'd have noticed. At least, I think I would've. I just couldn't see his face.

"You don't think so. Does that mean you might know him?"

"I didn't really look at his face. I was too busy getting out of there in case the killer was hanging around, waiting for seconds."

"Did you see someone else?"

"Yes."

"Can you describe him?"

"Short, maybe five-six, shaped like a fireplug, huge arms." I couldn't believe I'd been that close to the guy. I held my head, trying to concentrate on the memory and not the headache. "He was wearing a blue suit. Navy. No, not a suit. A uniform. Yes, a uniform. Oh." Comprehension dawned and I slumped. "He was probably one of yours, right?"

"Officer Bridges. Did you see anyone else in the alley?"

"What did he hit me with?" I had to know. The way I was feeling, it had to be police brutality. Maybe if Morris was happily busy suing someone, he'd forget all about me.

"Chin."

"Oh." I was embarrassed. "Well, he packs a punch for a guy who never used his hands."

"I imagine he does. Let's get back to why you were in the alley."

"Why was he there?"

"I'm asking the questions, Ms. Townley."

"Sara. Yeah. I get that. But why was Officer What's-his-name already there?"

"Why were you there?"

"You first." I crossed my arms over my chest. It was juvenile, I knew, but I tripped over a dead guy and felt entitled to something for my trouble, not to mention my terror.

"Officer Bridges was responding to a phone tip."

"Gunfire?" I guessed. Had that been a bullet hole? That was a really big bullet.

"Why were you there, Ms. Townley?"

Drip. Drip. Drip. This guy was the Chinese water torture of interrogation techniques. My head pounded.

"I was meeting someone."

"Who?"

"A phone tip." *Take that.*

The cop didn't so much as bat an eyelash.

"How did you set up the meeting?" he continued.

"He was just a voice on the phone. He said he had some information about a case I'm working on."

"What case?"

"I'm an investigator with Abercroft, Hamilton, and Sterns."

"The law firm?"

"Yeah."

"What is the case about?"

At the last instant caution reared its head. Caution and common sense. *Sorry, Mr. Policeman, but I was pursuing a hot lead on a missing furball and thought a war zone after dark would look good in the report.* This cop would buy it, no problem. Yeah, sure. I'd do what any sleazy lawyer—or in my case, innocent person who worked with too many lawyers—would do. I'd obfuscate. I'd fudge. I'd skulk behind attorney–client privilege. If there was one rule that Morris instilled in everyone from senior executive vice president to junior janitor, it was that client information was sacrosanct. Never discuss clients. Never discuss cases. Not even in generalities with the names changed to protect the innocent. Never, ever. God bless the evil minds of Abercroft, Hamilton, and Sterns.

"I can't say."

"This is an official police investigation of a homicide, Ms. Townley. I'd think you'd want to help us clear up this matter as soon as possible."

"You know I didn't kill him."

"This is the early stage of the investigation. I don't know anything for certain. Except that you were found running from a man who turned out to be stone-cold dead."

"He was cold. Really cold. Too cold for a night like tonight. It didn't penetrate then, but . . ." My hands flexed, as if they could still feel the soft cotton fabric of his suit, stripped of his body temperature. "How long had the guy been there?"

"Why were you in the alley?" he shot back, not about to be distracted.

"I can't tell you. I'm sorry. Really. Have you ID'd him yet?" My curiosity was getting the better of me, allowing me to ignore the fact that a mere hour ago I'd promised the Almighty immediate reformation of my character as I fled hatchet-wielding demons. This man handled real investigations. Not traffic accidents or custody disputes or, with apologies to Flash, cat disappearances. And I was in the middle of it. A real case.

"We are withholding identification pending notification of the family. Perhaps there is someone at your firm who could speak to me about this matter?" Sergeant Wesley clearly couldn't care less about what I wanted.

"No one will talk to you. Attorney–client privilege."

"Are you a lawyer?" he asked, his eyes icing.

"No."

"Then you're not bound by the privilege."

"Actually, I am." Abercroft, Hamilton, and Sterns practically demanded blood oaths during employee orientation. I'd have to be hit a lot harder to forget that lesson. "I don't have to be a lawyer. I just have to work for one."

"And this lawyer's name would be?"

"Morris Allensworth Hamilton the Fourth."

"Fine. I'll talk to him."

"Good luck."

"Thanks."

"No, I mean it. Good luck. Really."

Chapter Six

Too bad I couldn't sell tickets. Shabby civil servant versus pompous-ass senior partner. Morris would bristle with outrage at any suggestion that he might breach a valued client's private business to a lowly cop. His righteous indignation would reach epic proportions as he delivered an eloquent and incredibly loud discourse on attorney–client privilege as the bedrock of the greatest legal system on earth. That a policeman, a soldier in the battle for justice, could conceive of thwarting the very principles on which the nation was founded by intruding, without any just cause, into the sacred relationship between a legal adviser and a represented party evidenced a disheartening breakdown in the moral tenets that had built this country. Morris would be brilliant. All without the faintest recollection that his client was a cat.

"I understand you have someone at home who can watch for complications from your blow to the head?" A petite Asian nurse in a starched white uniform and comfortable matching shoes broke into my reverie, killing my amusement and replacing it with dread. While I had been chuckling over Sergeant Wesley's impending disaster, I had somehow managed to forget all about my own.

"I'm married."

"The paramedic checked the wrong box. He marked

'single' under marital status." Irritation crossed her bland face. "That's why they're supposed to give us a face-to-face briefing instead of just abandoning people in the exam rooms." She glanced at a clipboard of papers in her hand, all professional inquiry without any hint of personal interest.

"Honest mistake." I couldn't remember him asking me the question, but the answer sure sounded like one of mine. If I'd been thinking more clearly, I would've just told the nurse 'single' to stay consistent. Avoiding telling Connor about the evening's adventure for a few more hours would have been icing. I wondered if there was a soon-to-be-single box.

"And your next of kin is listed as Russ Smith."

"Yes. Absolutely." Maybe that blow to the head was a good thing.

"Then he's available to watch for symptoms?"

"No. I mean, yes, he is available, but he's at work right now." It would probably come back to bite me, but I couldn't think of an obvious drawback to using Russ to buy me a little time to get my act together before I faced Connor. Besides, Russ owed me for abandoning me to psycho killers and iron-jawed constables.

"He'll have to come pick you up. Hospital policy mandates anyone requiring observation to be signed out by a responsible adult." Her voice told me she wasn't going to bend her rules for me.

"It would be easier if I swung by to see him before heading home. He works the late shift." I had to at least try.

"Give me his number and I'll call him. Once I explain that you must be released to someone who can watch for danger signs, I'm sure he'll make himself available." I doubted there were many people with the nerve to be unavailable when this woman explained things to them.

"Really, it would be much easier if I just met him there."

"Hospital policy. Sorry. The number?" Five bucks said this nurse hadn't aced bedside manner.

I thought about Connor waiting at home. I needed time to come up with a story. Something good. Something that would explain everything. Bailing on him. My client the cat. The dead guy. The knife. The ambulance. The cops. Hell, Charles Dickens couldn't come up with a story that good. I needed Russ.

"He works at KSEA. I don't remember the number offhand."

"The late-night radio guy? He's your husband? I listen to him all the time." The nurse went from relentless professional to gushing fan in the time it took to blink. "I'll be happy to call him for you." She beamed at me before swishing out of the room.

If there was a way to come up with a convincing story, Russ was the guy to ask. Even if he was mad about my staying in Pioneer Square after he left, the guy would lie on a blood test. He was dependable that way. But he could be unpredictable. He might play along without missing a beat. Or he might spin some wild tale about an escaped mental-patient stalker who went around convincing professional health care workers that she was the wife of a local celebrity. I could be in the rubber room a week before I managed to convince anyone it was a lie.

I didn't want to think about why I had to avoid telling Connor. I didn't need Dudley Do-right to untie me from the tracks. I did fine on my own. Except for needing Russ to help me tell whoppers.

"Your husband's on his way," a red-headed nurse told me, coming into the cubicle just far enough to deliver her message before departing once again.

"Thank you, Russ." I whispered.

I spent several long minutes staring at the curtained walls of my cubicle. Where was the nurse? Wasn't she ever coming back? I had to get out of here. I glanced at my watch. Three twenty-six. Maybe Connor had gone to sleep. He might not even know how long I had been gone. Even if he knew, would he worry? Be angry? Where the heck was Russ? I needed aspirin. I needed sleep. I needed an accomplice with a felonious bent.

The Asian nurse finally returned with her sheaf of papers and a dreamy smile.

"Your husband will be here shortly. He was so concerned. And so sweet."

"That's nice," I mumbled, taking the clipboard from her and searching for the appropriate signature lines.

"And he's so sorry. He just couldn't stop saying it. He was so sorry."

"Sorry?" *Uh-oh.*

"He said it was all his fault. He never should have pushed you that way."

"Pushed me?" I was having trouble keeping up.

"Into having children right away. It's only because he wants such a big family. Not many men want six kids."

"Six?" Apparently Russ had started the lying without me.

"You don't mind that he told me, do you?" she asked, an anxious expression on her face.

"Told you what, exactly?" I tried to sound unconcerned, deliberately returning my attention to the forms in my hands.

"About your fight."

"Our fight?"

"On your anniversary, too."

"A fight on our anniversary." She was starstruck, glowing with inside information about her hero. I stared.

"He wanted everything to be perfect. That's why he hired the musicians. And why he flew the lobster in from Boston. He knew it was too much money, but it's your very favorite. He wanted your anniversary to be unbelievably romantic. That's exactly how he said it, 'unbelievably romantic.' "

"And unbelievable it was." Russ was allergic to lobster. It was generous of him to sacrifice himself that way. "What else did he say?" I was numbed by Russ's attention to detail.

"Just that he pushed you. He said that things were getting really intense and then he told you he wanted to make a baby on your anniversary. As a gift to each other."

"Just blurted that right out, did he?" I was going to get the big bottle of acetaminophen.

"Oh, please don't be mad at him for that." The nurse focused on me as she pleaded his case. "I know it's very personal. But he couldn't help himself. He was just so upset. You'd stormed out, and he didn't know where you were or if you would go back to that old boyfriend who's been calling. Or if you'd been in an accident in the new Jaguar he bought you for your last birthday. Or even if you'd gone to your mother's."

That would be tough, considering my mother died when I was seventeen.

"You know she's never liked him," the nurse stated emphatically.

The man was a menace. Of course, he had no way of knowing I wasn't up to being in on a lie of this magnitude. What was the deal with this woman? She was smart enough to get through nursing school, but a stranger could convince her white was black. You'd think she would've needed a bullshit meter before now. Instead, she'd swallowed everything Russ had said without question. There was no way I wanted her in charge of my medical care.

"Darling. Forgive me. Please. I was an unfeeling cad." Russ practically flowed into the room, gushing remorse.

Cad? Who used words like *cad*? And why was this woman still buying it? He was so over-the-top he had come back around the other side.

"Mr. Smith. I mean Russ." She blushed. "I'm Nurse Chang. Martha Chang. We talked on the phone."

"Of course, Martha. I would know you anywhere." Russ took the woman's hand, holding just the fingers as if he meant to raise them to his lips.

It was like watching an accident happen. I couldn't look away. The nurse practically vibrated with excitement, her face wreathed in smiles and her blush deepening. Russ's eyes remained locked with hers, his most charming smile firmly in place. For him, the gray linen slacks and matching loose-fitting jacket over a black

T-shirt were casual clothes. They were slightly rumpled from his shift at the radio station, but Nurse Chang didn't seem to notice. She continued to act as if she were in the presence of royalty. He was good.

"Ahem."

The nurse jumped at my intrusion, glancing toward me with unmistakable hostility before her professional mask dropped back into place.

"Darling." Russ dropped the nurse's hand and took two steps closer to me before crouching at my feet and taking the forms, placing them on the floor beside my chair. He reached for my hands. "I was so worried. Are you all right?"

I squeezed his hands hard, eliciting an almost imperceptible wince.

"I'm fine. Can we go?" I asked the nurse, who was subtly assessing Russ's backside, her head tilted to one side. Well, she was a medical professional. She abruptly straightened.

"I just need to check with administration. I'll get your paperwork," she said to me, her eyes never leaving Russ. He offered the discarded pages with his megawatt smile in place. She took them, deliberately moving so their hands touched. I wanted to gag.

"We'd appreciate that so much," Russ purred.

"Anything for you, Mr. Smith."

"Please call me Russ." He winked at her, standing up.

"Russ," she breathed before spinning and leaving the room.

"There oughta be a law." I rested my elbows on my knees and used my hands to prop my head up.

He struck like a snake. "What the hell were you doing?" Wow, that was really too loud.

"I told you. I was on a case," I whispered.

"You *said*"—he loudly stressed the verb—"you were leaving. You *said*"—again with the stress—"you were right behind me."

"And you listened to me? I am completely unreliable. Which you should know, since I learned it from you."

That took the wind out of his sails. His mouth opened, then closed. Quietly, thank goodness.

"I'm only forgiving you because you're not dead."

"Fair enough."

"And because it's our anniversary."

I started to laugh and stopped, holding my head. Laughing was not good. "I can't believe you sold that story."

"Can I help it if I am irresistible?" He took a couple of steps and lounged against the table.

"Liar, liar, pants on fire."

"Now, sweetheart, is that any way to speak to your beloved husband?"

"If you were really my husband you'd ask how I was before trying to seduce the hospital staff." Although I kept my voice low, the sounds seemed to echo through my aching head. I shifted in the uncomfortable chair, noting my ever-stiffening muscles. Getting hit by a car wouldn't have hurt this much.

"The nurse at the desk told me you were fine. Just a knock on the head. As I can personally attest to the fact that your head is harder than granite, I'm not worried." He grinned at me.

"I don't suppose they mentioned that I got taken down by a knuckle-dragging cop in Pioneer Square while running from a dead guy."

He laughed. "And you think I'm over-the-top."

"The truth is stranger than fiction."

"What are you talking about?" He straightened.

"Ssshh. Keep your voice down." I put a finger to my lips, looking toward the door and waiting before continuing.

"I'm not kidding. An old-fashioned double feature. A corpse and the missing link."

"Oh, my God." He returned to my side, crouching until we were nearly level with each other. "Are you okay, Sara?"

"I'm fine. You should see the other guy." I shuddered.

"No, thanks." Russ suddenly sat on the floor at my feet.

"How did he die?"

"Colonel Mustard in the alley with the knife?" I suggested.

"And the cop. You did say cop, didn't you?"

"Seattle's finest, on the job."

"Jeez, they don't think you had something to do with this, do they?"

"I don't know. Maybe." I was sorry the instant I shrugged. I wondered if I was going to be able to get out of the chair without help.

"You didn't talk to them, did you, Sara?" He read my silence and jumped to his feet. "You're never supposed to talk to the cops without a lawyer present. Don't you ever watch television? Of course not; you don't even own a TV. And look where it's gotten you. A murder suspect. We need to get you a lawyer right away. And no more talking with the police." His voice rose in agitation. His long legs paced the small area.

"Calm down, Russ. And keep your voice down." I stood up slowly, my body shrieking in protest. "And stop pacing. You're making me dizzy." I reached out and grabbed his arm. "I didn't do anything. All I said was, 'Talk to Morris.' You know I can't talk about cases."

"Do you think anybody's going to buy some lame story about an investigation for a bunch of stuffed shirts? No. Drugs. Gangs. Prostitution." Russ looked closer. "Okay, not dressed like that. Probably just drugs and gangs." He took an audible breath, his chest expanding. He held it for a second and then released it slowly. "It's no big deal. You didn't have anything to do with this guy's death, and the cops will figure that out."

"I don't even think I'm a suspect." I tried to wade through the pain in my head to figure out why I thought so.

"Why not?"

"The cop didn't act like he thought I did it."

"How did he act?"

"Casual. Fact gathering. You know, easy questions.

He didn't accuse me or anything. And he only read me my rights after I asked." I shifted a little, trying to stretch some blood back into my limbs.

"That's a trick, Sara. They always act like that."

I stared at him.

"Do you have a dark past I don't know about? Really, you could tell me. I can't repeat it. Marital privilege."

He laughed, his entire body relaxing.

"How did I ever get so lucky as to be married to you?" I stepped toward him, leaning my forehead against his chest. He put an arm around me.

"Oh. That's so sweet," Nurse Chang cooed from her position at the cubicle's opening, before moving toward us.

"I am the luckiest man alive to be married to this woman."

"Uh, your husband's here," a voice said loudly from the doorway. The redheaded nurse stood in the opening with a puzzled look. Behind her, grim-faced, stood Connor.

Chapter Seven

I wondered briefly if marriage had a mercy rule. When things got beyond hope—or, in this case, explanation— could we just shake hands and make peace over a hot dog? I looked at Connor. His entire body radiated suppressed energy. Nope.

"Ahem." Nurse Chang cleared her throat. "Would someone like to explain what is going on here?" She was mad. Fortunately, Russ seemed to be the primary target.

He smiled, slow and easy. As if he hadn't just been caught telling whoppers to a woman with unlimited access to scalpels, hypodermics, and all manner of pain-inducing devices. The guy had nerves of steel. I could practically see the wheels of his imagination furiously spinning, searching for a story. Twins? Connor's psychotic break with reality? Alternate religion? I glanced at Connor. When Russ started to speak, I jumped in.

"I'm a pathological liar. He's a pathological liar." I pointed an accusatory finger in Russ's general direction. "We met in a group." I stood completely still, waiting for my confession to sink in. It wasn't that far from the truth. Maybe they'd buy it. Even Russ took a minute to digest the new twist.

"How is that head trauma working out?" Russ inquired, a slightly bemused smile on his face. He shook his head gently, rolling his eyes in the direction of the nurse, who glared with blatant suspicion.

"Nurse Chang, perhaps I can clear this up. May I buy you a cup of coffee and we can discuss it? I would hate for you to have the wrong idea about this. Especially since I have literally dozens of follow-up medical questions to ask, and I simply will not be comfortable unless I know that a skilled professional of your caliber is the one to answer them." He threw in his best toothpaste smile and a gallant wave for her to precede him out the door. She melted like butter in the hot sun. Russ followed her out the door, his hand pressed solicitously to the small of her back.

Time to face the music. Lucky for me, medical help would be close at hand. I was relieved to see the red-haired nurse hadn't stayed to witness the carnage. Probably no stomach for it. My heartbeat thudded through my aching head. Connor's tight-lipped expression told me things weren't going to get better anytime soon.

He didn't say anything. He just waited. I couldn't meet his eyes. And he was unnerving the hell out of me. He should yell or something. I looked around the room, fidgeting.

"Did you get a prescription you need filled before we go?"

I thought of the prescription for pain medication the doctor had written and yearned for the reprieve the drugs could offer. It would be so easy to take one and play possum, but I knew it would only delay the inevitable. I shook my head. The sudden shrieking pain mocked my lack of verbal skills.

"No."

He sighed heavily. "Let's go home, Sara." He reached out, offering me his hand. I felt terrible, and it didn't have anything to do with my brief stint in the World Wrestling Federation. He sounded as tired as I felt, although he still looked crisp. He no longer seemed to be braced for impact. And his face, although not smiling, didn't look like thunderclouds. Maybe he was just going to roll with this whole thing. Nah. No one was that understanding.

I reached out and took his hand, surprised at the warm wash of security his touch gave me. He led me out to the car and helped me into the passenger seat. I was stiff and sore and would've killed for an acetaminophen.

"How did you know?" I asked.

"You must have given the home number to an intake nurse. The phone rang. I answered."

The paramedics. *Damn. Wait a minute.* He'd answered my phone? I glanced at him. Might not be the time to point out he'd been overreaching.

"I can explain." And I would, right after I was appointed pontiff.

"It can wait until we get home," Connor offered, maneuvering the car out of its slot and heading toward the exit ramp.

"I mean about Russ." I doubted Connor cared about having Russ explained. For some reason, people never did. He was embellishment and artistic license, forgiven in exchange for entertainment and joie de vivre. I was a bald-faced liar with social problems. No way around it. I leaned against the door, trying to find a position that throbbed a little less. I held upright as we descended "Pill Hill."

"He got a little carried away."

"You mean the part about having an alternative approach to marriage or the part where he practically seduced the Asian martinet in front of a roomful of people?" Connor's voice held a trace of amusement, but the expression his profile offered remained closed, his attention fully fixed on driving.

"I sort of told them he was my husband."

"Yeah, I'd figured that."

"It wasn't anything against you Connor, honestly." I pulled against the seat belt. "It's just that the cops were there and my head really hurt and I was all shaken up by the dead guy."

"The dead guy?"

"Yeah, the one in the alley. Pretty creepy, right?" I

shivered, the shudder carrying messages of pain all along my body. I wasn't all that squeamish, but I'd play the girlie-girl if it got me off the hook. I tried to look pathetic, then realized I didn't have to try that hard.

"Then the cops had questions. And the one I ran into, the big guy, was acting like I had totaled his car or something instead of giving him a couple of itty-bitty stitches. I was the one knocked flat."

"Sara?"

"And then in comes Russ, having turned my little white lie into a saga to rival *Gone With the Wind,* and there was that nurse eating it up with a spoon."

"Maybe we could talk about this at home?" he suggested.

"And then in you came, and everyone was staring like their next call was going to be to *The National Enquirer* or something."

"Sara?"

"Yes?"

"Let's talk about this at home."

"Okay."

I rolled down the window of the car, letting in a rush of cool air and the muted hum of late-night traffic. Anything was better than the tomblike silence. In minutes we were pulling into the parking lot behind the apartment. I'd used the reprieve to rack my brain for an explanation of the night's events that didn't make me seem like either a raving lunatic or a moron of seismic proportions. Nothing came to mind.

Tight with nerves and exhaustion, I gingerly preceded Connor up the stairs. Entering the apartment, I headed straight for the bathroom, wincing when I flicked on the light. I caught my reflection in the mirror and gasped, the unconscious flinch slamming against my bruises.

"Oh, my God."

My hair was wild. Don King tall and Bozo the Clown wide, the black curls were coated in dust and held bits of debris. One blue eye was shadowed by a darkening bruise, and I had a streak of something black across my chin. My T-shirt was spotted with dark brown spots that looked like blood. I yanked the shirt over my head, wincing at the sudden movement, and checked myself for wounds. Must be the cop's blood.

I dropped the T-shirt to the floor and put my hands on the sides of the sink, supporting myself as I moved closer to the mirror, turning my head to check the mottled skin around my eye. I groaned, closing my eyes and resting my forehead against the mirror. I was exhausted. The adrenaline had finally worn off. I sensed Connor behind me an instant before he rested his hand against my back.

"Kinda banged-up back here, too." He lightly touched one shoulder blade next to my bra strap before sliding his hand up to the back of my neck and rubbing gently. "Bet you've got a beaut of a headache."

"Yeah," I mumbled.

He guided me to the toilet, closing the lid and sitting me down. I dropped my elbows to my knees and held my head in my hands. My eyes stung with tears of pain and humiliation, and I swallowed hard to keep from crying. I heard water running and a cabinet closing.

"C'mon, babe. Take these."

I opened my eyes to see two capsules in Connor's palm. Manna from heaven. I reached for the medicine, accepted the glass of water he offered, and drank. Silently, I handed the glass back to him.

"Bath or sleep?"

"Shower."

He reached into the shower and turned the water on. I watched him numbly as he put one hand in the spray before adjusting the temperature. He reached for my hands, but I stopped him.

"I can do it."

"You sure? You're not dizzy or anything?"

"Just the headache. I've got it." I stood up slowly, meeting his eyes.

He reached out and tucked my hair behind one ear, his green eyes watchful.

"Okay. I'll be in the bedroom if you need anything."
He moved toward the door.

"Connor?"

"Yeah."

"Thanks. For not yelling or anything."

"I think I'll wait until you're feeling better." A half
smile softened his words before fading. "We are going
to have to talk about tonight, though, Sara."

"I know."

He nodded and left the bathroom, closing the door
halfway behind him. I stripped slowly and spent twenty
minutes steeping in the hot water. Washing my hair, I
carefully probed the knot on the back of my head. The
soap stung a scrape on my elbow. The drugs had dulled
my headache, but I still felt like I'd been in a brawl.
And lost.

I halfheartedly dried my hair and wrapped myself in
the blue bathrobe I kept hanging on the back of the
bathroom door. Connor was sitting on the edge of the
bed when I opened the door. The light on the bedside
table was set low.

"You okay?"

"I'm gonna live."

He stood and came across to me. He took my hands
and leaned down to kiss my forehead. I turned my head
and laid my cheek against his chest. His arm came
around me and he gently rubbed my back.

"Bedtime." Holding my hand, he led me to the bed,
pulling back the covers so I could slide in. He went to
his side of the bed and clicked the light out. I could hear
him rustling in the dark as he undressed before he
crawled in beside me and pulled me close. I turned and
turned again, trying to find a comfortable position.

"You okay like this? I'm not hurting you or anything?"

"No, this is good. G'night." Sleep was dragging at me.

"Try not to freak out when I wake you. Doctor's orders, remember."

"Hmmm."

"Sara?"

"Huh?"

I could feel his breath against my hair. He was warm and solid.

"When you're hurt, I'm the one you call."

Chapter Eight

Whoever invented the flashing message light had a lot to answer for. Despite two Starbucks quad venti lattes and six acetaminophen, the strobe from my phone drilled directly into my brain. It was barely eight o'clock and the only thing stopping me from pitching the evil device from the window was the fact that they didn't actually open.

I put my laptop and briefcase onto the desk. I picked up the phone and listened to four messages from Morris. Even with the volume turned to hangover level, they got increasingly abrasive and consisted of the same command: Report immediately to his office. *Oh, hurray.* Morris was the sort of senior partner who rose at the crack of dawn and was at his desk by six each workday. His wife probably insisted. I rubbed at my neck, my headache pounding behind my eyes. I felt like I'd been dragged through a bush backward and knew I looked it. Why me?

I took the elevator, my aching body rebelling at the thought of climbing stairs. Elizabeth sat behind her desk, the scarlet of her lips and nails matching her dress. The sheer brilliance of color assaulted my eyes. Without a word, she picked up her phone and informed Morris I was waiting. Her hard brown eyes never left my face, and a trace of a Cruella DeVille smile twisted her lips.

"You may go in now."

"Great. Thanks."

"My pleasure," she purred.

Sergeant Wesley rose from the visitor's chair as I entered the room. He looked worse than I felt. He wore an olive green sport coat and crumpled black trousers. His brown tie was crooked and sported a mud-colored Rorschach spot I doubted was part of a pattern. His big hand cradled the same dog-eared notebook he'd used the previous night, and he looked me over without any change of expression.

"Ms. Townley."

"Sergeant. Sir." I turned my attention to Morris, whose Brooks Brothers slickness was only enhanced by the company. He did not rise, and his eyes did not look kindly upon me.

"Miss Townley, Sergeant Wesley has been telling me about the incident last evening. As I've explained to him, while we are certain that this unfortunate episode is unrelated to any work you may have been doing for the firm, we cannot breach attorney–client confidentiality by discussing the specifics of any case." He leaned back in his chair, steepling his fingers as he looked down his bulbous nose.

"Yes, sir." I knew Morris was talking to me. I wondered if Wesley realized it, too. I could only pray the cop had told him I'd limited my responses to name, rank, and serial number. I couldn't tell by looking at Morris. He always wore that sour expression. I remained standing, not having been invited to sit. Wesley's appearance apparently belied good manners, because he continued to stand with me. Together we could be school-age delinquents called into the principal's office.

"I have also told Sergeant Wesley that any future questioning by the police shall be done only in the presence of counsel."

"She's not a suspect."

Although I'd pretty much figured out that the cops didn't think I'd killed the alley guy, it was reassuring to hear that Wesley hadn't come to haul me to jail. Not that I thought for a moment that the cop's statement would keep Morris from wreaking vengeance for my having inconvenienced him with this visit. Morris lived to discomfort.

"Be that as it may, Sergeant." Morris waved one hand in a regal gesture. "If there's nothing else . . ." He let the words trail off, making it clear that there would be nothing else. Morris finally stood, offering one hand to the cop in a here's-your-hat-what's-your-hurry gesture that couldn't be missed.

Sighing, Wesley stuffed his notebook into his pocket and shook hands, giving me a long look before shuffling to the door. It closed behind him with a click.

"What the hell is going on?" Morris boomed, collapsing back into his chair.

Ouch. "Well, sir, I was working on the Millinfield case. You know, the missing cat." The air conditioner hummed and I felt chilled.

"Why would you involve the police?"

No doubt it was only his paternal concern for my well-being that had him out of sorts. His point-the-finger approach was probably just an abundance of genuine concern.

"I received a call from Jeff Randall, the trustee in charge of the cat. Mostly his responsibility is to physically care for the animal. He got a call from someone claiming to have information. I went to meet with the informer. That's when I found the body."

"Did you meet with the alleged informer?"

"No. He didn't show up. Unless he's the guy I found." Having said it, I realized it was the most likely explanation. The informer had picked the time and location. If he'd been legitimate he'd have selected a nice office during business hours.

"What information did he offer you?" Morris voice returned to a normal decibel range. My head appreciated it. I would have appreciated being allowed to sit down even more.

"I didn't talk to him. Jeff Randall did. I'll reinterview

Randall this morning to see if I can find out anything else. In the meantime, I'd like to review the Millinfield trust, as well as anything we have on the Mastersons."

"That certainly won't be necessary. You have nothing to link this incident to the Millinfield case. If this corpse is your missing informant, he was obviously some con artist looking for a reward. More likely he was a drug dealer killed during the course of his illegal activity. A foreseeable end to a life of crime having absolutely nothing to do with Millinfield, Masterson, or this firm."

"We don't know anything for sure at this point, sir."

He was shuffling papers on his desk, already turning away from the case. I couldn't believe he was just going to blow off a dead body. I was supposed to be the investigator, and here he was totally dismissing significant leads on the case. There was nothing like having his opinion about my professional skills driven home to me the morning after I picked up a black eye working for him. I took a deep breath, stifling the urge to rant. I took a step closer to the desk, trying to regain his attention.

"Sir, the cat may have been taken deliberately. He is the beneficiary of a sizable trust. And since he lives at the Masterson estate, and the Mastersons were around at the time of the cat's disappearance, it makes sense to me to—"

"No. This is a missing-pet case, Miss Townley, not the Lindbergh kidnapping. The stupid thing has wandered off. Your job is to locate it, period. I will not compromise other clients, especially one as significant as Stuart Masterson, to satisfy your prurient curiosity. Limit yourself to the case. Find the cat. Have I made myself clear?" He was glaring again.

"Yes, sir."

What could I say? He wasn't going to listen. He was going to play ostrich. At least he wasn't taking me off the case altogether. Or firing me. Last night losing my job seemed like the worst thing that could happen. Today, facing Morris the Horse's Behind, I realized it wasn't. First, he wouldn't fire me. I wasn't important enough to fire. I existed to take metaphorical dictation, salute, and toe the company line. *Yes, sir. No, sir. Whatever you say, sir.* Second, everything that had happened didn't even register on his radar. Mysterious informant—childish prank. Murder victim—unfortunate coincidence. Police investigation—irritating irrelevance. Well, if he thought I was just going to ignore the first real case I'd ever had to keep this stupid job, Morris the Moron could bite me.

"Am I clear?" he bellowed.

I crossed my fingers.

"Yes, sir. Crystal clear."

Chapter Nine

The first step to successful career suicide is not to panic. It's not like I'd done anything, and he couldn't possibly know what I was thinking, right? My answer must have sounded reasonable, because I was still here, sweating outside his office. I wasn't going to do this. I was not going to risk my job. I wasn't.

Liz wasn't at her desk. With any luck she was on one of her hour-long smoke breaks and I'd be gone before she caught me not doing this.

I started with her calendar. Investigating for real sounded good, but here I was flipping through Elizabeth's mostly blank calendar without the faintest idea what I was looking for when it hit me. Only an idiot would believe in a coincidence big enough to cover the loss of a multimillion-dollar cat and a dead body in the space of a few hours. Only a moron would deliberately ignore an actual lead of the magnitude of a police investigation peripheral to the issue. Morris was many things. He wasn't stupid.

And what was all that about attorney–client privilege? I was covered by privilege. Why play coy? It was probably nothing. Simple I'm-an-important-lawyer-and-you're-an-insect philosophy. It wasn't his stance that bothered me so much. It was the vehemence. Maybe his elitism went that deep, but he seemed a little over-the-top.

Dead guys, police, air bag lawyers . . . maybe I was a little paranoid.

I flipped through the folders in the in-basket. I hesitated, debating the wisdom of rifling through Liz's files. I might actually be more afraid of Liz than I was of Morris. He could only fire me. Her revenge would probably include blackmail, job termination, and some sort of voodoo curse.

I slipped around her desk and stepped to the file cabinet. A quick perusal of the labels had me on my knees opening the lowest drawer, my fingers flying as I searched for the right file. I pulled a heavy brown folder marked MILLINFIELD TRUST from the drawer and flipped it open. I stared into the empty file. The sudden trilling of the phone had me whirling around, my heart in my throat and my breathing labored. I immediately whipped back, jammed the folder into place, and stifled a scream as I slammed my fingers in the drawer. I popped to my feet and managed to round Liz's desk and start toward the door before it opened to admit her, reeking of smoke. The woman was a walking vice. She gave me a dismissive glare and I fled to the hallway.

I nursed my throbbing hand in the elevator. When the doors opened, I took two steps toward my cubicle before I stopped. The file room was practically calling my name. Just because I hadn't found anything in Liz's files didn't mean the file room was a dead end.

The files were kept in the central core of the floor in a huge room with thousands of files housed on rolling metal bookcases. I walked down the length of shelves, trying to be casual while I checked for other employees. I could hear two women discussing the evil nature of men in general and their husbands in particular, but they were at the other end of the room. That topic could take a while.

I meandered toward the relevant section and, after a brief glance back at the gossips, pushed the file wall far enough to allow me to slip between sections. My eyes scanned past Masterson to Millinfield. I pulled the file and flipped it open. Inside were Morris's initials and nothing else. Disappointment swamped me. I pushed the file back into place and turned toward the end of the row, only to be startled by a bespectacled, gray-haired secretary in a frumpy green suit and sensible shoes—I could never remember her name.

"Are you looking for something?"

"Just putting a file back," I said casually despite a racing heart and sweaty palms.

"You're putting a file back?" Her voice dripped disbelief.

"Something strange about that?" I asked, passing her on my way to the door.

"No one ever puts them back," she muttered.

My heart tripped madly all the way back to my desk. I was astonished that the people I passed in the hall seemed unaware of my near miss. Surely heart palpitations were visible, yet no one seemed disturbed, and the file clerk didn't chase after me screaming, "Liar." The nearer I got to my cubicle, the more the fear gave way to blinding curiosity. Something wasn't right here.

I stopped at the opening to Joe's cubicle. He sat hunched over a stack of documents, his thick glasses barely hanging on to the end of his nose, both arms surrounding the files as if he expected someone to try to snatch them away.

"Joe?"

He jumped, his head coming up as his watery blue eyes tried to focus on me over the half-moons of his prescription lenses.

"You scared me. Nice eye. What did Morris want?"

"It was time for my annual review. I'm getting a monumental raise."

Joe snorted.

"Actually, it was nothing. I've got a question for you, though." I leaned against the fabric wall. "What does it mean when a file is empty but someone's initials are inside?"

"It means they checked out the contents. You're supposed to sign them out with the date, so if someone else needs the file they know where to look."

"What if there was no date?"

"Either it's a permanent sign-out or they just didn't bother with a date."

"Everything is also on the computer, right?"

"Sure. We save everything we draft and scan anything we get from anybody else. Whether or not you could see it is another story. The sensitive files are password-protected and can be accessed only by the assigned attorney." He leaned back and dug under a stack of papers, coming out with several pieces of candy, which he offered to me with an open hand.

I shook my head in refusal, careful to avoid his eyes. "What makes you think we're discussing a sensitive file?"

"I'm not discussing a sensitive file. I have never discussed a sensitive file with you. I will never discuss a sensitive file with you. Which is what I will tell anyone who cares to ask." He used his arm to shoo me out of the cubicle and returned to work.

I grinned and walked the few steps to my own cubicle.

My phone was ringing. I desperately wanted a few moments to think about Morris's weird behavior and the empty files, but I couldn't stand the ringing. I took a deep breath and picked up the receiver, dropping into my chair.

"Sara Townley."

"Spill." Russ didn't bother to identify himself before making his demand.

"I'm sure I don't know what you mean."

"When last we saw our heroine she was abandoning her husband of record to a truly unamused she-demon nurse while waltzing off with husband number two, who was wearing an I-am-not-happy-and-haven't-taken-my-Prozac expression."

"Oh, that." I didn't want to think about Connor. Just remembering how sweet he'd been made me feel like a heel.

"You sound terrible. Has something else happened? Since the dead body and the public bigamy?"

I laughed in spite of myself.

"Private bigamy really is the only choice. I never told you how much I enjoyed your performance last night. Oscar-caliber." I picked up a pencil and began to doodle. I could already feel Russ's good nature restoring my mood. I might have an irate boss and a disappointed husband, but I also had a best friend who could help me see the funny side of things.

"Thank you very much. Now stop changing the subject. What happened after you went home?"

"Nothing."

"I am your best friend and coconspirator. Start talking."

"He was mad."

"Well, you could hardly expect the guy to be doing cartwheels. He did walk in on his wife and another husband." Russ laughed.

I didn't respond, and the silence stretched.

"How mad was he?" Suddenly Russ didn't sound like he was having a good time.

"Nothing like that. He's not even much of a yeller."

"Okay. So he was mad. What did he say?"

I dropped the pencil, closing my eyes and leaning my head back against the chair.

"Nothing, really. Just that the next time I should call him."

"That sounds more like hurt than anger, Sara."

"I'm sure he was just mad. And embarrassed. I mean, that horrid nurse going on and on, and the story kept getting more and more ridiculous. Heck, I was mortified and I'm used to you."

"Hey, Sara, I'm sorry. I got a little carried away. But I would never do anything that—"

"It wasn't your fault, Russ." I pulled my legs up and rested my feet on the edge of my seat. "I knew the risks when I told them to call you. It's not like I haven't seen you in action before."

"I would give a million bucks for a picture of the expression on everyone's face when Connor walked into the room."

"A classic." I giggled.

"Better than the time we talked them into letting us run the cotton-candy machine at the Vashon Strawberry Festival?" he asked, choking on his own laughter.

"Definitely. Even better than the time you talked all those executive yuppies into a spontaneous polka party at the convention center."

"God, wasn't that a hoot?" We laughed for several long moments. I wrapped one arm around my waist, my sides aching, my headache pulsing dully.

"Enough." I gasped, using one foot to send my chair into a slow twirl.

"You're right. That is enough. Let's get back to the real dirt. What else did Connor say?"

I sobered.

"Just what I told you. 'I'm the husband. When there's trouble, call me.' He didn't dwell on the finer points."

"Like the corpse and the cops?"

"How did you know about that?"

"Nurse Chang. Very talkative and something of a fan."

"I thought she was going to dissect you once it became obvious you'd been lying." I reached into my desk drawer and pulled out a Snickers bar. If I was going to spend company time gossiping with Russ, I was going to go all-out.

"Let's just say I think best on my feet. I'll tell you all about it later. How did you happen to be in an alley with a dead body anyway?"

"It's a long story. The abridged version is, I'm looking for a cat worth millions."

"Liar."

"No, really."

"Bullshit. Is this because you hit your head?"

"I'm really not kidding. This woman left all her money to her cat, and he's missing."

Russ guffawed. "Beautiful. Not even I could have made that one up. Genius. Pure genius."

No sense protesting my innocence with Russ. His ability to perceive truth was severely limited by his desire for a good story.

"So, who was the guy in the alley? His vet? No, I know—he was a dog person."

"Still no clue." I unwrapped the candy bar and took a bite. Ambrosia of the gods. "I thought this was a nothing case, and suddenly I'm nose-to-nose with the afterlife." I reached over and dropped the wrapper into my garbage can. I always thought better under the influence of chocolate. I'd handled this case wrong from the beginning. There had to be a connection. Morris might not want me to pursue it, but an interrogation by the police surely earned me some right to check things out. A man was dead. It could have been me. Or Jeff. I'd been casual at the beginning, but no more. I was going be more careful. And vigilant. And, since Morris made it clear that he was not going to help me, devious. I could do that.

"As fun as this has been," I told Russ, "I have to get back to work." I was on a Snickers high. Who was the guy in the alley? Why had he ended up dead? Was this about the money? Was Jeff the target? Was I making all of this up? Did I have any candy bars left?

"I am so anxious to make sure my best friend is recovered from a very stressful evening that I get up at the horrific time of nine a.m. to talk to her—a sacrifice she doesn't even notice, by the way—and then I get the brushoff. Even a far less sensitive person than I am would be offended by such shoddy treatment. You should be ashamed." Russ's voice warbled with his dramatic intonation.

"I am. Feel free to divorce me on those grounds. Bye."

I dropped the phone back into its cradle without waiting for his reply. I clicked on my laptop and opened my notes from the previous day, looking for Jeff Randall's number. I picked up the handset, punching out the first few numbers before changing my mind and replacing the receiver. I didn't want to scare him by breaking the news over the phone. If things had been a little different, he could have been a chalk outline this morning. I threw my notebook into my briefcase, rose from my desk, and headed out the door.

I rode the bus back to my apartment, trying to come up with a plan of attack. First, I'd talk to Jeff, maybe have another look around the estate. A real search this time instead of just the dime tour. I had no idea what I was looking for, but maybe I'd know it when I saw it. And I should talk to the cop again. Maybe by then he could release the identity of the body. I was so focused on what I had to do I nearly missed my stop.

I went straight for my car in the lot behind the apartment, pulling up short at the blue sedan parked behind my green compact. I stared. It was probably Connor's, although I hadn't remembered seeing a car the previous night. I stared at the fourth-floor windows. I stood indecisively, starting as the rear door opened and Connor strolled through. He looked up and smiled slowly, walking to within a couple feet away from me.

"Hi."

"Uh, hi," I said, reflexively smiling back.

"Do you usually hang out in the parking lot in the middle of the day?"

"Beats working. Actually, Connor, I need my car and I think you blocked me in." I used my keys to point in the direction of the blue sedan.

"I don't have any plans. I'll play chauffeur."

"I'm working, Con."

"On the same case as last night? The one that's already required an ambulance and a hearse? Compared to that, my rental's pretty safe."

I shifted my laptop to my other shoulder, careful not to wince with the movement. It wouldn't pay to let Connor know I wasn't at the top of my game.

"That's hardly usual. There's nothing to worry about. Now, could you move your car, please?"

His smile faded, his arms crossing in front of his chest.

"I'm glad to hear that. And, since I'm going with you, I'm not worried."

"This is work, Connor. Do I ask to join you when you're off playing boy soldier? No. I don't think so."

"Sailor. It's boy sailor. And it's not the same thing."

"No, of course it's not the same thing. For me, bodies are an exception. For you, they're the rule."

"That's hardly accurate, Sara. And I'm trained for my job."

"You think I'm not?" Belligerence did not help my headache.

Connor stilled.

"I'm sure you're a good investigator, honey. The kind of savvy professional who is smart enough to take advantage of all your resources. In this case, a willing partner with some special skills." Connor dropped his arms, pushing his hands into the front pockets of his jeans. My eyes followed his movement, taking in his tight blue T-shirt, faded blue jeans, and battered lace-up boots before drifting back to his face. I couldn't see his green eyes behind his sunglasses, but his slow smile told me he recognized my distraction for what it was.

I mentally shrugged off his effect.

"Stop that," I said.

"Stop what?" His tone was total innocence. His smile was not.

"You know what. Trying to get your own way using . . . distracting me with . . . you know what I mean."

"Sara, I wasn't doing anything except pointing out my very reasonable concerns for your safety and suggesting—" I started to interrupt, but he raised his hand to stop me. "Suggesting an obvious solution."

"Well, thank you very much for your *suggestion*," I said gravely. "But I can handle this. Now, would you please move your car?"

"No." He crossed his arms over his chest and stared at me.

"You can't just block me in, Connor."

"Why not?"

"Because you can't." Rational female response number 147.

"We go together. Take it or leave it."

"Leave it!"

"Okay." Connor started walking toward the apartment.

I nearly choked. How dared he? Who the hell did he think he was?

"I could have you towed," I yelled at his back.

He stopped and turned around, shrugged. "Go ahead." He turned away.

He was leaving. *Jesus. Men.* I fumed. I wanted to stamp my feet but that would be completely juvenile, so I stuck my tongue out at his back. Looking over his shoulder, he caught me. I think the pain in the ass was trying to suppress a smile.

"I'm an excellent driver," Connor deadpanned.

So he had me in a corner. Fine. He could drive. And stay in the car when I got to Jeff's. It would give me plenty of time to share my mood.

"Since you offered." I gave it my best sarcastic tone.

He walked over and unlocked the passenger door, holding it for me. Pretty manners were not going to save him.

"Where to?"

"Hell in a handbasket."

Chapter Ten

I huffed all the way across the I-90 bridge. The thing was, he was better at waiting than me. Life was not fair.

"You can't do this again."

"What?"

"Push your way in."

"Sorry."

I sighed. "Okay, then."

"I meant I was sorry I can't agree to that, not that I'm sorry I'm here now. Actually, I'm not sorry about that either."

I glared at him.

"You going to tell me about this case?" Connor asked.

"No." Of course not, the patronizing jerk.

"You wouldn't want me to be unprepared when we get there, would you?"

"Since you invited yourself, I figure your level of preparation is sufficient." He didn't even seem to notice I was mad. He was so dense.

"Sara, I made a mistake I won't make again."

"Do tell."

"Last night you were running, and I thought you needed some room."

So much for revelation.

"Take this exit." I pointed.

"What you really needed was a leash."

"Excuse me?"

"No kidding, Sara. Last night could have been avoided if you'd told me where you were going, what you were doing."

"Let me guess. You'd have played Neanderthal and locked me in the dungeon."

"Does your apartment have a dungeon? Good to know."

"You are not the boss of me, Connor." I sat back in my seat and folded my arms over my chest. This was not going to work. No way. Nobody told me what to do.

"I'm your backup."

I looked at him suspiciously. He wasn't a backseat kind of guy. It must be a trick.

"Right."

"Really, I'm just here for security."

"You're not going to interfere?"

"No."

"You're not going to try to take over and tell me what to do and push me around?"

"I'm trying to sleep at night."

Great. Guilt. Okay, so maybe Connor was a more obvious choice for backup than Russ. Well, when it wasn't a verbal battle or a lying contest, anyway.

"I'm looking for a missing heir." That was sort of true, and it didn't make me look like an idiot.

"Okay."

"He's been missing for a couple of days. I'm going to talk to his, er, guardian, right now." That was pretty close to actual honesty.

"He's the last guy who saw your MIA?"

"MIA?"

"Missing in action."

"Oh, yeah. He was the last one."

"Where?"

"Here." I pointed to a driveway.

In daylight the houses seemed larger, the lawns lusher. We reached the gates of the Masterson estate and turned in, slowing the car to a crawl. Connor braked as Jeff emerged from the guesthouse as if he had been waiting for me. His polo shirt was blue, his Bermuda shorts a stonewashed sand. His deck shoes were dark brown leather and looked new. With his silver hair and blue eyes, he looked like a man on top of the world. I hated to ruin his day.

"Morning, Jeff." I smiled at him, reaching out to shake hands.

"Morning, Sara." He returned my handshake. "I was worried. You never called back last night. What happened to your face?"

"I had a little accident. It's nothing. I'm sorry I didn't call. It was really late and I didn't want to disturb you. I'd like you to meet my . . . colleague, Connor McNamara. Connor, this is Jeff Randall."

The men shook hands.

"Nice to meet you, Jeff."

"Colleague? Now there are three of us on the great feline hunt?"

Oh, that was bad. I avoided Connor's eyes.

"I need to talk to you, Jeff. Connor's going to"—I looked around for inspiration—"check the outside security of the house."

Jeff seemed confused. "If you think that's necessary."

I smiled brightly. "Absolutely. We're a full-service operation here." And I would do anything, absolutely anything, to buy myself enough time to come up with a good explanation for this.

Connor's sunglasses shielded me from what I suspected was a harsh glare. He hadn't made a scene last night, but today was a new day. A long moment passed. Then another.

"I'll be in voice range," Connor said, and moved toward the side of the guesthouse.

"He seems very diligent," Jeff said, gesturing toward his open front door. "Did you meet with the man who called?" I followed him along a stone walkway into the house.

"No. We never actually met," I hedged.

"That's too bad. I was hoping he'd have real information about Flash." He led me into the cottage's living room and gestured toward the couch. I took a seat on the striped cushions.

"Can I get you some coffee before we get started?" He stood in a doorway, and I could see the kitchen beyond.

"No, thanks. Too much caffeine makes me crazy." He sat on a chair opposite me. "Could we go over the phone call again?"

"Sure. Whatever you want. Do you think he'll call again?"

"I don't know. Something happened that we need to talk about."

"What?" He was sitting back, his arms resting on the arms of the chair.

"When I got to the alley last night, I found a body."

He sat straighter.

"A body? Whose body?"

"I'm not sure yet. Maybe the guy who called you. Maybe someone else."

He stroked his chin.

"Did you call the police?"

"I talked to them."

"What do they think? Do they think it's the man who called here?"

"I don't know. Is it possible . . . I mean, would there be anyone who might want to hurt you, Jeff?"

He sat straighter. "You think I was the intended victim? Is that where you got the black eye?"

"My eye was an accident." I really didn't want to talk about my collision. "Like I said, I don't know what to think yet." I shrugged my shoulders. "I don't want to scare you or anything, but it's a pretty big coincidence that there's a dead body in an alley where I'm supposed to meet someone with information about Flash."

"I see. No, I can't think of anyone who might wish me harm. Are the police investigating this as if I'm the intended victim? Will they be calling back?"

"I doubt it. So far, there's nothing linking the body to Flash. It could just be a coincidence. If they are connected it's not obvious, and since I can't discuss an ongoing case with the police—or clients, for that matter—I doubt the police will make a connection either. Unless you want me to discuss this with them. Would you feel safer?"

Jeff continued to stroke his chin. "What do you think?"

"Hard to imagine a missing-pet case becoming a murder investigation."

"Catnapping but not conspiracy. I agree. I'll leave it to you, then."

"Okay. For now, we'll just continue with our investigation. If the informant calls back, I'd like to try to trace the call. Just to see if he does have any useful information. Can you remember anything else about the call? Background noise? Another voice?"

"Noooo." He said the word slowly. "I don't think so."

"Is there anyone else who might be looking for Flash?"

"I don't know. Maybe. For the reward."

"What about someone else? A private detective maybe."

"I hadn't thought of that."

"Has anyone else been hanging around the house? Someone who might have seen Flash more recently than you?"

"There's a maid, but I think I told you about her. Her day is Friday, and I saw Flash on Monday. There is a gardener, but he comes only every other week. I expect him tomorrow."

"What about nonstaff?"

"No one other than the people I mentioned yesterday. Stuart the younger and Sterling Masterson, and Henry Jepsen, the partner."

"Any idea why they were here?"

"Not really. If I had to make an educated guess, I would say the children were looking for anything of value that wouldn't be missed right away. I believe Henry Jepsen came looking for Stuart Masterson Senior. He seemed to be spoiling for a fight."

"What do you base that on?"

"Intuition. I haven't interacted with them much, thankfully, but I'd have to say neither the children nor the business partner impress on character initially. And Millicent mentioned something similar when she first showed me around."

"I'm surprised a private secretary would be so chatty about her employer's personal life."

Jeff suddenly seemed uncomfortable. Then he smiled and gestured expansively. "She probably didn't say those exact words. Plus, I have had the dubious pleasure of their company on several occasions. It would color anyone's view."

"I'm sure it would. All in all, they sound like real characters."

"That's a generous way to put it."

"I thought since I was here, I'd have another look around."

Jeff's blue eyes opened wider.

"Of course. Would you mind if I asked why?"

"With everything that happened last night, I just want to make sure I haven't missed anything."

"So you're convinced this man from the alley is connected to Flash's disappearance."

"I really don't know anything yet. I'm not trying to be tight-lipped; I just don't know."

"Do whatever you think necessary. Shall I go with you?"

I stood. "I think I'd rather go through the house by myself. Sort of take it all in without distractions. Do you mind?"

"I don't mind. It's not my house. Since Stuart Masterson isn't here, I suppose he won't mind, either."

"Where is he, anyway?" I asked.

Jeff shrugged. "I have no idea."

He stood and went to the kitchen, coming back with

a key ring, which he handed to me. The ring was heavy, with at least a dozen keys.

"The house key has the red ring. Just drop them back when you're done."

"Sounds like a plan." I headed out the door.

"Sara. Wait," Jeff called, joining me on the porch. "Could you do me a favor?"

"Sure. If I can."

"Keep your eyes open for another ring of keys. Somehow I managed to misplace them. I'm pretty sure they are in the house somewhere, and it's no big deal, but I would really rather find them."

"If I come across them I'll bring them back with me."

"I appreciate it." He smiled his gleaming smile and gave me a jaunty salute.

I waved in response and went toward the main house. Connor appeared at my side.

"A cat?" he asked, falling into step beside me.

I sighed. "A cat. A millionaire but four paws, yes."

"Okay, then. You take the inside, I'll take out."

No ridicule, no laughter, no offer to send me to a shrink. Just "okay." He had to see how nutty this was, right?

"Okay, then," I said.

"I'm still in range. Yell if you need me."

"All righty, then."

Reasonable men creeped me out.

"Connor?"

He stopped and turned around.

"Don't you think it's weird? This cat goes missing and my boss puts me on the case full-time, but Stuart Masterson, a bazillionaire, drops off the radar and no one seems to notice."

"They've noticed. They just don't care."

"Yeah. Weird, right?"

"Everybody loves pets. Maybe Masterson is an ass."

He had a point. I climbed the shallow steps and inserted the key, turning the knob and letting myself into the kitchen.

I closed my eyes, deliberately clearing my mind. Yesterday, the Masterson estate was a Seattle Street of Dreams private viewing. Today it was a post-dead-guy maybe crime scene. If I was going to risk my job by ignoring my boss's direct order, I needed to figure this thing out. Investigate like I knew what I was doing. At least make it worth it.

I opened my eyes and took inventory in the kitchen. There was a huge, marble-topped island, complete with double stainless sinks and a grill top. Dozens of copper-bottomed pots hung from an elaborate iron rack in the center of the room. More marble was used in long countertops, and there were at least thirty cupboards with glass doors revealing crockery of all types. Unlike yesterday's walk-through, I took my time, carefully opening each cupboard and looking inside for the missing cat. I was methodical, forcing an attention to detail that would have felt ridiculous yesterday.

I thought about Morris and his theory. A stray cat, a drug deal gone bad, and all of it a complete coincidence. I needed to find Flash and figure out what was really going on. I needed to figure out how Connor did the cool-nonchalance thing. It was driving me crazy.

I finished searching the living room and moved into the pantry. Shelves lined every wall, crammed with food. I peered behind peanut butter and soup, boxes of pasta and cereal. I started at the higher shelves and worked my way down. I hesitated at the last shelf, eyeing a dozen cans of unopened cat food. He'd been missing seven days. The dead guy was going to stay dead, but the cat still had a chance. I wasn't really a cat person, but I hoped if I were missing for seven days without food, someone would be looking pretty hard to find me. I promised myself I wouldn't get so caught up in the bigger aspects of the case that I forgot Flash was counting on me.

I continued to search the house, moving from room to room. In the living room I checked under the couch and peered into the fireplace. In the den I snooped through bookshelves packed with classics, textbooks, and best-sellers. In the bathrooms I checked under the sinks and in the bathtubs. As they had been on the previous day, most of the doors were already closed. Maybe Flash sneaked in when the door was open and was trapped when the door got closed. A simple explanation in a case big enough to warrant murder. Probably not. Still, it wasn't like I really knew what I was looking for, anyway.

I reached the third floor before there were any signs of human habitation. I finally spotted personality in the first room on the right at the top of the ornate wooden staircase. Opening the door, I walked into a scene from *Aladdin.* The style was so different from the rest of the house, I assumed the room belonged to Millicent. Masterson must have allowed her free rein in her own quarters. A tragic, opulent mistake.

The bed was huge, its brass canopy draped in shimmering blue material. The bed itself was covered in a satin spread with a riotous print that forced me to squint against the visual assault. Dozens of pillows in various shapes, sizes, and colors were propped against the headboard. The bedside tables, wrapped in the same gauzy material as the canopy, held matching lanternlike lamps with green-tasseled shades. Both were stacked high with crossword-puzzle books, discarded magazines, and romance novels. Next to one of the bedside tables there was an enormous gilt mirror set in front of a dressing table swathed in purple velvet. The tabletop was bare but smudged. I leaned down and peered beneath the velvet cloth. Underneath was a pair of gray flannel slippers with rubber soles.

I straightened and moved to the closet. It was a walk-in affair with double rods on both sides. There were half a dozen polyester suits in boring blues and blacks and ten blouses, six white. Three pairs of shoes. The entire contents didn't use six inches of rod length. The only flash of color in the entire space was a pink silk robe embroidered with delicate flowers in yellow. The room of a madam and the wardrobe of a nun. Maybe the decor hadn't been Millicent's idea. Had Masterson decorated the room for her? For that matter, what was a personal assistant doing living with her boss? Did she really have to be on call twenty-four hours a day? In this room? Interesting job description.

I retreated from the closet and walked to a black-lacquered wardrobe. Opening the doors, I spotted a stereo, television, and VCR, all seemingly new. The lower drawers revealed video- and audiocassettes in a huge jumble, most of them having been pulled from their protective cases and tossed back into the mix with no thought to organization. I wondered how Millicent found anything in the mess.

The matching tallboy dresser was nearly as bad, the few T-shirts and jeans wadded up and jammed into the drawers with no regard for neatness. The only interesting thing I discovered was her penchant for Victoria's Secret lingerie in a size sixteen. Quite the contradiction, Millicent.

And then it hit me. If I excluded her underwear, there wasn't a single personal thing in this entire room. No pictures of family or friends, no memento from a vacation trip. No address book, no old bills, nothing. Millicent had been dead for a few months, but no one had gotten rid of her clothes yet. What happened to the rest of her things?

I started pulling open drawers in the dresser. Socks, support hose, one loose shoelace. Two empties. Who had empty drawers? Maybe some of her stuff was gone, but why? Where? Who? The last drawer handle stopped abruptly halfway open. I reached in to dislodge the mess and allow the drawer to open more fully. It finally yielded with a jolt, sending the drawer out of its housing and onto the floor with a clatter. I stared at a bloodred lipstick smear I had managed to get on my hand during my efforts before reaching for a tissue from the tabletop and wiping the mess away. I dropped to my knees and scooped up makeup, costume jewelry, scarves, and various other girlie-girl things.

I lifted a scarf, a blue-and-tan-checked silk with a Nordstrom price tag still attached. A hundred and twenty dollars. For a scarf. A scarf that now sported a lipstick accent. Makeup in a bottom drawer?

I slid the drawer back into its slot, imagining my own apartment. I wasn't a collector. I preferred my flat surfaces clean, but even I had a picture of Russ stuck to my refrigerator door with a magnet. My wedding picture, a blurry Polaroid obligingly snapped by a boozy tourist, I kept with my underwear.

I went back to the closet and stared at the empty rods.

I had no way of knowing if anything was missing. Maybe I should talk to Jeff about it. Then again, why would he know? I walked to the bed and sat down, trying to picture my own bedroom and superimposing my personal effects over Millicent's.

There was the picture. And a dog-eared, floral-covered journal I used to vent my frustrations. I had a hundred-dollar bill in my cookie jar for emergencies. And in the bottom drawer of my night table, I had the ugly rhinestone brooch Jimmy Wilcox had given me in the seventh grade. Millicent didn't have anything like that. No valuables of any kind. Of course, some of that costume jewelry could be real. I could be staring at the Hope Diamond and, unless it was on a velvet cloth in a museum, still think it was a Cracker Jack prize. But her stuff had seemed too gaudy. Too loud to be real. Then again, she hadn't spent her money on flashy clothes. What did a personal assistant make? Enough for a $2 million trust but not a designer suit? Would any woman buy real diamonds to wear with knockoff clothes?

"Ahem."

I jumped, my heart thundering into my throat.

"You scared me."

"Find anything interesting?" Connor asked, standing in the doorway.

"Not really. I'm not sure what I'm looking for." I gestured toward the room.

"Anything out of the ordinary, I guess." Connor came

in and went to peer into the closet. "This room doesn't match the house."

"Yeah. And the clothes don't match the room. Stranger still, Millicent has nothing personal, and I think maybe this room's been searched."

"Why?"

"She's got an expensive scarf in with the lipsticks."

"That's some sort of woman rule?"

"Common sense."

"Think they found anything?"

I shrugged. "I don't know. None of this makes sense. If someone wanted to steal, why leave some things and not others? And why search at all? Looking for Flash? I doubt it. You wouldn't look in the drawers. Money? She set up the trust. Maybe someone thought she had cash. Or jewelry or a bankbook or, I don't know, the Maltese Falcon. None of it seems linked to the body from last night."

Oops. I had been trying not to remind him about the body, but he seemed unbothered when I mentioned it.

"Anything else I should know about last night?"

"I don't think I'm going to be arrested for murder, but that might just be wishful thinking."

"Okay, then. You done here?"

"Pretty much."

Jeff was waiting for us in the living room.

"I can't stop thinking about what you said," Jeff began. "That I might have been the target last night. It doesn't make sense. I honestly don't have any enemies."

Connor and I took matching wing-back chairs.

"Which leaves us with Flash's disappearance as the motivating factor," I suggested.

"Or the trust." Jeff's fingers tapped against the silk.

"Plenty of reasons to be up to no good," I agreed. "Did you get a copy of the trust document when you became Flash's trustee?"

"I'm not trustee. A bank does that. They hired me to provide the day-to-day care. I might have seen the trust document. I don't remember."

"How do you get paid?"

"Wire transfer at the first of the month. It covers my salary and Flash's expenses."

I crossed my legs and folded my hands.

"What bank is it drawn on?"

He tipped his head to one side. "It's a wire. I'm not actually sure where it comes from. Is that important?"

" 'I don't know' seems to be my answer of the day. I don't suppose you kept copies?"

"No."

"What do you do if there's a problem?"

"Until now there's never been a problem. When he went missing I called your law firm. They represent Stuart Masterson."

"And Millicent." I thought about the empty files.

"Millicent?" Connor asked.

"She's the one who left her money to the cat." I turned back to Jeff. "Do you know anything about the trust?"

"Such as?"

"I'm wondering where a personal assistant got two million dollars."

"Stuart Masterson is rich." Jeff shrugged. "I assumed Millicent . . . well, um . . ." He cleared his throat.

"Was she the type?" I asked.

"Is there a type?" Jeff asked, exchanging a look with Connor.

Men. Honestly.

"Maybe she inherited it from a generous uncle," Jeff suggested. "I don't know. Do you think any of this will lead to Flash?"

"I've got my doubts he just wandered off," I told him. "When was the last time someone was in Millicent's room?" I leaned against the table, carefully keeping my tone casual.

"I don't know."

"Have you ever been in there?"

"Sure. When I was looking for Flash."

"What happened to her personals?" Connor asked. He'd been letting me lead the conversation. Background was definitely not his strong suit. I tried to drill him with my eyes.

"Everything is still in her room, I suppose."

"No one disputed the will?" He remained oblivious to the drill, so I reached across and tapped the back of his hand.

Jeff was looking back and forth between us like we were at Wimbledon.

"Not that I know of."

"What happens to the money if . . ." I tapped Connor with more force and a fingernail. He looked over at me.

"What happens to the money if Flash doesn't come home?" I grinned evilly at Connor before turning back to Jeff.

His eyebrows were raised.

"I mean, surely Millicent didn't expect Flash to run through the whole stash on catnip."

"He was spoiled." Jeff shrugged. "As for the rest, I don't know."

"Not you?" I asked.

"Definitely not. Millicent and I were acquaintances. I think she chose me only because I was already living in the guesthouse and I'm fond of animals."

"Why were you living here?" Connor asked.

"I'm working on my dissertation at the university. Psychological disorders and criminal victimology. Specifically, I'm researching the techniques employed in confidence crimes. The guesthouse is convenient and free. I think Masterson had some sort of alumni connection."

I stood up. Connor and Jeff rose, too.

"I think that's all I have for today, Jeff."

"Are you staying on the case? I mean, with last night, I would understand if you wanted to quit. Flash might be okay. If he's loose, his instincts will probably take over and he'll fend for himself. I'm not sure you should risk yourself for him. I'm very attached, of course, but you're a stranger."

"I promised you I would find your cat. That's what I'm going to do."

Jeff sighed. "I am grateful, Sara. Please be careful, though."

"I will. You might want to keep your doors locked, too." I offered him my hand. He took it and held on.

"You don't have to tell me twice. I've definitely picked up a taste of the house paranoia. Rumor has it Stuart Masterson checks under his bed every night."

Jeff and Connor shook hands. "Connor, it was a pleasure to meet you."

"You, too," Connor murmured.

As we were pulling out of the driveway, Connor said, "Interesting guy."

"What's that supposed to mean?"

"He lives on-site but doesn't know anything. He gets paid to take care of some cat. He doesn't pay rent. He's a poseur."

"Connor, he's a student." I rolled down my window.

"Dresses pretty well for a student, Sara."

"Fine. He dresses well. What did you think of the house?"

"Rich-guy place. Security's a joke. Everything's wired but nothing's on. Dead bolt is decent but new, and there was no key in the back of the lock."

"So?"

"People who use them keep the key there in case of fire. Or close to the lock, anyway. I didn't find one. My guess is they're for show. What's next?"

"I'm going to check with the animal-control people again. And then I thought I'd try to talk to the Mastersons and the business partner, Henry Jepsen."

"What do you hope to get from them?" Connor merged onto the bridge. I stared at the lake, shimmering blue in the sun.

"They were all here in the last few days. They could have seen Flash. They probably knew about the money. They'd know who to call to get it."

"Talk as in phone?" Connor asked.

"Probably."

"If it's only probably, I'll stay with you."

"No."

"Yes."

"No. I'm not being difficult, Connor. These are probably phone calls. At worst, it means a couple of office visits. Public buildings, bright light of day. Short of my being run down by a caffeine addict lunging toward a Starbucks, I'd bet real money on coming back in one piece. Besides, if I do end up face-to-face, any one of these guys could call my boss, and it will be hard enough to explain why I'm there without having to come up with a reason for you."

Connor merged onto the freeway without needing my directions. In fact, he'd driven us home without once asking for them. I envied him his internal atlas. I was born without a sense of direction.

"Just desk time and a couple of business types during office hours?" Connor asked.

"Absolutely." I crossed my fingers just in case I was lying.

Chapter Eleven

Connor dropped me at the office. I stopped by the break room on the way to my office, picking up a bag of chips and a soda for a belated meal at my desk. While I munched, I surfed the Internet until I found the newspaper article about Flash. It was pretty light on facts. It mentioned Millicent and millions along with a beloved pet, but no details about the trust. I looked for the byline, then pulled the phone book off my shelf. I reached for the phone.

"You never did say what happened to your face." Joe strolled into my cubicle and sat down.

"Walked into a door."

"You might try opening it next time."

"I'll do that."

"I hope that's not a personal call." Joe shook his head. "Big brother is watching. You remember Stan Intuak? Litigation paralegal on the forty-first floor? He got canned last week for playing computer games online during work hours. And Marta Blake, the summer law clerk, had her full-time offer withdrawn yesterday when they found out she'd been making copies of personal stuff."

"You're kidding."

"Nope. There's some sort of software that tracks employee activities. Phones, copiers, fax machines. Elizabeth personally reviews the printouts. And you know what that means."

"She is such a bitch." I couldn't believe somebody had actually been fired for making a few extra copies. It was practically an employee benefit. Elizabeth probably thought it was the height of power to be able to crush people for stupid stuff like that.

"Hmm." Joe rose and ambled out of my cubicle.

"Hey, Joe. Did you want something when you came in or did you just stop by to nap in my chair?"

He shrugged. "Just thought you might want to, you know, talk or something."

"Talk?"

He tapped next to his eye.

"Oh, that. It's nothing."

"Okay." He shrugged again.

"Thanks for asking." I was touched and a little embarrassed.

"Sure." He flushed before wandering away.

I called the reporter, a guy named Bill Forester. His one-second baritone "Leave one" was followed by a computer-generated voice telling me his voice mail was full. How many messages did it take to fill voice mail? Frustrated, I took two preboredom, postconcussion pain relievers and tried to come up with a game plan. Flash was a missing heir. Routine. Of course, most heirs were happy to be found, lured by the temptation of money. Even though I'd never met him personally, I somehow didn't think Flash was the mercenary type.

I swiveled my chair back and forth. The motion was soothing, almost hypnotic. I took a couple of minutes and closed my eyes, swaying with the chair. The phone rang.

"Sara Townley."

"This is Elizabeth. Mr. Hamilton wants a daily progress report on the Millinfield matter."

I opened my eyes and sat up.

"Um, of course."

She hung up.

I stared at the phone in my hand, embarrassed at drifting off even though Elizabeth couldn't have known that

I'd been on the verge of sleep. I stood and stretched, doing neck rolls and shoulder shrugs to wake myself up. I reached toward my bookcase. The shelves groaned with the tools of my trade: phone books, reverse directories, and atlases for legwork. Binoculars, camera, and crosswords for surveillance work. Dictionary and thesaurus for paperwork. Nerf basketball. Joe had installed a hoop that was perfect for blind three-point shots at the buzzer from the comfort of my chair. Even worker bees needed diversions.

I flipped my dog-eared yellow pages. If Flash had been an actual person, then after checking with his beer-drinking, male-bonding buddies, his longtime mistress, and his new girlfriend, I would check the local jails and hospitals. For a cat on the lam, that meant the pound.

There were a dozen animal shelters, welfare societies, and halfway houses for pets listed in the phone book. I'd called half the previous day without success. That left six for today's mind-numbing chore. I dialed the first number.

"Animal Astrological Commune, Astrid speaking." She had a soft, breathy voice barely audible over the New Age background music.

"I'm looking for a cat."

"And what is your sign?"

"My sign?"

"Or your birthday would be better. I could consult your chart for last life connection and psychic empathy, too."

"He's male, gray and white, and weighs about ten pounds. Answers to the name Flash." I drew a cartoon cat's head on the yellow-lined pad.

"I'm sure that can't be right."

"I beg your pardon?"

"Forgiveness is a gift of the spirit," she replied serenely.

"This cat is missing." I felt like Alice in Wonderland.

"Perhaps his spirit needed to travel along its true path. Rejoice in the journey."

"Is there someone else there that I could talk to?" I asked, using shading to give Flash's features a feral quality.

"I am but one," she said sadly. "Melissa won't be back until after her honeymoon."

"Let me guess: You're new." Her unflappable serenity made me want to spit nails. "Do you have any animals without known owners?"

"One spirit cannot own another."

"Could I come look at any cats you do have?" I was starting to feel desperate to get off the phone and back to normal people. Flash's body was a little disproportionate, but I was satisfied with the overall aesthetic of my rendition.

"You must reach out to the world around you."

"When?"

"Your psychic energy is ever flowing."

"When are you open?" I asked, deliberately pausing between each word.

"Whenever."

"I don't suppose 'whenever' happens on a regular schedule?"

"Not usually, no."

"Thanks."

I dialed the next number. The phone rang ten times before being answered by a harassed receptionist with a harsh, "SHARPO."

"Excuse me?"

"SHARPO."

"I'm looking for the pound."

"We don't call it the pound anymore. This is the Society of Humans Achieving Responsible Pet Ownership."

"Uh, sorry. I'm looking for a cat." Was it a full moon?

"Identification tattoo?"

"No visible marks." My doodle began to sport an ink *Mom* near his shoulder.

"Microchip?"

"What?" Did she think he was the feline version of 007?

"Does he have a microchip for identification?" She used the same you-are-an-imbecile-wasting-my-time pause between syllables I had used on poor Astrid. Microchip? Maybe it was like a LoJack for pets. Maybe all I had to do was follow the signal to find Flash.

"I don't know. If he has one, could I use it to track him?"

"The microchip is for identification only. If he's found"—she emphasized *if*—"we would know where he lives and who his owner is by the information on the chip."

"Oh."

"Yeah, oh. Name."

"Sara Townley."

"His name."

"Flash." I added a banner with his name in a flowing, graceful font.

"Description?"

"Gray and white, male, approximately ten pounds." I shifted in my chair, leaning back to peruse my drawing.

"Altered?"

"I have no idea." The file hadn't contained any information about Flash's medical history. Probably too personal. My pen raised, I briefly considered incorporating this idea into my sketch but decided against descending into pet pornography.

"Some people shouldn't have pets." She slammed down the phone.

I carefully returned the phone to its cradle. My head ached, but at least I'd have something to put on the daily report Elizabeth had demanded.

I spent a half hour running cursory criminal and credit checks on the Masterson offspring so I'd have something for Morris's report before deciding that my promise to Connor didn't mean that I couldn't follow hot leads. Well, not hot exactly, but a lawsuit claiming wrongful termination, and the eldest child of a billionaire spending a three-day weekend in jail because he couldn't make bail were mildly interesting. More interesting than getting browbeaten by strangers for my pet-parenting skills. Besides, a little fresh air would help my headache. It was practically a medical intervention.

I went in search of Joe. I found him at his desk, his face inches from a stack of papers with tiny print.

"How go the crusades?" I asked him, leaning against the opening to his cubicle.

"Bloody," he said, not looking up.

"I thought you lawyer types loved that sort of thing?"

He did look up then. "We do. We really, really do," he said in a monotone.

"Can I borrow you car?" I asked.

"Got any more Snickers?" he asked, looking back down at the work in front of him.

"No."

"Call a cab."

"If I had wheels," I drawled, "I could get some."

"The big bag and a full tank." He tossed me his keys.

"You need a twelve-step program."

"Yeah, I'm on that."

"Joe?"

"I'm in withdrawal here."

"What would you say if I told you I got married?"

Joe looked up and blinked. Then he went back to work.

I could have stayed in my office and rode the phones, calling the rest of the shelters in case Flash had turned up. On the other hand, since Joe seemed to be in hypoglycemic withdrawal, the least I could do was go on a mission of mercy and pick up some of the poor overworked guy's favorite treats. I hadn't taken a lunch break either, and after the stress of last night and the fight—if I could call it that—with Connor this morning, a little alone time was just what the doctor ordered.

Chapter Twelve

J epsen worked out of the Bank of America building downtown. I took the elevator to the twenty-eighth floor and stepped out, momentarily stunned by a hideous electric blue vase stuffed with stiffened orange feather boas. I looked right and then left. In either direction there were heavy glass doors inscribed with multiple names of law firm bigwigs. I didn't see Jepsen's name on either door. I double-checked the address. Bank of America building, twenty-eighth floor. I was in the right place, so where the heck was his office? I picked left and pushed my way through the doors, stopping in front of an elegantly dressed blond woman wearing a phone headset and speaking in melodious tones. She raised one manicured hand to stop me from speaking while throwing me a brilliant white smile of apology. I waited for her to finish while taking in the expensive furnishings and original art on the walls. Morris's ambient approach to the rich and powerful. Maybe they taught it in law school.

"May I help you?" the secretary asked.

"I'm looking for Jepsen Entrepreneurial Opportunities. Do you know where it is?"

"Sure." The secretary's blue eyes did a quick assessment of their own, taking their time and moving from the top of my head, past my navy blazer and wrinkled chinos to my black penny loafers, a puzzled expression on her face. I fought the urge to straighten my clothes.

"His office is in the core. Go out this door and turn left, past the restrooms, and it's on your right."

"Thanks."

A discreet buzz sounded and she answered another call, her expression once again completely bland.

While the law firms had paid premium prices for their amazing views, Jepsen had contented himself with the cachet the address offered. Not that it had helped him. Before the split with Masterson, Jepsen's name was all over the business section. Afterward, he couldn't deal cards. Which was probably when Jepsen took up the sport of suing.

His office was in the center of the building. While the heavy wood door boasted a scrolled brass plate with the firm's name and Jepsen's name and PRESIDENT, the inner vestibule was small and cramped, decorated in muted purple and gray. I stood between a bleached oak desk too big for the narrow room, and two large overstuffed chairs in fake leather. A framed Munch print screamed at me from behind the unmanned desk.

I noted the empty wire mesh in-basket. The desk held a beige desk blotter, a stapler, and a tape dispenser in precise alignment. I didn't see a computer. There was a small brass bell, and I raised my hand to summon attention before stopping. Snooping was like eating potato chips: Now that I'd started I was having a little trouble stopping myself. I couldn't resist the temptation the undefended desk afforded. I looked around oh, so casually. I shifted slightly to peer at the two doors behind the desk, both closed. After a quick glance over my shoulder, I stepped behind the desk. The chair squeaked when I pulled and I reassessed my chances of getting caught. My heart pounded. A moment passed, and when no one appeared I pulled open the top desk drawer. It had pencils and Post-it notes but not much else.

I turned my attention to the upper right-hand drawer, spotting a day planner. I liberated it, flipping open to the current date, then paging back one day at a time. The schedule included meeting times, places, and associates, each with a reference to the purpose of the meeting. Most of the pages were empty, and the appointments seemed to consist primarily of bankers and investors, with an attorney thrown in. The legal appointments were noted with a capital M. Masterson, probably. At the rate this guy was meeting with his lawyers, he'd be broke even if he managed to hoodwink some jury.

There were also two appointments in the month before Flash disappeared that I couldn't understand. One was just initials with a phone number, and the other was a lunch meeting at the Rock Salt with a lowercase d next to the time. Both were written in a different hand from the rest of the entries. I pulled my notebook from my pocket and pilfered a pen from the middle drawer, carefully copying the two messages. I closed the diary and returned it to the drawer. I made a quick search for a Rolodex or phone book without success. Oh, well, I guess I couldn't expect the mother lode every time. Deciding I had pushed my luck far enough at the moment, I slid the middle drawer closed and replaced the chair in its previous location. I returned to stand at the far side of the desk and had just raised my hand to ring the bell when one of the inner doors abruptly opened and a rather disheveled flame-red-haired girl in a tight lime green dress and matching spike heels emerged. A rush of success left me nearly giddy. Timing and presentation really were everything.

The woman sauntered toward me smoothing the form-fitting lines of her dress with a hand adorned by three-inch-long black-lacquered fingernails. It took a moment to pull my eyes away.

"You want somethin'?" the woman asked, snapping her gum.

"My name is Sara Townley. I'd like to speak with Mr. Jepsen."

"You wanna leave your name?"

"I was hoping to actually talk to him."

"He's unavailable."

"Perhaps you could explain to Mr. Jepsen that I am

with Abercroft, Hamilton, and Sterns. The law firm that
represents Stuart Masterson." A technical truth, maybe,
but still intriguing enough to get Jepsen's attention—I
hoped. I really hoped he wasn't going to call and check.
I pulled a business card from my jacket pocket and offered it to her. She took it and stared at me for a moment, still snapping her gum, a shrewd look on her ebony
face. I made sure mine remained expressionless.

"I'll ax him. Wait here." She pivoted on one of those
deadly spikes and returned to the door from which she
had emerged. She knocked, then stepped inside, closing
the door behind her. A minute passed before the door
opened again and she gestured me inside.

"Mr. Jepsen will see you now."

I stepped around the desk and entered Jepsen's office.

A man greeted me at the door with an outstretched
hand and a creepy smile baring yellowed teeth. He was
about sixty years old, dressed in an expensive blue suit
designed to hide what I suspected was serious middle-
age spread. His white hair was worn long on one side in
a comb-over style. Why was it that men never understood how dumb that hairstyle was? I shook his hand
and surreptitiously wiped on the leg of my trousers the
moisture his sweating palm had left.

"Henry Jepsen. You're one of Masterson's mouth-
pieces, huh? A girl? Well, it don't matter. I'm not gonna
be sidetracked by a little thigh. Took you damn long
enough. I assume you're here to talk settlement. That
son of a bitch owes me."

"Mr. Jepsen, I'm afraid there's been a misunderstanding."

"There's been a misunderstanding, all right. That bastard thinks he can steal from me and get away with it.
Then he hides behind a bunch of candy-ass, butt-wipe
lawyers. Don't think that just because I'm willing to talk
deal that I'm gonna let that motherfucker off cheap. No
goddamn way. He better settle pretty quick or I'm gonna
personally see to it that he never does business in this
town again. Does he think anybody's gonna deal with a

little pissant like him after I get done? He settles quick and I'll think about lettin' him keep his pretty little reputation. He stalls, and I'm gonna make sure that there isn't a dealer in this town that doesn't know all his dirty little secrets. And I mean all of 'em.''

Jepsen's tirade came upon waves of bad breath heavily laced with alcohol. I took a step back to get out of range and bumped into the doorjamb. I wanted to ask Jepsen some questions, but not badly enough to subject myself to physical contact. I already felt like I needed a shower.

"Mr. Jepsen, there's been a mistake. I'm not here to discuss your lawsuit against Stuart Masterson. I need to ask you some questions about something else. Could we sit down?" I used my hands to urge him back to his chair on the other side of the desk, careful not to actually touch.

He glared at me through bleary eyes. I took one step sideways, placing myself in the doorway for a quicker exit in case it became necessary. He continued to stare for a long moment before abruptly turning and dropping back to his chair. It squeaked in protest.

I settled myself into the only other chair in the room, a heavy oak with ornate scrolling and no padding in the seat. I looked around the room. The furniture was too big and cramped for the small space. His desk was awash with stacks of papers. I didn't see a computer here either. The Stone Age, complete with Neanderthal man. *Great.*

"What the hell do you want?"

"I'm investigating the disappearance of an associate of Mr. Masterson. I was hoping you could help me with some background."

"Who's missing?"

"I'm not at liberty to say." I was glad I'd rehearsed my story on the way over. Even I thought I sounded coolly professional. It was a mismatch against a drunk, but still impressive.

"Look, I'm a very busy man. I haven't got time for some chickie asking stupid questions."

"I was wondering when you were last at Stuart Masterson's house."

"His house. Why the hell would I go there?"

"A witness saw you there quite recently."

He reached over and picked up a coffee cup sitting amidst the debris of his desk. I angled myself closer to the desk to try to read some of the papers. He took a swallow and returned the cup to its place on the desk. He smacked his lips. No way was that coffee.

"Yeah, okay. I've been there."

"When?"

"I dunno. Couple days ago. The bastard's hiding. Thinks he can just pull a Howard Hughes and get away with it."

"Away with what, sir?"

"Stealing. He's nothing but a goddamn thief. My ideas, my contacts. Without me he'd still be conning widows out of their savings."

"I'm sorry. I don't understand."

"I knew him. Really knew him. Before the nose job and the phony accent. Before he became Mr. High and Mighty Businessman of the Year. No one else knows, but I do."

Jepsen was drunk and probably spewing sour grapes, but what if he really did know something? Flash was missing. There was the dead guy in an alley, and when was the last time anybody had seen Stuart Masterson? Jepsen, if he was telling the truth, had gone to Masterson's house looking for him. Someone at his office must know where he was, but who? I made a mental note to find out. I slid farther forward in my chair and casually turned my head to make reading upside down easier.

"Do you remember the exact day that you were last at the Masterson house?"

"Tuesday, Wednesday. I don't know."

"Did you go into the house?"

"No." His voice was emphatic, clearer, suddenly more alert. I looked back into his eyes. They were green. A flat peridot green, totally different from Connor's emerald. Connor's were fringed with gold-tipped lashes thick as paintbrushes. They had laugh lines at the edges. . . . *Jeez.* I shook my head, trying to dislodge Connor's image. What was I doing? I forced myself to smile and try to ease Jepsen back into his previous cooperative stupor.

"Did you see anyone else at the house when you were there?"

"No."

"Did you see anything out of the ordinary?"

"Like?"

"A strange car, people in the neighborhood, animals roaming loose."

"No. I didn't see anything. I knocked on the front door, and when no one answered I went home."

"You don't have a key?"

"Why the hell would I have a key?"

"You and Masterson were partners. He worked from his house. It would make sense if you had a key."

"Well, I don't."

"And you didn't see a cat?"

"No, I didn't see no goddamn cat. Nasty thing. Gray, right? Never did understand why he put up with it."

"Put up with it?"

"The bitch's mongrel cat. Always biting and spitting." The bitch or the cat?

"You knew Millicent Millinfield?" A shot in the dark.

"He's got enough to screw anything he wants, and he spends his time with that ugly old bitch. He's losin' it. Mark my words. He ain't what he was, and he wasn't nothin' without me. Stupid bastard, lettin' her move in like that. And that mangy damn cat, too. I told him then, 'Big mistake. Hump what you want, but don't shit where you eat.' You got me, girlie?" Spittle collected at the corners of his mouth. The little troll appeared to be frothing.

"Do you know anyone else who might have keys?"

Jepsen steepled his sausagelike fingers. He rolled his eyes toward the ceiling, and I took the opportunity to read the top page of the stack of paper at the desk's front edge. The phone bill. Ugly red demand to *pay now or your service will be discontinued*. I glanced up to see that Jepsen's gaze had returned to my face.

"Did you check with the brat?"

"Mr. Masterson's children?"

"Yeah, them. A couple of weeks ago I saw them coming out of the house when I went by to drop off some papers."

"Were they coming out of the house or just knocking?"

"Coming out."

"Anyone else?"

"Did you talk to that sponge who lives in the guesthouse?"

"Sponge?" Jeff?

"I don't know what the hell his name is. All I know is he acts like he owns the place. A real superior bastard, if you know what I mean. Thinks his shit don't stink."

"I see. When was the last time you were actually in the house?"

"Couple months ago."

"Do you remember the exact date?"

"No."

"Maybe it's in your Day-Timer," I suggested with total innocence.

Jepsen pulled a notebook from the stack of papers without looking. Impressive. The book was open, and I half rose from my chair to scan the entries as he flipped back a day at a time.

"Nothing. Satisfied?"

"You've been very helpful, sir." I stood and reached my hand out to shake his, deliberately toppling the paper stack near the edge of the desk. The pages showered my feet and I dropped to my knees, scooping up the mess.

"I'm so sorry. How clumsy of me." I scraped at papers. I heard Jepsen rise from his chair but he made no move to help me. The hairs on the back of my neck stood up as I could feel him staring at me. I gathered up the paperwork and stood, extending the documents to him with a smile.

"Leave them. The girl will do it."

"Thanks again for your time, Mr. Jepsen."

He plopped back into his chair without trying to shake my hand again.

"Yeah, whatever." He dropped his head into his hands. I turned and left the room, closing the door behind me. I passed through the once-again-deserted reception area and into the hallway. I strolled to the elevator and waited until the door closed before checking my pocket. I grinned at Jepsen's phone bill. It was amazing how fast I was developing light-fingered tendencies. Next time, maybe I wouldn't even feel like throwing up.

Chapter Thirteen

If I hadn't known from the credit check, this house made it clear that Daddy apparently didn't share his economic good fortune with his progeny. Unlike the elder Masterson and his palatial estate, Bud and Stewie Masterson worked out of a dumpy little house squeezed between two equally dilapidated residences. It didn't emit an aura of power or convenience. It felt more like desperation. A quick check of the file I had put together revealed that the house was owned by Sterling "Bud" Masterson, the younger son, and that it doubled as his home. Stuart Junior, or Stewie, rented a one-bedroom off Aurora Avenue. Note to self—drugs and temper do not a good time make, and big brother Stewie was the one who liked to cut things. For an instant I remembered my promise to Connor. Well, they did use it as an office, and it was daylight. Maybe I was a little beyond the spirit of the promise, but on a technical basis I was still innocent.

I slid the file under the passenger seat and opened the glove compartment. Surprise, surprise—Joe didn't keep pepper spray in his car either. I still didn't have anything resembling a weapon. I wrote the words *pepper spray* on my hand in ink. Stuart's last rap sheet entry was more than three years old. Stewie hadn't been to jail in two. I crossed myself and said a quick prayer to whatever saint protected the truly stupid and totally unprepared and got out of the car.

I walked toward the house on a cracked sidewalk erupting with patches of weeds. I climbed the sloping concrete steps and pulled open the torn screen door, knocking loudly. After waiting a long two minutes without a response, I tried again. I leaned close to the door, listening over the din of the nearby freeway.

"He ain't home." I jumped at the sound of the voice, my heart pounding. My coronary inducer turned out to be a tow-haired boy of around four years old, sitting on a rusty blue tricycle at the end of the walk. So much for high alert.

"Do you know Mr. Masterson?"

"Bud is a butt-head."

I tried to keep my face bland. I didn't have kids, but I was pretty sure *butt-head* wasn't part of the preferred vocabulary. I didn't want to encourage his delinquency, but I'd seen the rap sheet, and *butt-head* was an astute call. I moved down the stairs and along the walkway toward him. He flashed deep dimples with his sunny smile, and I couldn't help but grin in return.

"Bud is a butt-head, Bud is a butt-head," he sing-songed.

"You don't like him, I guess?"

"He says bad words." My young informer's solemn expression showed his lack of appreciation for Sterling Masterson's verbal abilities.

"Oh. Well, that's not good."

"Bud's dumber than Stewie, and that's not even possi-ble." He laid long emphasis on the word *even,* unconsciously adopting a censorious tone I was sure he had learned at home. I made a pledge to never voice opinions in front of preschoolers again.

I took a final step closer to the boy and sat down on the sidewalk, folding my legs Indian-style. It probably wasn't quite ethical to pump little kids for information, but he was offering pretty freely.

"Why do you think Bud is dumb?"

"He pees money. I can pee in the toilet like a big boy." He seemed very pleased with his accomplishment, once again beaming at me.

"Good for you. You seem like a big boy to me."

"I'm four." He held up his pudgy hand, spreading his fingers so I could tell he hadn't actually learned to count yet.

"Four is definitely a big boy. Do you know where Bud is right now?"

"The resation."

"I don't know where that is."

"The resation. Wif da Indyans."

"Ah."

"I never seen a Indyan; have you?"

"I think they call them Native Americans." Never too young to numb him with political correctness. I reached out toward a tuft of grass, pulling a few blades as I considered. "So Bud went to the reservation, huh?"

"Yup."

"Of course. And he pees money. Do you mean he pisses money away?"

"That's a bad word. You're not 'sposed ta say that." His blue eyes rounded, his voice a hush as he shifted around on the seat of his tricycle.

"You're absolutely right. I won't do it again. Who said Bud pees money?"

"Mommy."

I started to strip the thin blades of grass into even thinner slivers. The credit check had made it clear both sons owed large sums to legitimate creditors, but if Bud had a gambling problem, his debts could be the sort that led to violence. How that could have led to my dead guy in the alley, I couldn't really see. Besides, Stewie was the one with the penchant for assault with grievous bodily intent. Maybe they were involved in something together? Nothing made sense.

"Did your mom ever say anything else about Bud?"

"Bud is a butt-head, Bud is a butt-head."

"I'm pretty sure that's another one of the words you shouldn't say."

" 'Kay."

"Did your mom say anything else about Bud?"

"Bud kicked Yips."

"He kicked Yips?"

"Yup. Hard."

"Yips is a dog?" I guessed. Bastard. If he'd kick a dog, what would he do to poor Flash? Maybe this wasn't a swipe. Maybe it was a serial killer wannabe taking out his antisocial behavior on a helpless pet. I didn't want to think about it. The little boy nodded again, beginning to rock on his seat, nearly throwing himself off. I dropped the grass and leaned forward, prepared to make a mad grab if the boy actually managed to launch himself.

"Yips is a 'treaver. He's Mikey's dog. Mikey got him for his birfday."

"That's a nice gift."

"Mikey's daddy gave him to Mikey. Mikey's got a new daddy."

I doubted they were actually connected, but I didn't suggest it to my new friend. For all I knew, divorce might frequently follow pet adoption.

"And Bud kicked Mikey's dog."

"Yep. And Yips had to go to the doctor."

"Is he all right now?"

"Yup."

"Tony," a woman's voice called urgently. "Tony."

"Bye." The little boy pumped plump legs, quickly generating a head of steam as he raced toward the call. I looked toward the woman several houses away; her face was indistinct but her mood carried.

"I thought I told you to stay in the yard."

"But, Moooom . . ."

Ah, the universal retort of youth. Rising from my seated position, I brushed the seat of my pants. One look told me Tony's mother had no interest in a conversation with a stranger who'd approached her son on the street. I couldn't blame her. She glared until Tony was safely in the house, then slammed the door loud enough for me to hear. Accepting her decision with good grace, I went back to my car. If I bolstered my energy with some french fries, I had plenty of time for evil son number two.

Chapter Fourteen

The heavy security door on Stuart Masterson's apartment had a broken lock and a spiderweb of cracks in the thick pane of cloudy glass. I opened the door, stepping into a dingy foyer that reeked with the sweet smell of marijuana. The hall was even gloomier, completely denying the August sunshine I had left behind. The floor was cluttered with garbage, the walls scarred. I followed the hall to a stairway at the end, hesitating for a moment before pushing the door open, tripping my way up three flights with the negligible aid of a low-watt bulb. This was not the sort of place any rational woman wanted to run into someone she didn't know. Or someone she did know, for that matter. I doubted a scream for help in this building was either unusual or successful. I shook the can in my hand. One drive past the building and I'd headed straight for the local pawnshop. There were plenty in the neighborhood. When the counterman realized I didn't have three days to wait for a weapon, he'd sent me to REI. There, under the guidance of a Rasta granola guy in a tie-dyed T-shirt, I'd bought the Magnum of immediate personal protection—Counter Assault Bear Deterrent. Guaranteed to take out a PMSing grizzly from fifty feet away. Bad neighborhood, addict to interrogatee—no problem.

Peering into the fourth-floor hallway, I was relieved to find it empty. Well, at least it didn't have any people in it. Empty it wasn't. This floor looked like a tornado had blown through, depositing refuse in every corner. It smelled of sweat and urine. I forced myself to breathe through my mouth, gagging a little. I found Stuart Masterson's door and knocked loudly, looking around to see if I roused anyone else. I lifted my hand to pound a second time just as the door swung open, barely catching myself before rapping my knuckles against a barrel chest covered in wrinkled cotton. His khaki pants were soiled and crumpled. He squinted at me through the pudgy folds of his face.

"Whaddya want?" His breath was heavy with alcohol while his eyes were dilated into tiny pinpricks. Drugs and alcohol, breakfast of champions. I suddenly wondered how important anything he had to say might be. Probably not important enough to linger very long.

"Mr. Masterson, my name is Sara Townley. I'm with Abercroft, Hamilton, and Sterns." I pulled a card from my jacket pocket, handing it to him. He held the card out, tipping his head and trying to read the fine print.

"Yeah, so? I ain't got all day." He took a swig from the beer bottle he held in one hand.

"Abercroft, Hamilton, and Sterns is the law firm that represents your father." Once again I was playing fast and loose with my employment status. I was also losing my ability to feel terror at being caught doing it.

"Bastard. What about 'im?"

"When was the last time you were at his home on Mercer Island?"

"What the fuck is this? What's the son of a bitch been saying?" His face took on a mean, pinched look as he reddened. His voice was belligerent.

"It's just a routine inquiry, sir. I'm looking for something that was last seen at the Masterson estate."

"Routine. Right. Accusing his own son of stealing. Paranoid, worthless bastard."

I took a small step back as his voice boomed into the narrow hallway. He put his hands on his hips, a trickle of beer spilling onto the soiled carpet.

"I didn't mean to suggest—"

"Suggest." Even his short laugh was mean. "Like the last time he suggested something was missing and called the fucking cops. Tried to have me arrested. Bud, too." He was swaying a bit, his squat body quivering. He reached out one meaty hand and grabbed hold of the door frame, steadying himself. His face was crimson now, the veins in his neck standing out. I glanced out of the corner of my eye, measuring the distance to the stairway at the end of the hall. Swallowing hard, I edged back. With a running start I had a chance to get away. If he caught me, the size mismatch would not be pretty. I'd have to gas him. I should have taken the cap off first.

"It's not like he hasn't got plenty. I'm his son." He pounded the bottle against his big chest.

"I'm sorry, sir. I'm afraid I've given you the wrong impression." I tried a weak smile, hoping to calm him a little. He was too wasted to be useful, and I could see some definite drawbacks to exchanging chitchat with a violent drunk.

"He's hiding it all away. Like a fucking chipmunk. In his little hidey-hole. Bastard."

"Hidey-hole?" I'd just keep him talking as I eased away.

"You don't know about that, huh?"

"No, sir, I'm afraid I don't."

"He's got someplace he hides the good stuff. Like Adolf fucking Hitler. My old man and his motherfucking secret stash."

Paranoids of the world, unite.

"Do you have any idea what he keeps there?"

"How the hell would I know? I'm only his eldest son. His heir." He spit the word out.

"Is that why you were at the house the other day?"

He looked closer at me, leaning forward, his breath assaulting me in a wave.

"How d'you know I was at the house?"

"I think someone mentioned it."

"That prick at the house. Acting like he owns the

place. Telling me—*me*"—he banged the bottle against his chest again—"that I need permission to be there." He used the back of his hand to rub at his forehead, the bottle still clenched in his fingers. He slumped toward the door frame, his eyes half-closed.

"Did you see your father when you were at the house?"

"No." His voice was quieter now, a huge yawn splitting his face.

"Did you see the cat?"

"Whadthafuck?"

"The cat."

He stared. Maybe he'd burned through too many brain cells to keep up with the conversation. Which would be handy if I had to spray him. No permanent damage.

He was half passed out, turning away and stumbling back into the apartment.

"Just one last question, Mr. Masterson," I called loudly. He stopped, turning to look at me over one shoulder. "Why were you in Pioneer Square last night?"

A feral look crossed his face and his eyes opened wider. He suddenly didn't look nearly so impaired. I grabbed for the cap and raised the can as he slammed the door in my face.

Chapter Fifteen

I went straight for a Starbucks iced tea and a cranberry scone. It took the place of the shower I craved after standing too close to Stewie for too long. A drunk called Stewie. That suddenly struck me as funny and I started to laugh. Hard. Loud. Inappropriately.

A man reached out and pulled a woman closer, moving between me and her. Protecting her from the dangerous, crazy woman. Me. The laughter wouldn't stop. My sides ached, and I had to set my drink on a nearby table. They were right. I was crazy. Certifiable. I'd tripped over a dead guy. I had a black eye. I was risking the first straight job I'd ever had for a damn cat, and, God help me, I was married.

I gasped for air, slumping into a chair. Two teenage girls from the next table gawked openly. I waved. They bent their heads together and started whispering fiercely, their eyes darting back to me again and again. Best friends sharing secrets. Every thought, every experience pored over in minute detail. Together. I shook my head, fighting tears. Since when had I become Miss Mood? It was nothing. Just teenagers. So what that I'd never been that young? I had things to do.

Bud Masterson made his brother look like a temperance society elder. Bud smelled of stale sweat, beer, and cheap cigars. My stomach roiled in protest. I wanted to know where he'd been last night, but I wasn't sure I wanted to know that bad. He hung on to the door frame of his little house and looked at me through bleary, bloodshot eyes.

"Took you long enough." His response to my knock came with a spray of saliva. I took a step back.

"My name is Sara Townley. I work for Abercroft, Hamilton, and Stearns." I handed him a card.

"Fifty bucks." He handed me a fifty-dollar bill, dropping the card.

I stared at the money, then handed it back.

"I'm sorry, sir. I'm from the law firm that represents your father."

"My father. Hell, you'd be lucky to get a fifty from that bastard. Fucks for minimum wage and bennies." He lurched forward, grabbing my arm. The money fluttered toward me.

"I just have a couple of questions to ask." I tried to pull away but his grip tightened.

He reached for his zipper, yanking me into the house.

"Hey." I knocked into the doorjamb, dropping my bear assault spray. *Shit*. It rolled away. In the next instant he'd pushed me to my knees, still fumbling with his zipper.

I tried to get up and he grabbed my hair.

"Let go."

"I paid you." He pushed me back and I slammed against a hall table, knocking something off it to crash against the tiled entry.

"I don't care." I pushed back.

He grabbed me by the shoulders and jerked me hard toward him. I used the momentum to put everything I had into the knee I gave him in the groin. He squeaked, his eyes bulging, and then dropped first to his knees, then to the fetal position, clutching himself. I dusted my hands in satisfaction. The old ways really were the most reliable.

I took a step back and straightened my clothes, rubbing at the knot on my head where he'd pulled my hair. I picked up the can.

"No means no." I pointed it at him.

"Paid you." He gasped, the discarded bill lying next to him on the floor.

"You don't have that much money, buddy." Another guy who couldn't afford to lose any more brain cells. I lowered the can.

I stepped over his prostrate form to get to the door. A woman was tottering on high heels down the walkway. She was all platinum hair and blue eye shadow, her forty-plus years shoehorned into a fuchsia minidress.

"I don't think he's up to company."

She stopped, one hand on an outthrust hip. "There's still a charge. If I come, I get paid. It don't matter nothin' if he can't get it up or whatever; I still get paid."

I turned and looked. Walking over to a half-dead shrub next to the porch, I plucked the fifty-dollar bill from its branches. I handed it to the woman.

"Here you go."

She tucked it into the top of her dress. "Gotta have rules, you know."

"I understand completely," I assured her, moving toward my car. "I have rules myself."

"Me, too," a man in coveralls said from the curb. He was standing next to a tow truck, winching a black Corvette into position. With a scream of gears, the car was up and the man touched the brim of his cap before levering himself into the driver's seat. Smiling, I watched the repo truck take Bud's car away before I got into my own car.

I drove back to the office. A Mariners game had traffic tied in knots, which gave me too much time to think. I rolled the window down all the way, but I wasn't moving fast enough to stir any type of breeze. Too many near misses. My misplaced furball had been hanging around some pretty unsavory types. Meeting Jepsen had left my skin crawling, and I wouldn't be caught again in the same area code with either Masterson offspring without a SWAT team. Or maybe one Navy SEAL.

In the last twenty-four hours I had a missing cat, a

dead body, and a live husband. In the last four hours alone I'd managed to do the meet-and-greet with a snake-oil salesman, a nut-job junkie, and a potential rapist. I had a black eye, an expedition-sized can of bear spray, and an urge to scream. What the hell happened to my life?

Traffic crept along as the pain at the back of my head crept forward. I reached over and opened the glove compartment, hoping to find a bottle of acetaminaphen waiting for just such an occasion. No such luck. Figured. I wanted to be sharp. Lying took a lot of energy, and the truth about my day would not make the husband a happy guy. I might not be an expert on him, but I was pretty sure his definition of a safe afternoon at the office wouldn't include mail theft and felons. Maybe I could distract him with sex. He was a guy. And pretty interested. That thought helped my headache a little. Things weren't so bad if a great-looking guy wanted to jump my bones. I'd had worse days. Remembering, I groaned, reaching for the rearview mirror and taking a look at myself. Wild hair, ghostly pallor, a dark circle under one eye, and a shiner around the other. Per-fect. Forget the Mata Hari routine. Connor was interested, not blind.

Traffic finally loosened up, and I parked Joe's car in the lot. I considered just going home. It was already four o'clock, and a nap sounded good. Then again, if Connor was up there, there'd be no rest for the wicked. I went back to the office. I was on the way up in the elevator when it occurred to me: I hadn't checked all the files. Sure, Masterson's main file was missing or hidden or just not there or whatever, but the billing files were kept separately. Lawyers were anal about billing. Every tenth of an hour or six minutes, a client got billed. And with that time came a description of the work done. Most of the lawyers at the office couldn't stop talking if their lives depended on it. Maybe the same was true for pontificating on the amount of work they did to deserve such exorbitant fees.

I sauntered into the file room as if I were out for a

casual stroll. This late in the afternoon it was deserted.
I walked past the movable aisles to the back of the cav-
ernous room where the billing files were kept. A quick
search showed no file for Millicent Millinfield, but that
didn't surprise me. I'd gotten the impression that the
firm hadn't done much work for her directly. I moved
to the Masterson files. One for the company, inches
thick, and one marked PERSONAL, much smaller. I pulled
out the business file, checking the last several months as
quickly as I could. Employment agreements, worker's
compensation claims, contract disputes, financing plans.
Several telephone conversations with M. Millinfield. If
there was something obvious here, I couldn't see it.
There were two lawsuits in progress: *Masterson v. Masterson,* some sort of family dispute, and *Jepsen v. Masterson Enterprises.* Both were being handled by the same
firm. Maybe they specialized in suing Masterson Enterprises. I flipped to the Jepsen tab. There were lots of
letters, responses to subpoenas, interrogatories, a deposition that got canceled in March. Then nothing, really. A
couple of letters, but they must have been follow-ups,
because none took longer than a few minutes to draft.
The only other interesting thing was Masterson's failure
to pay. I guess if you're fabulously wealthy, you can wait
six months to pay your bills and no one hunts you down.
Sort of like being the Queen of England.

Footsteps echoed down the hall and I held my breath,
carefully sliding the file back into its spot and standing
still. There was some rustling in the next aisle, a muttered curse; then the footsteps moved away. I took a
deep breath and pulled the personal file. Masterson
hadn't used the firm personally in months. He was probably running the legal fees through the company. On
March 5, Masterson had been charged for a missed appointment with M. Millinfield. Millicent. Just days before
she died. The notation was *ep.* Masterson was paying for
Millicent or she was acting on his behalf? *Ep, ep.* Escrow
prep? Land, maybe, or some new business venture.
Maybe they were having an affair and legal services were

thrown in as a perk. Some women liked diamonds; some might like sound legal advice. I could only hope Millicent got dinner first.

I put the folder back and checked to make sure the coast was clear before leaving the file room and going back to my office. I dropped into my chair and closed my eyes, rubbing my shoulders. It didn't mean anything. I was sneaking around my own office, risking my job, for a whole stack of I-don't-knows. It was crazy. I could lose my job. Jeez, I'd even taken to stealing other people's mail. A federal offense. What was I thinking?

The phone jarred me. Jumping, I snatched at the receiver, unsettling a stack of papers on my desk that threatened to avalanche.

"This is Sara Townley."

"Where are you?"

"Russ?"

"You were hoping for Ed McMahon? Or maybe a certain green-eyed god we both know?"

"Where are you?" I shifted the papers into a more upright stack.

"It's five o'clock on Tuesday. Where would I be? Where am I every Tuesday at five?"

"Oh, God." I glanced at my watch, catching the corner of my paper pile. I made a grab for it. "I'm sorry. I lost track of the time."

"So get your butt down here."

"Russ, I'm really—" The buzz of the disconnect sounded in my ear.

The phone rang again. *Grand Central Station, may I help you?*

"This is Sara."

"It's Joe." His usual tenor was lost in a whisper. I turned to look at the cubicle wall. I knew he was over there, so why the heck would he call me?

"Why are you calling me on the phone?" I whispered back.

"I just talked to one of Morris's paralegals. Lady Liz is on her way down to see you."

I sat up straighter, dread sliding along my spine.

"She never leaves the forty-second floor."

"Well, apparently she's making an exception today. For you." He drawled the last syllable.

"Do you know why?"

"No idea, but I wouldn't hang around if I were you."

After the previous evening, I just wasn't up to crossing swords with the she-dragon. I would, in fact, prefer the cops any day. My head pounded with a renewed vengeance.

"I've got one quick question. What does 'ep' stand for?"

"What's the context?" Joe was all business.

"I saw it in a billing file."

"You taking up accounting? You can't add."

"You should take your act on the road." I stood up, peering over the cubicle wall, on the lookout for Elizabeth. She'd be wanting that daily report, no doubt. What was I going to say? *Gee, sorry, but I spent the day skulking through our file room and stealing other people's mail?* Somehow I didn't think that would improve my employment situation.

" 'Ep' means estate planning. Wills and health care directives and—"

"Trusts." My adrenaline surged. "I'm outta here. Distract her for me, okay?"

"I wouldn't, except you already look like people have been pounding you for fun. Use the back stairs."

"You're a pal."

"Sara, about before . . ."

"Before what?" I grabbed my laptop and jacket, peeking out of my cubicle.

"The marriage thing."

"What about it?"

Joe stepped out of his cube and moved closer. "Is it true?"

"You don't believe it?"

"It's just . . . well, you work as many hours as I do. I've never seen you with anyone but Russ. You never talk about anyone, and I thought . . ."

"You thought I'd never get married?" I asked.

"I thought you were gay."

It was stifling in the stairwell. I walked down three flights, my mind fixated on Joe's assumptions. So my personal life had been a little slow lately. Except for the quickie marriage, of course. But Joe didn't know about that. In a Victorian environment like Abercroft, Hamilton, and Sterns, an alternative lifestyle wasn't something you'd bring to work, so maybe Joe's conclusion made sense. But I considered Joe a friend. I spent a lot of time with him. Or next to him, anyway. How could he get it so wrong?

Already slick with sweat, I bolted down the last two stairs before the landing just as the door was opening. Reaching past the startled man, I grabbed for the knob, grateful that I wasn't going to have to clomp down all forty-one flights.

"Do you mind if I go in this way? I'm really not up to walking all the way down."

"Stupid to lock them, isn't it? It's got to be against the fire code." The man waved me through.

"No kidding. You one of those morally opposed to elevators?"

"Claustrophobic." He sighed. "Have a good one."

"You, too."

Blasted by the arctic blow of the air-conditioning, I hurried toward the elevator. Catching the doors as they started to close, I pushed myself into the crowded car, ignoring the irritated looks of my companions.

I was first out of the elevator. The foyer was crowded with nine-to-fivers heading out for the day. I swam upstream, making my way to the Starbucks in the lobby. Russ waited at our usual table against the windows with a Frappuccino in front of him and a Tiazzi waiting on my side of the table.

"Sorry I'm late," I huffed.

He stood, staring. Then he reached out and took my chin in his hand, turning my face. He whistled.

"Nice shiner."

"Thanks, I grew it myself."

"You've missed your calling."

I looked toward the window, trying unsuccessfully to see my reflection in the metallic glint. On second thought, I didn't want to know.

"Maybe I should try some makeup or something?" I sat down in the chair, using the empty chair next to me to hold my jacket and computer case. Reaching up, I probed the swollen lid of my sore eye.

"It's barely noticeable."

Russ was an excellent liar and a good friend. Picking up my glass, I slurped juice and tea through the straw, shuddering as the frozen berry taste slid down my throat and cranked my headache up to blinding.

"Russ, did you ever think I was gay?"

"What?"

"Joe didn't believe me when I told him I was married. He said he thought I was gay."

"You told him?"

I thought back, sipping on my juice.

"Well, not exactly."

"What does 'not exactly' mean?"

"I asked him what he'd say if I told him I'd gotten married."

"And he said . . . ?" Russ prompted.

"Nothing. He went back to work."

"So where did the gay thing come in?"

"Later. He asked if I meant it about getting married. Then he said it."

"Oh."

"What's 'oh'?"

"I never thought you were gay. A repressed white woman, to be sure, but never a member of the tribe."

"What did you mean by 'oh'?" I repeated.

"You have secrets, Sara. Things you don't talk about. Subjects that close you down. It's not subtle, honey. That's all I meant. Joe sensed the secret. He just guessed wrong."

"I talk about things with you," I defended.

"Not everything. Not even with me."

I squirmed uncomfortably. He was right. He knew it and I knew it.

"So are you going to tell me or do I have to ask?"

I choked a little on my juice. I just couldn't get myself to speak.

Russ took a long swallow from his own drink, his brown eyes fixed on my face.

"What about the dead guy?" Russ's voice boomed, startling a couple of secretarial types moving past. They were middle-aged, dressed in frumpy suits, one gray, one blue, with low-heeled pumps and purses the size of grocery carts. They stopped to look at him, then me, then back at him, tentative smiles draining from their faces as they shared a quick look between them. Russ's megawatt meeting-the-public grin failed to thaw them. It was a rare day when that look didn't work on every female within range. The women went to a nearby table and sat, whispering and gawking.

"Keep your voice down," I whispered, exchanging darting glances with our neighbors, who continued to stare.

He rolled his eyes, leaning forward, hands wrapped around his drink, elbows on the table.

"Sor-ry. So what happened with the dead guy?"

"I don't know." I shrugged.

Russ sat back, surprise touching his features.

"C'mon. You mean to tell me you found a body in an alley last night and you didn't do anything today to try to find out what happened? You? Liar."

"Okay, so maybe I did check around a little. I still don't know who he is or why he was there. And that's off the record."

"Of course." His brows rose in indignation.

"There's no 'of course' with you. You're as discreet as the local tabloid."

"There's no reason to be rude." He leaned back, crossing his arms across his chest and adopting a haughty expression.

"Rude is the only thing that works with you." I out-stared him.

He chuckled. "You know me so well. So what's next?"

"I don't know. Go home, I guess." I shrugged, the late night and my lack of progress during the day weighing me down.

"Too bad Connor's not there. It would make going home a lot more fun." Russ wiggled his eyebrows lecherously.

"What do you mean, he's not there?"

"He went to talk to the cop. Didn't he tell you?"

"No. He didn't tell me." My hackles rose, indignation straightening my spine. "He most certainly did not tell me." How dared he interfere? I hadn't asked him to talk to Sergeant Wesley. It didn't have anything to do with him. "I've gotta run."

"Aren't you going to ask me about my day?"

"Did something big happen?"

"Well, nothing to compare to an estranged husband and a corpse."

I caught a hint of something in his expression. Used to being the center of attention, he seemed a little put out that the ritual Thursday coffee break hadn't focused on him. I didn't usually have much to share other than paper cuts and office gossip. On any other day I would have made time to listen to his stories. Today, however, I had a husband to yell at.

"I really have to go, Russ."

He rose, reaching out to catch my arm.

"Wait, Sara, I wanted to tell you about—"

"Take your hands off her, you creep," the gray suit muttered between clenched teeth, pushing her bulky frame between Russ and me. The blue suit hovered be-side me, chewing at the nails of one hand.

"Excuse me, ma'am. Do I know you?" Russ dropped his hands to his sides, looking from one woman to the other before shifting his glance to me with eyebrows arched in silent inquiry. He looked back at the woman, a friendly smile lighting his golden features.

"No. And you're not going to, either, mister." The gray suit spun around, thrusting balled fists onto her hips. She took a step closer to me, and I took one back, bumping into her companion. The aggressive woman's faded blue eyes snapped with indignation, and red flames lit her pale cheeks.

"You don't have to take it from him, honey. No woman does."

"Excuse me?" A glance at Russ revealed a hurt expression, his smile tinged with pain.

The avenging angel reached into the depths of her black leather purse, digging for a moment before pulling out a dog-eared card. Handing it to me, she turned and threw a glowering look at Russ before hustling off, her mute blue twin following closely behind. I looked down at the card, gasping. Russ reached out and I gave him the card, watching as he read the name of a local shelter for battered women.

He sighed, sober-faced. "Yesterday I was Prince Charming; today I'm the frog."

Chapter Sixteen

Connor was leaving the Department of Public Safety building just as I walked up. I stopped three feet from him, my temperature spiking beyond the level induced by my dash across town in ninety-degree heat. I'd been too mad to wait for the bus. My pulse pounded in my head, and the heavy computer case cut into my shoulder.

"What do you think you're doing?" I puffed.

Connor stopped short, raising his eyebrows at my greeting. He looked good—calm and cool, and in that moment I really hated him.

"Whatever happened to 'hello'?"

"What do you think you're doing?" I raised my voice a notch, wincing at the shrillness, my vision blurring a little around the edges.

"I had to get information somewhere."

"I didn't ask you to . . . Oh, man." Really dizzy now, I reached out to support myself against the building's exterior. The shoulder strap fell and the computer hit the ground with an ominous thud, before I slid down the rough brick and sat on the sidewalk. I closed my eyes, letting my head droop, shutting out the curious looks of the people hurrying past.

"Hey." I could feel his hands in my hair, lifting the crushing weight away from my head and neck. One hand moved to my chin, tilting my face back toward the burning bright sunlight.

"Sara, open your eyes."

I ignored him, concentrating on taking deep breaths and praying the sudden nausea would pass without embarrassing me.

"Sara, open your eyes." His voice was insistent, calm but determined. I forced my eyelids up, trying to bring his face into focus. He was crouched before me, his big body blocking out the worst of the light.

"Okay, that's good. Do you know where you are?" His cool hand seared my cheek before rubbing gently up and down my arm.

"That's a stupid question."

"But do you know?" The nausea faded and my vision cleared.

I pushed him away. He dropped his hold on my hair and managed to crab-walk back without landing on his butt, which just figured. I pushed myself back up the wall.

"Wait a minute." Connor rose with considerably more grace, reaching out to help me. I shrugged his hands away. He took a step back.

"I don't need your help."

"Why don't you just sit here and I'll flag a cab." Connor turned to scan the flowing traffic.

"I don't need a cab. You need to start explaining." I leaned over, reaching for my crumpled jacket before thinking better of it as dizziness descended again. Straightening, I blinked the waves away.

"You've got a concussion. We need to get you back to the doc." Connor turned back to me.

"We don't need anything of the kind. I'm fine."

"You are not fine." He shook his head.

"Did I ask you?"

"You shouldn't take chances with concussions."

"You're going to get a concussion of your own if you don't start explaining what the hell you were doing down here."

"Let's at least get you out of this heat." Connor reached down, grabbing my jacket and computer in one hand before steering me toward the Starbucks two doors away. He reached past me to pull open the heavy door, and a wave of frigid coffee-scented air blasted me. Connor swept me along, seating me at a table next to the window in the nearly deserted shop. He put my things on the table and headed toward the bored teenage girl standing behind the counter without even asking me what I wanted. *Men.*

He returned in an instant, unscrewing the cap on a bottle of water and handing it to me. I rested the cold glass against one cheek while Connor returned to the counter.

Setting the bottle down, I fumbled through the pockets of my computer case, finally coming up with the bottle I had snagged before leaving my office. I pried the lid open and freed two tablets, washing them down with a gulp of icy water. Connor chatted with the girl, who seemed in no hurry to lose his company by doing anything as mundane as actually working. I drank the rest of the water before putting the aspirin away, closing my eyes and rubbing at my throbbing temples.

"Here. Drink a little more. You're probably dehydrated." I opened my eyes. Connor had returned with a plastic tray loaded with two tall, ice-filled glasses, two bottles of water, and a selection of pastries. I reached for a bottle, unscrewing the lid and taking another long drink. Connor moved the computer and jacket to an empty chair and placed the refreshments on the table. Taking a glass, I poured the rest of the water over ice. Connor drank slowly, assessing me. Suddenly I remembered my black eyes and wild hair. *God.*

"Well?"

"You seem better now." He took another swallow.

"That's not what I meant. Well, are you going to explain what you were doing at the Public Safety building? I know it has to do with last night, so don't try to deny it."

"Why would I try to deny it? I went to see the cop in charge of the case."

"What did you think that would accomplish?" I set my glass down with a clunk.

"Well, among other things, I wanted to make sure I got the full story. I was worried, Sara."

I was a little fuzzy about the sequence of events last night, but I was pretty sure I had filled him in on the relevant details. I knew I'd told him about the body. Maybe that was this morning at the Masterson estate. God, was that just this morning? Did I tell him the rest at the hospital? When had I told the cop? I could swear the cops were there when Connor arrived, but maybe it was just the starstruck nurse, the bigamist, and me. The Three Stooges of Pioneer Square.

"I told you about the body this morning. You didn't seem mad then. Why are you now?"

"Let's just say that between Sergeant Wesley's fuller recitation of the facts and your near miss with the pavement just now, I'm losing my mellow."

I wasn't buying it. His voice was the same even tenor, his body leaning back in the chair, completely relaxed. So I'd told a couple whoppers in the last couple of days. Big deal. I wasn't the one meddling where I didn't belong. No, I was the injured party—bad phrase—and here he was trying to distract me with . . . I don't know . . . some sort of man logic.

"When you mentioned a body this morning, I thought you must have been in the emergency room when they brought him in, or maybe you'd overheard the staff or something." He shrugged. "I was a little distracted at the time."

"I thought I'd told you."

Connor sipped from his water, his eyes steady on mine.

"I really did," I said.

"Okay."

"Okay?"

"Yeah. This time."

I faked a laugh. "Hey, my next dead body, I'm getting a billboard."

"No next time."

I sobered. "It doesn't explain what you were doing going to see Sergeant Wesley behind my back. I didn't realize I hadn't told you all the details. You deliberately lied."

"I didn't lie."

"You didn't know you intended to see Wesley this morning?"

"I knew."

"A lie by omission. Same difference."

"No, it's not. You're my wife."

"What's that supposed to mean?"

"It means I won't be on the outside of your life looking in."

I stiffened. Connor's face was composed, his hands loose around his glass. The tingle along my spine told me he wasn't as calm as he looked. I didn't know how to deal with him. I let my gaze wander while my mind whirred. Except for us and the fresh-faced, ponytailed barista behind the counter, the place was deserted. Sighing, I turned back to him.

"What do you want me to say?"

"I'd love to hear, 'Yes, Connor. It won't happen again, Connor. Please can I tell you everything, Connor?' But since I haven't completely lost my mind, I don't actually expect that."

"That's good to know." I took a quick drink, crunching a piece of ice and trying to buy some time. *What the hell do you want from me?* seemed like the wrong tone. Part of me was dying to know what he really thought. The other part of me wanted to scream, *Mind your own damn business*. This marriage stuff was tricky.

Connor set his glass down, his gaze never leaving my face. I felt like a bug on a pin. It was as if he were trying to reach inside my head. I squirmed as the silence dragged.

"I give up. I have no idea what you want from me."

"I want you to invite me in. But since you're obviously not ready for that, I'll settle for being in any way I can."

"In where?"

"In on whatever is going on with you. Your job, your friends, your life."

"You can't just come here and demand total access." I plopped the glass on the table in emphasis. It really was sweet in a three-hankie-movie kind of way. Not that I would ever admit that. He'd take it the wrong way. I needed to start as I meant to go on, which definitely didn't include checking in with him every time I went anywhere.

"Sure I can. I'm your husband. Why do you think we had to get married?"

"We didn't have to get married. You make it sound like a shotgun wedding or something. And keep your voice down." I glanced over at the girl behind the counter, who didn't even try to hide the fact that she was eavesdropping. I glared at her. She colored and scurried back behind the relative safety of the coffee grinder.

"We did have to get married."

"We did not. We got married because great sex impaired our better judgment."

"Speak for yourself. There was nothing impaired about my judgment."

I leaned back and folded my arms.

"Amazing sex notwithstanding"—he smiled slowly—"I knew that if I left it up to you, we'd be old before we got this far."

"And where exactly are we?"

"Together."

"You're making absolutely no sense. And none of that has anything to do with your going behind my back and sticking your nose into my case."

"Our case. Community property."

"Are your missions our missions, too? Because I don't exactly remember you sharing the details of your last little work-related adventure. Or even where you were for the last four months."

"I'm not choosing to keep you in the dark. I'll tell you everything I can. And everything I'm thinking is yours for the asking."

"Nice little double standard you've got going there."

"Yeah. I'm sharing and you're still shutting me out."

"That's not what's happening."

"That's what it looks like from here, Sara."

He was irritating. He was also incredibly sweet. And I didn't feel up to arguing with him. I usually enjoyed a little verbal tussling. Somehow he managed to take all the fun out of it. I picked up a muffin and stripped the paper wrapper, more to give my hands something to do than because I really wanted it. The muffin was dry against my tongue. I glanced up at him, but his attention hadn't wavered. Quickly, I dodged the pressure from his eyes by looking back at the muffin. Without realizing it, I'd managed to reduce it to a pile of crumbs. I dusted my fingertips with the napkin.

"What are you thinking right now?" Connor's deep voice lured me.

"I can't do this," I whispered.

"Sure you can. You tell Russ. Tell me."

I knew I could never explain about Russ. Russ was a good friend who listened if I wanted to talk, but rarely asked about the things that were important to me. I didn't mind. Russ always called me Miss Low-maintenance. But low-maintenance didn't mean no-maintenance, and sometimes I resented his self-absorption a little. Russ never pushed his way into places he wasn't invited, and when I said I didn't want to talk about something, that was it. Connor was different. I wasn't sure I could cope with different.

Connor reached across and took my hands, ignoring the crumbs still clinging to my fingers. His thumb rubbed slowly along my knuckles, gently soothing. But I knew he was waiting. I pulled my hands away, for once seeing his touching as the trap it was. If I was going to be the one drawing lines around what was and wasn't his business, I'd need my wits about me.

"I'm not a sharer." I cleared the lump from my throat before lifting my head and staring defiantly at him. He refused to take up the challenge. I pushed my chair back a little from the table, feeling the bulwark of the wall behind me. A minute passed, then another. Connor steepled his fingers and continued to wait. I finally had to look away. When it came to the waiting game, Connor made me look like an amateur. That Connor's determination came wrapped in desire and affection scared me. If I gave him an inch . . .

"All you need is a little practice. I figured we could start with your job."

"Oh, you figured, did you?"

"Yeah. It seems like that's the biggest part of your life. Besides, it was either your job or the reasons you felt compelled to invent a husband, or maybe how eager my parents are to meet you. I thought you'd prefer starting with your job."

I gulped. His parents? *Oh, my God.*

"Are those my only choices?"

His smile was gentle, but he showed no signs of backing down. And given my options, I'd choose talking about my job every day and twice on Sunday.

"So why did you go see Sergeant Wesley?"

"You weren't talking, so I went to the source. I figured that the cop would see me as useful to his investigation and maybe share some information in the interest of keeping me cooperative."

"Why would he care? You don't have anything to do with this case."

"My wife does, and unlike her, I'm not asking for a lawyer. Wesley sees me as his best chance at inside information without legal heartburn."

"That sort of makes sense. Did you learn anything useful?" I reached for another napkin and started wiping the mashed bran from the table.

"Did you?"

I crumpled the napkin. I thought I'd managed to divert him by asking questions and turning the focus, but his dry rejoinder told me he wasn't buying it.

"Well, if we're going to go through all ten rounds, I'm going to need some real food."

"That's a plan." We got up, and Connor picked up my jacket and computer, gesturing for me to precede him while throwing a friendly smile at the drooling sales-clerk. I sent her a withering look and she moved away.

"So you knew after a week that I wasn't an instant bonder, huh?"

"Actually, I knew that after two minutes." He reached beyond me to open the door, his hand slipping to the middle of my back. "It took me a week to realize that it mattered."

Rendered mute, I led him to the bus stop.

I took him to Mama's, my favorite Mexican restaurant, only a few blocks from my apartment. The booths had cushy brown upholstery, the lighting featured dim tabletop candles, and the tortilla chips were warm. The smell of cooking meat wafted through the room on the currents generated by overhead fans. For a moment, when our waiter, Tino, was giving me a long look with raised eyebrows, I regretted making a public appearance look-ing like Mike Tyson.

I hid behind salty chips and spicy salsa, grateful for the weak candlelight and the fact that Tino had put us all the way in the back, away from prying eyes. I ordered fajitas and a lemonade without looking at the menu. Connor asked for fajitas and a beer.

"You are totally giving me the willies with that lie-in-wait thing, Connor, so knock it off."

A look of surprise crossed his face and his lips twitched. He leaned back against the booth's dark upholstery.

"That was a subtle change of subject."

"The only subject we were on was your going behind my back to the cops." My earlier moment of weakness had passed with the introduction of food, and I no longer felt like sharing.

"You make it sound like I turned state's evidence and you're on your way to the big house." Connor ran a finger up the side of his water glass, streaking the con-densation. One corner of his mouth remained upturned. My temper spiked.

"It's not a joke. I never gave you permission to meddle in my case."

"Obviously, permission isn't going to play a big role in our relationship. And I don't think it's meddling to find out what's going on with you. Especially when whatever it is lands you in the emergency room." His lips setting in a firm line, he pushed his water glass away, all amusement gone from his face.

I took a deep breath and dropped my eyes to the table. I fidgeted with the silverware, twirling the fork in my hand. I looked around the room, nodding to a neighbor and his wife in a table a few feet away, really seeing a moody landscape that had probably been on the wall forever. Everything seemed so alien somehow.

"I'm sorry about the emergency room thing, Con." I felt small. If someone had embarrassed me the way I'd embarrassed him, I wouldn't have wanted to show my face for a week.

"Why didn't you call me?"

"I don't know. Russ knows me, and I didn't want to make a big deal out of it, I guess."

"I don't mean then. Although from now on I would appreciate being your only husband of record." I glanced up and met his sardonic expression before breaking eye contact. "I mean, why didn't you call me before you went into that alley? Jesus, Sara, when I think about you walking into that place by yourself . . ."

I held his gaze. I didn't know how to tell him. I didn't want to hurt him, and I didn't want to look like an idiot. Russ would have had a great lie, a slick escape from the corner I'd boxed myself into, but I couldn't come up with it.

"I didn't do it deliberately. Well, not exactly. Russ was there. Before. Right after he left I saw the cigarette. I thought, No big deal. It's a missing cat, not a mob hit. I really did think it was no big deal." Okay, that did make me sound like a moron. I pushed my hair back behind my ears and crossed my arms over my chest just as Tino came with our entrées. We waited while he put sizzling platters on hot pads and placed a basket of fresh tortillas on the table.

"Can I get you anything else?" Tino asked, looking from me to Connor and back again. His thick black eyebrows practically disappeared into his hairline as he rolled his eyes in my direction, backing away from the table without waiting for an answer.

"I keep forgetting this whole thing is about a cat." Connor sighed, lifting a tortilla out of the basket and covering it with fajita mix. He straightened the meat and peppers, aligning them just so on the tortilla.

Watching him, my heart ached. I'd hurt him. It hadn't been deliberate, but I'd hurt him all the same. Wanting to apologize, I reached across the table and touched the back of his hand. He stilled, and I held my breath until he set his fork down and turned his palm toward mine, squeezing for a moment before releasing my fingers. Suddenly I felt . . . reprieved. I put my hand in my lap, my thumb rubbing the spot where he'd touched me behind the shield of the table. I cleared my throat.

"So, honey, how was your day?" I asked the question in my brightest June Cleaver voice.

The corners of his mouth twitched, and a teasing gleam returned to his eyes.

"Interesting."

"A word that covers a multitude of sins. What did you do today, other than try to pry information from tight-lipped cops?" I took a bite of the fajita. It was the first food I remember tasting since Connor's unexpected arrival, and it was delicious.

"I reconned your neighborhood."

"Oh, good. Now if you need to get out of Dodge in a hurry, you'll have the perfect escape plan."

He smiled. "I'm not anticipating a middle-of-the-night bunk. I will have to go back to San Diego in a few days. I wanted to take more time, but scheduling was a bit tight."

"I know, I know. Dictators to overthrow, hostages to rescue. You guys really ought to come up with new lines. Those are getting so old." I tried to keep a straight face.

Connor chuckled, dabbing at his mouth with a napkin. "I'll do my best. Why don't we talk about what you did today? Anything new with the case?"

I sighed. How much to tell? I'd hate for détente to fall in the face of detail.

"Well, I nearly got myself fired." Just thinking about my near miss flattened my mood.

"How?"

"My boss, Morris, called me onto the carpet first thing this morning."

"He was probably just worried you were hurt last night."

"Obviously you've never met my boss." I pushed my empty plate to one side and brought my lemonade closer, cradling the cold glass in my hands. "No, he was more interested in humiliating me in front of Sergeant Wesley. He didn't mention it when you talked to him?"

"Not a word. Why would your boss undermine you like that with the cops?" Connor's smile had disappeared.

"Morris doesn't think much of my abilities. Oh, and he's a lawyer. Enough said."

Tino came back and cleared our plates without a word.

"Maybe it's time to work for someone else."

"I like the job, Con," I rushed in. I didn't want him to start thinking I would be happy to just drop everything in Seattle. "Morris is an ass, but I can handle him. Until this case, I'd never even had a real conversation with him before."

"So what's so important about this case?"

I leaned forward, resting my arms on the table and taking a quick glance around to see if anyone was listening.

"I could tell you, but then I'd have to kill you."

Connor's green eyes went wide; then he threw his head back and laughed. "Good luck with that."

I laughed, too. It made my head ache a bit, but it was worth it. "I don't know. I thought it was about the money, but now I'm not so sure."

"What do you mean?"

"You should have seen my boss when I asked him for the files. He was . . . I don't know . . . odd. Masterson's business partner, Henry Jepsen, turned out to be this Donald Trump caricature. And Masterson's kids—good grief. Silver spoon gangbangers. The body in the alley and these people, it just feels . . . ." I struggled to find an accurate term.

"Off?" Connor suggested.

"That's the word," I agreed.

"Okay. Any luck finding out what happens to the money if the cat doesn't come back?"

"Nope. Morris wouldn't let me see the trust document."

Connor held his glass at an angle and poured the beer. "Why not?"

"Client confidentiality."

"Doesn't that apply to you anyway?"

"Oh, yes. A point he was quick to make to both me and the cop."

"Curiouser and curiouser."

"That's what I thought. In fact, when I really started to dissect exactly what Morris said when I asked him for the files, my imagination went into overdrive. I began to wonder what he had to hide." I took a drink, shuddering a little at the tartness.

"He's a lawyer. He's probably used to denying everything. It could be habit."

"Possible. On the other hand, he totally dismissed the dead guy as a coincidence and told me in no uncertain terms to stick to the cat-chasing business. He really was over-the-top. Which is what I was thinking when I nearly got caught trying to snag the files from the file room."

He arched one golden eyebrow.

"Interesting career choice."

I shrugged.

"It seemed like a good idea at the time. Although I was really sweating it when the file clerk practically popped up beside me."

"Honey, rule number one is don't get caught." Connor raised his glass and took a sip of beer. A tiny line of foam marked his upper lip for an instant before he wiped it away with his napkin.

"Now you tell me."

"Learn anything good?"

"Nothing. The files were gone. Although I did go back to look at the billing files later."

"Gone where?"

"According to Joe, who's the exploited junior associate in the next cubicle, the hard files are probably in Morris's office under lock and key. He also thinks there are computer files with the same information, but they require a password, which no one has seen fit to share with me. When I went back to look at the billing files, though, I might have found something. Flash's owner, Millicent, had an appointment to talk about estate planning with Morris. She missed it."

"Anything else, Sara?" Tino was back.

"Not tonight, Tino. Thanks." Tino winked at me, sliding the bill next to Connor and drifting away.

"Is there any way to know specifically what she wanted to talk about?"

"I don't think so." I leaned back against the upholstery.

"So what are you going to do now?"

"I guess I'll just follow the money."

"The last time it led to the emergency room. I don't want you taking chances, Sara."

"What are the odds that twice in a week I'll run into an inanimate object and end up knocking myself out? I'm thinking pretty small. I would really like to see the actual files, though. I can't help but think there's something in there that would at least put me on the right track."

Connor pulled a few dollars from his pocket and

dropped them on the table. He picked up the bill and we rose, walking toward the cashier, where I helped my-self to a some butter mints from a small dish. He leaned against the counter.

"I don't suppose I can say anything to make you change your mind about staying on this case."

"I've got a job to do, Connor. Besides, I want to know."

"Maybe we could make a deal." He reached for a mint, sliding it between his lips.

"What kind of deal?"

Tino came to the cashier's desk and took the money and bill Connor offered to him. He handed Connor his change and disappeared. We left the restaurant and started down the street toward the apartment, the eve-ning summer sun still golden, the air still warm.

"I help you get a look at the files. In exchange, you let me back you up. Make sure you're safe."

"How could you help me get at the files?"

He reached out and took my hand, lacing our fingers as we walked along. "As it turns out, I've got a little experience going places I haven't been invited."

"How?" I asked, punching my code into the keypad of my apartment building.

"Very carefully and late at night."

"How late?"

"Two a.m."

"Why two?" I asked, climbing the stairs.

"Bar time is one thirty," Connor said, crowding be-hind me.

Made sense. "Clever."

"Thank you, ma'am."

I looked at my watch. "That gives us six hours. What do we do until then?" I unlocked my apartment door.

"Rest."

A euphemism if ever I heard one. It sent a tingle down my spine. I turned around and put my arms around Connor's neck.

"You're kidding?" I used coy. I recognized that hint of a smile.

"No."

"Rest or *rest*?" I asked.

He swept me, Rhett–style, into his arms.

"Both."

Four and a half hours later, we were sitting bleary eyed at the kitchen table. At least, I was. Connor looked like he'd had a solid ten hours. That was just wrong.

"There's no guarantee the files have anything to do with your missing cat," Connor said.

Connor rocked back in the kitchen chair, studying the building map I'd drawn without the appreciation I thought it deserved. He was so methodical about breaking in to see the files I wanted to scream.

"I know that, but Morris was acting so squirrelly, and Millicent missed that appointment, and somebody searched her room. If you don't want to help me with this, Connor, that's fine with me, but I'm going."

He looked up. "I'm in, honey. I just don't want you getting your hopes up."

"My hopes aren't up. Well, maybe they are a little. I know I'm new at this investigation thing. I get that no one takes me seriously. Not Morris and not you." I held up a hand to stop the argument I saw coming. "But I take me seriously. There's a lot more going on here. I can feel it." I put my hand against my stomach. "And I'm going to figure it out."

"Were you this persistent in your last job?"

I thought about my last few jobs before getting my degree and finally landing with the firm. Obituary writer. Sonics mascot. Space Needle ticket taker. Phone-sex operator. That one hadn't even lasted a week. No, persistence hadn't been big in my career path. This job was different. A real job. A grown-up job. Testament to my finally getting through school and working at something I was actually interested in. I knew I was taking chances with Morris. He could fire me and I'd be back to scraping by. But I was done going through the motions. I was done with jobs I didn't care about and spending my time waiting for the day when my past was past and my life began.

"Okay."

Easy agreement took the wind out of my sails. I gave him my best what-are-you-up-to look. "Okay?"

He dropped his chair back on all fours with a thud. "That's right, Sara, okay. You're not exactly leaving me with a lot of options. I could stay here and wait for a call from the cops or the hospital, providing that I am the one you call this time. . . ."

I winced at his hard look.

"Or I can help."

"I don't need help."

"So humor me."

The guy could be in the waiting hall of fame. And he hadn't even taken off his clothes to convince me. What could it hurt?

"It's my case."

"Roger."

"My case means I'm running things."

"Whatever you say."

His face was a mask of innocence. I wished I could perfect such an angelic countenance. It would come in handy. It obviously did for him.

"I mean it."

"Okay." He folded his hands in front of him, resting them on the place mat. He could pass for an eager-to-please third grader. Except for the sexy grin, which was entirely adult.

"So how does one breach the security of a downtown office building?"

Chapter Seventeen

"It makes a lot more sense if I do it," Connor pointed out with an inescapable logic I resented.

I beamed death rays to where his shadow loomed next to me against the building across from my office. The two hours of sleep I'd managed before we started our adventure hadn't made a dent in my exhaustion, and Connor's offer struck the wrong chord. Here we were in our matching, up-to-no-good black outfits, casing my office, and he was still trying to take over.

"My case, remember. If there is any breaking and entering to be done, I will be the felon to do it."

"It's safer if I do it."

"Oh, so it's not safe for mere mortals, but for Mr. I Can't Talk about My Job but James Bond Has Nothing on Me, it's perfectly fine."

"That's not what I said. I have experience. You don't."

"You can always go home." I peeked around the building, staring at the glass doors of the building across the street. I could see the security desk in the entry, but I didn't see a guard.

"Fine."

"Fine." He leaned close, his body against my back, his voice a whisper in my ear.

"First rule of reconnaissance: Don't get caught."

"So you keep saying."

"I'm not kidding, Sara. It's impossible to control what happens after you get caught. And it tips the bad guys off to your strategy."

"Don't get caught. Check." I grinned. The adrenaline from this spy stuff was perking up my mood. The security guard came back into view, and Connor checked his watch.

"You'll only have ten minutes, max. You're sure there're no cameras?"

"Yep. Morris bought fakes and put them up, but everyone knows they're just props. Office theft didn't drop either. I lost a bag of Snickers every week for a month. People can be so evil."

"Even without cameras, people can return to an office unexpectedly at any time. Watch for that. And the cleaning woman. She's enterprising. Watch for her, too. Do you have your key?" Connor lacked a chocoholic's innate empathy for my loss.

"It's a code. One-two-three-four."

"What a bunch of morons. Typical, though." Connor pulled me back behind the shield of the building. "Most people have the security sense of a chicken crossing the road."

I laughed. "Sometimes I forget that you don't actually know them."

"I guess one code works for everybody?"

"All for one and one for all."

"Good. That means they aren't tracking who comes and goes by when the codes are entered."

"So what if they were?"

"Remember rule number one?"

"Don't get caught. Right." I winked at him. "I remember."

"What about the computers?" Connor asked, winking back.

"What about them?"

"Are they networked together?"

"Yes, but I already tried to access the information on Millicent and Masterson. They're password-protected.

And we know the hard copies are missing. Morris might have them in his office, but it's probably locked. Really locked, I mean, not just coded. Even if he had a code, I'd bet he'd be as big an idiot as Masterson and never actually use it. Keys are probably more his speed."

"Could we stay on task, here? Does your boss have a secretary?"

"Elizabeth the Evil."

"It's probably in her desk. Is her office locked?"

"It's not a real office, just a sort of waiting area outside Morris's office."

"Good. Check under the phone, her coffee cup, in the desk drawer. It may be pushed out of sight or mixed in with the paper clips. Try not to think too hard and you'll probably find it."

"I'll do that." I poked him in the chest.

"Once you're in the office, close the door and lock it."

"Yes, all-knowing one." I did a half salaam in his arms.

"It's important, Sara. Don't forget the dead guy. I'd hate for that to happen to you." He kissed my nose. "At least until you change your will."

"Needless to say, I'll rush right off to do that. I'm ready." I shifted from one foot to the other. Between Connor's proximity and the thought of breaking into Morris's office, I tingled all over.

"Look for your boss's password first."

"We've been over all this. The password means we can try to hack in without having to be in the office."

Connor rested his hands on my shoulders. "His password's probably in plain sight. Check his calendar and his computer screen. He might even have preprogrammed his password into his computer. Try that last, though. It could take a while to find the files in the computer, and you won't have much time. Remember that first rule."

"I know, I know. Don't get caught. Still, it would be safer if I just take the computer disk."

"What disk?"

"Every client is supposed to have a master disk with

all their documents since we had this big computer crash last year. There were things that couldn't be recovered, and it caused all kinds of havoc. If I find the file, I find the disk."

"Don't take it. Copy it."

"Which is why I brought this." I pulled a blank disk from my jeans pocket with the flair of a magician producing a rabbit. "I'm ready."

"If you're stopped, act like you have every right to be there, but don't overdo it." He tightened his grip on my shoulders.

"Me? I don't overdo things."

"This from an acknowledged bigamist."

"That was Russ. I can't be held accountable for him."

"Whatever you say. Just stick to the game plan, okay?"

"Aye-aye, Cap'n. Shall we synchronize our watches?"

"That won't be necessary." Connor glanced at his wrist anyway. He kissed me on the forehead and pushed me toward the sidewalk. "Go get 'em, tiger."

Chapter Eighteen

Connor had been right: Morris was obnoxious, but not security-conscious. The key to Morris's office was in Liz's front desk drawer beneath a *Vogue* magazine. I pulled it from its hiding place, only to have it bang against the metal drawer handle. The clang seemed amplified and I froze, straining to hear the guard's footsteps. Several long moments later I released the breath I was holding. I walked to Morris's office door and let myself in.

I continued to use the flashlight, afraid the desk lamp would be seen under the door. Morris had never struck me as a driver on the technology superhighway, so I started with his desk. I lifted the blotter and shone the flashlight underneath. It was too easy. I spotted a small sheet of paper neatly printed with Morris's log-in, password, and key code. Like taking candy from a baby. A stupid baby.

The top drawer wasn't locked. Apparently my boss thought a locked door was adequate protection. It wasn't his fault. He'd never met Connor. The center drawer held paper clips, staples, and pens, all carefully arranged in neat compartments. It's anal precision gave me the willies. I stuck a yellow Post-it note to the blotter and used Morris's engraved silver pen to write down the password information.

The rest of my boss's desk was a revelation. A worn

deck of cards, a doodle pad with really bad art, a dog-
eared copy of *Playboy,* and an enormous bag of Gummi
Bears. Resisting the urge to help myself to his nutritional
supplements, I slid the drawer closed.

The lowest drawer held the mother lode. I slid into
Morris's leather chair and let my fingers do the walking.
I jumped to the M section. No Millinfield file. I pulled a
bulky folder marked MASTERSON and another labeled
MASTERSON ENTERPRISES from the drawer and placed
them on the desk. I glanced at the clock. Five minutes
left. I flipped open Masterson's personal file.

The folder was divided into sections. I started with
general information: name, address, date of hire, Social
Security number. I scratched another note with the facts.
I added Masterson's Social Security number and date of
birth. Another glance at the clock had me flipping pages.

I moved to the section marked ESTATE PLANNING. Masterson's will was loose on top. Dozens of pages. I started
rifling through them, trying to glean the bottom line
without reading through all the legalese.

Identification of family. Both sons were listed. I
laughed softly to myself before smothering the sound.
*For reasons well-known to them, I make no provisions
in this will for either of my sons.* Succinct. I liked that
in disinheritance. I wondered if they knew.

Specific bequests. Finally, I was getting somewhere.

*To my personal assistant, Millicent Millinfield, I leave
my best wishes.* So, Millicent hadn't hit the lotto. So
much for her female charms.

*To my valued friend and associate Mitchell Burke, I
leave the sum of one million dollars in recognition of his
contribution to my success.* Wow. Talk about your bo-
nuses. Maybe he knew where the bodies were buried. I
added his name to my note.

I skipped past two more pages of nominal gifts to
servants, friends, and colleagues. *Ah, here we go. The
payoff.* Soap operas should have plots this good.

I leave the balance of my estate, both real and personal,

to my former business partner, Henry Jepsen, in memory of all he has done for me.

Holy cow! Jepsen. I reread it, sure I had gotten it wrong. Why would Masterson leave everything to Jepsen? Jepsen was suing. Had been for months. It didn't make sense. Then again, maybe Masterson had the will drafted before the big fallout. Jepsen couldn't possibly know. If he had, he would have found a way to collect. I swallowed hard. Maybe Jepsen did know. How long had it been since anyone had seen Masterson? *Jesus.* Maybe the guy hadn't pulled a Howard Hughes; maybe he'd done a Jimmy Hoffa. I flipped to the last page. Unsigned. A new will. Did Jepsen know about the will? Did he think Masterson had signed it?

I flipped another page. Beneath the loose will was another will fastened into the file. I turned pages frantically. The kids. There it was, the residuary estate in equal shares to his children. I turned to the last page. Signed two years ago. Jesus, he was getting ready to cut them out of the will. All he'd have to do was sign the new will and Stewie and Bud were out millions. Did they know? That couldn't be good.

"Tick-tock," Connor remarked from the doorway.

Chapter Nineteen

The internal scream started at my toes and slammed upward like a runaway train. I tried to rise, only to bang my thighs hard on the wooden desk and slam abruptly back into the chair.

"Jeez, Connor. You scared me half to death. Next time make a noise or something," I hissed, my pulse pounding, my breathing shallow.

"What is the first rule of reconnaissance, Sara?" Connor stepped into the room and silently closed the door behind him.

"You'll never believe this. I read the will. Both wills, actually. Masterson is getting ready to cut his kids off without a dime. Guess who hits the jackpot? You'll never guess, so I'll just tell you. Well, as long as you promise not to tell anyone else. My boss would kill me. So who do you think it is?" I paused for dramatic effect. "Jepsen. The scumbag business partner gets it all." My words tumbled out on top of one another. I searched his face for a reaction. His expression never changed. He walked to the far side of the desk before planting a hand on either side of the file and leaning forward until his face was inches from mine.

"Don't get caught."

"What?"

"The first rule of reconnaissance is don't get caught."

"I know, I know, but I haven't finished."

"That's what the disk was for. Copy your files and let's get out of here. I figure we have about two minutes before the cleaning lady comes in." He turned and stalked back to the door, standing on the hinge side of it with his back to the wall, his head tilted as he listened.

"It doesn't matter. She'll never come in here. This office was locked."

"She's enterprising. Now get moving."

"Fine. Whatever." I opened the file and pulled the disk out, slipping it into the computer. I clicked the computer on, and the whirring motors seemed deafening in the quiet of the room. Probably panic giving the hum a symphonic quality. I punched in Morris's password, remembering at the last moment that a professional such as myself wouldn't use her own code on a covert mission like this one. It'd be a good way to get fired. I clicked with the mouse, copying the files into a temporary folder.

"She's on the floor," Connor murmured.

I was sweating, fumbling as I tried to hurry. I copied the files onto my floppy and yanked it from the drive. I clicked, waiting interminable seconds while the computer shut down.

"She's next door."

I glanced up. Connor was still, his head now turned away from the door toward the wall. "We're trapped," I whispered.

"Finish."

The hourglass icon still blinked steadily on the screen. A muffled clang came from the outer office. I stuck my foot out and turned off the system at the surge protector, stuffing the disk into my pocket and jamming the file into the desk. Connor made the universal hurry-up gesture, his attention once again trained on the door. *Oh, my God.* There was a scraping sound at the door as someone worked the lock. I snatched the flashlight and the note and leaped from the chair, clicking the room into total darkness. I raced toward Con's outstretched hand, his hard pull slamming me into his chest just as the door opened, shielding us from view.

Soft, off-key singing preceded the sudden beam of the overhead light. I scrunched my eyes closed, wet pants and unemployment imminent. The chair creaked, a drawer opened, and my neck and back tingled in reaction. Shudders made their way through my body as Con tightened his hold. He used the pressure of his arms to shift me an adrenaline-jolting inch. He had an eye pressed to the crack between the door and the jamb. I was on the verge of ignoble downfall by cleaning staff and he was playing peekaboo. Another drawer opened before I heard a sigh. The singing stopped and was replaced by the distinct sound of chewing. Chewing. *Damn.* My missing candy bars. Did no one respect the bounds of professionalism anymore?

Connor craned for a better angle. I stiffened, grabbing at his shirt to keep him still. I lost my grip on the flashlight and it slid an inch, trapped between our bodies. I grabbed onto him, wedging the flashlight. Connor shifted, moving us an inch farther behind the door. I froze, peering up at him. The light went out and the lock clicked. She was gone. I sagged against Connor's chest. He patted my back in soothing circles. I hugged him hard, relieved and grateful. He reached between us and pulled the flashlight free with a grin. The loss of adrenaline was like having my strings cut.

"She should be gone by now," Connor whispered. I stepped back, out of his arms.

"Right. Let's go home," I whispered back.

Getting out of the building proved to be a complete anticlimax. No confrontational security guards, no pilfering maintenance people, just quiet, empty hallways and an unattended security desk.

We passed through the heavy glass doors and onto the street. Nonchalantly, Connor released my hand and threw his arm over my shoulder. We strolled to his rental car five blocks away. We got in the car and sat silently for a moment. I looked over at him and laughed.

"God, that was fun." Still laughing, I crawled onto his lap and kissed him.

After a couple of mind-blowing moments, he pulled back.

"Ten minutes. Isn't that what we agreed on, Sara?"

"Absolutely. Ten minutes. Maybe I ought to get a digital watch. Then I wouldn't get confused by Winnie the Pooh's hands."

He cleared his throat, unsuccessfully smothering a laugh.

"It's not like I was going over Niagara Falls in a barrel, Con. I was a couple of seconds late. Actually, the scariest moment was when you showed up." I leaned back against the steering wheel, crossing my arms across my chest.

He kissed my neck, just under my ear, and my train of thought derailed. He shifted me back into the passenger seat and started the car.

I shook my head. "How did you know?"

"Know?"

"You knew how to get in before we even got there. Give."

He glanced at me and smiled slowly.

"That's what the debrief is for."

I giggled. "I bet you say that to all your partners. Oh, God, you don't, do you?"

"Can't say it's ever come up before."

I giggled harder. "Now, that is funny."

Chapter Twenty

"So, how did you get into Morris's office?" I rolled toward him, pulling the sheet up under my chin and propping my head up on my hand. Connor rolled toward me and mirrored my position except for the modesty of the sheet. Art. The man was art.

"Does it matter?" He ran one finger down the length of my arm, and my skin rippled at the contact.

"What are you hiding?"

"You'll get mad."

"I will not get mad." I was feeling so relaxed and he was looking so good, I couldn't imagine ever getting mad again.

He moved closer, putting an arm around me and nuzzling against my neck. I definitely didn't feel mad.

"Connor."

"I used my key."

"Your key? How did you get a key?" I pulled away, sat up straight against the headboard, and crossed my arms over my chest. "When did you get a key?"

Connor rolled onto his back and sighed, closing his eyes.

"Tonight." He lifted his head and glanced at the bedside clock. "Last night, I guess."

"While I was taking the nap you insisted I needed to be at the top of my game?"

"You're mad."

"No kidding, Sherlock. How did you figure that out? And what was tonight all about? You get in a good laugh, Connor? Watch the little woman play detective?" I got out of bed and stomped to the dresser, throwing on a pair of worn sweats. When I turned back, he'd pulled on jeans and was sitting on the edge of the bed.

"I wasn't laughing."

"Yeah, right."

"I wasn't laughing." He held his hands up in surrender.

"Oh, and the cleaning lady. Let's not forget the cleaning lady." I was on a roll now. "Enterprising. Isn't that what you called her?"

"Sara, it's not a big deal."

"How did you know she was enterprising? Or a woman for that matter?" I put my hands on my hips and glared.

"Sara."

"How did you know?" I punctuated with dramatic pauses, my teeth clenched.

"I followed her earlier."

"You followed her earlier. How enterprising of you, Connor. So you knew all along about her light-fingered tendencies and that even if she did see me, she wouldn't be in a position to do anything about it."

"I'm sorry."

"Sorry? About what? Lying to me? Manipulating me? The whole dog-and-pony show you arranged? No wonder you weren't worried about getting caught. There was no chance of that, was there? Of course not. What was I thinking?" I stepped around him and he reached out and grabbed me. I stared at his hand on my shoulder, then squinted up at him. He released me.

"Last night, the call from the hospital. You scared me, Sara. And nothing scares me. I had to at least try to keep you safe." He tucked my hair behind my ears. "I had to try."

My eyes stung.

"I'm sorry. I should have been straight with you."

"Yes, you should have." I cleared my throat. "Maybe, after the whole disaster at the hospital . . . Well, you might have had a legitimate reason. This time."

"So I'm out of the doghouse?"

"I guess."

"Partners?" He held out his hand.

"Partners." We shook.

"There's only one real way to seal a deal like this."

"Really?" His eyebrows were raised, a half smile playing around his lips.

"Food." I led the way to the kitchen, stopping to take the disk out of my jeans which lay abandoned on the living room floor.

I loaded the kitchen table with all the junk food I could find and poured lemonade while Connor booted up the laptop. He pushed the two chairs close on one side of the table and we peered at the screen together. We started with Masterson's wills. I munched while Connor read.

"Tell me about the players, Sara. You talked to them yesterday. What was your read?"

Talk, I would admit to. Visit, not so much. There was such a thing as too much detail.

"Just what I told you—the partner, Jepsen, was like a get-rich-quick infomercial without the class. He and Masterson went their own ways about a year ago. Henry didn't take it well. He's suing."

"The American way," Connor said, turning another page.

"Exactly. As for the kids, they both have records, although neither's done any real time."

Connor peered at me over the paper, eyebrows arched. "Protected by Masterson senior?"

"Maybe, but protection doesn't stretch to financial independence. Both are in debt up to their armpits."

"What are the criminal records about?" Connor went back to reading.

"Drugs. Brawls. Bad checks and DUI." I shrugged. "A cornucopia of criminal activity."

"Something for everyone," Connor agreed. Connor set the papers down and picked up his glass. "From what you told me the kids are no prize, so I get why the old man would disinherit them. But why leave everything to a guy who's suing him?"

"That's the sixty-four-thousand-dollar question. Or in this case, a couple million. Do you think the kids know Dad is getting ready to end their lotto dreams? Maybe Masterson's dead, not missing. If they knew he was getting ready to make a new will, they'd have plenty of reasons to get rid of him on a more permanent basis."

"I'd buy that if Masterson washed up on the tide. Dead works great. Missing doesn't work at all. They can't get the money and they can't mend fences. If Masterson were dead, and the kids knew about the change in the will, the body would have turned up by now."

I sighed. He was right, much as I hated to admit it. Did I think the Masterson sons were capable of murdering their own father? In a New York minute. But without a body, they had nothing. Given the level at which they were living, I just couldn't see them calmly waiting for Dad's body to be found. If they had offed him, they would have called the cops anonymously to tell them where to find the body. It was a dead end.

"Do you think Jepsen knows?" I asked. "Maybe Masterson did steal the company from the guy and wants to make it up?" The lemonade was a good match for the pretzels.

"If he wanted to make it right, why wait for the will? It doesn't get read until the guy dies. And it was never executed. It's not a done deal."

"They started out together. Maybe the business dispute didn't taint the friendship? Of course, Jepsen wasn't exactly gushing with affection when I talked to him. Oh, God, I almost forgot." I got up and went to find my jacket, returning to the kitchen to hand Connor Jepsen's phone bill.

"I picked this up when I was there."

"There?"

Busted.

"Office visit."

"An office visit where you happened to steal Jepsen's mail?"

"I prefer to think of it as reallocating the informational resource."

"You have had a busy day." His eyebrows were raised. "What do you expect to find?"

"I don't know. I was thinking about the call to Jeff Randall to get him to that alley. I knew the numbers would be older than that, but . . . well, it was there, and so I just thought . . ."

"What the heck, he doesn't really need his phone bill," Connor suggested.

"Something like that. I'd still like to know who he was calling. Maybe there's a hit man on the list. Or a famous catnapper."

"Maybe." Connor grinned, putting his arm along the back of my chair. I turned back to the computer and pulled up a directory of the disk's files.

Nothing jumped out at me. I started opening files. After five minutes we'd scanned all the files on the disk without learning a thing.

"So, no trust document." I was disappointed. "Think it's a public record?"

"Not if she did it during her life. It doesn't have to be recorded."

"How do you know that? You a trust-fund baby, Connor?" Lemonade and chocolate brownies weren't nearly as bad a combination as I'd feared. I took another bite.

"You mean you didn't marry me for my money?"

I laughed. "I married you for your body."

"It's hard being a sex object." He sounded so oppressed I nearly choked.

"I'm sure I can't imagine how difficult it's been for you, Connor. So what do you think happens to Millicent's money if Flash doesn't turn up?"

"I don't know. Maybe it goes back where it came from originally. How did she end up with so much?"

I nibbled a pretzel as I thought it over.

"I guess I assumed she got it from Masterson, but maybe it was hers before. She could have come from money or hit it big in Vegas or something. You know, Connor, we could be completely off base here. Ever since that guy showed up dead, I've been all over the place with this case. Who is he? How does he connect to Flash? Is Masterson involved? Maybe we're missing the point. Maybe we should follow the money."

"Makes sense. Flash is worth a bundle. So is Masterson. Greed is one of the seven deadly sins. People have been killed for less than a million bucks."

"Right. So let's assume for the moment that Millicent got her money from Masterson. Stock options, sexual favors, whatever." I moved my chair so I could look at him without craning my neck.

"I'm with you." He rocked onto the back legs of the chair.

"Where does the money flow from there? Jepsen and this other guy, Burke. But not his kids. Or at least, that's the way the new will reads. Maybe Masterson was going to execute this will. Maybe he was going to change it. Lots of motive there."

"So we know who does and doesn't benefit from Masterson's money, but we should probably look at all the options," Connor suggested.

"Like?"

"If Millicent had millions, why was she still working as a personal assistant?"

I thought about that. If I hit the lotto, I'd give Morris my letter of resignation in bold print. Then again, what would I do after that?

"Maybe Millicent was bored," I said. "Maybe she liked working."

"Is Flash's trust all the money she had? Her room . . . it didn't look like she was on a spending spree."

The polyester suits, the crossword-puzzle books. He was right. If Millicent had millions, she wasn't spending like she did.

"We need to know more about that trust."

"Ideas?"

"The bank will know."

"They won't tell us," Connor said.

"Don't be too sure. Tomorrow I'll make some more calls before I talk to the Masterson brothers." I actually meant to see them again, but I didn't want to put too fine a point on that. "If someone took Flash deliberately, it's got to be about the money. If that's true, why haven't they called?"

"Maybe they did," Connor suggested.

"What do you mean?"

"Randall told us he doesn't handle the money. If someone snatched the cat for cash, they'd call the checkbook."

I nodded. "We're back to the bank."

"Roger that."

"I also want to go talk to this Burke guy, and I'll need to run more comprehensive background checks on Stuart Masterson, his two kids, and Jepsen. Then I'll check with Joe, an attorney in my office. Maybe he's got an idea about how to find the terms of the trust."

"That's a plan. I'll do the interviews with you."

"No need. You're going to be busy checking out these phone numbers." I pointed at Jepsen's bill. "I'd also like you to go see Sergeant Wesley, since you and he are such good buddies. We need to know if they've identified the alley guy."

"I can do that and still go with you to the interviews. You don't know what these people are like. There's a killer running around out there."

To say nothing of the weed-smoking thug or the lecherous alcoholic. I hadn't told Connor about the Mastersons because I didn't want him all wrapped around the axle, but I wasn't in a big hurry to go bond with them again.

"Okay, you take the Mastersons and I'll take Burke. I couldn't get much fairer than that, could I?"

Connor laced his fingers behind his head and looked

up at the ceiling as if considering. If he was suspicious of my sudden acquiescence, he didn't say so. He dropped his chair back to the floor with a thud.

"That still leaves Randall."

"I don't think he knows anything about the corpse. Besides, it could have easily been him in that alley instead of me. For all we know, he was the target."

I drained the last of my lemonade before rising and putting my glass in the sink. Connor got up and started putting the food away.

"We only have his word that there ever was a call." Connor voiced the idea even as it occurred to me.

"I know, but it doesn't make any sense. If he were really up to something, why send me to that alley? And what does he have to gain? Nothing."

"There is another possibility." Connor leaned against the counter, his expression grim.

"I walked into a drug deal gone bad?"

"Okay, so there are two more possibilities. Bad neighborhood, bad timing. Or, somebody wants this investigation over."

"Why?"

"Maybe they were afraid you'd come across something else, something completely unrelated to Flash's disappearance. Or it could be that the cat's up to his collar in something dangerous." Connor smiled. "If you got arrested or hurt, what would happen to Flash's case?"

"Morris would reassign it." I tipped my head back against the refrigerator, fighting a yawn.

"To someone more likely to take the boss seriously when he says it's a nothing case?"

"Yeah, probably."

"So the case would be over. The kids could go on stealing silver and Jepsen could go on trespassing and whoever could continue doing whatever."

"All of which works better if it's Jeff Randall in that alley instead of me. Without somebody with a connection to the great and powerful Masterson pushing, there's no way Morris would leave me on this case." I closed my eyes, the intricacies of the case adding their weight to my fatigue.

"Maybe things will look clearer in the morning." Connor glanced toward the clock on the stove. "Which, by my calculation, will be here in exactly two hours and twenty-seven minutes."

"I probably only need an hour and twenty-seven minutes of actual sleep. You?"

"I'm a Navy SEAL. I've been trained to forgo sleep in the name of duty."

"Hurray for duty." I took his hand and led him into the bedroom.

Chapter Twenty-one

The next morning the phone rang just as I was coming back from updating Morris. It had been a repeat of the previous day's tongue-lashing without the limiting witness. Fun, fun, fun. I snatched up the phone, dropping into my office desk chair.

"This is Sara Townley."

"The plot thickens."

"Con?" His voice played deliciously down my spine despite my no-sleep headache.

"One of the numbers on Jepsen's phone bill was a private investigator named Cort. He worked out of San Francisco."

"Worked?"

"He doesn't do anything anymore. Turns out he had a little trouble on his last business trip. Died in an alley."

"He's the guy."

I slumped back in my chair. The dead man was now a person with a real name. I shivered.

"Yep."

I picked up a pencil and started tapping it against the ceramic mug on my desk, trying to chime Cort's image out of my mind.

"So our dead guy, Cort, ties to Jepsen. What's the date on that call, Connor?"

"A week before you tripped over him."

"Any chance we can find out what he was working on

when he died?" My pencil drumstick moved to the side
of the phone, where it elicited a hollow *click, click*.

"You think it's something other than Flash?"

"Jepsen looking for the cat doesn't make any sense,
Connor. Why would he care?"

"Maybe Cort's wife will know. I'll try calling. The
woman in his office wasn't the chatty type. Anything
more on who would care if Flash didn't come back?"

"Maybe. Maybe not." I opened my top drawer, pulling a rubber band out and loading my pencil catapult
for an assault over the cubicle wall on Joe, whose indistinct voice indicated that he was on the phone. "There's
a bank account. It's in New York. I couldn't verify the
balance but it's definitely there." A return volley came
over the cubicle wall, tinging against my abandoned
teacup.

"How did you get that?"

"Billing records."

"So the trust exists."

"Yeah. There is something funny, though."

"Funny ha-ha or funny strange?"

"The latter." A rubber band pinged off my computer
screen. I picked it up and zipped it back over the cubicle wall.

"Well?"

"There's a newspaper article talking about the trust.
It even mentions the two million."

Ping. Ping. Two more rubber bands whizzed into my
cube, one missing my head by inches.

"I called the paper. The guy who wrote the article is
a freelancer and out of town, but I talked to a friend of
mine over there. She checked their system. The fact-
checker is an editor known as a tight-ass. If he approved
the story, he knew it was true. Only one way I think he
could know the facts were accurate."

"He saw the trust document."

"I think he must have."

"Will he share?"

"Not with me, but my friend is going to see what she

can find out. It still begs the question of who would give the trust document to the newspaper. Someone had to. I can't imagine it was anyone here. Forget the secret lawyer code for a second. What would be the point?"

"Meaning there's at least one more copy floating around somewhere," Connor added. "Here's another one for you, Sara. How come Flash gets to stay in Masterson's house?"

"I thought of that, too. As near as I can tell, he gets to stay because no one ever objected."

"No one meaning Masterson."

"Right. The same Stuart Masterson who cannot be reached by phone, fax, or smoke signal. I spent an hour on the phone to his office today. Maybe I'm just not important enough, but no one claims to have seen him lately. I asked my reporter friend when I talked to her. It's apparently a case of when you're poor you're weird, but when you're rich, you're merely eccentric."

A heavy sigh came through the line. I could picture Connor sitting on the couch, his feet propped up on the coffee table, head tipped to one side as he used his shoulder to cradle the phone. It would be nice to be there instead of chasing useless leads. I dug in my drawer for aspirin as Joe's counterattack flicked off my hand with a sting.

"What next?" he asked.

"Talk to that private detective's wife. Find out what Cort was doing in Seattle and why he was talking to Jepsen. It might also be interesting to see who else Jepsen was talking to in the last few days. Maybe find out if Cort's appearance sent Jepsen scurrying."

"I could call the phone company. Pretend I'm Jepsen. Tell them I am having a problem with the bill."

"Good idea. You have a way with subterfuge. I like that in a guy."

He smiled. "It's nice to be loved for my mind."

I smothered a laugh. "That, too."

"And what are you going to be doing, Mrs. McNamara, while I am getting cauliflower ear?" *Mrs. McNa-*

mara. Weird. I switched the phone to my other ear, rubbing at the exposed one.

"Well, Commander Townley, I plan to spend my time trying to track the source of the Flash trust story. I'd like to lay my hands on a copy of that trust document. It would be interesting to find out who inherits after Flash."

"Motive."

"Exactly. That detective ended up dead. It can't be a coincidence." Dropping the pencil, I pulled my laptop closer and clicked away from the spreadsheet I had left up to fool visitors; the report I had put together on the Flash case appeared before me.

"You're assuming the detective was killed because he was investigating Flash."

"Not really. There are hair balls aplenty around this case, and I'm not talking about Flash. There could easily be another reason Cort ended up dead, but it sure feels connected somehow. I don't think waiting to be surprised is such a good idea."

"Roger that. How are you planning on finding out this information, if a paranoid and protective husband is allowed to ask?" It sounded like he was teasing, but I wasn't absolutely sure. I didn't want him parked in the lot, watching all day. There was no need to worry him unnecessarily, so I lied.

"Don't worry, Connor. I think I can handle these tasks from the office. What's the worst thing that could happen to me here? I might get sued. Very scary."

"Strictly office work, right?"

"Aye-aye, Cap'n."

"I'm a commander."

"Relax, Con. Strictly office work. Scout's honor." I crossed my fingers.

"When you're ready to come home, call and I'll come get you."

I groaned. "You really are paranoid. I'm perfectly safe on the bus. It's only thirty blocks or so. I'll see you when I get home."

"Sara."

"Gotta run. Bye."

Following the money made complete sense last night, but after a day on the phones without so much as a glimmer of progress, checking out the players held more appeal. Somebody was out there killing Californians and leaving them in alleys for me to trip over.

I turned to my laptop, linking to the Internet. I loved the information age. If the general public had any idea that all it took was a Social Security number and the right databanks to get birth certificates, death certificates, and everything in between, they'd stop giving them out to every eight-dollar-an-hour telemarketer who called. Yesterday's check had been cursory. Today I was going for the dirt under their fingernails.

I started with Jepsen: credit check, criminal records check, court records check. I ran his driver's license, his last ten addresses, and, with a little luck, even managed to tap into a central clearinghouse database that tracked all the purchases the guy had made at his local super-market: booze by the gallon, no fresh vegetables. What a surprise. I ran similar checks on Stuart Masterson, Millicent, and both Masterson kids. Stuart Masterson had less than I expected. He had majority control of Masterson Enterprises, valued in excess of a billion, but how anyone would know that about a private company I couldn't tell. Masterson had eighty thousand in the bank, another two hundred thousand in CDs. Pretty tame investments for an eccentric billionaire. Maybe the rest of his fortune was offshore or buried in layers of trust funds and holding companies. Millicent had a bank account with eighteen thousand and change. No real estate, no debt. Not even a credit card. No sign of the trust and no extra millions lying around, unless she'd stashed them somewhere discreet. The Masterson kids had few assets, horrible credit, and no ownership in Daddy's company. None. After a quick glance at my notes from the break-in, I also ran Mitchell Burke, the million-dollar winner in the Masterson death sweepstakes.

"Damn, Sara. What are you printing? The Gutenberg Bible?"

I jumped at Joe's voice. His hands were full of papers, which he shoved in my direction.

"You're hogging my printer," he grumped. "The least you could do is check to see if it's out of paper. Why are you using my printer anyway? What's wrong with the one in the hall?"

The problem was, it was in the hall. In the open. My current course of action required a greater degree of discretion. Joe looked like hell. His brown suit, which even I knew wouldn't make the cover of *GQ,* had unintended accordion pleats in complex, discordant patterns. The knot on his tie was pushed off to one side, and the material sported a mysterious darker patch I didn't remember from previous wearings. His face was ashen, and his hands quivered with the fine tremor of too much caffeine.

"When's the bar exam?" I asked, changing the subject.

"Next week." Joe heaved a heavy sigh, his shadowed blue eyes ravaged by exhaustion. "Just check the paper next time, okay?"

I got up and went to him, taking the papers and slinging an arm around his shoulders. I pushed him toward my empty guest chair. He slumped into it, closing his eyes. I leaned back against my desk.

"Maybe you should take a couple of days off. Rest up before the big day."

"Can't. Not with this thing exploding on us." Joe laid his head back against the chair and I thought he'd drifted off to sleep.

"And I still have that antitrust case besides," he mumbled, his eyes still closed.

"They gave you something new? Couldn't it wait?" I leaned more comfortably back against the desk, trying to be as good a friend as he'd been to me about the black eye.

"Gotta clear up the Masterson mess, then the antitrust problem, then the bar exam."

I stood a little straighter.

"Stuart Masterson?"

Joe rubbed his hands over his face before opening bleary eyes.

"The same. You still working that missing cat?"

"Yeah. What did you hear?" I moved to red alert but Joe still seemed half-asleep.

"We've been sworn to secrecy."

"I'm included in attorney–client."

"I got the distinct impression she meant no chatting even amongst ourselves."

"She who?"

"The lovely Elizabeth."

"You hate her."

"I fear her. It's not the same thing."

I got up and walked around my desk, opening my drawer and reaching into my stash of Snickers, pulling a bar from the pile. I approached Joe, whose blue eyes sparkled with interest. In his weakened condition, he was no match for the call of caramel and peanuts.

"C'mon." I waggled the candy just out of his reach. "You can tell me. I won't tell anyone."

His arm flashed out, belying his exhaustion, his hand grasping air as I jerked the Snickers farther out of reach. I'd seen his act before.

"Quid pro quo, Joe. It's Latin. Totally lawyerly." I kept the candy in his line of sight but out of reach.

"There's no such word as lawyerly. Chocolate first."

I nodded before breaking the candy bar in two, ripping the paper and tugging as caramel stretched enticingly. I offered one of the pieces to Joe.

"Half now, half after."

He took a second to peel the wrapper, then inhaled the treat. He licked his lips, then his fingers. I waited.

"Talk."

"You really do have to keep this to yourself."

I crossed my heart with the remaining bribe. Joe stared at the candy bar as if he could see civilization after years in the desert. Chocoholics were all alike.

"Did I ever tell anyone you were the one who spiked the punch at last year's Christmas party? Even after Morris's wife jumped up on that table and started doing the shimmy? Did I?" I let my indignation at his lack of trust come through.

"Okay. Masterson Enterprises has a little accounting problem."

"An accounting problem? What sort of an accounting problem?"

"The kind where the pension plan doesn't get funded on time."

"I don't get it."

"It's probably no big thing. Sometimes, with certain types of plans, the employer is a little late when making the contribution." Joe shifted closer to an upright sitting position, smoothing the front of his suit. The wrinkles were undeterred.

"I'm not sure that's worth all the secrecy." I handed him the reward, returning to my desk to get one for myself. I threw the wrapper into the trash and dropped into my chair.

"Typical attorney paranoia. It's not like Masterson Enterprises isn't worth a ton of bucks. If worse comes to worst, they'll just borrow from Peter to pay Paul. Right now we don't want to have to deal with a bunch of irate employees. They probably don't know yet, so we're not talking, trying to keep the lid on until it gets straightened out."

I gripped the arms of my chair, a hint of understanding stirring my senses.

"How much is missing?"

"Not missing. Temporarily unaccounted for."

"Okay, how much is temporarily unaccounted for?"

"The last two years' worth."

I racked my brain in calculation. Math had never been my strong suit.

"Two years times a couple of hundred employees. My God, Joe, that's gotta be millions."

"For now, it's just a clerical error."

I pulled myself closer to the desk, then pushed away. Rocking back and forth, I let my mind fly in a thousand directions. Joe seemed to pick up on my mood, sitting up and leaning toward the desk.

"No one's going to believe it's a clerical error." I took another bite.

"It probably is a clerical error, Sara. Like I said, it's not that unusual."

"If it were something nefarious, who would be on the top of your suspect list?"

"It's not."

"Just for fun, then. Who would you be looking at?"

"Masterson, obviously. Others, who knows? The cat lady you've been checking out is dead. The longtime chief financial officer, a guy named Mitchell Burke, died several months ago. A lot of would-be bad guys are conveniently—or inconveniently, depending on your point of view—no longer among the viable suspects. But it doesn't matter, Sara. I'm telling you, we'll find the money. It's missing, not gone."

"Mitchell Burke is dead?"

"Yeah, car accident."

I digested that information with a bite of chocolate. Mitchell Burke was dead. Before or after that new will was written? Burke was dead. Millicent was dead. Another car accident. And then there was my alley guy. Not a car and definitely not an accident, but at the rate it was going, Seattle cemetery space was going to be harder to come by than a sunny day in February.

"So what does Masterson say?" I asked.

"He's conspicuous by his absence."

"Have the cops been called?"

"For a paperwork problem? No."

I finished my candy bar, licking my fingers. "You must really be in the loop to know all of the great Stuart Masterson's business." I grinned.

Joe pushed himself up from his chair, his empty wrapper clenched in one fist. I extended my open hand, and he gave the paper to me. Turning, he shuffled toward the door.

"I think people just forget I'm in the room."

I put his wrapper in the wastebasket, buzzing with the new information. Millions in missing dollars, a billionaire no one could find, one murder, a convenient accident, and a catnapping. Busy week. I paged through my research until I found Mitchell Burke.

Chapter Twenty-two

I parked at the curb and got out of the car. The Burkes' house was a two-story Georgian with ivy-covered pillars. The lawn was neatly mowed, but the flowers along the walkway drooped. I stepped around a moldering pile of newspapers, pulled open the screen door, and knocked. No one came. I tried to peer through a shuttered window, then banged a second time with considerably more force. I leaned closer to the door, putting my ear against the wood just before it swung inward. I straightened.

"Mrs. Burke?"

"Who are you?" I guessed the woman was in her fifties, although the grayness of her skin and the dark circles under her eyes made her look years older. She was dressed in an old pink bathrobe and big pink slippers. I wondered if she was ill.

"Mrs. Burke, I'm Sara Townley. I'm an investigator. I have a couple of questions about your husband."

Her pale blue eyes filled with tears, and her expression crumpled as she lifted her hands to her face. I didn't know what to do. I hated when people cried. I reached out a tentative hand and patted at the shuddering chenille-covered shoulder.

"I'm sorry, Mrs. Burke. I didn't mean to upset you."

"I just miss him so much." She sniffled loudly, reaching into her pocket for a crumpled handkerchief.

"I know." What the heck was I supposed to say? I was glad to see that she seemed to be getting her control back.

"I'm sorry, Miss . . ."

"Townley. Sara Townley."

"Please come in." She made a sweeping gesture with one hand, and I preceded her into the cramped living room. Most people didn't just invite strangers into their houses anymore, and I was a little surprised she had. Then again, maybe she wanted to talk to someone about him. Grieve a little. Even a door-to-door psycho killer could lend an ear.

The drawn shades left the room shadowed, but I could feel eyes on me from every corner of the room. The hair on the back of my neck stood up. As my vision adjusted, I could make out the room's contents. Dolls. Dozens, hundreds of them. They sat on every table, in every chair, and on the fireplace mantel. Each was dressed with infinite care and an obvious attention to detail. I took a step farther. They were like one of those velvet paintings with eyes that followed you everywhere you went. I shivered. Mrs. Burke stepped around me and picked up two dolls from a nearby armchair, one a fair-skinned blonde in a long blue gown, the other a black infant in a fuzzy yellow sleeper. She cradled the dolls in her arms and moved to the couch, where she sank into a narrow gap between a three-foot-tall Raggedy Ann doll and a Cabbage Patch Kid.

"I feel better when they're around me. They're the only family I have left." Her eyes filled again, but the tears didn't fall. She hugged the dolls closer to her chest and took a deep breath.

"I understand." I would have said anything to keep her from crying and to get out of this room as soon as possible.

"You wanted to talk about my husband?"

"Yes, ma'am." I perched on the vacated armchair and pulled the notebook and pen from my pocket.

"How long did your husband work for Stuart Masterson?"

"Fifteen years."

"He was the controller?"

"Yes. He was always so good with numbers. He used to say the world needed people to cross the t's, dot the i's, and add two plus two." Another loud sniffle and a quick swipe with the handkerchief.

"I understand your husband died in a car accident."

"Who did you say you worked for, dear?"

"I don't think I did. I work for the law firm that represents Stuart Masterson." I reached into my pocket and handed her my card.

She looked from the card to me and back again. "It wasn't an accident."

"Excuse me?"

"It wasn't an accident."

So much for my stellar research skills.

"I thought your husband died in an automobile accident?"

"He was so upset. He had been for weeks before he died. There was something going on and someone killed him. He wouldn't have left me like that. He was very upset those last few days."

"I thought the police called his death accidental?"

"Oh, they did. Said the tests were inconclusive. He didn't hit his brakes. They couldn't figure it out. An accident or suicide." She sniffled. "He would never have done anything like that. Not to me."

Suicide. Oh, man. What the heck was going on at Masterson Enterprises? I shifted in my chair.

"That still leaves an accident," I suggested as gently as I could.

"Then why was he there? He didn't have any reason to be on that road at night. He didn't like to drive at night. He only did it if there was a business emergency. His secretary told me he didn't have anything scheduled for that day. He would have written it down. He was always so meticulous about writing things down." She leaned down to kiss the blond curls of the doll in her arms, laying her cheek against its head. It was hard to give much credibility to a grief-stricken woman who played with dolls.

"You said he was upset in the days before he died. Do you know why?"

"He wouldn't tell me. Why wouldn't he tell me? I would have supported him. Helped him. I was his wife." Her voice warbled an octave higher. She set the blond doll down and moved the black baby to her shoulder, holding it up against her as if she were burping it.

"Did your husband ever talk about Stuart Masterson or Henry Jepsen?"

"He thought very highly of Mr. Masterson. Just a couple of weeks before he died, Mitchell told me he couldn't believe how clever Mr. Masterson was. He said no one understood finance better, that Mr. Masterson had made a fortune from nothing. Even Mitchell didn't understand how he could have been so successful."

"And how did your husband feel about Henry Jepsen?"

She leaned back against the cushions and shook her head.

"He didn't like him. Mitchell said that without Mr. Masterson, Henry Jepsen would never have made it. Even so, Mitchell was so distressed about the lawsuit, one partner suing the other and all. Mitchell was putting together the numbers, you know. He was going to be the star witness. He was so proud to help Mr. Masterson like that."

"Did he tell you anything about the case itself? Maybe he mentioned some improprieties at Masterson Enterprises?"

"No, nothing like that. He was putting together some documents for Henry Jepsen's lawyers. He had to go and meet with them and answer their questions. He didn't want to do it, but he said he had to. He got a notice to appear."

"A subpoena?"

"Yes, that's it."

"He never mentioned anything about the case at all?"

"Not really, no. I wouldn't have really known anything about it if Millicent hadn't mentioned it."

"Millicent Millinfield?"

"Yes. After my Mitchell died, she came to see me. She was such a dear. Really, a very sweet, kind woman. Then she died, too." The old woman's lips trembled, but she pressed them together and raised her chin.

"When did Millicent come to see you?"

"Two days before her own accident."

That couldn't be a coincidence, but it had to be.

"Do you have any idea where your husband was going the night he died?" I asked as gently as I could. "Could he have been visiting friends or relatives, maybe?"

"No." Her chin wobbled. She pressed her lips together and sat up straighter. "I was his only family. I don't know why he was there, but I'm going to find out."

"How are you going to do that?"

"I hired a private investigator. Actually, it was Millie's idea. I thought . . . well, I suppose I was too upset to see things clearly at first. I mean, I knew my Mitchell would never commit suicide. I knew that. But I thought it must be an accident. Then I talked with Millicent. She was very concerned for me. She thought it would give me comfort, I suppose, if I did everything I could to find out what happened to my darling husband. The next day I hired him."

My heart sank. "Do you mind if I ask who?"

"A man named Matthew Cort. He and Mitchell went to school together."

I had to get out of there.

"I'm so sorry for your loss." I rose. She reached up and rubbed the baby doll's back in circles. I let myself out of the house but hesitated on the porch. Dead investigators, pension shortfalls, missing executives, suicides. Cabot Cove had never seen a crime wave like this one. What the heck was going on at Masterson Enterprises?

Chapter Twenty-three

I took deep breaths as I went back to the car. Pulling my cell phone from my pocket, I called Connor.

"Matthew Cort was hired by Emma Burke, the widow of the financial guy mentioned in Masterson's will. Get this: It was Millicent's suggestion."

"Widow?"

"He died in a car accident a couple of months ago."

"I see."

"I . . ." I cleared my throat. "I couldn't tell her."

"The widow?"

"Yeah. You should see her, Connor. She's a wreck. I just couldn't tell her about Cort."

"See her? Where are you?"

"At her house in Magnolia." There was a long silence, but I could hear him breathing. "Connor?"

"Pretty good trick, being at her house when you're also at your desk, like you promised."

I squashed the pang of guilt I felt at his quiet comment.

"I guess this is where I say I'm sorry."

"Since you're okay, I'll forgive you. Don't worry about the widow, babe. The police will tell her."

I thought about Sergeant Wesley. He'd been a consummate professional but not exactly warm. I looked over at the house, shuttered in the bright daylight.

"I have to tell her."

"Want some company?"

I swallowed hard. "That'd be nice."

"What's the address?"

I leaned against the car, trying to come up with what I would say. The sun baked down on me, and my nose started to sting with the early signs of a sunburn. I couldn't believe I was actually going to tell that sad old woman that the man she had hired to find out about her husband's accident was dead. Worse, murdered. That fact alone raised a lot of other questions. The police had told her that her husband's death was an accident or suicide. With this much coincidence, we should be in New Orleans. Still, murder might be better than thinking your husband killed himself, right? A killer could be caught. Prosecuted. Punished. Made to sit in a house full of dolls and grief and consequences. It would never be enough but it would be something.

Twenty minutes later, Connor parked behind my car and got out. He came over and leaned against the car next to me.

"Hi." He put an arm around me.

"Hi."

"Know what you're going to say?"

Dread knotted my stomach. "I thought I'd go straight at her with, 'You got that detective friend of your husband killed.' "

"Sara."

"She's just sitting in that house with these dolls. I mean, it should have been ridiculous, or absurd, or something. Instead it was just so sad. God, I really don't want to do this."

"You don't have to be the one to tell her. The cops are going to do exactly what we did. Make the same connections. Then they'll tell her."

"I don't want her to find out that way. At least she'll know her husband didn't choose to leave her. I guess there's no point in putting it off." I straightened and headed toward the house. Connor caught up and took my hand.

We climbed the stairs and crossed the porch. Pulling the screen door open with a sense of déjà vu, I knocked on the door. The door cracked open, then was thrown wide. Mrs. Burke stood in the doorway dressed in flattering navy trousers and a pink blouse. She'd used makeup to cover the dark circles. I took a small step back in surprise, bumping into Connor. She could have been a completely different woman.

"Mrs. Burke?"

"Miss Townley. How nice of you to come back. I was planning on calling you later. Oh, and you've brought someone with you. Please come in." We entered the foyer and were led to the living room. Mrs. Burke moved to the sofa and gestured us into the matching armchairs across from her. Both were now empty of dolls. A place for human interaction. Connor pressed my hand and released me.

"I wanted to apologize for earlier, Miss Townley."

"Sara, please."

"Sara. That's a lovely name. And your friend is?"

"Oh, I'm sorry. This is, um, a colleague. Connor McNamara."

Connor rose, holding out his hand. They shook.

"It's my pleasure, ma'am." A delicate pink stained her cheeks, mirroring the pastel of her shirt. Connor's thing, whatever it was, apparently knew no age limits.

"How do you do? You must call me Emma." She smiled shyly, dropping her eyes. He released her hand and took his seat.

"Emma, I have some—"

"No. Wait. Please. I must apologize first. I was feeling sorry for myself this morning. In fact, I've been feeling sorry for myself since my husband died. Sitting around moping. Surrounded by my dolls. You must have thought I was a silly old woman."

"I didn't think that."

"You didn't say it. In fact, you were very sweet. But having someone ask about Mitchell—ask and really listen—I can't tell you how much it helped."

"I'm glad, but—"

"After you left, I gave myself a mental shake. I've spent too much time wallowing. I mean, I even hired an investigator. It didn't matter what the police said or what my friends said. I just couldn't accept that my husband was gone and nothing was going to bring him back. Nothing. So I just sat in my house and moped."

I shifted in my chair, uncrossing my legs and leaning forward. If my first visit had given her the impetus to get dressed and moving, my second visit was likely to send her back to the bedroom. I sent a quick, pleading glance at Connor, who gave a small shrug of his shoulders, leaving the decision to me. I hated being the bad guy.

"Then I saw myself through your eyes."

"I didn't mean to—"

"Of course you didn't. You're too nice a person to do that. But I heard myself going on and on about Mitchell. I heard all the things the police must have heard when I ranted about how he shouldn't have been on that road at that time, how he must have been killed by some evil maniac no one knew anything about. It's no wonder no one believed me. Well, Millicent was receptive, but I think she was just being kind. Even Matthew, the investigator . . . I knew he was just humoring the wife of his old friend."

"The thing is, Mrs. Burke," I said gently, "we do believe you."

Chapter Twenty-four

"**Y**ou believe me?"

"Yes, ma'am. Well, at least I . . ." I glanced at Connor. "We think there's more going on."

I searched the older woman's face. She seemed calm, a little confused, but not in danger of being pushed over the edge. I hoped like heck I was reading her right.

"I'm afraid I have some bad news, Mrs. Burke." I choked a little on the words, pushing them past a lump in my throat. "Matthew Cort was killed on Wednesday night."

"Killed?" Her pale hands twisted around each other, the only outward indication of a rising stress level.

"I'm so sorry."

"He was murdered, wasn't he? It was the same man. The same one who killed my Mitchell." She put one hand over her heart as she gave me a stricken look. "It's my fault, isn't it? If I hadn't asked him to help me . . . Oh, dear Lord."

Connor and I rose simultaneously. I moved from the armchair to take a seat next to her on the couch. Dolls stared at me from the mantel, their eyes glassy, as if from tears. I reached out to cover Emma's hand. Connor disappeared into the house.

"It is not your fault. You need to remember that, Emma. The only one to blame is whoever killed him." I gave her hand another squeeze.

Connor returned with a glass of water in one hand

and a box of tissues in the other, He handed the glass to the older woman and set the tissues on the coffee table within easy reach before resuming his position in the armchair.

She lifted the glass to her mouth, and I could see it tremble slightly as she took a quick swallow, then a slower one. She set the glass on a gold-edged coaster and pushed the Kleenex farther away. Her husband's death had obviously devastated her, but underneath her grief was a pretty tough woman. She squeezed my hand and I smiled at her.

"We think your husband's death might be connected to a case I'm working on."

"Something tied to his work?"

"We don't really know."

"Millicent. Oh, no. Her accident . . ."

"Really an accident," I assured her. "Millicent was in a major collision. Dozens of cars, and hers wasn't the first. Millicent's death was definitely an accident."

Tears rolled down her pale cheeks. She clutched at the front of her blouse, wrinkling the pink silk.

"I'm glad. How foolish is that? She was a good person and she's passed and I'm glad she wasn't murdered, as if that matters at all. I want to help. How can I help?"

"We appreciate your offer, ma'am." Connor interrupted. "But it's important that you consider the risks. Matthew Cort was murdered. If it is connected to the work he was doing for you—and that's a big if—it's possible that helping us could put you in danger."

"He's right, Mrs. Burke. We don't want anything to happen to you."

"Something has already happened to me, Sara. And it's not right that whoever killed Mitchell and Matthew should get away with it. What can I do?"

"If you're sure . . . ?" I waited until she gave me an emphatic nod.

"Okay. Did your husband have an office at home? Did he keep a computer or files or anything here at the house?"

"He never brought his work home. He did have a computer, one of those newfangled laptop ones. But he never really used it. He would just carry it back and forth from work, then leave it in the hall closet. He called it his daily workout."

"Is that computer here now?"

"No. At least, I don't think so." She rose and disappeared for a moment, returning to the room empty-handed.

"Is it possible it's still at his office?"

"No. I cleaned out his office a couple of weeks after his death. I took all his personal things. They're in storage. I couldn't face having them in the house, so I just taped up the box and dropped them off."

"Maybe we could have a look?"

"The storage facility requires a signature. I'll get the box for you. What else?"

Talk about your needle in a haystack. Without knowing what we were looking for, there was no way to eliminate any item. We'd have to see everything and hope the significance occurred to us.

"What about a date book or Rolodex?" I suggested.

"That would all be with his office things."

"Well, ma'am, it's possible that your husband brought something home for safekeeping."

"I don't remember anything."

"It might not be obvious. It could be a key, a computer disk, anything, really," Connor said.

Until that moment it hadn't occurred to me that Burke knew the importance of whatever it was he might have found. It could be an accident. Or even suicide, although I'd hate that for this woman's sake. Maybe her husband had known something. Maybe the killer just couldn't take the chance that Burke would tell. On the other hand, what if Burke had tried to use the information? I really hoped I wouldn't have to tell Emma her husband had been killed because he'd been a black-mailer.

"I'll look. I'll go through the house room by room."

She seemed eager now, the concrete tasks strengthening her resolve.

"Good. Emma, what did you tell Matthew Cort when you hired him?"

"Just that I thought Mitchell's death wasn't a suicide."

"Did he ask to see your husband's personal items?" Connor picked up on my train of thought, leaning forward, resting his chin on top of his steepled fingers.

"No. He was more interested in the information from the accident scene."

"What information?" I jumped back into the interviewer position.

"Photographs. The medical examiner's report. Some other reports. I called the police and insisted on seeing everything. They didn't want to give me a copy of the file, but I called the insurance company and they helped me get it. I gave it to Matthew."

"Did you make a copy?"

"No. He said he would make a copy and return the originals to me."

"Do you remember anything specific in the file?"

"I couldn't look. I just couldn't bear to see him like that."

"I understand. Don't worry about it. I'm sure we can get a copy." I wasn't sure of anything of the sort, but I didn't want to sidetrack her. "Did Matthew Cort tell you what he had found?"

"No. I talked to him a couple of weeks ago. He said he thought he was making progress, but we didn't discuss specifics."

I turned to Connor.

"Maybe we should get the police reports from Cort's files. It'll save us from having to reinvent the wheel on anything he's already checked out." It would also save me from having to ask Sergeant Wesley for them.

"I tried to talk to Mrs. Cort earlier, Emma. She wouldn't discuss particulars of the case with me. But maybe, if you called her and explained that it was okay to talk to us, she'd be willing to fax a copy of the file."

"Oh, my goodness. Roberta." The color had once again drained from the older woman's face, leaving her ashen and shaking.

"Mrs. Burke?" I asked, alarmed. Connor was already out of his chair and kneeling at her feet, gently rubbing her hands in his.

"Are you all right, ma'am?"

"We've never been close. She's so much younger and all. But I never even thought . . . It never occurred to me."

"What?"

"I made Roberta a widow."

"Roberta is Matthew Cort's wife?" I was confused.

"She was his wife. Now she's his widow." She shook her head slightly and threw her shoulders back. She looked at Connor as if realizing for the first time that he was there. "I'm fine . . . Um. I can't believe this. I've forgotten your name. How rude of me."

"It's Connor, ma'am."

"Well, Connor, you can get up now. I very much appreciate your concern, but let me assure you that I will be fine. Now, however, I will have to ask you to leave. I need to call Roberta."

Connor stood and I did, too. Emma rose from her seat and ushered us in front of her toward the door.

"Are you sure you are all right, ma'am? Maybe we should call someone to come keep you company."

"That won't be necessary. I need to help Roberta through this difficult time. After all, no one understands her pain quite like I do. Then I need to gather those things I told you I would get for you. After that, I'm going to search this house from top to bottom for something I might have missed."

"You'll call us when you have something? Or if you need anything?" I was nervous about leaving her alone in case she fell apart as soon as we left. Widow crusher wasn't a title I aspired to.

She reached behind me and pulled open the door, sliding her arm into the opening to push the screen door open. *Here's your hat; what's your hurry?* She was pale and retained her air of fragility, but her posture and expression told a different story. This woman was taking her life back.

"I will call you in a few hours. You call me if you think of anything else I can do."

"We will," Connor assured her, using one hand to urge me onto the porch and down the steps. The door closed behind us with a click.

We walked to the curb and I turned to look back at the house.

"She's going to be okay, isn't she?"

"She seemed pretty tough to me. At least now she knows she isn't crazy."

"You think the detective's wife will blame her?"

"I don't know. People do things in times of grief that don't make sense. Even if the Cort woman doesn't hold Emma responsible, a little guilt is probably inevitable." He patted me on the back. "She'll feel better when we find the bastard."

I stared at him. *When* we *find him.* I leaned forward and kissed his chin.

"What was that for?"

"I think you're cute."

"Works for me. So, Madam Investigator, what do you want to do now?"

"Emma said her husband was under subpoena in the Jepsen case. With Cort's number on the phone bill, I think I should pay Jepsen a little visit and try to find out where he was on Wednesday night."

Connor leaned back against my car and folded his arms across his chest. I crossed my arms in response.

"I know I agreed to let you make the decisions in this case, but just hear me out," Connor began.

"Yes, you did. And I'm holding you to it."

"Jepsen's already seen you. He knows you're tied to Masterson. If he killed Cort he's proven he's ready to kill anyone who gets too close to whatever it is he's hiding. And it would be pretty easy to jump to conclusions about how much you know if you turn up again so soon."

He had a point, much as I hated to admit it. "Do you have a suggestion, or are you just going to rain on my parade?"

"I'll go see Jepsen."

"What makes you think he'll tell you anything?"

"I can be sneaky when the situation calls for it."

I looked at him with my best you're-kidding expression.

"Which we've agreed I will use only against outsiders." He held his hands up like a robbery victim happy to give up his cash. I didn't believe it for a second.

"Any ideas on how you're going to get Jepsen to talk?"

"You told me he was a wheeler-dealer. I figure he'd be interested in a new player in town, one with a big deal in the works."

"A deal where you need to know where he was last Wednesday night? That'll never fly."

"Okay, boss. Do you have a plan?"

I thought for a moment. I'd show him sneaky.

"Okay, how's this?" I smiled, wanting to show off a little. "You work for an insurance company. You have a client who thinks he may have hit Jepsen's car on Wednesday night. Then ask him where he was on Wednesday."

"That's good. What kind of car does he drive?"

"Black Mercedes. That's the beauty of this particular lie. A status guy like him will immediately want to check his precious car. Maybe you get a look at the car as a bonus."

"Smart and beautiful." He grinned, clearly impressed. "You think we can tie it to the alley?"

"No way. A car like that would've been noticed. Not to mention stripped."

"I'll check it out. What will my colleague be doing?"

"Hopefully I'll be getting a copy of Mitchell Burke's accident file. How about if we meet back at the apartment in"—I glanced at my watch—"three hours?"

"Five o'clock. Check."

He held open my car door and I got in.

"Be careful, Sara."

"You, too, Con. Remember this guy is the bad guy, okay?"

"Roger that." He leaned into my window to give me a quick, brain-scrambling kiss.

"See you at five." He turned and walked away.

"Oh, and Connor?" I yelled, half hanging from the open window.

"Yeah?"

"If that she-devil in the front office leaves so much as a fingerprint, there's gonna be trouble."

Chapter Twenty-five

I stopped by the apartment and dropped off the car. There was no sense paying twenty bucks for a couple of hours' parking. A quick trip upstairs for a peanut-butter sandwich and I was on my way back to the office. I stepped into my cubicle and stopped short as Elizabeth casually closed my desk drawer.

"Find what you were looking for?"

"Where is your status report on the Millinfield matter?" She was in an ice blue suit with matching eye shadow; very befitting of her personality.

"I briefed Mr. Hamilton personally this morning." Which she damn well knew. "I'll have a written update by the end of the day." I walked around the desk and she was forced to skirt me to get out. It was a petty victory but still sweet.

"It's hard to imagine it takes a professional investigator"— she laid mocking emphasis on the noun—"days to track a missing pet."

I wanted to reach over and push her face in. I was hot and my head hurt. I'd spent the morning emotionally beating up on a woman I liked more in an hour than I could like this woman in a year.

"Maybe you ought to—"

"Elizabeth, I think the boss is looking for you." Joe appeared over her shoulder, a too-bright smile on his exhausted face.

She glared at him, then threw me a venomous glare and swept away. I slammed into my chair, running my hands through my hair.

"Ugh. You should have let me do it. It would have been a public service. No one would hold it against me."

"She'd call the cops."

"They wouldn't hold it against me either."

"I'm thinking Sergeant Wesley might not be your biggest fan, although he's a hard read." Joe slouched against a filing cabinet.

"When did you meet Sergeant Wesley?"

"At lunch. I ran into him in reception."

My peanut-butter sandwich molded into a fist in my stomach. "Was he here to see me?"

"Yep."

"What did you tell him?"

"What could I tell him?" Joe shrugged. "I don't know anything. I never know anything. I did tell him I didn't know where you were."

"He say anything else?"

"Asked if I knew where your husband was."

Joe was giving me an odd look. I didn't blame him. I knew I was married, and I didn't believe it either.

"You're not married, are you?"

"Well, actually, I am."

"Shotgun?"

"Of course not."

"Arranged?"

"No."

"Nervous breakdown?"

"Joe!" I yelled.

He held his hands up. "Just checking. The cop asked you to call." Joe pulled a card from his pocket and handed it to me.

"I'll get right on that." I put the card in the top drawer of the desk.

"Oh, and Sara? Stay away from Lethal Liz. She's got a serious jones for you."

"I don't know why. I didn't do anything to her."

"I doubt she needs a reason." He left.

I spent a useless minute fuming over Elizabeth's unreasonable hatred of me. She might be only a secretary, but she had the big man's ear. She could cost me my job. Then again, pretty much everything I'd done in the last couple of days could cost me my job. I dismissed Elizabeth from my thoughts.

It took only one phone call to get Cort's office to agree to fax me the file. Emma had been there before me. While I waited, I got on the Internet and searched the newspaper databases for articles about Mitchell Burke's accident. There was only one reference.

Seven people including two teenagers were killed and four others injured in a three-car collision on Highway 2 near Leavenworth last night. Identification of the victims is being withheld pending family notifications. A police spokesman said bad weather and road conditions may have contributed to the crash. In an unrelated accident, Mitchell Burke, chief financial officer of Masterson Enterprises, also died when his car plunged down an embankment less than a mile from the site of the three-car accident. According to local police, Burke, 54, was alone at the time of the accident. For months local community groups, through an active letter-writing campaign, have been urging the Washington State Highway Division to place new reinforced guardrails along an eight-mile stretch of Highway 2 that has been the site of several traffic accidents over the last few months, including two other fatal accidents. Timothy Manus, spokesmen for the Leavenworth chapter of the Elks, said his volunteers plan to redouble their efforts in the wake of these new tragedies.

Millicent Millinfield, speaking on behalf of Masterson Enterprises, said Burke was a key player in the success of the multibillion-dollar conglomerate. Burke is survived by his wife of thirty years, Emma Burke.

I stared at the screen. A man's entire life boiled down to a couple paragraphs. Emma's face flashed into my mind. There had to be something I could do to help her, some closure I could give her.

Inspiration took hold. I highlighted Millicent's name and pasted it into the search box. A moment later a list of five dozen articles appeared. I opened the first. It was a long account of Millicent's fatal accident. Like Burke, she'd died in a car accident. There was a lot of that going around. Deciding I wouldn't have made it far on the Warren Commission, I started reading.

Ten articles later, I had to concede that accidents really did happen. Millicent's crash was nothing like Mitchell's. She'd died in a twelve-car pileup that included a chemical truck. HazMat had responded to the scene. And if the volume of newspaper attention was any indication, there'd been more professionals on the case than Dalmatians had spots.

I got up and stretched, heading to the fax machine. My fax from California was just coming through. I looked around and, not seeing anyone peering over my shoulder, I read as the pages printed. All three of them. Picking up the phone, I made three calls: one to Emma, one to the police detective listed on the report, and one to Information. Stuffing the papers into my pocket, I left for the day.

I stopped short when I reached my kitchen doorway. It had been a long day. I knew it was going to get longer. All I wanted was a quick shower and eight uninterrupted hours of sleep. Okay, seven postcoital hours. Marriage was turning me into a sex maniac. It was a pipe dream and I knew it. Instead of Connor and the sandman, I had road trips and the men of my life bonding over bottles of beer. Worse, Russ knew just about everything there was to know about me. Much more than Connor needed to know. And Russ, bless his heart, had the discretion of Aldrich Ames. I needed to break this up fast.

"Hi, honey. How was your day?" Russ asked with his bad-boy smile.

My stomach clenched. I sneaked a look at Connor, but he didn't seem mad. I wondered if there was a way

I could throw Russ out before I ended up explaining the unexplainable for the rest of the night.

Connor straightened from his leaning position against the counter and came over to me. As he bent to kiss me, I caught sight of Russ's avid expression and turned my head, offering my cheek. No sense putting on a show. I sank into the chair across from Russ, admiring the view over his shoulder, as Connor bent down to retrieve a beer from the refrigerator.

"Any luck on the great feline caper?" I looked back at Russ, only to realize he'd turned his head to watch Connor, too. I kicked Russ under the table, and he turned back to me with an angelic countenance.

"Not much."

Connor handed me the open bottle and I gripped the chilled glass, savoring the wet coldness.

"That's too bad. I think it's a career-maker. Definitely the direction you want to be going." Russ raised his bottle in salute before turning to face Connor. "Which is surprising, since she has no sense of direction. In fact, she's lucky if she finds the house from the driveway."

"At least I can find my own apartment once I'm actually in the building," I jabbed at him.

"Subtle. Did I mention how subtle your wife could be, Connor?"

"I think it came up after you told me she hadn't had a date since Carter was president."

I choked on my beer. I looked from one to the other and back. If I had more energy, I'd be mortified. As it was, I could only shake my head at Russ and promise myself I would get even later.

"Which is probably a good thing, since she's already apparently married to two men," Connor added.

"Don't help him. He doesn't need your help. And stop ganging up on me."

Russ laughed, reaching over to chuck my chin.

"You'll be happy to know that Connor and I have decided to behave like gentlemen about the whole marriage thing." Russ began to peel the label from his beer, dropping the shreds onto the tablecloth. "There's no sense letting things get out of hand. After all, Connor is a reasonable man. And we all know that I am the definition of enlightenment."

"Besides, he could kick the crap out of you," I muttered.

"Which shows I'm also one of God's brighter bulbs."

"I said *could*. He won't because I'm saving that pleasure for myself."

"She also likes to threaten people. I don't take it seriously."

"That could be a mistake," Connor suggested, sipping his beer.

"I just put it down to her passionate nature." Russ grinned lasciviously at me. I bit my lip to keep from laughing.

"Passionate. Definitely." Connor's voice was jazz smooth.

"I don't suppose you'd consider a request for details? No? I didn't think so. Although I must tell you, I think personal privacy is incredibly overrated, especially when it keeps me from hearing all the good parts. Anyway, except for a few aggressive tendencies and a deplorable sense of style, she's not so bad."

Connor murmured noncommittally.

"You want another beer?" Connor raised his bottle inquiringly.

"I don't mind if I do."

"Don't you have a job or an apartment or a life you have to get back to?"

"I don't have to be at the station until eight. And, since Connor is only going to be here for a short time, I think I really ought to make getting to know him a priority."

"Prioritize this." I used my favorite traffic gesture.

Russ laughed and Connor kept his head bent, clearing his throat. I looked from one to the other and gave up, shaking my head in exasperation.

"So are you going to tell me what agreement you two

gentlemen have made with regard to my company? Is it Monday, Wednesday, Friday, every other weekend? Or are we working on a six-month-on, six-month-off schedule?"

"I have graciously decided to forgo future sexual relations with you," Russ said. "It's an unsafe world out there, and monogamy is really the right answer."

I finished my beer.

"And what did you get in exchange for such a big concession?"

"He doesn't do anything that would make it impossible for me to have a monogamous relationship with someone else in the future," Russ said dryly.

I swallowed a laugh. Actually, it was kind of sweet in a caveman sort of way. I sneaked a glance at Connor, who winked at me, a smile playing around his lips.

"You got the better part of that deal," I told Connor.

Russ left a few minutes later. Connor walked him to the door and came back smiling.

"How about a pizza for dinner? Easy, no dishes."

I leaned back in my chair. "We can grab something on the way."

"On the way where?" He leaned against the refrigerator.

"Leavenworth, Washington."

I got up and went into the bedroom, pulling jeans and a T-shirt from the dresser. I changed clothes in the bathroom, coming back out into the bedroom to find Connor slouched against the headboard.

I sat down and put on my shoes.

"What's in Leavenworth?" he asked.

"Other than the best fudge in the state?" I tied my laces and stood, fishing the fax out of my discarded pants before leading Connor out of the apartment and down the back stairs. "I was thinking it was time for another mission."

"What kind of mission?"

"Reconnaissance. That's what you call it, right? Recon?"

"Yeah, that's what we call it. What are we re-conning?"

"Mitchell Burke's accident scene. Or, more particularly, his car." I unlocked the passenger door and handed him the keys. "While I was waiting for the fax, I checked out Millicent's death," I told him.

"She's the cat owner?"

"Yeah. She died in a car accident less than a week after Mitchell Burke."

"That's a bit of a coincidence."

"That's what I thought." I merged onto the freeway in light traffic, picking up speed. "But in this case it really is a coincidence. Millicent died in a big accident in downtown Seattle. There were a dozen cars involved. An entire hazardous-materials team was dispatched. There were at least ten specialists assigned. So we know that Millicent's death really was an accident."

"Either that or the best-planned murder in history."

"What did you get from Jepsen?"

Connor groaned. "The things I do for you."

"You insisted on being the one to talk to him." I leaned my seat back, the days of no sleep hitting me hard. "What story did you give him?"

"Told him I was interested in investment opportunities. The guy's vermin. Desperate vermin." Connor took one hand off the wheel and laid it on my thigh.

"Desperate?"

"He's got a big development of office buildings in a neighborhood a few miles from your apartment. They're about three-quarters complete. The only problem is, according to my investment broker, office space in downtown Seattle isn't exactly a hot market. With all the dot-coms going under, and all the empty Boeing space, prices have dropped and vacancy rates have skyrocketed."

"You have an investment broker?"

"He's a family friend."

"That's handy. What kind of investor is Jepsen looking for?"

"The bail-me-out kind. I had my friend make some

calls. Jepsen put up all his Masterson Enterprises stock to secure a note for this project. He's already had to sell off his other stuff to make his interest payments. Without another investor, he's toast."

I was having trouble keeping my eyes open. *Yes, Sara, you are officially too old for all-nighters.* "Did you find out where he was on Wednesday?"

"No. I did get a look at the car, though."

"Anything interesting?"

"He has a fifty-thousand-dollar pigsty."

I shuddered, picturing it. "I'll bet."

"I did get one more piece of intel."

"Hmmm?" I sighed, trying to get more comfortable.

"Both Masterson children are investors."

I sat up straight, shaking my head to push the sleepiness away. "That's cozy."

"They invested after Jepsen filed suit."

"Nice. I wonder where they got the money? Everything keeps coming back to it." I rubbed my eyes and tugged the seat belt away from my neck. "Well, that and revenge. When I met with Jepsen, every other sentence was more diatribe against all the ways Masterson has screwed him. Got to love that testosterone."

"Hey, don't lump me in with them."

"Except for you, then."

"Thanks, I think." Connor grimaced. "My take, based on what Jepsen was saying, is that he's suing to force a payout on his shares of Masterson Enterprises. Apparently, there is some big case where minority shareholders got a court to mandate dividend payments to keep the majority shareholders from holding their investment hostage. For Jepsen, it would be a win-win. He'd have enough cash to bail out the project, and, with the court overseeing payments tied to the shares, they'd be worth a lot more and there'd be an actual market for the things."

"Definitely a win-win. And the kids?"

"Siding against Daddy."

"That should make for fun holiday gatherings." I digested this new information while we drove. "Did you get a chance to meet the heirs apparent?"

"I did. I take it you did, too. Or at least, I've got a feeling the 'nosy lawyer bitch with the great tits' was an oblique reference to you. Why didn't you tell me?" He glanced in my direction, but he seemed more curious than judgmental.

"I was trying to forget. The only thing I got out of them was an overwhelming need to shower. Did you get anything?"

"Bud the gambler has an alibi. He was losing his shirt at the Tulalip Casino. Apparently a pretty regular thing, since the blackjack dealer I talked to knew him by name. Most of the waitresses knew him, too. A couple have the handprints to prove it. He bother you when you met him?"

"Nothing I couldn't handle."

"Hmm." We rode in silence for a mile or two, measuring the likelihood that we wouldn't agree on what I could handle. He let it go.

"Stewie has no alibi. Neither one has a nice thing to say about their father, and both seem like pretty good candidates for incarceration to me."

I couldn't agree more. I'd personally sleep a lot better knowing they weren't out pouncing on unsuspecting women. "You get anything else?"

"I asked my investment buddy about the lawsuit and what Burke's role might be. His best guess is that Burke was doing a valuation of Jepsen's stock and/or the company." The city slipped away in the rearview mirror and the landscape became rural. The windows let in a warm breeze, and the view soothed me. We came to a small town and slowed for the speed limit. It was like a dozen towns bisected by the highway leading to the mountains. They were Mayberry in appearance, two-pump gas stations and tiny post offices.

"We should stop," Connor suggested.

"Are you hungry?"

"I could eat. It's probably also a good idea if we wait

until it's dark. I assume we aren't on a guest list for this place?"

We pulled into the parking lot of a local diner. "That would be an accurate assumption."

I followed him into the restaurant. Definitely Mayberry. There was a long chrome counter with matching stools. A grizzled old man sat on the last stool, drinking coffee and shouting small talk at the kitchen doors. There were booths along two walls, covered in red Naugahyde and scarred with age. Three small tables filled the center of the room.

We made our way to a booth near the back and sat down. An instant later a beehived waitress in her early sixties set water and silverware in front of us. I couldn't look away from the platinum blond hair. It added a good twelve inches to her five-foot frame.

"Hey. How you doing?" She wore a starched blue uniform covered by a white apron with the name Vera stitched over the pocket. She moved with the grace of a dancer, offering an easy smile with the menus.

"We're fine. How are you?" Connor asked.

"Happy to be waiting on somebody with your smile, honey."

His cheeks flushed and his eyes dropped to the table briefly before he glanced up at me, mischief dancing in his eyes.

"You're gonna hafta watch this one, sugar. Imagine flirtin' with me while he's out with you. This one's a bad 'un, all right. I always liked that in a man."

"Please don't encourage him. He already knows he's cute."

"Cute?" Connor choked on his water.

"Them's the most dangerous ones. Now, what can I get you kids?"

"What do you suggest?" I figured she would steer me away from anything questionable.

"Meat loaf for you, sugar. I know it's hot as a griddle cake out there, but there ain't nothin' like Dave's meat loaf. I married the man for his meat loaf. 'Sides, a skinny li'l thing like you can use a bit of cushionin', you gonna hold on to a man like him." Her hair nodded toward Connor while her head seemed to stay still. I was awed.

"And what can I bring you, darlin'?"

"The same. And a couple of lemonades."

"You drivin'?"

"Yeah."

"Smart boy." Her crayoned lips smiled. "Two meat loaves, two 'ades comin' right up."

She turned and walked away to greet a family of four as they took their place at one of the center tables. Connor spread the fax pages on the table between us.

"This is all there was?"

"Yep," I conceded. "If you have a one-car accident in a hick town you get a county sheriff and a coroner who doubles as the funeral director."

"Great."

"It gets worse. The regular coroner is an MD, which I gather is pretty rare. It's an elected position. No medical training necessary if you've got the votes. Unfortunately, he was away when Burke died. So his replacement, the local funeral director, answered the call."

"So, we think a mistake is not out of the question," Connor said.

"It doesn't seem like a huge stretch to me."

Connor leaned back as Vera placed our drinks in front of us. As soon as she was gone, he leaned forward conspiratorially, resting his arms on the table.

I reread Burke's file, taking my time. The first page was a police report dated March 1 listing a single-car accident on Highway 2 at approximately nine p.m. The weather was described as snowing with bad visibility. Under road conditions, there was one word: *Ice.* Page two was a medical report. Mitchell Burke was described as a Caucasian male, forty-five to fifty-five years old, five-seven, and a hundred and fifty pounds. The cause of death was listed as traumatic head injury. Toxicology was listed as negative. Page three was a towing report, which showed that a Mercedes registered to Mitchell

Burke was removed from the accident scene on Highway 2 and towed to the impound lot in Leavenworth at eight seventeen a.m. on March 2. There were two photographs, both on the same sheet, rendered almost indecipherable by fax. One showed the broken barricade through which the car had apparently plunged before dropping two hundred feet into the ravine below. The second photo showed the car resting against a rock, its nose crumpled, its sides pleated, the windows shattered by the impact. The last page was a two-paragraph final report written by the officer called to the scene, with his conclusion that the accident was an accident.

"So, in Leavenworth, somebody dies and all he gets are two lousy paragraphs?" Connor looked at the gritty photos.

"He actually died outside of Winton, but you've got the rest right. It was a busy night. Two fatal accidents. One with kids. There were at least a dozen follow-up stories to the other accident, but Mitch wasn't a local. There was the bigger obituary in the Seattle paper, but he didn't rate much interest from the hometown cops. The two paragraphs he did get seemed like an imposition on Officer Laura Stanley."

The smell of meat loaf announced Vera's arrival with our dinner. The plates were heaped with the entrée, creamy mashed potatoes, and peas. All the comforts of home.

"It looks delicious. Thanks."

"Don't let that boy's sweet whisperin' distract you from your dinner, honey. I got a feeling you're gonna need all your strength."

I laughed, embarrassed myself this time.

"She sure is," Connor agreed.

Vera laughed in delight. "He's a bad 'un, all right."

"So, how do you know the cop thought it was an imposition?" Connor ate his meat loaf plain. I drowned mine in ketchup, then forked up a large mouthful. Vera was right: The cook was definitely a catch.

"I talked to Officer Stanley on the phone. I also talked to an Officer O'Neal."

Connor moaned softly, clearly savoring the mashed potatoes. I took a bite of my own. We lifted our glasses, clinking them together in mutual appreciation of the cuisine.

"Let me guess. Officer O'Neal is a guy."

"You had a fifty/fifty shot."

"Actually, I was pretty confident."

"Because I have Jean Harlow's voice?" I gave my breathiest impersonation.

"Maybe."

He finished his dinner and began to eye my remaining potatoes. I curved my arm protectively around my plate. He smiled, picking up his lemonade and draining it. I set my own fork down long enough to toast him mockingly with my lemonade before finishing it as well.

"So, if we're going to do this, we ought to run by the local grocery store."

"Why?"

"Supplies."

"Right."

Connor signaled to Vera. "We need another order of meat loaf and the check."

"Sure thing, hon."

"Let me guess; felonies make you hungry."

We drove through deserted streets. The setting sun skewered dark shadows with rays of light. The houses were small, the yards littered with abandoned toys. It was apparently an early-to-bed, early-to-rise sort of place, although I detected the gleam of televisions behind the picture windows. Connor and I didn't talk. I tingled with adrenaline. This sneaking-around-on-the-verge-of-being-caught stuff was incredibly seductive—addictive, even. I wondered if Connor felt it, too. I turned to look at him, tugging at the seat belt as it cut across my throat. Compared to his real life, breaking into an impound lot was probably as interesting as watching paint dry. This case

was the most exciting thing that had happened to me . . .
well, ever, with the possible exception of meeting him.
I let my eyes linger, my thoughts shrouded in the deepening gloom. Meeting Connor was definitely the
exception.

"You got the bag?"

"Felony implements. Check." I lifted the bag we'd
gotten at the all-night convenience store we'd stopped
at on the way. I lifted the yellow rubberized gloves and
waved them at Connor.

"We don't want to leave fingerprints."

"Or have dishpan hands." I emptied the bag, setting
the items inside between us: duct tape, two flashlights,
and Ziploc bags. I picked up a small plastic case. "Eye
shadow? What's this for?"

Connor parked behind a gas station a couple of blocks
from the impound lot, far away from its lights.

"Fingerprint powder."

"Cool." I grinned at him. "How do we get in?"

I looked past the gas station to a high fence, beyond
which sat hulking vehicles in a variety of shapes. Of
course, why would anyone put high-tech security in for
a few broken-down cars? A tall fence would be plenty
of protection.

"The old-fashioned way, right?" I answered my own
question. "I haven't climbed a fence since I was a kid."

I threw our tools back into the bag, popping out of the
car and striding to the fence, while Connor rummaged in
the car. I looked left and right furtively, humming the
tune of "Secret Agent Man." I looped the bag's handle
over my arm and reached for the fence, pulling myself
up and scrambling toward the top. It wasn't as easy as
it had been when I was twelve.

"Sara, no, wait." A harsh whisper.

"C'mon."

"Sara."

Just then a fast-moving shadow separated itself from
the others and, with a deep-throated growl, launched
itself at me.

"God." I yelped, propelling myself off the fence and landing with a thud. The ground was hard and I knocked the wind out of myself. My attacker barked his head off.

Connor dropped down beside me.

"Sara? Are you okay?"

"You should see the other guy." My head hurt, my butt felt bruised, and both elbows stung like mad. Not my best moment. The dog continued to sound his alarm.

"Connor, the dog. We'll have the entire neighborhood out here. We've gotta go." I began to struggle to my feet.

"No, just sit. Take a minute."

Connor got up and picked up the Styrofoam container he'd gotten at the diner. He walked toward the fence, murmuring to the dog, who abandoned barking for a menacing growl. Connor opened the container and tossed it over the fence. The dog sprinted out of the way, dropping to its haunches and keeping both the man and box in sight. The dog eased its way closer to the white plastic, its growl now barely audible. I sat up and then stood, ignoring the shooting pain in my left elbow. I brushed myself off and looked around for the bag, spotting it twenty feet away. I retrieved it and moved closer to Connor, close enough to see the dog wolf down the meat loaf dinner Dave had so lovingly prepared. Mashed potatoes, even the peas were consumed. I never knew dogs ate vegetables.

We stood and watched the dog for several more minutes. He continued to growl intermittently, staring at us with a fixed gaze from four feet inside the fence. He let out a halfhearted bark and dropped abruptly to a lying position. In another minute he was snoring.

"That explains the cold medicine, I guess. It won't hurt him, will it?"

"He'll be fine. Do you still want to do this?"

"Sure. Only bruised my pride. How did you know they'd have a dog?"

"In my experience, everybody's got a dog."

"Any more educated guesses I should know about?"

"The dog was it. Are you sure you're okay?"

"I'm fine. Let's do this."

Connor took the bag from me and we moved to the fence. Getting over it was a lot easier without the ferocious flying dog. Connor managed it in half the time with a fraction of the noise, but I refused to be irritated by his easy competence. I dropped inside the fence and took a long, careful look at the dog. Summoning my courage, I took a couple of steps closer, crouching over the prone animal, not convinced he wasn't playing possum. Reaching out, I poked him, prepared to run at the first twitch. He didn't move. Not even a little.

"God, Connor, I think you killed him." I leaned closer, kneeling as I put my face close to his snout, one hand resting on his fur. His side rose on a deep intake of air, reassuring me an instant before his doggy breath assaulted me. He might not be dead but he could kill people with that breath. I almost preferred when he was attacking me physically. Straightening, I waved my hand in front of my face to dissipate the reek, my yellow-gloved hand flapping.

"He's okay. Let's start at the back," Connor whispered, handing me a flashlight.

"It'll be quicker if we split up."

"We are not splitting up."

"Don't be such a scaredy-cat. The dog's been disabled. Do you actually think there are psycho killers lurking in remote impound lots?" I peered at him in the gloom. His testosterone-induced overreaction was taking some of the fun out of the adventure. We started down the wide center path together.

"There's no reason to chance it."

I directed my light, chasing looming shadows. The cars were parked in neat rows, the center aisle splitting the lot into distinct halves. My beam skimmed along the hulking shapes, caressing expensive imports and old beaters. I fixed the light on a faded red number in front of an old pickup truck.

"Too bad we don't know which slot it's in. We should split up. You take the left side; I'll take the right."

"We should stay together."

"Connor, you're being ridiculous. No one is out here waiting for us. No one knew we were coming. Let's start at the back and move forward," I whispered. It was probably an unnecessary precaution, but paranoia was so contagious.

"Sara . . ."

"That was our deal, remember? I'm working the case. You're along for the ride."

"I'm sorry I ever agreed to that stupid deal."

"Be sorry after we find the car. It's a black Mercedes. License plate 857 HJZ." I checked the cars along the way, counting the rows as I went. Twenty-six in all.

"Right."

"No, you're left. I'm right." I nudged him. The back fence glinted as we neared the last row. I turned my beam toward the cars to my right, starting down the row.

"Yell if—"

"If I run into anyone lurking between cars, I'll do my best screaming meemie. Go."

The gravel crunched behind me as he moved away.

I checked one side of me as I walked, quickly realizing that I could make better progress if I didn't keep jumping from one side to the other. The lot was pretty full. Many of the cars looked like they'd followed Mitchell Burke off his steep cliff. Some appeared perfectly fine. Drug seizures? DUIs caught before they had an accident? Why would anyone leave a perfectly good Jaguar moldering in this lot? I turned and retraced my steps, checking out the other side of the row. A flicker of illumination showed Connor's progress as he turned the corner toward the next aisle.

Picking up my pace, I stopped a couple of times to identify cars so badly damaged I had no idea what make they were. Back and forth I walked. A dog howled in the distance and the hair on my arms rose. Pressing my back against a hulking SUV, I flashed the light toward one end of the row, then the other, making sure the Doberman wasn't coming at me from behind. It took a moment to realize the sound had come from much farther away. Taking a calming breath, I fought the shudder that worked its way up my spine. I walked faster, counting the rows as I moved toward the front. The Mercedes was in the tenth row, nestled between a rusting station wagon and a truck perched on wheels the size of small buildings.

"Connor," I called, cringing as the sound carried loudly into the night.

I approached the car from the driver's side, mentally matching it to the one I'd seen in the photographs. The front end was smashed and the windshield was a spider's web of broken glass. Both windows were missing from the driver's side. The headlights were broken. I walked slowly around the car, carefully examining every inch, letting the flashlight play along each scrape. Dropping off a cliff made for some pretty extensive damage. I rounded the trunk and returned to the driver's door. I reached my arm through the window and studied the passenger side, then the backseat, probing the shadows. The seats and footwells were littered with shards of shattered glass. The light strobed against their irregular shapes.

"Sara?"

I jumped, choking on a scream as I slammed my arm against the inside of the car, dropping the flashlight. I pulled my arm free, cradling the throbbing limb against my stomach.

"Must you keep sneaking up on me? You could've given me a heart attack. Not to mention breaking my arm."

"You were supposed to be paying attention. I could've been anyone."

"You are anyone." I rubbed the ache.

"Are you okay?" Connor reached out, his fingers lightly touching the spot I was sure would end up black and blue.

"Yeah, yeah, I'm fine."

"You're sure?"

"I'm sure. I need my flashlight." I leaned into the car, searching. The light had gone out. I hoped it wasn't broken. The driver and passenger seats were empty, so I reached farther in, trying to feel for the flashlight in front of the driver's seat, carefully patting against the glass chips.

"I'll get it." Connor handed me his flashlight and pulled the door open, reaching into the footwell. Coming up empty-handed, he shifted and dropped into the driver's seat, seemingly unconcerned about the sharp edges of the broken window. As he searched, I stepped closer, shining the light past his long legs and into the passenger side.

"Maybe it rolled under the seat."

Connor got out of the car and crouched near the door, yanking on the lever that would move the seat. It didn't budge. He got to his feet and gave another yank, slamming his hand against the back of the seat, but it still wouldn't move. I stepped forward, handed him the flashlight, and moved him out of the way. I knelt beside the seat and reached underneath.

"Connor?"

"Yeah."

"How tall are you?"

"Six-three. Why?"

I scrambled off my knees and sat in the driver's seat with my legs stretched out. "According to the police report, Burke was five-seven. I'm five-seven." I looked at Connor, then back toward my feet. He followed my gaze with the beam of the flashlight.

"So how did he reach the pedals?" Connor asked.

"Maybe the seat got jammed during the accident?" I suggested.

Connor shook his head. "The pictures."

"Right. The car landed on the front grille."

"Yeah, and the car seat's jammed back. It could have happened when the rescue guys removed the body."

"And I'm next in line for the pope's job."

He laughed. "For the record, I'm against any job that requires you to be celibate."

"You have a one-track mind."

He started a slow search of the dashboard with his flashlight. "It's the best track, though, don't you think?" The circle of light rested on the passenger side for a moment before he rounded the car and tugged the door open. He sat in the seat with his back toward me, his legs stuck out the door. He moved closer to the headrest and the upholstery. He pulled the seat belt out and away from the door, then leaned back, holding the seat belt with one hand and the flashlight with the other. He looked at me over his shoulder.

I stared at the irregular stain, barely visible against the dark material. "Blood?"

"If I were guessing."

"So Mitchell Burke was already dead when he got moved."

"Or he was already hurt. And his killer was at least six feet tall."

We got out of the car and closed the doors, brushing the plastic pieces of safety glass from our clothes. Connor took my hand and we walked down the aisle, past the still-sleeping dog and to the fence. I reached out and grabbed the chain link.

"Head bashing? My money's on the loving children. Bud, the gambling cretin with the assault record, is pretty short. The other one, Stewie the glue sniffer, is tall." I swung one leg over the top of the fence. "He could have killed Burke, drove him out here, and then had his brother drive him back." I dropped to the ground, where Connor was already waiting.

"Next stop, Sergeant Wesley." Connor took my hand and we headed back to the car.

Chapter Twenty-six

"At least six feet tall isn't much to go on, Connor. We need proof before we go to the cops."

We were out of the parking lot headed back to the freeway when I finally spoke my thoughts aloud. My motives weren't pure. I wanted Emma to know she'd been right. I wanted her to have some closure. The evil sons were pond scum. I knew they had something to do with Mitchell Burke's death. The cops hadn't done anything before. Would Wesley bother to investigate if the local police stuck with the easy accident explanation? It wasn't his jurisdiction, and what if the blue wall held? Would he question another police officer? Would he take over? Could he take over?

"We've got the car." I insisted. And Emma. Besides, it's the police's job to investigate and make the case, not ours. We'll do the good-citizen part and tell them what we know, and they can take it from there."

"Emma is a distraught wife who doesn't want to believe that her husband could have committed suicide. And the car isn't proof."

"It's still a police problem." We wove slowly through dark streets.

"We found the car."

"It's not ours. Neither is this murder."

"So you admit Emma's husband was murdered." I

pointed at him in the darkness, a prosecutor catching a witness in a revealing statement.

"I'm convinced," he stated matter-of-factly, concentrating on the road. "I'm sure the police will be, too."

"The police"—I laid emphasis on the word—"wrote the whole thing off as a suicide. They didn't investigate when the evidence was fresh." I tugged at the seat belt.

"Sara, you're becoming obsessed with this thing."

"I'm not."

"You are."

"Not."

"Sara . . ." His voice held a warning tone. My peripheral vision caught his glance in my direction, which I deliberately ignored.

"Okay, so maybe I am into it a little. But we're close, Connor. Can't you feel it?" I reached over, gripping his arm, trying to infuse some of my enthusiasm into him.

"That's the part I don't like." His voice was dry. I dropped my hand back into my own lap.

"I really hate to be critical here, but aren't you the one who spent four years at the Naval Academy and another two training to become a SEAL just so you could feel like this?"

"I joined the navy for a lot of reasons. And it's different when my very impulsive wife is involved."

"I am not impulsive."

"You define impulse. Jesus, you married someone you knew a week."

"So did you."

"For me, it was an aberration. With you, it's a lifestyle."

"I don't think I like being referred to as an aberration." A flash of light caught my eye as we turned a corner getting onto the highway. "Connor, stop." My feet pressed against the brakes I didn't have.

"What?"

"We just passed the diner." I grabbed my armrest, feeling the car slow.

"You're not hungry again, are you?"

"Actually, this spy stuff does whet the appetite, but that's not why I want to stop."

Connor pulled off the side of the road, checking his mirrors before heading back toward the little building. He pulled into the lot, parking between two pickup trucks in the half-full lot. He released his seat-belt and turned toward me.

"Okay, Holmes, why have we stopped?"

"The other driver."

"I don't follow."

"Let's assume for a moment that somebody did drive up here with Burke in the car and pushed the thing over the cliff. He couldn't have done that alone. At a minimum, the killer would need some way back to town. A wheelman. Which means our killer had an accomplice he could trust. For grins, let's imagine he has a brother."

"Babe, we don't have any reason to believe that the Masterson kids had a motive for killing Mitchell Burke."

"One's a druggie and the other is a thug. Their father is missing. His right hand at the company is helping the lawyers investigate. Who knows what they think? Maybe they're the reason Dad can't be found. Maybe they took his walkabout as an opportunity to help themselves to the corporate coffers. Who could figure that out? A controller. It would make Mitchell Burke a threat to them." I hated that he was poking holes in my theory.

"Only if your assumption is correct, and we have no basis for that. No proof, Sara."

"Humor me. Say it was six-foot Stewie who did it. He puts Burke in the passenger seat and drives him up here. Maybe he remembers one of the previous crashes, or maybe he just knows this is a risky stretch of road. He gets lucky or, depending on the timing, creates his own luck by staging the accident near where another has already happened. Small police force already stretched thin. No one will think twice. He gets the brother to follow them up and drive him back after it's over."

"That's all guesswork, and neither of these brothers struck me as either that smart or that controlled."

"Maybe, but say I'm right. Or even say I'm wrong about who did it. No matter who you were, would you take a second car to the scene of the crime?"

"No." Connor shook his head, his eyes searching mine. "Too conspicuous."

"Exactly. So if it were me, I might go somewhere where a stranger wouldn't look out of place." I stared deliberately at the brightly lit building.

"Like the parking lot of a diner open late-night. Got it." We went into the restaurant. One of the bookend codgers still sat on a stool at the far end of the counter. Two middle-aged women were playing cards at a central table, and a couple of handholding teenagers necked discreetly in a far booth. We hesitated in the doorway as Vera came out of the kitchen.

"Guess you two just can't stay away, huh?" She approached, patting her beehive and winking at Connor.

"We missed dessert." Connor winked back.

"What did you have in mind, honey?" She waggled pencil brows at him, including me in a broad smile. I smiled back. Who was I to stand in the way of a little harmless flirting? I didn't have the impression that Connor's taste ran to sexagenarian Marge Simpsons.

"Ice cream and a little conversation."

"We got plenty of both, sugar. You know what you want?"

"Whatever's the house specialty will be fine."

"Comin' right up. Why don'tcha grab a booth and I'll be right over."

"Great." Connor steered me toward a booth near the front plate-glass window, far from the other customers. We sat side by side. I drummed my fingers impatiently against the Formica tabletop. Connor reached out and took hold of my hands, stilling their restless movements.

Vera came to our booth with two hot-fudge sundaes and a cup of coffee on an orange plastic tray. With a big smile she placed a sundae in front of each of us. Then she slid opposite us and set the tray down, lifting the cup and gulping at the steaming brew.

"Thanks." Connor picked up his spoon, taking a quick bite of whipped cream. "We want to know if you remember anything about an accident that happened not far from here on March first of this year. A man was killed."

Vera swallowed, nodding.

"Sure. It even made the city papers. Seven people killed, including two sweet little high school kids. They was so young. It was terrible."

"I'm sure it was, but we're actually interested in another accident that happened that night. One fatality."

"Course, I remember that one, too. Comin' the same night after them other people died. You'd think the police would have figured out how to make that road safer by then. Why you interested? You two reporters or somethin'?"

"Nothing like that," I assured her. "The victim's widow is a friend of ours." I spoke slowly, trying to decide how much to tell her. I swallowed a spoonful of ice cream, taking my time, holding the icy dessert on my tongue for a second before allowing it to slip down my throat.

"Poor thing. I hope she's doing okay. I wouldn't want to be losin' my Dave; that's for sure." She dabbed at her lips with a napkin, her eyes dark with sympathy.

"She just has a lot of unanswered questions, you know. We told her it didn't matter why her husband was up here, but she just can't let it go. We were wondering if you remember any strange faces in the diner that night."

"Maybe you oughta just tell her he was on business. Even if you don't know for sure. I mean, it ain't gonna do nobody no good to go telling some poor widda woman that her man was cattin' around right before he goes off and gets hisself killed." She lifted her cup to her lips, her eyebrows raised.

"You're probably right. The thing is, if he was meeting someone, and it was innocent, she could ask about his last hours, you know? Maybe he mentioned her or told a funny story or something she could hold on to." I felt Connor's arm slide behind me. I took it to mean that I was believable without being schmaltzy.

"I suppose that would be a comfort. Lemme see. We got lots of skiers up here that time of year."

"It would have been pretty late. The car was found around two in the morning, but we think it happened earlier."

"Place was really empty with the big accident and all. Everybody wanta' to be home with their lads, y'know." She closed her eyes as she considered for a moment before opening them again. "Oh, my Lord, yes, there was one woman."

A woman. Damn.

"No one else?"

"Not a soul. Like I said, it was real quiet that night."

"Was there anything else out of the ordinary that night? Anything at all?" I was deflated. I'd been so sure I was on the right track.

"Jus' that she couldn't take that cell phone out of her ear. Talkin' real loud and all. It wasn't like we had lots of customers to disturb or nothin', but she could keep her personal business private, if you know what I mean. If you ask me, those cell phones are ruinin' this world."

"Did you hear what she said?"

Vera rolled her eyes. "I'm not an eavesdropper. I don't go listenin' to people's private conversations 'less they force me to by talking loud enough to wake the dead."

"I'm sure that's true." Connor added his agreement with a nod.

"She was waitin' for somebody. Kept askin' him where he was, like he was keepin' her waitin'. I tell you, that woman did not like to wait. Finally she said, 'I'll be right there,' and dashed off like she was bein' chased."

"What did the woman look like?" Connor asked, switching his empty sundae dish with my half-full one.

"She was young, black, pretty in a city kinda way."

"Probably just skiers on their way back to Seattle." I

sighed again, letting my hand fall to rest against Connor's jeans-clad thigh. I'd really thought I was onto something. There was no way either of the Masterson kids was going to be mistaken for a pretty black woman.

"Oh, she wasn't no skier. Not with those nails."

My own nails dug deep into Connor's thigh.

"Something I said?" he muttered into my ear, pulling my hand free from its grip.

"Nails?"

"Beauties. Bloodred and at least a coupla inches long. Bet they cost a pretty penny."

"We've got to go." I pulled a crumpled twenty from my jeans pocket and set it next to the empty sundae dish before pushing against Connor's shoulder to get him moving.

"Did I say something to upset you folks?" Vera was looking at me in confusion, her penciled eyebrows and painted-on lips adding an element of whimsy to the expression.

I sent my brightest smile in her direction.

"Absolutely not. You've been a big help. I just remembered somewhere we have to be." Connor was standing, and I jumped up beside him, continuing to prod him into motion. Vera looked from him to me and back again before turning up the wattage on her own grin.

"Like that, is it?" She rose, chuckling. "I'll just get your change." She reached for the twenty.

"It's yours." Connor finally started moving toward the door, and I urged him to pick up the pace.

"Have a good time. Where is that man of mine? Dave?"

The door jangled as we stepped through. Connor pulled the keys out and I reached for them, striding to the car. I jumped in, clicked his door lock, and started the motor. The second he closed his door I set the car in motion, peeling out of the parking lot and onto the highway. Connor reached across to pull my seat belt across me before clicking his own into place. I kept the gas pedal near the floor.

"You realize that our friendly neighborhood waitress thinks you're dragging me off to bed."

I leaned closer to the steering wheel, trying to see beyond the darkness, trying to keep the too-fast car on the road.

"If that's your intention, I really don't mind."

A flash of lights blinded me for a moment and I took my foot off the gas, blinking rapidly. As soon as the car passed by us, I depressed the accelerator, quickly climbing back above the speed limit.

"I think I can wait if you wanted to slow down enough to get us there in one piece."

I took a corner too tight and the reflectors clicked against the wheels.

"That would be the wrong side of the road."

My mind was shooting down the road faster than the car. Jepsen, the bastard. He'd killed Mitchell Burke. It was his fault that Emma was sitting alone in her house with a bunch of dolls, for God's sake. And he thought he'd gotten away with it. That burned me the most. Well, he wasn't going to get away with it any longer. His time was up.

"That's it, Sara. Pull over. Pull over." Connor was shouting. I glanced at him and the car skidded wildly. Connor grabbed for the wheel and we struggled to keep the car on the road, ricocheting back and forth across the asphalt, spinning gravel on both shoulders. I took my foot off the gas, careful not to slam on the brake as we worked on straightening the car. Thank God the road was deserted. Finally slowing, we gently rolled onto the shoulder, the motor still idling. Connor pushed the gearshift into park and turned the engine off, yanking the keys out of the ignition. I took a shuddering breath and leaned back against my seat, my heart hammering in my ears. I pulled my shaking hands from their death grip on the steering wheel and twined them in my lap. There was no movement beside me. I could still hear my own breathing coming in harsh gasps, but Connor was deathly silent. A tingle crawled up my spine.

"Nice night for a drive, huh?" My attempt at humor fell flat.

Total silence for another full minute. My heart pounded louder. Finally Connor pushed open his door and got out. The overhead light in the car was on just long enough for me to get a good look at his clenched jaw and the white-knuckled fist he had wrapped around the keys before he closed his door and it went dark again. I blinked. A gentle knock on my window had me practically ejecting through the roof. One hand clutching at the front of my T-shirt, I used the other to roll down my window. Without a word, Connor reached through the open glass to unlock my door. He leaned in and undid my seat belt before pushing me toward the empty passenger seat. I shifted, swinging my legs over the gearshift. Mutely, I fastened my seat belt and waited as he started the car and deliberately pulled back onto the highway. We drove several long miles in deafening silence. I couldn't take it.

"Aren't you going to yell or something?"

"Or something." We got back on I-5, heading toward the city. The highway was so well lit, I could see him almost as clearly as if it were day. A muscle twitched in his jaw, and despite the relaxed hands he kept religiously at ten and two on the wheel, his rigid posture told me he was still pretty upset about our near miss. We drove in silence for a long time, each lost in our own thoughts.

"Hey, Connor, take this exit." I pointed.

"We're going home."

"But, Connor, don't you get it? Henry Jepsen killed Mitchell Burke."

"We're going home."

"But he did it. It was her. The secretary. Jepsen's secretary. She was the one in the diner. Pretty city girl with killer nails. Killer. Literally. Didn't you see her when you went over there?" I pulled on the confinement of my seat belt, shifting so that I could half face him. "She's black, she's beautiful, and she has nails to die for. Claws, really."

Connor continued past the exit as if he hadn't heard me.

"Connor, Jepsen murdered Burke in cold blood. He probably killed Cort, too." I reached out and gripped his forearm to try to reach him. He took an audible breath.

"Why?" Connor clearly didn't share my sense of urgency.

"What do you mean, why?"

"Why would Jepsen kill Burke?"

"Burke was involved in the lawsuit. He found out something."

"What?"

"I don't know what," I yelled. "What difference does it make? Burke knew everything about the company. Maybe he did just what you said. Maybe Burke valued the stock low or something."

"So Jepsen killed him? How would that help? If Burke's valuation was correct, the new accountant would just come up with the same number. If Burke's calculation was incorrect, Jepsen could hire his own guy and challenge it. The only thing that Burke's death accomplished was a delay, and I don't see how that could possibly help Jepsen. He needs the money now. Waiting hurts him."

"It's no coincidence. That was his secretary waiting for him. It was Jepsen. It has to be." The wind leaked from my sails. "He's a murderer, Connor." I let go of his arm and slumped back into my seat, crossing my arms and staring out at the brightly lit city. I hated logic.

"A pretty woman with long fingernails isn't a video-taped confession."

"Vera can pick her out."

"Maybe. But we've still got as much on Stewie and Bud as we do on Jepsen. I think we should let the police handle it from here."

"You wouldn't think that if it were your case."

"It's our case, remember?"

"No." I said it petulantly but I didn't really mean it. Connor was right. I had suspicions but nothing else. Jepsen may have killed Burke, but I couldn't prove it.

We drove the rest of the way to the apartment in silence. I shuffled up the stairs with Connor behind me. I brushed my teeth and got ready for bed, sliding beneath the sheet. Connor got in beside me and we lay spoon-fashion. I could feel the sting of frustrated tears behind my eyelids.

"Tomorrow we'll call the cops and tell them what we found out about Burke's car. Then we'll take another look at everything and see where we are." He cuddled closer to me. "Sara?"

"He made her a widow."

"I know."

Chapter Twenty-seven

"**A**s near as I can tell, Masterson hasn't been seen in public since before Burke died."

"Maybe he's the shy type," Connor suggested, taking a seat at the kitchen table.

I logged off the Internet news page and shut the lid to my laptop, rubbing my tired eyes. "If he is, he had a personality transplant. He was in the papers at least once a week for years before this missing-in-action thing. Even when he dropped out before, he managed to stay in the headlines. Both the mentally deficient, knuckle-dragging eldest son and the sleazy business partner mentioned that they hadn't seen him, although Masterson's absence was pretty much put down to avoidance."

Connor pulled a file toward him, flipping through documents. He'd picked up two cartons of files from Emma before I'd even gotten up. Court documents, affidavits, deposition notices, financial records. All with neat identifying tabs and manila file folders. Emma had found them in the storage shed behind their property.

Jepsen had filed suit for wrongful termination and demanded an accounting as minority shareholder. A subpoena duces tecum, demand for document production, had been filed on Masterson Enterprises. Mitchell Burke had carefully kept copies of the documents he sent in response. Halfway through the stack was a copy of bank transfers to the pension fund. The dates leaped off the

page. The transfers stopped in December. Jepsen was
fired in April. He immediately filed suit and pushed the
case hard. Burke answered the subpoena on May 20. He
died on May 22. Right afterward, Jepsen's lawyer started
to drag his feet. The May pension payment was made.
A clerical error, my ass.

"How much nerve do you think Jepsen has?" I asked.

"He came from nothing. I doubt he's in a hurry to go
back. Why?"

"The pension money. It stopped going into the account while Jepsen was still at Masterson Enterprises. It
makes it look like he was siphoning off the funds and
Masterson caught him."

"But Jepsen's the one who sued," Connor said.

"Could be a smoke screen. Payments were missed
after he left, too. That's where the nerve would come
in. It's a serious game of felony chicken. Once he was
fired, Jepsen had to know someone would figure it out.
Probably Burke. He was the natural suspect. So he went
on the offensive and sued."

"Why not just bail if he had the cash?"

"That's where I keep getting hung up."

"So work it backward," Connor suggested.

"What do you mean?"

"If you had a few million and the house of cards was
crashing, you'd go missing."

"Right," I agreed.

"Who's missing?"

"Stuart Masterson."

"It also means the lawsuit Jepsen filed was probably
legit."

I nodded, getting up from the couch and stretching.

"So Jepsen files suit. Burke supplies the information
that lets Jepsen know Masterson's looted the company.
Why slow down? Why not go to the cops?"

Connor just looked at me.

"Jepsen didn't want the cops. He wanted the money."

"And probably Masterson's head on a pike," Connor
agreed. "He also couldn't afford to have the pension

swindle go public. What assets he has now are leveraged by his interest in Masterson Enterprises. If ME is suddenly under investigation for financial wrongdoing . . ." Connor trailed off.

"His other business tanks," I concluded. "Mitchell Burke and his neat tabs. All the papers in nice orderly files." I slumped onto the couch.

"A threat," Connor conceded.

"I hate these guys."

"I know."

"We have to find Masterson. He's the key."

"What about Masterson's business contacts? Isn't anyone asking questions about his disappearance?" Connor asked.

"No one is screaming about it. I couldn't find any record that he had much contact with staff. It's like Masterson Enterprises was built in silos. No one had visibility outside their own piece of the puzzle meaning no one saw a big picture. Stuart Masterson also liked to maintain old-school distinctions between poo-bahs and peons. He never had much contact beyond a couple of key people, mainly Jepsen, Burke, and Millicent. Even Morris was hired by letter."

"Morris never met him?"

"I don't know that for sure. The engagement letter was signed by Millicent. I'd love to ask, but I just can't see myself walking up to him and saying, 'Hey, boss, is there a reason your oh-so-famous billionaire client has never bothered to actually meet you face-to-face?' I could follow it up with, 'By the way, how's the search for the missing pension millions working out?' "

Connor laughed. "That shows a stronger instinct for survival than I would have credited you with."

"Gee, thanks. So nice to know I can still surprise my soul mate of three days." I saluted him with my coffee cup. He raised his and we clicked ceramic.

"Four months and three days. Just because I wasn't here doesn't mean we weren't actually married." He winked, sipping at his coffee.

"So you keep reminding me."

"You keep forgetting," he said matter-of-factly, reaching across the table to push my hair back behind one ear.

I kept my eyes glued to the pale blue tablecloth, gripping my coffee cup with both hands as he traced the outer shell of my ear with his forefinger, lightly stroking. My train of thought derailed with the gesture.

"But I digress. We were talking about your case."

"Right. Okay. Yes." I took a gulp of coffee, scalding my tongue.

"So how did you find out that no one had seen him?"

"Most of it's in the affidavits the kids filed." I sat up straighter, attempting to appear as nonchalant as he did, disgruntled but still relieved to be returning to safe ground. "I can't believe they actually think some judge is going to give them the keys to the kingdom. Anyway, it's the crux of the claim. Dad doesn't return calls. He ignores business. His financial affairs are in disarray. Dad must need his faithful and loving children to babysit his billions. The fact that he doesn't send his adoring family love notes on their birthdays is a clear indication that he has gone around the bend. Until you have the misfortune of actually meeting the relatives."

Connor leaned back in his chair. "It muddies the water some. The kids' lawsuit would have had a much better chance of succeeding without Burke, especially if Masterson wasn't around. No one close to him to testify he didn't howl at the moon. That could sound like the kids had their own reason for killing Burke. Maybe we should try this another way. Someone must be making decisions. Who's paying the bills?"

"It's on autopilot. Masterson's personal expenses are electronically paid. Probably preauthorized, although I haven't seen any bank records. The business side is paid by the company. Day-to-day decisions are made by a chief financial officer. I forget his name." My gaze drifted involuntarily to his mouth and I lost the flow of the conversation again.

"Let me guess. Our moneyman has never met his employer."

"What? Oh, right. Give the man a cigar. Although taking into consideration what happened to his predecessor, maybe it's a good thing."

"How long did Burke work for Stuart Masterson?"

"Nearly fifteen years."

"That's a long time." The doorbell rang. Connor got up and went out into the hall, returning a moment later with a large envelope. "It's from Emma." He ripped open the back and pulled out several sheets of paper, reading aloud. " 'Dear Connor and Sara. I found this tucked into my late husband's Day-Timer after you left. I don't know what it means, but I thought you should see it. I'll let you know if I find anything else. Best regards, Emma Burke.' "

Connor handed me the first page and I reread Emma's note. "What did she send?"

"It's a Post-it note. It says 'Private Placements Employment Agency' and has a phone number." He handed it to me.

I looked at it. "Well, he probably hired temps all the time. Wait a minute. It's a two-one-two area code. Where is that?"

"New York City, I think."

"Why would Burke need a New York employment agency?"

"Maybe it was a big job. Could be they were advertising nationally for a vice president or something."

Thinking through Connor's idea, I got up and refilled my coffee mug, offering some to him before sitting back down at the kitchen table. "I suppose anything is possible. We still need motive. Why would Jepsen want Burke dead? It has to tie into the lawsuit, don't you think? Jepsen demanded financial disclosure. He'd scheduled Burke for a deposition, for Pete's sake. What was he hoping Burke would say? Maybe Burke came up with the wrong answers." I shrugged.

"Who knows?" He shook his head. "I keep coming

back to what really started the whole thing. One minute Jepsen's got Masterson's six; the next Jepsen's taking range and distance."

"Is it me or did you just stop speaking English?"

"Sorry, babe. I keep forgetting you're a civilian."

"Well, I could use a translation, G.I. Joe." My stomach rumbled loudly and I got up to check the cupboards for food.

"G.I. Joe was army. I'm navy."

I rolled my eyes at him.

"One minute Jepsen's signature is necessary for important financial transactions; the next he's out in the cold and Millicent is running everything. Why? What set Masterson off so much that he axed his partner of ten years?"

"Maybe it wasn't about Jepsen. Maybe it was about Millicent," I offered. "Masterson thinks with his other head. He's a guy. Good-bye, best friend; hello, lady love." I crunched some oyster crackers. They were incredibly stale but I was starving. Connor reached out with his palm up. I gave him some.

"Ugh. These are worse than C-rations."

"They're not that bad." I had a couple more. The phone rang. I gestured to Connor to answer while I washed the salt from my hands.

"McNamara. Thanks for getting back to us. No. Have you had breakfast? Where? We'll be there in fifteen." He hung up. "That was our favorite cop."

"You think he's psychic?"

"I called him while you were in the shower."

"You were right last night, Con. We don't have proof. Or a motive. I'm not sure confessing to breaking and entering, tampering with evidence, obstruction, and felony assault with meat loaf is such a great idea."

"They're not even looking into Burke's death. We have the blood in the car and the driver's seat. We have motive all over the place, even if we can't definitively link it to any particular person."

"It was Jepsen."

"We need proof. The cops have resources we don't have—forensics and manpower. We need to give them the car, Sara. Sergeant Wesley wants us to meet him at the market for a chat over breakfast. I think we need to go."

"I think I lost my appetite."

Chapter Twenty-eight

Sergeant Wesley was standing next to the brass pig in front of Pike Place Market when we arrived. He'd abandoned his sport coat in concession to the August temperature, already uncomfortable at ten in the morning. The market was teeming with people, tourists and locals, searching through the food and flower stalls for the best picks of the day before the unseasonably warm temperatures drove the crowds to seek cooler locations.

"Good morning, Sergeant." Connor might think this meeting was a good idea, but my stomach was jumping with butterflies.

"Ms. Townley. Commander."

Connor shook hands with him. "Thanks for meeting us. Do you mind if we eat while we talk?"

"There's a pretty good bakery."

"Yeah, we could get doughnuts." I offered. The cop grunted. "Lead the way." Connor and I followed behind him to a glass case full of pastries. My appetite resurfaced with a vengeance. We got muffins and coffee, then meandered toward the Totem Park. We found an empty bench and sat down. I maneuvered so that Connor was between me and the cop.

"You want to tell me why you wanted to meet?" The cop's voice was laconic, his squint fixed on Puget Sound as he sipped at his coffee.

"Have you identified the man in the alley yet?" I was going to have to work up to confession.

"He was a PI named Matthew Cort. Worked out of California. You heard of him?"

"I don't think I ever met a Matthew Cort. Except for the alley, of course. Do you have any idea what he was working on?"

"He was helping a friend of the family look into a suspicious death." He took a bite of muffin, crumbs dropping onto his sweat-stained blue shirt.

"Have you established a cause of death?" Connor asked.

"A thirty-eight-caliber bullet to the heart. You don't happen to own a gun, do you, Ms. Townley?"

"Nope. I don't like guns."

"Commander?"

"Just my issue. A nine-millimeter Glock. Do you have any leads, Sergeant? Witnesses, motive, anything else?"

"Nothing but the case he was working on." He finished his muffin and brushed at his shirt. He looked directly at me. "Mrs. Burke sends her regards."

I flinched. I leaned back, shielding myself behind Connor before exchanging a look with him. Unfortunately for me, I couldn't read any advice through his mirrored lenses. I got up from the bench and took a couple of steps before turning and facing both men. "Okay, so maybe we've heard the name before."

"Yeah, maybe you did. You're dangerously close to interfering in a police investigation, Ms. Townley. Not to mention meddling in something that may have already cost one man his life."

Connor leaned back against the bench and raised his hands to cradle the back of his head. So much for gallantry.

"I wasn't meddling."

Connor turned a half laugh into a loud throat clearing, and I glared at him. "This investigation started with a case at work. I have an obligation to a client."

"Even if the client is a cat?" Wesley crossed his arms over his spreading middle, a trace of amusement in his gray eyes.

"If you already know everything, why did you want to talk to us?"

He sighed. "I wanted to talk to you because what I don't know about is last night."

"Last night?" I used my most innocent tone.

"Yeah. Last night. After I talked to Mrs. Burke yesterday, I called the impound lot that was holding her husband's car. This morning, bright and early, I'm out there with a local deputy who tells me someone else was asking about the car yesterday."

"Really? How interesting."

"Where were you last night?"

"Are we under arrest?" Connor's quiet voice filled me with dread. I hadn't meant to get him in trouble.

"Do I need to arrest you to get some cooperation, Commander?"

"Mitchell Burke's death was ruled an accident months ago," I said defensively. "The car's not even evidence. So no crime was committed. No crime, no arrest." Maybe I ought to apply to law school. I was pretty good at this logic stuff.

"When you have to drug the guard dog, you can be pretty sure you've committed a crime."

"Maybe we should stick to hypotheticals, Sergeant," Connor suggested.

"Hypotheticals. Yeah, that sounds good." I agreed. "Hypothetically speaking, how's the dog?"

Sergeant Wesley chuckled softly, shaking his head. "In a bad mood. Tell me about the car."

"Hypothetically, I might think blood on the passenger side and a jammed driver's seat is a little peculiar, given my victim's height," I offered.

"I might think"—Connor grinned at me—"hypothetically, that the waitress in the local diner might know about someone out of place the night of the so-called accident."

Wesley took his worn notepad out of his pocket and scratched a few notes. "Anything else I should know?"

"You might check out the secretaries of any bigwigs you run across," I said.

"What have you been doing besides visiting impounds in the middle of the night?"

"Me? Nothing. Have you been doing anything, Con?"

"Not me."

"I'll need you to come down to the station so we can do some elimination prints."

"Hypothetically, Sergeant, neither my wife nor I would be foolish enough to leave our prints if we were, shall we say, straddling some sort of legal standard."

"No. We'd definitely wear gloves."

"Of course you would." Wesley groaned. "I'm going back to work, and you should go back to looking for your missing cat. No more impound lots, no more business partners, no more background checks. You do your job and I'll do mine. I'm not joking. If I find out you've done one more thing, made so much as a single call to New York, I will arrest you." He was looking straight at me.

"Arrest me? How come you're not threatening to arrest him?" I pointed at Connor.

"I think I've got a pretty good idea who's driving this particular bus. I mean it, Ms. Townley. No more."

"It could've been his idea."

"No way."

"How do you know?"

"I'm married."

Chapter Twenty-nine

Connor and I wandered around the market for another hour, hand in hand like high school sweet-
hearts. This couple stuff had some real upsides. My face
hurt from grinning. Around noon, the sizzling sun finally
drove us back up the hill toward the apartment.

"It's not usually like this," I said, mopping at my forehead as we climbed the stairs.

"You don't like it warm?"

"I didn't say that. It's just that Seattleites can over-
dose on ten minutes of sun a day. An entire week of
actual summer might put me into a coma."

"We can't have that." Connor led the way into the
kitchen and poured two glasses of lemonade.

I took a big gulp, and an ice-cream headache slammed
against my eyes. I shuddered as the pounding in my head
made a delicious counterpoint to the quenching of my
thirst. "Oh, that's good." Holding the glass against one
cheek, I moved back into the living room before slouch-
ing in the armchair. Connor remained standing.

"I hate to do this, honey, but I'm going to have to
check in here pretty soon."

My cheek felt suddenly cold and I took the glass away
and placed it carefully on the side table. "You've got to
go back."

"Eventually. Actually, it's likely to be sooner rather
than later."

"How soon is sooner?"

"A day. Maybe two."

"Then what?"

"I go back to work."

"Oh." I closed my eyes and laid my head back against the chair. I hadn't really thought about him going back. I'd always known he had to go. Of course he did. He couldn't just stay here and be my Dr. Watson forever. He had things he had to do. Important things. Dangerous things. The lemonade soured at the back of my throat. I opened my eyes and sat up straight in the chair, my smile plastic.

"What are you thinking?" He sat on the coffee table facing me.

"I'm going to have to go back to making my own coffee."

He smiled. "I'll miss you, too. After I figure out what the duty schedule is going to be, you could come visit me."

"In San Diego?"

"Sure."

"I guess I could do that. I hear they have a pretty good zoo."

He reached out and lightly touched my hand. "Don't forget Shamu."

"And Shamu." I cleared my throat and jumped up from the chair. "You're probably going to want a little privacy. You can use this phone." I picked up the cordless receiver and handed it to him. "You'll just need to dial one first for long distance. That was stupid. You already know that. I'm just going to go into the kitchen. Maybe I'll look for something for lunch."

"You're babbling."

"It's rude to notice."

He stood and walked to where I was hovering in the kitchen doorway. He kissed my forehead; then lifted my chin for a soft kiss on the lips. "It's going to work out, Sara."

"Sure it is. Go make your phone call."

He turned his back on me and moved toward the window, dialing.

I swallowed hard and went into the kitchen. The cupboards held the same stale crackers I'd tried to pass off as breakfast. Eight days since Flash had had a meal. He'd probably welcome stale crackers. That's what I needed to do. Concentrate on him. Finding him. And Jepsen. Getting enough evidence to put him away forever. They were a lot more important than some stupid phone call in the next room. I just needed to focus.

I moved to the sink and rinsed coffee cups, running the water at high speed to try to overcome an overwhelming need to eavesdrop. I wanted to know and I didn't want to know. I dried my hands and went to the kitchen table. I was pushing the papers from the case file into a stack when Millicent's employment agreement caught my eye. It had been in the initial file. I hadn't thought about it since. I picked it up and stared.

"We have at least another day." Connor spoke directly behind me and I jumped, whirling around. I put a hand to my pounding heart. "Sorry. Maybe I should wear a bell."

"No, better not. That sneaky thing probably works pretty well on the job."

"It does have its uses. What've you got there?"

"A gift from our friend Sergeant Wesley." I handed him the paper.

"Maybe next time we should register somewhere."

"Funny. Don't you get it?"

He looked down at the page. "It's Millicent's offer of employment. The Private Placement Employment Agency." He looked up, astonishment on his face.

"Signed by . . ." I pointed at the signature.

"Henry Jepsen, vice president." He shrugged.

"Yes. And just this morning Sergeant Wesley warned us not to call New York."

"Actually, he warned you."

I put my hands on my hips and gave him my megawatt smile. "New York. He knows about New York."

He grinned. "Pretty big leap there, Sara."

I went into the living room and picked up the phone, dialing the employment agency. After six rings a machine picked up. I left my name and number with a request to call back as soon as possible.

"It's Saturday," Connor remarked.

"I know it's Saturday, but some people work on the weekend. Heck, we're working."

There was a knock on the door and Connor went to answer it, returning a moment later with Russ in his wake. He came over and gave me a hug.

"Your door was locked."

"What?"

"Your door was locked. Your door is never locked."

I pointed at Connor. "New security system."

"We should all be so lucky. How goes the gumshoe business?"

"We're getting close. I can feel it. If somebody would just call me back." I shouted at the handset I still held before flinging it to the couch.

"Feeding time?" Russ asked, looking over at Connor.

"Maybe," Connor mumbled.

"Then I arrived just in the nick of time." Russ held up a two bags I hadn't noticed before, swinging them in front of my face. "I've got all your favorites. Chicken salad, crusty rolls, some ice cream."

I lunged for the smaller bag, taking it and peering inside. Butter pecan. My mouth watered.

Russ moved over to the armchair and sat down, setting the bag on the coffee table. "I thought I ought to bring lunch in case she hadn't given you the standard ptomaine warning about things in her refrigerator. You could easily have ended up at the hospital with the same Nurse Chang who so enjoyed our last visit. The bigamy story would get out, and then that sergeant friend of yours would arrest me. There'd be this big trial with CNN and Larry King hanging around. I would look tragic, but very well dressed." He sighed, putting a hand on his crisp ice blue polo shirt directly over his heart.

He crossed his legs and pulled at the crease in his khaki pants. "I'd be famous, but at what price?"

Connor and I laughed.

"I wouldn't want to inconvenience you," Connor said.

I laughed again, walking into the kitchen. Russ and I had been a two-person team for so long, I was surprised Connor fit so well. It seemed almost too easy. I hummed a little as I went into the kitchen and put the ice cream in the freezer. Then I got plates, napkins, and silverware and brought them back into the living room, where Connor and Russ were opening Styrofoam cartons on the coffee table. I took a seat next to Connor on the couch, helping myself to generous servings of salad and bread. I took a bite of the chicken.

"Mmm. Good."

"From abuse of telephonic equipment to one-word murmurings with just the introduction of a little sustenance and the anticipation of a sugar high. I hope you're paying attention, Connor. The skills you learn here could save your life someday."

I rolled my eyes in Connor's direction but his gaze remained fixed on his plate even as his cheek twitched. I nudged him hard.

"That's enough out of you." I pointed at Russ with my fork, using my most menacing expression even though I wanted to laugh.

"Yes, of course, Sara. Whatever you say, Sara. Can I get you anything else, Sara?" Russ leaned toward Connor. "Meek submission is another effective technique."

I threw a roll at Russ. It hit him in the head and bounced onto his plate. He picked it up with two fingers and a disdainful, long-suffering expression, and put it on the coffee table.

"On the plus side, she doesn't throw like a girl."

We all laughed.

"So what are you doing today? Other than bribing us with food to put up with you over lunch."

"The radio station is sponsoring a concert on the pier and I'm hosting."

"Who's playing?" Connor asked, looking up just long enough for me to steal his roll from his plate. He glanced at me with upraised eyebrows.

"James Taylor."

"Oh, I like him." I took a bite of the roll, grinning at Connor.

"Maybe you ought to come by, then. I could add your name to my list of people at the gate. I have another friend coming, and he'll be alone in the staff box."

"That sounds great, but we're kind of waiting for this phone call. Maybe we'll track down some other leads."

"We're probably not going to get a callback until Monday, Sara."

"I know. I just think there might be some other things we could do. Besides, Russ isn't going to be all alone. He's got his friend coming, and there's always his adoring audience."

Russ stood, setting his plate on the table. "All work and no play makes Sara a very dull girl." He came over and kissed the top of my head. "But if you feel you must keep your nose to the grindstone, who am I to try to talk you out of it? Just because you're luring some poor, unsuspecting fool"—Russ looked at Connor—"nothing personal—into your no-fun, no-life web, I'm not going to say a thing."

"It takes you more words to say nothing than anyone I ever met."

"I'm eloquent."

Russ moved toward the door.

"Thanks for lunch," Connor called.

Russ stopped and turned. "You're welcome." He pointed at me. "You owe me."

"What about the ice cream? Aren't you staying? I think I've even got chocolate sauce and maybe even some whipped cream around here somewhere."

Russ leered. "The mind boggles, but three's a crowd." With a cheery wave, he left.

Chapter Thirty

"Since we've apparently got some time to kill, why don't you tell me what you expect to learn from this call to New York?"

Connor followed me into the kitchen, watching as I riffled the papers in front of me. I pulled the fax of Cort's file out of the stack, and stood reading.

"I plan to prove motive in the murder of Mitchell Burke," I told him.

"Which is?"

"Jepsen killed Burke to keep him quiet about the insider."

Connor frowned. "What insider?"

"The one stealing from the pension plan." I held the fax to him.

"You think Burke figured out there was an inside man?"

"Better. I think Mitchell Burke figured out there was an inside woman."

Connor looked up. "Was the secretary with him at Masterson Enterprises?"

"Not the secretary, Con. Millicent. Millicent was the inside woman." I pointed to the fax. "Cort made a list of all the people he was going to check out. Millicent's name was on that list. Look, there are check marks next to everyone else's name. She's the only one he didn't clear."

Connor looked back down at the fax. "Okay, but she was dead by the time Cort came on the scene. Maybe he was leaving her for last. What would be the point of blaming her if she was already dead?"

"Things happened after that, Con. The money going missing, for one. And Masterson's disappearance. Millicent might have been dead, but her partner wasn't."

"Jepsen."

"Yeah, Jepsen. So, I've got Millicent tied to Jepsen. He murdered Cort. Cort works for Burke's wife, which leads to Burke and his murder. I honestly can't see how Flash fits into any of this. So where is he?"

"He's a cat, babe. He might have gone native."

"It's a long time between meals. What about water? It's been so hot. . . ."

"He could have figured it out. Mice, puddles, sprinklers. I don't think he's got anything to do with this either."

"First thing tomorrow, I'm checking back with all the shelters."

"That's a good idea."

Connor moved back into the living room and sat on the couch. I followed him and sat down. His eyes were far away as he processed my theory. He leaned back against the cushions, pulling me back to spoon against him.

"I'm thinking . . ." I began.

"Dangerous."

I poked him. "I'm thinking," I repeated, "that the relationship between Jepsen and Millicent might go further back, before she was ever hired. If we could show that Millicent and Jepsen were in on something together, we'd have a smoking gun."

"Hardly. Still, motive is important. Convince me."

"I think it's all connected. Burke's murder, the dead investigator, Masterson's disappearance, the missing pension money, the whole thing."

"What missing pension money?"

I clapped a hand over my mouth. "I wasn't supposed to say anything."

"I can keep a secret."

"I know. It's just the guy—I mean person—who told me . . ." I looked at Connor. He'd never tell. I could trust him. "Forget it. The Masterson Enterprises pension fund has an accounting irregularity."

"Nice euphemism."

"Right now my firm thinks it's just a computer glitch, but I was thinking maybe it was the 'something' that Millicent and Jepsen were in on together."

"Lay it out," Connor said, rubbing my shoulders.

"It's the timing. Jepsen hires Millicent a few weeks before he's forced out of Masterson Enterprises. Do you think he didn't see that coming? He was a longtime partner of Stuart Masterson. Don't you think he would have seen the handwriting on the wall?" I leaned forward, dropping my head toward my chest and closing my eyes.

"Probably."

"So Jepsen knows he's on his way out. He has a minority interest. Masterson controls everything, and there's nothing Jepsen can do but hire a bunch of lawyers with money he doesn't have to try to take on Mr. Billion-dollar Masterson with his high-powered law firm. He's got to know it's a long shot. Go a little to the left. Yeah. Right there. Oh, that's nice." He had magic fingers. "Anyway, even if he wins, it'll be years before he collects. By then he'll have lost everything. So maybe he decides he's not going to wait. He's going to get his payout up front. Since he knows he's about to be pushed out, he'll need help."

"And that's where Millicent comes in."

"Exactly. He hires her. He makes a big deal about how much he hates her. She makes a play for Masterson. Jepsen gets fired but Millicent's still there to do the dirty work."

"So why file the lawsuit? It invites scrutiny." Connor moved his hands from my shoulders to my upper back, kneading gently.

"Smoke and mirrors. He went through lawyers like socks. He made a lot of noise, but very little was actually accomplished. He distances himself from Masterson, so when the brown stuff hits the fan . . ."

"He's well away. Frankly, babe, he didn't strike me as that smart."

I agreed. "Which brings me back to the original point. I think Millicent was the brains of this particular operation. You're right. Jepsen's as dumb as a bag of rocks. Could you go a little lower?" I sighed, arching my back to give him better access. "So, what was I saying? Oh, yeah. Jepsen's no computer genius. I think it would take some technical skill to pull this thing off. I also think that's how Mitchell Burke ended up at the bottom of that ravine."

"You lost me." His voice was a whisper against my neck.

"What did Jepsen do when Millicent died? Walk away?"

"No. For some reason, he stayed in Seattle. He set up shop and continued to chase the scheme."

"Yeah. But without Millicent, Jepsen couldn't finish the job. Burke figured out about the embezzlement, all right, but he didn't know Jepsen was still in the game. If he had, he never would have told everything to Jepsen. Do you think we'll be like them?" I leaned my head back against him, and his arms went around me.

"Jepsen and Burke? You think you'll have to eliminate me because of what I know?" He kissed the top of my head.

I opened my eyes, turned my head, and peered up at him with a mock scowl. "Maybe." I put my feet up on the couch and lay back against him. "I was actually thinking about Emma and Mitchell Burke. Married for thirty years. Still happy about it."

"Absolutely." He kissed my ear.

A chill went through me. They'd been happy. Until one of them didn't come back. I jumped up, startling Connor. "You know, that ice cream is calling my name. You want some?"

"What just happened?"

"Ice-cream withdrawal. Chocolate sauce?" I asked over my shoulder as I went into the kitchen.

"Sara?"

I dug in the refrigerator, pulling out a can from the back before turning to him with my brightest smile. "I wasn't even lying about the whipped cream."

He looked at me for a long moment, his expression serious. "Okay. I'll get the bowls." He went to the cupboard and took out two bowls. I scooped up large helpings and he added toppings. We took our bowls and sat at the kitchen table.

I took a bite of ice cream, letting it melt on my tongue, savoring the sweetness of chocolate as it washed the bitterness of my earlier thoughts away.

"So do you think Flash's trust fund is the pension money?" He asked, stirring vigorously at his ice cream, melting it into soft-serve.

"You're ruining that. Philistine." I shook my head, taking another bite. "I hadn't thought of that, but it makes sense. That's another loose end. The newspaper article. The trust. The contingent beneficiary. I don't even know how to track it down. No bank is going to admit that they have the account. Lots of people have made a killing with stock options and things. The trust money could have come from there. Besides, there's a lot more missing than just what's in the trust. We're close and we're not, you know?"

"We're close. Odds are, we'll never know everything." He emphasized the pronoun, his eyes twinkling. He'd caught me. I'd used the word *we*. Somehow it seemed sort of natural. It wasn't even this easy with Russ. With Connor it was like having a partner. I decided to forget about what the future might hold and concentrate on the now, even if he did ruin perfectly good ice cream.

"What?" Con asked, becoming aware of my scrutiny.

"Nothing."

"You're staring."

"It's nothing."

"Okay." He got up and rinsed the bowls before putting them in the dishwasher.

"Aren't you going to ask?"

"I just did. You said nothing." He dried his hands on the dish towel hanging next to the stove, then resumed his place across from me at the table.

"You're going to leave it at that?"

"Sure." He leaned his elbows on the table. "Oh, I get it. This is one of those times when I am supposed to read your mind and continue to probe even after I have asked you a direct question that you answered with a euphemism for 'mind your own damn business.' "

"Exactly." I was amused by his rational interpretation of the completely illogical.

"Do I get a hint?" He smiled back, obviously humoring me.

"Since you are not very good at this, I suppose I could help you just a little." I leaned across the table, boosting myself out of the chair with one arm until our faces were mere inches apart. Then I reached out with my other arm and used my index finger to outline his ear. My eyes never left his, watching them as they darkened from emerald to forest before closing briefly.

He reached up and captured my wrist, stilling my hand, before pushing his chair back and rising. By the time he was upright, I was already standing, stepping closer to him. He caught my free hand and started backing out of the kitchen.

"You're right. I'm not very good at this." He leaned forward and kissed me very softly at the corner of my mouth. He never stopped walking. "I'm going to need another clue. Several, in fact."

Chapter Thirty-one

"He doesn't have a reason to run, Sara. Jepsen'll be there tomorrow. We have to wait for the phone call to even confirm your theory about Millicent and Jepsen." Connor had propped himself up against the headboard, the crumpled sheet tossed across his lap.

For a second I hesitated at the picture he made, shaking my head a little at the resurgence of desire. The man was dangerous. He was turning me into a sex fiend. I took clean underwear, a blue T-shirt, and a pair of shorts into the bathroom, leaving the door open.

"Sure he does." I closed the door halfway, standing behind it to dress. "We know he killed Mitchell Burke," I called to him. "We're gaining on him. He'll run."

"He's not going to run now."

"I don't know. Maybe Cort's death has him spooked. Maybe having the cops pay him a visit and ask about Burke will be enough to send him running. I don't know why he'll run; I just know he will." Stepping into the bedroom, I put a fist against my chest. "I can feel it in here."

"He doesn't know we found the car. He doesn't know we know that Burke's death was murder. He's doesn't have the money." Connor put his hands behind his head.

"The money." I moved to the bed and dropped onto the sheet. "He doesn't have the money."

"Exactly."

"God, I never even thought of that. Of course he doesn't have the money. That's the reason he hasn't bolted." I slapped my forehead. "I am so stupid."

"No, you're not." Connor tugged on the sheet, pulling me a little closer. I slapped at his hand.

"We've got to get this guy."

"There's nothing we can do until we get that phone call. We might as well catch up on a little sleep while we can." He tugged again.

"Sleep?"

"Sure. What were you thinking?" He was all innocence. I shook my head.

Connor walked out of the room without a hint of modesty, returning a minute later with two tall glasses of ice water. He handed me one, took a long drink from his, and placed it on the bedside table before sliding back under the sheet. He patted the spot beside him and I moved over, covering myself without removing my clothes. He put his arms around me. I scooted lower, finding a comfortable spot in his arms, pulling my pillow beneath my cheek.

"He got away with it."

"Not yet he didn't. We'll get him, Sara."

A yawn nearly split my face.

"He's thinking he got away with murder." A second yawn and I was shaking my head to try to clear the exhaustion.

"Tomorrow." Connor kissed my ear, burrowing into my hair, bringing our bodies into closer contact. I could tell sleep wasn't the only thing he was thinking about.

"Connor?"

"We're sleeping, Sara." Just mention of the word *sleep* sent waves of exhaustion rolling through me. How long had it been since I slept more than a few minutes? Two days? Three? What day was today? Now that I'd let it in, the tiredness was taking complete control. My eyes stung with the effort to keep them open. I rolled over, laying my head against his chest, letting my eyes close.

Chapter Thirty-two

The alarm clock read 5:07 when I woke. For a second I didn't know if it was morning or evening. I was wrapped around a pillow in the middle of the bed, having kicked the covers free. The room was still semidark. Connor must have closed the drapes to keep the afternoon sunshine out. Definitely evening. Twisting, I looked for him, but he was gone.

It was the phone ringing. In my exhaustion, my muddled brain thought it was morning and the alarm.

"Sara," Connor called from the living room. "It's some guy from the office."

Morris. Shit. There goes my job. I flashed on Emma's face. My job wasn't everything. I reached for the extension.

"Hello?"

"Sara?"

"Joe. Wow. You called me at home."

"Your cell phone isn't on."

"I had a long day. What's up?" I sat up against the headboard and propped a pillow behind my back.

"The shit's hitting the fan, here."

"Where?"

"Work."

"Why are you working on Saturday night?"

"When things are this screwed, the day of week is irrelevant."

A sense of dread settled into my stomach.

"Tell me."

"Masterson Enterprises' payroll bounced."

"Bounced?"

"As in there's no money there."

"How is that possible?"

"I don't know much. Just that there was some sort of automatic transfer from the regular payroll account to an offshore account. It had been happening for a couple months, slowly. It would have been picked up with the quarterly financial review, but it started right after the last one and wiped out the bulk of the account before payroll on Friday."

"How much?"

"At least eight million."

"Has anyone seen Stuart Masterson?"

"No, but both he and Henry Jepsen are definitely on the cops' I'd-like-to-see-you list."

He'd run now. Money or no money, he'd fly.

"I've gotta go."

"Wait, Sara. Elizabeth is looking for you."

"Why?"

"She's an evil bitch? Seriously, watch your back. If she finds out you've been snooping around Stuart Masterson, she'll be gunning for you before you can get her."

"Get her how?"

"Let's just say what Morris doesn't know about Elizabeth's sex life doesn't hurt her or you."

Of course. Rich, lecherous old man and gold-digging social climber. A match made in hell.

"Thanks, Joe." I hung up.

I stepped from the bed, stretched, and went in search of Connor. I found him sitting at the kitchen table, its glass top covered with stacks of files, my laptop humming before him. He had the phone trapped between his shoulder and his ear. I stepped behind him, putting my arms around his shoulders and leaning down to kiss his free cheek. He turned his head, redirecting the kiss to his lips.

"Thanks a lot. Yeah, that number'll work. When? Great. Thanks. Bye."

Connor leaned over, hanging the phone in its wall cradle.

"Hi."

"Hi. Sleep well?"

"Like a log. You should've woken me." Releasing him, I walked to the counter, where I helped myself to a cup of coffee from the pot he'd made. Taking a sip, I closed my eyes and savored the caffeine surging gloriously through my system.

"You needed the rest."

"Did you sleep?"

"I don't need much."

"That call from the office . . ."

"Anything good?" Connor asked.

"The payroll at Masterson Enterprises bounced."

"Hmm. That's not good."

"Especially if you work there."

I leaned against the counter, cradling my favorite ceramic mug and sipping the rich coffee slowly.

"What are you doing?"

"I thought I'd work on putting together our stuff for Sergeant Wesley. Sooner or later we're going to have to give him everything we've got and let him run with it."

I moved to the table and pulled out the chair opposite him. Sitting down, I glanced around the stacks of documents.

"Any revelations since this morning?" I asked.

"Maybe."

I sat up straighter.

"Maybe?"

"I've been thinking." Connor pushed the laptop to one side, leaning his forearms on the table.

"You've been thinking . . ." I prompted, enjoying the suppressed excitement I could see in his eyes.

"What are the chances that Mitchell Burke's death and Matthew Cort's death aren't connected?"

"Slim to none." I took a deep drink.

"Okay, so say we're right about Henry Jepsen. He kills Mitchell Burke and makes it look like an accident."

"The slimeball."

"Why?"

"Why is he a slimeball?"

"No, why did he kill Matthew Cort?"

"Because Matthew Cort discovered that the pension plan was looted."

"That's just it. How could he have discovered that?" Connor searched the stacks, finally pulling out a court document and flipping pages. "Babe, I've looked through every piece of paper. Nothing talks about the pension. You told me your firm was treating it as top-secret."

I sat down in the chair opposite Connor, resting my arms on the table.

"So if Cort didn't know about the pension . . ." Connor began.

"We don't know that he didn't know." I played devil's advocate.

"True, but for the sake of argument let's assume Cort didn't know. Why would Jepsen kill him?"

"Maybe Jepsen just thought he knew. Cort's asking questions; Jepsen's afraid it will bring the cops. So, he panics and kills him." I leaned back, not thrilled with my reasoning. It held together, sort of.

"He hasn't panicked before. Why now? And why there?"

"The alley?"

"Yeah, why would Cort meet Jepsen there? He's investigating the guy for murder. He thinks he's got something to prove the case. So a seasoned investigator agrees to meet his suspect in the middle of the night in a drug zone. I checked his bio. He was in the army. Served in Vietnam. Two tours. No soldier with that kind of time in makes a mistake like that."

"I think you're putting too much faith in the military brain of a fifty-some-year-old guy. It's been a long time between wars, Connor. He probably thought he could handle it. He was a big guy, and look what he did for a living. Macho city. Maybe he just didn't think it through."

"He gave up home-field advantage. I just don't buy it." Connor ran his hands through his hair, giving it a spiky look.

I pushed back from the table. Connor was right. There had to be a reasonable explanation for what Cort had been doing in that alley. How would Jepsen have convinced him? What did Jepsen have for leverage? I snapped my fingers.

"Blackmail."

"What do you mean?"

"Maybe Cort did figure it out. Maybe he told Jepsen all about his suspicions. What would a bottom-feeder like Jepsen do? He'd offer a bribe."

Connor got up and went over to the sink, refilling his water glass and taking a drink before turning back to me.

"Maybe. We don't know what Cort was like, or his financial condition. He might give up Emma for a quick buck. But where would Jepsen get the money?"

"We're back to the missing money."

"Yeah."

"Maybe the pension's not all that's missing. Joe said the embezzlement could have been done by computer. Maybe the same is true of the tax fund and the office fund and whatever else. Jepsen could have still had the codes or whatever and helped himself after he got canned." I knew it was weak.

Connor turned the computer toward me, hitting a couple of keys. I stared at the screen, scanning the notes I'd made after first going to Jepsen's office. "He didn't have a computer."

Closing my eyes, I pictured Jepsen's office. "He didn't have a computer," I repeated, disheartened. "Maybe he just promised the money but wasn't actually intending to give it up. 'I'll meet you in the alley for your payoff and I'll bring a little something for your thick skull'?" I made it a question. "Or maybe there was another accomplice. Maybe it was her. The secretary with the claws."

"Your notes say there wasn't a computer in the office. If she were the computer-literate type, wouldn't she have one on her desk?"

"I doubt her skills were primarily clerical." I half smiled.

"Even so"—Connor's lips twitched—"there's no sign either one of them knew how to hack into Masterson's system. And there's no evidence that Masterson was stupid enough not to change his security codes when he threw Jepsen out."

"I don't know about that. He bought state-of-the-art security gear but that doesn't mean he used it. Look at the burglar alarm." I got up and refilled my cup, needing the extra caffeine to bolster my spirits as they sagged in the face of his irrefutable logic. I hated logic. Especially since I knew Jepsen had killed Burke and I didn't want anyone poking holes in my theory. Not even Connor.

"So, if we stick with our assumption that Mitchell Burke got killed when he discovered the embezzlement, how did Jepsen steal the money? And where is it now?"

I started to pace in the small room. Four steps to the window, turn, four steps back to the table. Back and forth as I thought. We were missing something. I could feel it.

"He had help," I suggested. "Someone other than the most personal of personal assistants."

"Yeah. Which brings me back to my first point. Are we sure the deaths of Mitchell Burke and Matthew Cort are connected?"

I sat back down, setting my cup on the table and running my hands through my hair. "Matthew Cort figured out that the pension plan was short. No. We've already concluded that there was no way he could have found that out. It's all handled by the lawyers, and they don't tell anyone anything. Joe practically forced me to sign a confidentiality agreement in blood."

"Let's forget the blackmail scenario for a second. Is it possible Cort found out something entirely different that got him killed?"

I stared, watching as Connor shuffled through the papers.

"Like?"

"Like where is Stuart Masterson?"

I dropped my head into my hands. "My brain hurts."

"Jepsen's asking for a meeting in that alley would have rung all kinds of bells with Cort. It just wasn't his kind of place. Who would blend in in a place like that? Who had reason to want Masterson out of the way?"

I reached into the stack of papers, pulling out the credit reports I'd run the morning after I found the body.

"Bud and Stewie."

"Bud and Stewie," he agreed, raising his water glass to me in salute.

"What about the woman at the diner?"

"Jepsen's secretary can't be the only black woman with a manicure in the state of Washington."

"It's Jepsen." I felt defeated.

"All I'm saying is, maybe it's both."

The phone rang but I didn't have the energy to get up to answer it. Connor raised eyebrows in my direction, then stood to pick up the receiver.

"McNamara. Yes, she is. Hold on." He held the phone out to me. "New York," he whispered.

"This is Sara Townley."

"Ms. Townley, my name is Elspeth Siwicki. I'm the owner of Private Placements Employment Agency. You left me a message." She had the strong nasal accent of a native New Yorker.

"Thank you for returning my call so quickly, Ms. Siwicki. I was calling to ask about one of your employees, Millicent Millinfield. She worked for you some months ago."

"She is one of our most reliable people, but I'm afraid she won't be available until the end of September. We do have several other highly qualified people who might suit your needs. What position are you looking to fill?"

"Excuse me. I think there must be some mistake. I wanted to ask about Millicent Millinfield." I looked at Connor and he shrugged.

"As I said, Ms. Townley, Millicent is unavailable. I think I should also tell you that she doesn't accept out-of-town placements."

"I'm sorry to have to tell you this, Ms. Siwicki, but Millicent Millinfield is dead. She died four months ago in Seattle."

Silence.

"Ms. Siwicki?"

"Is this your idea of a joke?"

"No. I'm sorry to have to be the one to—"

"Millicent Millinfield is alive and well. I saw her yesterday."

"I'm afraid that's not possible. Millicent Millinfield was killed in a car accident in April. In Seattle."

"Millie's never been to Seattle."

"Is it possible you could be mistaken?" Either she was or I was, or there were two Millicent Millinfields working at the same temp agency. Not much chance of that.

"Of course not." Her accent flayed me. "We've been friends since our first day at Miss Ella's Boarding School."

"And you're sure she never came to Seattle?"

"Of course I'm sure. Ever since her mother's stroke last year, she's spent all her time with her. I had the hardest time convincing her to take some time off now that her mother is gone. I took her to the dock myself yesterday."

"Dock?"

"Yes. She's on a six-week cruise."

"Is there any way I could talk to her?"

"I don't think so," she said doubtfully. "What is all this about?"

"There was a woman in Seattle named Millicent Milli-nfield who died last April. She worked for a local business-

man, and she listed your agency on her job application."
I leaned against the wall.

"I see. I don't know what you are up to, young lady,
but I can assure you it will not work." Siwicki's tone
had taken on a frosted edge.

"I'm not up to anything. I'm just trying to figure this
out."

"Well, figure it out without trying to get my agency
involved. We don't want any trouble. We insist on
speaking directly with all of our clients before placing
anyone with them. Our Web site includes complete résumés with photographs of all of our personnel. If
you've been taken in by some con artist, it hasn't got
anything to do with us. We are not responsible if you
failed to make reasonable inquiries into someone you
hired, and if you have anything more to say to me, you can
speak with my attorney." She slammed the phone down.

I held the receiver away from my ringing ear, dumb-
founded.

"What?" Connor asked, taking the phone from my
hand and returning it to the cradle on the wall.

"Millicent Millinfield."

"What about her?"

"She's not."

"She's not what?"

"She's not Millicent Millinfield."

"What are you talking about?"

"According to her"—I waved at the phone—
"Millicent Millinfield still works for the Private Placements Employment Agency and was seen very much
alive just yesterday. Alive enough to be on a cruise,
anyway."

"Who's the woman calling herself Millinfield?"

I went into the living room and looked around. I
grabbed my cell phone from the hall table. I lugged my
laptop into the living room and set the computer on the
coffee table, attached the phone, and logged onto the
Internet. Connor sat down on the couch next to me.

"What are you doing?"

"The agency owner said they have photographs on the Web." I typed in my query.

"What kind of jobs are they filling?"

"Beats me. Anyway . . ." I found the Web page and went to the personnel site. I started clicking through résumés, scanning faces. "If our Millicent isn't the real deal, then she must have known the actual woman."

"Not necessarily." Connor went into the kitchen and came back with a copy of the photo that Jeff had given me, the one with Millicent and Flash. Connor laid the picture next to the computer and resumed his seat. "She could be a total stranger."

"No way." *Click, click.* "The agency woman said that Millicent was home taking care of her dying mother. She hadn't been working. The impostor must have known that. If they had both been using Millicent's name at the same time, somebody would have figured it out. Social Security, the agency, somebody. Whoever took Millicent's place was relying on her not turning up. That means it's either a friend or . . ."

"Someone she worked with," Connor finished.

"Exactly." I flipped to the last résumé. None of them looked even vaguely like Millicent. I sighed. "I was so sure."

"Don't give up yet," Connor advised, moving his hand to the mouse. He went back to the home page and clicked on the group photo on the main page. He zoomed, then zoomed again, enlarging the photo enough so I could make out the slightly blurred features of a middle-aged woman standing in the back row of a posed photo of the entire staff. Connor moved the cursor onto the photo and a small pop-up box appeared. It read, *Margaret Trilling, clerical support staff.*

Connor looked over at me, a smile on his face. "Allow me to introduce Millicent Millinfield."

I stared for a long moment before adrenaline surged through me and pushed me to my feet. I paced back and forth from the windows to the kitchen doorway and back. Connor leaned against the cushions, resting his arms along the back of the couch.

"Talk about your curveballs. The murders aren't part of the theft. They're the consequences of it." I tunneled my fingers through my hair. "It would be so easy. Just like Joe said. Simply change the routing information for the deposits. Any clerk with the right signature could do it."

"I'll buy that. Jepsen picks his stooge in advance. Probably approached Margaret what's-her-name with the plan." Connor leaned back on the chair again, rocking, staring at the ceiling as he did the mental gymnastics. "There've got to be checks in place for that, Sara."

"Yeah. A reference check. Which Margaret probably couldn't pass, but Millicent did with flying colors. The other fail-safe was requiring two signatures. While Jepsen was still around it was easy. They were partners. After he left, things got trickier, but they're enterprising individuals."

"So Millicent forges Burke's signature . . ." Connor suggested.

"Or Masterson's," I shot back. "It doesn't really matter which. What matters is that Burke found out when he was getting ready for his deposition."

"And then Mitchell Burke, honest man, tells Jepsen, scumball. Why didn't Burke go to Masterson?" Connor was looking directly at me, and I could practically feel the intellectual pulse as we pulled at opposite ends of the puzzle.

"Masterson's nowhere to be found. He's missing or maybe dead. Anyway, Burke was under subpoena as part of that whole court case thing. He was going to have to tell. And in the absence of his friend and mentor, Stuart Masterson . . ." I spread my hands like a preacher reaching out to his congregation.

"Mitchell Burke tells Masterson's former partner." Connor laced his fingers behind his head, once again seeking inspiration in the ceiling tiles before turning back to me.

"Giving Henry Jepsen a motive for killing Mitchell Burke. And that probably went down just the way we figured it. Burke turns his back. Jepsen clubs him with something handy, then stages the accident with the help of the secretary."

"Or she could have hit him. Either way . . ."

"Right. Either way, they're off pushing the car over a steep cliff on an icy night. They catch a break with the local cops, who are overworked, understaffed, and have seen real accidents happen just that way a hundred times. The report comes back a possible suicide."

I sat in an armchair, tucking one leg underneath me. "That's when their luck runs out. Emma doesn't believe Mitch killed himself. She hires Matthew Cort to check it out." I rested my chin on my folded hands, watching as several expressions washed over Connor's features. "Matthew Cort looks at everyone around Burke at the time of his death. Which includes those who are now dead, as well as the living."

I nodded.

"He makes calls to everyone's former employers. Including a certain temp agency in Manhattan. Where he discovers that Millicent Millinfield is caring for her dying mother."

Connor leaned back and stared at me, a half smile on his face. "So, Sherlock, how are we going to prove it?"

"Prove what?"

"There has to be a trail. Something that connects your greedy partner to his moll."

"What's a moll?"

"The lady friend of a guy with a questionable reputation."

"Like me?"

He reached over and pushed a curl of my hair back behind one ear. "I don't have a questionable reputation."

"Really? That's too bad. I was hoping maybe you knew somebody who knew somebody who could run a background check on our impostor secretary."

"There's always Sergeant Wesley."

I grimaced. "I don't think he's too anxious to be doing me any favors, but you might have better luck." I disconnected the computer and handed him the phone. I listened as he left a message, asking Wesley to call and leaving both the home and cell phone numbers.

"Any other ideas?"

Connor dialed again. He talked to someone for a couple of minutes, asking for background on Margaret Trilling. He told the other person about the agency and her picture on the Web site. Then he hung up.

"Now we wait," Connor said.

"I hate waiting."

"Really? You don't say."

I swatted at him. "You don't like waiting any more than I do. Admit it."

He shrugged. "So, it's not my favorite thing."

"Let's not," I said.

"Let's not what?"

"Wait."

"We haven't got any proof."

"I'm not going to arrest him. I think we should just go over there and make sure he's not headed for Rio or Canada or wherever."

"It's Wesley's case, babe. We should let him handle it from here."

I got out of my chair. "I should do lots of things, Connor. Are you coming?" I held out my hand.

He shook his head slightly, letting me pull him up from his chair. He followed me out of the apartment and down the stairs, opening the passenger door for me to get in. He leaned into the car as I put my seat belt on.

"What?" I asked.

"Smart is very sexy."

I giggled, leaning forward to kiss him deeply. His hand cupped the back of my head and he let the kiss linger. He tasted like coffee. I loved coffee.

"I don't suppose you'd consider going back upstairs and leaving the felon chase for another time?"

Connor's phone rang. He answered it. From the side I heard, he could have been doing a survey for laundry soap. A lot of okay, reallys, yeahs.

"What?" I asked the second he was off the phone.

"Margaret Trilling is really her name."

"And?" He was killing me.

"Three arrests, no convictions."

I grabbed at his T-shirt. "For?"

"Fraud. Seems she liked the husband-wife con. Always worked with a partner until her last caper. She got a walk. Her partner got three to five."

"So Millicent—I mean Margaret—if she were still grifting, would need a partner."

"Yes."

"Jepsen."

"In the current context, I'd say that's an affirm."

"Bingo!"

"Okay, tiger. Let's go play your hunch. Just remember that we're only sitting on Jepsen until Wesley gets there. He's a killer. Probably armed. We're just watching, and I'm calling the shots."

Yeah, right. "Roger that," I told him.

"Smart-ass."

Chapter Thirty-three

"I told you he'd run. Coward."

Connor and I were crouched behind the hedge that ran alongside the driveway, fifty yards from Henry Jepsen's open garage door. Jepsen's black Mercedes had been backed half inside, half outside the garage with the trunk open. We watched as Jepsen, dressed in wrinkled suit pants and a short-sleeved white shirt, came and went through the garage's interior door to the house, moving boxes into the trunk. The contents of the boxes seemed to spill out the tops, but we were too far away to make out any of the specific items.

Connor turned my chin toward him, and I watched as he pointed at me before raising a hand to his ear, mimicking a telephone call. I was shaking my head before he pointed back in the direction of the car. The cops weren't going to be any help. They were the reason this psycho was still walking the streets.

"No." Connor placed his hand over my mouth, peering back in Jepsen's direction. I looked, too, waiting for a moment as Jepsen brought another box to the trunk.

I turned back to Connor, who glared at me. I shook my head. I pointed to him, to me, then finger-walked for a second before pointing to Jepsen and twisting my hands as I pretended to wring his fat neck.

Connor shook his head emphatically. He pointed to

me and back toward the road. I mouthed the word *no*.
He put his palms together as if in prayer before placing
a hand over his heart. A total manipulation. Crossing
my arms over my chest, I shifted, my knees and legs
beginning to ache from the squatting position. He touched
his chest again before reaching up to cup my face, leaning over to place a soft kiss on my lips. He kept his
eyes open, the green plea unwavering. He was totally
cheating, playing the endearing-husband card, but I
could feel myself softening. I scuttled back a step, creating a scant few inches between us. After making him
wait for a long moment without looking away, I rolled
my eyes and shrugged. He should have kept the smile
to himself.

I checked for Jepsen. He'd disappeared back into the
house, so I took the opportunity to drop to my hands
and knees and crawl away from the house, following the
hedge as it curved along the driveway toward the street,
using the same screen of bushes we had used to creep
closer to the house on our way in. Reaching the thick
stand of pines that lined the street, I stood, keeping the
boughs of one tree between me and the house while I
rubbed at my bruised knees. I brushed at my clothes,
stopping at the bulge in the front pocket of Connor's
brown windbreaker. Reaching into the pocket, I pulled
the cell phone out. Damn him, he knew we had the
phone all along.

I dialed Sergeant Wesley's number, having committed
it to memory days ago. I probably should just put it on
speed dial. It rang twice before connecting to voice mail.

I pressed zero to bypass the mail and go back to the
operator, waiting impatiently while Muzak played. Two
minutes later I was still on hold. Impatiently, I ended
the call and redialed. Reaching voice mail a second time,
I left a message.

"This is Sara Townley. We're at Henry Jepsen's house
in Magnolia. He killed Mitchell Burke, and we've got
proof." Maybe not proof, exactly, but I was in a crisis.
"Unfortunately, he's packing to go on a trip. A long trip.

If you don't want to let him to get away a second time, I suggest you get out here ASAP. We're gonna try to stall him, but you'd better hurry."

I clicked off, zipping the phone back into my pocket. Staying within the shadows of the pine trees, I used the grove of trees as cover, moving toward the back of the property, past where anyone in the garage could see me. Connor had insisted on staying behind cover the whole way to the house, but now that I knew Jepsen was moving between the house and the garage, I didn't see any point in skulking. The garage didn't have a window on this side, so, after another visual sweep of the lawn, I ran for it. I dashed across the lush grass, straight toward the garage wall. Once there, I put my back against the wall, catching my breath. I signaled a thumbs-up to the bushes where Connor was hidden, knowing he'd be fuming over my failing, once again, to take orders. He didn't move.

Dropping to my knees, I crawled to the end of the wall. Taking a deep breath, I peered around the corner, darting back when I saw Jepsen walking toward the interior door of the garage. My heart pounded at the close call. I checked to see that my near miss hadn't sent Connor charging from the bushes. There was no sign of him. I heaved a sigh, grateful that I hadn't exposed his position to Jepsen.

I heard a door slam. They must be getting ready to leave. I did a quick peek around the corner, relieved to see that the trunk was still open. Jepsen must have gone back into the house through the garage. Jepsen was nowhere to be seen, so I risked rising, noting through the rear window the boxes filling the backseat. What the hell was I going to do now?

Pulling back out of view against the outside garage wall, I gestured madly, trying to get Connor's attention. I'd never be able to face Emma with the news that Jepsen had gotten away. Where the hell was Connor? And why wouldn't he come? He wouldn't have just left me.

I stared at the bushes where we'd secreted ourselves.

No movement. No sign that anyone was there. I knew Connor wouldn't just leave me hanging. He must have a plan. God, I was such an idiot. Of course he had a plan. Which was exactly why he'd gotten rid of me. Well, if he thought I was going to play the helpless female waiting while a man did all the dirty work, he was in for a shock. I looked for a stick or a rock, anything I could use as a weapon. Nothing. Damn those lawn services, anyway. Why the hell did they have to manicure everything to within an inch of its life? Wait a minute. What better place to find a weapon than a garage? Listening carefully, I waited a full minute without hearing a sound. I took the chance. On the other side of the wall I'd been leaning against, I hit the mother lode. Rakes and shovels leaned against the wall, three-quarters of the way into the garage.

"What are you doing?" Connor whispered behind me.

I slapped a hand over my mouth to keep from screaming. I turned and glared, then hit him on the shoulder.

"You scared the hell out of me."

"We're going. Right now." Connor pulled on my arm.

"No way. We're here. We might as well look around." I moved to the open trunk of the car.

"They could come back any second."

"So, we'll hurry. We won't get caught. Rule number one, remember?" I undid the zipper on a suitcase and started going through the clothes.

"Women," Connor muttered, taking the lid off a box and starting to go through the papers. "Can't live with them; can't shoot them."

"I heard that."

I finished rummaging through the suitcase and went around the car. The backseat was locked, so I reached through the open driver's window just as the muffled sound of voices heralded Jepsen's return. I dropped onto my hands and knees, behind the shield of the car. Connor came from the back of the car and pushed me flat against the concrete. The door opened. Two voices and the click of heels against concrete. Connor rammed me under the car and crawled under after me. My face was turned toward my side so I couldn't see Connor's expression. Probably just as well.

"We'll get the money. We'll take the disk and pay some kid to hack for us. He'll never even know what we're looking for," Jepsen's voice boomed into the small garage. I could see two pairs of shoes, one highly polished black loafers and the other stiletto pumps.

"That's all we need. More loose ends," the secretary sarcastically flung back.

The heels started to walk out of my field of vision but were yanked back, one shoe flipping off and landing just inches from where I was hiding. I swallowed hard, my throat dust-dry.

"I don't want to hear any more crap from you. We're gonna get the fucking money and then we're getting the hell out of here."

"You've been promising that for months. We're still here." The secretary didn't take his threat seriously. The sound of a slap and a surprised cry from the woman had me flinching.

"Hey, why'd you do that? I didn't mean nothin' by it."

"Shut the fuck up, Arlene."

"Why do you always have to go hittin' on me?" *Click, clomp*—she moved away from the loafers, heels tapping against the concrete. "I treat you real good and then you go beatin' on me. It ain't right, Henry." She *click-clomp*ed over to her discarded pump. A hand reached for it and her purse fell, a lipstick clinking against the floor. The tube rolled under the car within an inch of my nose. Before I could react, she'd knelt down and was looking under the car.

"Hey," she cried. "What are you doin' under there?"

Connor was already moving, sliding out from under the car like smoke under a door.

"What the fuck are you doing in my garage? Get out." Jepsen spewed real venom.

"There's no need for the gun," Connor said calmly. "Sara, stay under the car."

The secretary was half under the car with me, reaching out and trying to grab me. I slapped at her hands. I snatched at her purse, pulling it under the car. Desperately searching for a weapon, anything I could use, I started yanking things out of the little clutch bag. Compact, makeup bag, tissues, Day-Timer, keys. Nothing. No gun. No pocketknife. Not even nail clippers. I grabbed the keys. Putting the little plastic remote entry gadget and the key ring in my palm, I laced the keys between my fingers. She made another grab for me but I kicked at her.

"Get out from there," Jepsen ordered. "Get out or I'll shoot him."

"Don't do it, Sara."

He fired a round that pinged off the concrete, and I flinched.

"The next one I'm putting in his head. Get out of there."

I couldn't let him die. Connor might kill me later, but I just couldn't hide under the car while Jepsen shot him. I would have gone out toward Connor, but he'd positioned himself halfway along the car's side, his legs and feet blocking the way. I inched over to the secretary's side, keeping my makeshift brass knuckles out of view. The secretary grabbed my arm and yanked me as I emerged. She pulled so hard that I fell into her and we slammed against the wall, sending tools in all directions.

"Hey," Jepsen yelled, before another gunshot and the sound of bone hitting bone.

I was running toward the open garage door with the secretary behind me when I stepped on the tines of a rake that had fallen from the rack on the wall. The handle flew up on the fulcrum and I dodged aside just in time for the wood handle to make thudding contact with the secretary's nose. I stopped, staring, as she screamed and blood gushed.

"This is the police. I want to see everyone's hands." I turned around, my hands raised high. Sergeant Wesley had arrived.

I looked at Connor and our eyes caught. He didn't seem hurt. His hands were up, and there was a tear in his T-shirt near the collar, but other than that he seemed fine. Fuming, but fine.

Chapter Thirty-four

Connor closed the apartment door behind us with a click. I walked through to the living room and headed straight to the cupboard for a glass. Moving to the refrigerator, I reached for the pitcher of lemonade before changing my mind. Nine o'clock in the morning notwithstanding, I needed a beer. Setting my empty glass next to the juice, I reached for a bottle.

Sergeant Wesley had grilled us all night, taking shifts with an even more irritable lieutenant from the homicide division. They wanted to know everything and they wanted to know it ten times over. Connor had more patience than I did, obviously believing that cooperation gave us a better chance of dodging arrest for obstruction, interfering with police, or whatever else they could charge us with. I figured they wouldn't charge us with anything, since they'd probably need us as key witnesses in the murder trial of Henry Jepsen, and they'd want us to at least appear credible.

Wesley walked us out the door of the Public Safety building with the news that Henry Jepsen was being held for felonious assault for the shot he took at Connor. The secretary was already looking for a deal, and Wesley assured us that Mitchell Burke's death was going to be reinvestigated with an eye to charging both of them with murder. There was Cort's murder, too. Maybe they'd get the hat trick and find the money. It wouldn't bring

Mitchell back to Emma, but it was something. Wesley was almost human about it.

I twisted off the top and drank half the beer while absorbing the cold blast of the open refrigerator. Finally pushing the door closed, I returned to the living room and dropped into an armchair. I could hear the shower running. Connor had spent the entire drive from the police station in controlled silence. I preferred yelling. This silence was making me crazy. We'd caught the bad guy, hadn't we? He should be happy. I was. Or I would be after I got a little sleep. I was just tired. Maybe he was, too. That was it. A quick shower, a short nap, and we'd be ready to celebrate Jepsen's impending incarceration.

Connor came into the room, his blond hair darkened to sable by the shower. He was wearing a crisp white T-shirt that hugged the muscles of his chest and tailored khaki shorts with a plain brown belt. He was strapping his watch to his wrist as he settled onto the couch. Exhausted or not, I could certainly appreciate the view.

"Do you want to grab a shower before?" Connor asked.

"Before what?" A shiver of anticipation slid along my spine. Maybe I wasn't that tired after all.

"Before we have the fight we've been headed for all week." He wasn't smiling.

"Fight?"

"Fight." A second look confirmed that he wasn't just not smiling; he was actually looking pretty grim.

"Why would we be fighting?" I stayed slouched in my chair, but I could feel my entire body brace.

"Because you didn't do what we agreed on. Because it nearly got you killed. Because you ended up without a weapon, face-to-face with a guy we knew was a murderer." His voice was so deep and calm, I might have missed how enraged he was if I weren't carefully watching him. It was in his eyes. The beautiful emerald had darkened almost to black. Eyes really could shoot sparks. I'd never actually seen it before. I was more fascinated than alarmed. Gripping the arms of my chair, I pushed myself a little farther upright.

"Look, Connor, things were happening kind of fast."

"You should have waited for me. Like we agreed." He stressed the last three words.

"He was going to get away."

"I had it under control. If you'd just let me protect you . . ."

Now I was getting mad. I pushed myself out of the chair and stood next to the coffee table, my hands on my hips, glaring down at him.

"Let you protect me? I don't need your protection. This may come as a surprise to you, Connor, but I managed fine before you got here. I can even tie my own shoes, if it comes to that."

He stood and faced me, his arms hanging loose at his sides.

"This was different. This was a guy with a gun."

"And I was handling it."

"You wouldn't have had to handle it if you had just done what you were told," he yelled, his outward composure finally cracking. "Look—Sara," he tried in a gentler tone.

Finally catching fire, the tinder of my own anger exploded.

"Done what I was told? What I was told? What are you now, my lord and master?" I yelled back, the blood thundering in my head. I stepped around the coffee table, coming within inches of him, my hands clenching.

Connor held his hands out to his sides, his palms facing me. "This is not about that, Sara."

"What is it about then, Connor? If it's not about keeping the little woman under your thumb, then what is it about?"

"It's about you in the same room—the same zip code—with a known killer." Connor reached out and held my shoulders, managing to get an edge of calm back, but mine was out of reach.

"You don't need to do anything about it. In the future, if there is something to be done, I will do it." I spun and strode to the side table, snagging my beer and slamming the remaining liquid in one long drink.

"In the future? There's not going to be an 'in the future' for this, Sara. The case is over. This is over."

I carefully set my bottle back on the table before turning to face him.

"Oh, really." My heart pounded in my chest, but I deliberately kept my words even. "Well, brace yourself, Connor, because I'm pretty good at this job. And I don't see any reason to be doing credit checks the rest of my life. I don't intend to be pushing papers forever. And who knows? Felons may become part of my daily existence." I crossed my arms across my chest and waited.

"No." Connor's voice was a croak, and his skin had gone gray.

"Yes."

The phone rang and we both flinched. Neither of us moved as the phone rang again and again. Each shrill turned the tension in the room higher. After several rings, the answering machine finally picked up with a click.

"You can't ask me to—"

"I'm not asking," he exploded. "I forbid it."

Chapter Thirty-five

The door was slamming behind me before I even thought about my keys. For that matter, I hadn't bothered to grab my wallet, either, so my financial resources were limited to whatever I might have in my pockets. I didn't care. I wasn't going back in and looking like an idiot. I was already feeling plenty stupid. He was so maddening; I just wanted to strangle him. I could actually see my hands reaching for his throat. I waited at the door. He should be out here begging my forgiveness. He was wrong, wrong, wrong. There should at a minimum be sounds of crashing glass and thwarted temper seeping around the door's edges. Nothing. It was quiet as a tomb in there. I leaned my ear up against the thick wood. Silence. First he was wrong, then he was calm about it? Strangling was too good for him. I needed something that would last longer. A lot longer.

I marched down the stairs to Russ's apartment. I pounded on the door. Connor was a relic. He should have been born in the caveman days. He would have fit right in with the rest of the Neanderthals. The door opened abruptly and I stormed through, practically pushing Russ out of my way.

"Did I wake you?" Russ was pulling at the sash of his navy robe. "Sorry."

"I wasn't asleep."

"He forbids me. He actually said it that way. Forbids me! Of all the egocentric, chauvinistic, pigheaded—"

"Sara, honey, now is not really a good time."

"He's my lord and master and I should do whatever he wants."

"I'm sort of in the middle of—"

"Who the hell does he think he is? He can do anything he wants and never even has to discuss it with me, and I am supposed to not only tell him every little detail, but then I need his permission." Russ began to tidy the room, picking up a pair of trousers left next to the sofa. I began to pace, dodging a pair of polished loafers and a silk tie.

"I would really like to help, but now isn't the—"

"Marriage is not slavery. Do you think marriage is slavery?" I pointed at him. "Of course not. You are an enlightened man. You understand that women actually come equipped with brains."

Russ removed a wine bottle from the coffee table and placed it on the counter separating his lushly appointed living room from the kitchen. "I'm definitely enlightened. I'm also a little busy."

"Stop with the cleaning already." I rounded the overstuffed armchair and strode the length of the room before turning to face Russ. "You wouldn't keep taking your clothes off every time you wanted your own way. You would *not* try to blind me with sex."

"He blinds you with sex?"

"Sounds like someone I should meet," a new voice interjected from the hallway.

I pivoted, staring at the stranger. Short and dark, with teeth that flashed white against his tan. His hair was rumpled, his oxford shirt misbuttoned, and his feet were bare. Horrified, I turned back to Russ. His hastily sashed robe finally registered.

"You're busy. I'll just come back later." I wanted to slink from the room. I headed for the door, not daring to look at Russ's guest.

Russ stepped in front of me, barring my progress.

"I've really got to go now," I muttered.

"No way you drop a line like that and then race out

the door. Tony, meet my best friend, Sara Townley. Sara, this is Dr. Anthony Martelli."

Tony joined us in the foyer and offered his hand. I shook it without looking up.

"How do you do?" I mumbled.

"Nice to meet you, Sara."

Russ put his arm around my shoulders and steered me toward the sofa, settling me onto a cushion before dropping down beside me. Tony opted for the armchair, leaning forward and resting his elbows on his thighs.

"So what's this about seduction? And don't leave anything out."

"This can really be handled at a later time. I'm sorry I interrupted." I tried to stand up but Russ yanked my arm and I was forced back into a sitting position.

"Don't worry about Tony. I told him all about your shotgun wedding."

"Oh, God." I hid my face in my hands, using my hair to further shield me from scrutiny.

"It's a great story," Tony offered.

"Except when you're living it," I muttered into my hands. Russ rubbed my back gently.

"C'mon. Head up. Tell Uncle Russ."

I raised my head.

"We won't tell anyone. We promise. Don't we, Tony?"

Tony's response was to cross his heart and hold up the Boy Scout salute.

"He's driving me crazy," I confessed.

"And that's a bad thing?" Russ seemed perplexed. Of course, he thrived on crazy.

"He tells me what to do. He follows me everywhere I go. Every time I turn around, there he is."

"At least the scenery's good."

I glared at Russ.

"I'd heard the same thing, although I haven't actually met your husband yet."

"Is there anything you won't tell people? What did you do? Describe his butt on the air?"

"Can't. The FCC is very prudish when it comes to that sort of thing."

"Don't worry, Sara. Russ discussed your situation with me only in confidence. It won't go any further. We doctors are used to keeping things confidential." His voice and manner reassured me. A quick glance at Russ yielded a confirming nod.

"I only know you through Russ. And I don't know Connor at all. I do know that new relationships are hard work. They take some getting used to. Particularly if you haven't been with anyone in a really, really long time," Tony suggested helpfully.

I jabbed my elbow hard into Russ's side and he winced, using his free hand to rub at his sore ribs.

"Thank you very much, Rona Barrett." I glared at Russ.

"I felt honor-bound to explain my marital situation to Tony," Russ said slyly. "Explaining a wife later could prove awkward."

"Really?" I freed myself from Russ's arm and got up from the couch to resume pacing.

"Do you want a drink or something, hon? Something to cool you off maybe?"

"No, I'm fine." I moved to the open cabinet where Russ kept his CD collection, idly flipping through the cases. "It's not just that it's new. It's . . . well, Connor's so into it, y'know? Or he was into it. Now I don't know what he is." I straightened the cases, matching them to the edge of the shelf with careful precision.

"I'm not sure I understand." Tony said.

"I don't think I'm the marriage type."

"A little late for second thoughts, don't you think?" Russ's contribution was more practical.

"What do you mean, you're not the marriage type?" Tony steered the conversation back into a serious vein.

"I just mean"—I turned and walked to the window, staring across the street at the dance club the Romper Room, where the sunlight glinted off its oversized picture window—"well, he's good at it. The marriage thing. I don't agree with him. I am definitely not letting him follow me around everywhere, but part of me sort of likes it. That he worries, I mean. Not worries, exactly . . ."

"He makes you feel cared for." For someone who didn't know either of us, Tony had managed to hit the bottom line with amazing ease.

"Yeah, I guess. Like I should tell him where I'm going. Then he says something stupid, like I *have* to tell him, and I just want to deck him."

"I'm putting five bucks on you. He's a Navy SEAL and all that, but I've seen you in a mood," Russ said.

I turned to look at them. Russ had moved to the arm of Tony's chair, draping himself casually, one arm slung around Tony's shoulders.

"Russ." Tony shook his head slightly, looking at Russ before returning his attention to me.

"And just when I start to think maybe I ought to cut him a little slack, he can't take it."

Russ sat straighter. "He can't take what?"

"Me, I guess."

"You guess? He said that to you?" Russ was standing, his hands clenched at his sides. Tony reached over and took one of his hands, tugging him back into a sitting position and smoothing the fist against his thigh.

"What did he say?" Tony's eyes were chocolate soft, his voice soothing.

I couldn't remember exactly what Connor had said. Something about he couldn't take it. But what? I'd been so angry at his dictate I'd nearly missed it. I pushed my hair behind my ears, shivering as I suddenly noticed the air-conditioning. I paced one length of the living room before dropping back onto the couch, my legs weak with realization.

"It sounds like you need to talk to Connor," Tony suggested. "Listen, too. Maybe ask him to slow down a little."

"The man is incapable of slow."

"That's more sex talk, isn't it? You're such a tease."

Russ's smile couldn't cover the concern in his eyes. He winked at me but it lacked its usual merry zeal.

"That's not exactly helpful, Russ." Sitting beside Russ, Tony responded to his words without having the advantage of seeing his expression.

"You're the psychologist, not me. I don't do touchy-feely." Russ got up and came over to me, capturing my hands with his, before sitting on the coffee table.

"He can handle it, Sara. If you're not getting what you want, tell him. If you're mad at him, fight. And if you need him, lean. He's not going to bail."

"And you know that, with absolute certainty, based on two hours' acquaintance?" Despite Russ's reassurance, I wasn't convinced, but I did feel a little better.

"I've watched him watch you. You should try it sometime. It's quite enlightening. Now it's time for you to go upstairs and make up."

"He was wrong."

"Absolutely. Which is why you're going to make him do the no-clothes thing when he says he's sorry."

Russ squeezed my hands, waggling his eyebrows. I couldn't help but grin as I pressed back. Freeing myself, I hugged him hard.

"Thanks."

"Anytime."

"Oh, and thanks, Tony. You were a big help." I stepped toward him and offered my hand. He stood and took it in both of his, shaking gently.

"My pleasure. Good luck, Sara."

"I'll probably need it. Are you really a psychologist?"

"As a matter of fact, I am."

"Then good luck to you, too. You might need it more than me." I glanced back at Russ meaningfully for a moment, smiling away the sting.

"Go back to whatever you were doing. I'll see myself out."

With that, I left.

Chapter Thirty-six

The knock on the door boomed through the apartment. Popping up like a jack-in-the-box, I managed to drop the book I'd been pretending to read, slam my shin against the coffee table, and slosh lemonade out of my glass and onto the table and carpet. Ignoring the mess, I raced to the front door. My hand on the knob, I took a moment to collect myself, taking a calming breath and using one hand to try to tame my hair before opening the door with a bright smile.

"Russ."

"Tone down the enthusiasm a bit, okay, Sara? It'll go to my head."

"Sorry. C'mon in."

I gestured Russ toward the living room. He preceded me, forced to take an awkward step as he noticed the sticky pond on the carpeting only at the last second. He turned toward me, eyebrows raised. I shrugged and he shook his head in disgust. Placing the shiny package he had been carrying on the side table, he went into the kitchen, coming out with a damp washcloth and a roll of paper towels.

"I was just about to do that." I dropped into an armchair and watched as he crouched, dabbing at the carpet.

"I'm sure. So where is he?"

"He went for a run. At least, that's what the note said."

"Note. I guess that means you didn't get a chance to patch things up?" Russ gave the beige carpet a last swipe and rose, returning to the kitchen.

"He didn't apologize yet, if that's what you're driving at."

"Not exactly." Russ returned with a beer in one hand, stooping to pick up my discarded book and making himself at home on the couch. He glanced at the back cover of the book.

"The college roommate did it. Revenge for a fraternity prank years earlier." He set the book on the coffee table.

"Thanks. That'll save me the bother of reading the rest of it."

"It's not that good anyway." Russ reached to fondle the yellow ribbons on the package, deliberately drawing my attention to the gift. I couldn't generate any enthusiasm.

"Maybe next time you might let me figure that out for myself."

"It's probably a good thing he went for a run. Give him a chance to cool off." Russ sat up straighter, moving the box to the coffee table. "Then when he gets back you can go straight to that blinded-with-sex thing."

"If he comes back."

"He's coming back. He's only been gone—"

"Two hours. At least." I glanced at my watch, trying to confirm my calculation. "Okay, well, maybe not quite that long, but a long time, anyway."

"To a guy like that, it's probably just a short run. Relax. He's coming back." Russ centered the package exactly in the middle of the table, reaching up with his hands to frame the configuration.

"Of course he is. Tony seems nice."

"Subtle change of topic, but I'll play along. He is nice." A blush crept along Russ's cheekbones, and he shifted a little on the cushions.

"Cute, too."

He waggled his eyebrows at me.

"So why didn't I hear about this nice, cute guy before I was running into him coming out of your bedroom?"

"You know what they say about gay men, humping like rabbits night and day?" He crossed his legs, leaning back and adopting a haughty expression.

I laughed. "That press agent is worth every penny you're paying her."

Licking his lips, he put one hand to the back of his head and stared passionately at something a couple of inches to one side of me.

"And then some." I laughed harder. "Stupid stereotypes aside, it's been a long time between overnight guests for you."

Russ dropped his hand and returned to his semislouch.

"I like him." Russ's voice was soft and he stared at his hands, refusing to make eye contact.

"That's good. So why have you been keeping him a secret?"

I felt disconnected from everything. It was as if Connor's existence had wrapped me in cellophane, one degree separated from everything but him. Even Russ. I was on the outside with my best friend. I stood and rescued my abandoned glass from the coffee table before returning to my chair. I wrapped both hands around the sticky glass, hiding in the prop to hide my hurt feelings.

"I haven't known him that long. And you've been busy."

I knew he didn't mean it as a slam, but it bruised a little nonetheless.

"I'm never too busy for you."

"Well, anyway, I ran into him at the radio station. We talked, had coffee. The next day I called him and asked him to dinner."

"You called him?" Russ had been so gun-shy over the last couple of years, I was surprised.

"Yeah."

"You must really like him."

"Like I said, he's a good guy. And I'm lonely."

I was broadsided and for a moment couldn't even respond.

"Russ. God, I didn't realize." My throat felt tight and my words came out in a croak. I got up and went to sit next to him on the couch, reaching out to hold his hand, squeezing until he met my gaze. "I mean, I've been all caught up in this case and Connor and—"

"It's not your job to make sure I never feel lonely, Sara."

"I'm your best friend. I'm supposed to be there when you need me."

"You are there when I need you. I never would have gotten through the last couple years without you." He dropped my hands and draped an arm around my shoulders, scooting lower against the sofa. I settled lower, too, resting my head against his arm.

"But I didn't know you were lonely. I should have known."

He kissed my head and gave me a quick hug.

"Getting married was the best thing you could have done for either of us."

"What do you mean?" I shifted so that I could meet his eyes. For once there was no humor in his expression. It saddened me.

"Neither one of us was going to get a life. We were relying on each other for everything. Friendship, companionship, laughter, concern. Pretty much everything but sex."

"You never offered," I told him.

He laughed, leaning forward to give me a hearty kiss on the cheek.

"Having you to do things with made it easier for me to not look for anything else. And you were doing the same thing."

"I do love you." I reached up and took his face between my hands.

He leaned forward and rested his forehead against mine.

"I love you, too, Sara. But you can't be my boyfriend. And I can't be your husband."

"We're still best friends, though, right?"

"Always." He kissed my hand. "And that's why I thought I should bring you your wedding gift." He took the package from the table and placed it in my lap.

"This is the first wedding gift we've gotten. In fact, it's the only one we've gotten." I swallowed hard, not quite ready to shift gears. I cleared my throat and sat up, staring at the shiny silver paper with its big yellow bow. I threw a quick smile in his direction, determined to show him how much I appreciated his thoughtfulness.

"Then it'll be the best one you get. Go on; open it." Russ nudged me with his shoulder.

"Maybe I should wait for Connor. For when he gets back."

"There're actually two boxes there. The top one is for you. The bottom is his. Go ahead and open yours."

"Our first his-and-hers." I shook the boxes a little. Nothing. *Damn.*

"Open it."

"Okay, but only because you insist." I smiled at him, still trying to clear the lump from my throat. Turning my attention back to the package, I untied the bow and the two boxes slid apart. Taking the top box, I tore the paper and lifted the top of the box. Pushing delicate lavender tissue paper out of the way, I stared. From inside an elaborate silver frame, Connor's unsmiling face and grass green eyes stared back.

"I had to borrow his military ID. It's actually friendlier than his driver's license. You'd think a guy as beautiful as him would work the camera a little."

I laughed. And laughed. And laughed until tears ran down my cheeks.

"It's wonderful." I hugged him hard.

"I figure every woman should have a picture of her husband."

"Definitely." Smiling, I returned my gaze to the picture, running my hand along the frame.

"I hope you used a better picture of me."

"Ugly bridesmaid dress, party last spring. You wore that orange dress with the big poofy sleeves and the matching bow in your hair."

I groaned, closing my eyes in momentary horror. "Thanks."

"Think nothing of it."

Seeing the funny side, I started to laugh again, my sides aching. Russ joined in.

"At least he's got a picture that accurately reflects his wife's sense of style." Russ pushed the heckle out between gasping breaths. I sat upright, my humor fading as I tried to calm my breathing. I stared at the picture.

"A picture of his wife."

"Yeah. Of course. That's the point."

"He had a picture of his wife. I am so stupid." Connor was right. Wesley was right. Jepsen was the guy. He had to be the guy. Didn't he? Rising, I set the pictures on the table and started looking around for my keys, stepping over Russ's outstretched legs.

"What?"

"I've gotta go. Where are my damn keys?" I paced around the living room, checking tables, moving things, trying to catch a glimpse of my keys.

"Go where?"

"Do me a favor. Tell Connor I'll be back as soon as I can."

There were two sets of keys sitting on the hall table: my rubber sneaker shoe ring and another. I picked up the second set. The key ring was an embossed gold M. There were a half-dozen keys and a black plastic remote-entry device. It took me a minute to remember where I'd seen them before. The secretary. They'd fallen from her purse and I'd tried to use them as a weapon. I stared at the key ring, tracing the gold with my finger. Of course, the letter M. M for Millicent. Or maybe, just maybe M for Masterson. I grabbed my cell phone and headed out the door.

"But where are you going?" Russ called to my back. Ignoring him, I picked up my pace.

Chapter Thirty-seven

I parked along the road several blocks from the Masterson estate. If I had to run for it, I was going to regret leaving the car so far away. I pulled the cell phone from my pocket as I made my way through the trees that screened the houses from the road. The sun was up and I began to sweat. I called the apartment first, leaving another message for Connor to meet me at the Masterson estate. I wondered where he was and if he was on his way. I'd left two messages for Sergeant Wesley, too. I hadn't told him everything. I wasn't really holding out on him, but without the money I didn't think he'd believe me.

I circled around the back of the property. Everything looked closed up tight. No cars sat in the driveway, no shades were up, the gatehouse looked deserted. I took a deep breath and ran across the lawn. I clicked the electronic fob at the garage door and it began to go up with a squeak. I glanced over my shoulder. I slipped inside and pressed the switch to drop the garage door behind me. I leaned against the door, breathing hard, listening for sounds of movement in the house. When I didn't hear anything for a full two minutes, I slipped into the house, moving across the kitchen, through the shadowed living room, and up the stairs. At some point, someone had pulled all the shades in the house, whether to keep out the August sun or prying eyes, I wasn't sure.

Still, I was grateful. Nervous sweat ran into my eyes even in the stuffy coolness of the house.

I ran upstairs, turning the knob to Millicent's room. I meant Margaret's room, I guess. It was locked. It hadn't been the first day I came out to the manor, but now it was. I tried the keys on the ring one by one, holding my breath each time a key ground in the old lock. Finally the lock turned and I let myself into the room. I stared in disbelief. The room was a shambles, drawers over-turned, clothes dumped all over the floor. This wasn't like the first search. Whoever had searched then had at least tried to be discreet. This new search was done without any attempt to hide the fact. Jepsen had grown sloppy, desperate, as the cops asked questions and he couldn't find the money.

I knew he didn't have it. He'd said as much in the garage before Connor'd jumped him. What had he said exactly? Something about a computer. That was right. They'd take the computer and hire a hacker, Jepsen had said. I didn't remember a computer in the house, but I moved across to the office anyway. This room was in the same condition as Millicent's. Everything had been torn apart. I went to the desk. The drawers were all open, their locks pried loose. Beneath the desk the carpet had been cut away to reveal a floor safe. The keyhole was gauged, the metal scraped but unyielding. I tugged at the metal handle. It was locked.

I thought I heard a squeak and froze. Floorboard? Mouse? I held my breath, moving farther beneath the desk. I couldn't see the door from my position, and I couldn't stand not knowing. I crept out from my hiding place and moved to the side of the desk on my knees, staying crouched and watching the door. Nothing happened.

"You're letting your imagination run away with you, Sara," I muttered to myself, going back to the safe.

I took the smallest key and tried to insert it in the lock. It didn't fit. I swayed a little as the adrenaline crested. I took the next key, then the next, until I'd tried every one on the ring twice. None of them fit the lock on the safe. I couldn't believe it. I sat down on the wood floor.

I'd been so sure. The computer had to be in there. It had to be in there. There wasn't anyplace else it could be. Jepsen had the disk, but I'd bet a night with Connor that there was still a copy on a hard drive somewhere. Well, maybe not great sex, but something valuable anyway. I knew I wouldn't keep only one copy of the account number where millions were stashed.

I wanted to pull at my hair in frustration. I yanked at the handle on the safe. I pulled again and again. I took the handle in both hands, the remote-entry device gouging my hands as I pulled with all my might. I let go of the handle and slammed the little plastic device on the table. I heard a click and a bookcase moved, revealing a shadowy recess behind it.

I stared. I picked up the remote control and pushed the button. The bookcase closed and the lock clicked. Another push and the chamber beyond was once again revealed. I shook my head. Of course. Masterson had been a gadget guy. He wouldn't use a key. Stewie had told me: a hidey-hole. I'd dismissed it as drug-induced delusion. Note to self: Even lunatics occasionally talk sense. I moved from the desk toward the narrow opening.

A frigid draft raced into the office, carrying a strong wave of must and urine. The odor was thick and suffocating, causing me to gag. The elegant leather-bound books flanked the darker space beyond like sentinels on watch. I went closer, coughing harshly as the smell got stronger. I jerked my T-shirt collar up over my nose and mouth, holding it like a makeshift mask with one hand. My throat began to close up and I coughed, again trying not to breathe. I took baby steps over the edge.

It took a minute for my eyes to adjust to the darkness of the little room. This was crazy. A wild-goose chase. No way were female intuition and dumb luck going to get me to the answer faster than careful investigation by professionals. The cops had Jepsen. They had the secretary. This was a wild hair. I heard a creak behind me and froze, my sweat chilling as I got closer to the source of frigid air. I waited, my eyes searching out the gloom of the room, trying to see past shadows. It was nothing. Just an old house, probably cringing at the god-awful stink. A high-pitched scream preceded a flying projectile, and I threw my arms up to protect my face, swallowing a scream as the object hit me full force, gouging my forearms before ricocheting off and landing nearly at the door to the hallway. The scare had forced putrid air into my lungs, sending me into another round of coughing spasms as my stomach pitched and rolled. Intent eyes were transfixed on me, and I reached up a hand to rub at the stinging scratches left on my neck, feeling the blood the attacker had drawn. Flash. He stared at me for a long moment before walking to the door and reaching up to scratch his demand for release, yowling piteously.

"So the prodigal returns."

He stopped long enough to fix me with a look of disdain before returning to his eloquent scarring of the door's old oak.

"What's in the room, Flash?"

He never even turned around. I turned back to face the opening. Having a cat trapped in that little room for a week probably made quite a mess, but I somehow doubted that smell could be entirely blamed on feline hygiene. Jepsen had found the computer in that room. I knew it. I walked to the opening, careful to keep my body behind the protection of the bookcases. I swallowed hard, then jerked my head into the opening for a quick peek before resuming my position behind the shelves. I waited a minute, then darted in for another quick look. Discerning no lurking murderers, I stepped carefully into the room.

It was small, barely twelve-by-twelve but it seemed to be fully equipped. The room had an eerie green glow provided by a dimly illuminated set of nine closed-circuit video screens, set up like a tic-tac-toe board. I could make out the study, the kitchen, three bedrooms, two bathrooms, the front of the house, the rear of the house, and the living room in the guest cottage. Bud Masterson had been right: His father did have a little place of his own. One that let him play voyeur with his guests.

That wasn't its only use, though. The room was a sort of bunker, and it offered all the comforts of home. I could make out the dull outlines of a bunk and a drop-leaf table, both of which appeared fixed to the wall but could obviously be opened when needed. There were built-in cupboards, nearly black against the far wall of the room. I reached for the light switch. Whatever that smell was, I didn't want it on my shoes. I started breathing through my mouth, through the filter of my shirt, but it didn't help. I turned on the light, blinking in the glare.

A computer sat on the desk, surrounded by a variety of other gadgets neatly stored in the recesses of the wooden desk hutch. This place could give Radio Shack a run for its money. With my eyes adjusted to the light, I looked around and gasped, choking on a combination of surprise and foul air. The carpet underneath my sneakers was soundproof-thick, which explained why no one outside the room had heard Flash's yelling for freedom. I figured it was probably the bullet wound in the head that had kept the man inside the room from offering assistance. It also explained the smell. Something had died in here.

Somehow his being the second body I'd practically tripped on in a week took away some of the horror. Maybe I was getting used to it. It was kind of fascinating in a way. I took a step nearer the body propped up in the far corner. The wound gaped at me, a perfect crimson hole ringed by a darker smudge. The skin of his temple had pulled back from the wound, leathery and dried. His skin was nearly black, sunken like an old apple left in the sun. I had to admit, I did manage to stumble across exceptionally well-dressed corpses. This one's navy pin-striped suit could have come from the same tailor who had designed the first dead guy's gray ensemble. His navy-and-gold silk tie still held its Windsor knot; his patent-leather shoes still gleamed with polish. I wondered how long he'd been dead. How long did it take a dead body to turn into *Tales from the Crypt*? I hunched down nearer the body and craned my head to look at the face turned toward the wall. I couldn't recognize him. Stuart Masterson, probably. The grainy newspaper photograph that I had seen had been of poor quality, but long-term decomposition was infinitely worse. I had guessed he was probably dead, but there'd always been the chance that he'd just headed for a nice tropical island to forget his troubles. I continued to stare at his face until I noticed the green mold forming along his eyelashes. *Gross.* I jumped back.

I glanced back at the desk, considering my options. The guy had been dead awhile. I doubted he would mind if I had just a quick look around before I called the cops. He wasn't going anywhere. Amazing. Less than a week ago I was practically losing my cookies because I had seen a dead body, and here I was contemplating a leisurely little search with a reeking corpse for company.

I walked to the computer and sat in the leather chair. I needed to find the money. I crossed my fingers, hoping that Masterson had the same approach to security as my boss. I wanted to find the money, but I didn't want to commit to a long-term relationship with a moldy dead guy who stank to high heaven. I couldn't wait to tell Connor I'd found the money. Maybe not. He'd probably be ticked that I went off on my own. Wesley, too, since I'd had to resort to a little breaking and entering. Still, they could hardly complain about the end result when I found the cash. If I found it. No, when I found it. If a techno-idiot like Jepsen could find it, I certainly could. I just needed to think positive. I booted the computer.

A creak sounded behind me and I whirled, the leather chair squeaking a loud protest. On second thought, discretion was the better part of valor, and I wouldn't want anyone to think I was stupid. Maybe I should just let the professionals handle it. I'd done all the hard stuff. I knew where to look, and I had found the cat to boot. The cops could handle the bodies. I would call in the troops. At the rate I was going, I should probably get Wesley's direct line. I spun back to the desk and picked up the receiver. No dial tone.

I sat up straighter, suddenly realizing that Flash had also gone quiet. No howling, no scratching, nothing. I dropped the receiver into its cradle and rose from the chair, pushing away from the desk and spinning toward the door. The first step brought me face-to-face with the biggest gun I had ever seen.

Chapter Thirty-eight

"**Y**ou don't seem surprised to see me." Jeff, dressed in tailored pants and another polo shirt, this one a deep forest that enhanced the bronze of his tan, said casually from the far side of the gun. I closed my eyes, willing his image away, internally screaming at my own stupidity. When I opened my eyes, the gun was still there. I raised my hands. Connor was right: Sooner or later my headlong approach was going to get me into serious trouble. Welcome to sooner.

"It's more like disappointment." It was, too. I'd thought he was such a nice guy. So much for my judgment. It wasn't like I'd had any proof. Just a picture. The sort of picture only a parent or a significant other would put in a silver frame. I'd wanted so much to be wrong. The gun in his hand told me that I'd finally gotten it right.

"How'd you figure it out?"

"It was the picture of Flash, the one you used to make the posters. You kept it in a fancy frame. In your cottage, not the main house. What was Margaret Trilling to you? Was she your wife? Your lover? I know she was your partner. Did you plan the whole thing together?" I could still talk myself out of it. Maybe some of that nice guy was real. All he wanted was the money. He wasn't a killer; he was a thief.

"Plan it together? She tried to leave me. She took my

money and cut her deal and went all boring on me. I did five years and what did she do? She took typing. She bought ugly suits. She forgot that everyone's on the con." He glanced over at the body. "The late, unlamented Stuart Masterson, I presume."

"That would be my guess." He seemed surprised. Amen to that. "You haven't killed anyone, Jeff. This thing can still go away as long as you don't do something crazy."

He smiled slowly, the light in his eyes telling me he was way past crazy. "You're standing three feet from a moldering body on the wrong side of a gun and you're going to try to talk your way out of it?" Jeff laughed, genuine amusement rippling through the room in waves. "I'm afraid I seriously underestimated your moxie, my dear Sara. It's too bad about the husband and your penchant"—he pronounced it *puhn-shunt*—"for doing the right thing. A lack of imagination is the worst sin, Sara. On the other hand, you have much better nerves than the last investigator did."

"I know you didn't kill Masterson." Last investigator? What was he talking about? *Stay cool, Sara. Just take it easy.*

"How could you possibly know that?"

"You didn't know about this room. You don't have the money. You wouldn't have killed Masterson before you had the money. You're too smart for that. My money is on Henry Jepsen. He's under arrest for murder and fraud."

Jeff laughed. It made the room colder.

"Murder? Maybe. He is of questionable temperament. Fraud? No. Henry Jepsen doesn't have the brains. It takes a certain level of intellect to run a good con, Sara. Intellect and imagination."

"Millicent?"

Jeff made a sound like a buzzer. "Wrong again. My less-than-lovely wife could never do it on her own. She needed someone to do her thinking for her. For ten years she did what I told her, and I made more money than a hundred Harvard Business School types. Then she went stupid and I paid the price. Now I'm going to get mine."

"The two million in trust."

"Much more than that, my dear girl."

"You said she took your money. That's what you meant. You came to get it back."

"Originally, yes. Only that stupid slut put it into an irrevocable trust. Told me she couldn't spend it. It was blood money. Of course, she didn't give it back either. She gave it to the cat." Jeff laughed again and I wanted to retch.

"She named a bank as trustee," he continued. "Do you have any idea how hard it is to remove a bank as a trustee? She knew that. She knew I'd come for it. She knew I'd make her give it to me. She'd never be able to deny me anything."

"So Millicent made sure you'd never get the money." I didn't want to provoke him, but I kind of admired Millicent's—Margaret's—determination to remake her life. She did bad things under the influence of an evil man, but, on her own, she'd tried to be a decent person. She'd been surrounded by snakes and liars, but she'd still tried.

"She showed you the trust document, didn't she?"

"Yes. I made her call the bank while I listened in."

I could imagine it. Millicent scared out of her mind. Jeff coldly holding his ear to the phone.

"I was going to strangle it in front of her."

I swallowed the nausea.

"Flash?"

"She'd brought it on herself. She'd always been obsessed with that stupid animal. I never wanted it in the first place, but it fit our image at the time. She acted like it was her child or something. Sentimentality is a waste of time."

My knees felt weak, and I leaned against the desk.

"The cat ran away. It kept disappearing and reappearing. Like smoke. It's how she named it. It would be just a flash and then it would be gone."

Gone. The cat had gotten away.

"Why did you stay once you knew the money was gone?"

"She needed to make it up to me."

"You were going to con Stuart Masterson?"

"She was already in place. There were deep pockets." Jeff gestured with the gun. "Unfortunately, Masterson was unavailable."

I nodded. "Henry Jepsen killed him when he realized Masterson was setting him up to take the fall for the pension theft. How did you figure out the pension money was missing?"

"Margaret knew. Some bean counter figured it out and wanted to warn her." Jeff chuckled. "Warn her. Like she was the Virgin Mary."

"She didn't have anything to do with taking that money."

"Are you sure about that? I trained her well."

I wanted to punch him in his smug mouth. Two people had been killed for this stupid scheme, and he wanted to take credit for its inventiveness. My fear was fading fast. Too fast. At least fear kept me from doing something stupid.

"Not well enough, apparently. She didn't find the money. And her death left you scrambling. She needed you? More like you needed her. How did you get the bank to appoint you as guardian? Did you force her to write a letter? Or maybe you forged one after she died."

One of his eyelids fluttered just a bit. It wasn't much of a reaction, but it showed he knew his back was against the wall.

"It's evidence. That letter. It's a way the cops can tie you to this. A link in the chain. Did you like prison? Looking forward to going back, are you?"

His finger tightened on the trigger and I flinched. I needed to push him but I didn't want to die.

"Margaret died before I could help her on her way." He lifted the barrel of the gun an inch. Sweat rolled down my back. "You, however . . ."

"I know where the money is."

He hesitated. A feral look crossed his face. It lasted only a second before the smooth facade slid back into place. He looked so normal. Average. Sane.

"You know where my money is?"

"It's why you called the firm in the first place, isn't it? Flash wasn't missing, or maybe he was, but you didn't care about that. You wanted someone in this house, searching. You made sure that the firm would send someone inexperienced. It was a missing pet, for God's sake. Then you hooked me. You sent me to that alley. It was a novice investigator's dream. A real case."

"It was very clever of me, I must say." Jeff preened a little. "When that investigator called I knew I was running out of time. I had to know what the police knew and how close they were getting. I had to get rid of the investigator. And I needed additional resources. You were perfect, my dear. I had thought that the police would suspect you, at least initially, in the death of Mr. Cort. Your firm would have been forced to rally around the troops. It is such a litigious society. In the end, they cleared you right away, but it didn't matter. You wouldn't let it alone. You were like a dog with a bone, Sara. Really very determined, and such a clear view into the police pursuit."

"Why did you kill Matthew Cort?"

"His interest was personal."

It made a sick kind of sense. Cort was investigating for his old school friend, for his widow. For Jeff, a personal agenda meant Cort wouldn't likely be bought off or manipulated into giving up. Killing him was the only choice. Jeff took a step closer and pressed the gun to my forehead. I could barely breathe.

"Where is my money?"

I raised my hands a little higher, a lump swelling in my throat. A chill slid through me, and I shuddered.

From now on I was going to do everything Connor told me. I wasn't even going to question him. *Please, God. Just let me get out of this and I promise I won't give him another minute of worry. I'll eat right and exercise. I'll mind my own business. I'll floss after every meal. Anything to get out alive.*

"It's here." I made a wave at the computer without ever taking my eyes off the gun. *Please let me be right about this.* Stall. I had to stall. Slowly, so slowly that he wouldn't feel the least bit threatened, I lowered my hands until they rested on either side of me on the desk. What had been on the desk? I couldn't turn around and look. *Remember, Sara. Picture the desk. That's good.* A phone, a stapler. Was it heavy enough to use as a weapon? A stapler against a gun. *Brilliant, Sara. Why don't you just offer to jump from the roof?*

"Now, Sara." Our eyes met, sending another shudder through me. Calm. I had to stay calm. *Connor. Please, God. Or Wesley.* If the cop showed up at this moment, I'd gladly confess to all the things I'd done since birth in thanksgiving.

"The Caymans." When it doubt, lie. Lie big. Lie often. Lie convincingly. "I was just about to log onto the computer to access the account number." *Wow.* That had almost sounded legit even to me.

"Do it." He used the gun as a pointer.

"Sure. Just stay cool, okay?"

I stood, turning my back to him with my internal alarm shrieking. I flinched as a sliver of sweat rolled between my shoulder blades, icing my spine. Carefully I pulled the chair out and slid into it. My eyes did a desperate inventory of the desk. The stapler was a plastic, portable model. The phone was hooked on the wall. Other than the computer, which would be held down by its various cables, there wasn't anything with enough heft to put a dent in him. He rested the gun barrel against the back of my neck. Bile rose in my throat as I went statue-still.

"The account number." I pulled the keyboard closer,

noticing for the first time that it was cordless. I shifted it, subtly testing its weight. The gun jammed harder against my head.

"I'm trying. But I'm having a little trouble concentrating with that thing shoved against my skull like that."

"Just get going or you're going to end up like the last man who crossed me—dead in some alley."

A murderer. That was really starting to sink in. *Oh, man.* The muzzle of the gun caressed my cheek. He'd kill me. Finding the money wouldn't matter. He was going to kill me anyway. I needed a plan. Fast. I clicked a couple of keys, pulling the keyboard a couple of inches off the edge of the desk as casually as I could, shifting in my chair to shield the move. I turned my head slightly, risking a glance toward Jeff to gauge his distance, freezing when my gaze met an angry stare from the shadowed recess of a bookcase. Flash.

His eyes glowed like coals, pulsing with liquid fire. The energy in the room shifted, alliances were formed, and I looked up at Jeff with a renewed sense of calm. I needed to stall. A plan. *Think, Sara, think.*

"Jepsen couldn't find it either," I babbled. "He knew about this room, of course." I pointed in the general direction of the decomposing evidence of Jepsen's inside information.

"What the hell are you talking about?" His voice was harsh as he leaned farther over my shoulder toward the screen.

"That's why he was always hanging around. He was looking for the money, too. After he killed Burke, anyway." Talk. Nice, casual conversation. Keep him calm. Like hostage negotiators on TV. It could work.

Jeff pushed his face close to mine. I caught a whiff of improbable mint even as I sat up, trying to edge the chair farther away. He stared at me, his pupils dilated, his skin still slick with sweat. His mouth was set in a fixed line, his lips narrowed to a sliver. I froze. He was crazy. *Hail Mary, full of grace.* What was the rest? Damn it, what the hell was the rest of the prayer?

"You're stalling. You don't know where my money is. You lied to me." He was whispering now, his blue eyes blazing. Give me screaming lunatics any day. His quietness was freaking me out. He placed one hand on my shoulder near my neck, squeezing hard enough to bruise. I was going to die.

"There." He pointed at the screen to a file named *Millicent.* I stared. I found it. Oh, my God, I'd actually found it. I moved the mouse to open the file.

"Open it, goddamn it." He pushed me away, moving the mouse himself.

"What the hell?" Jeff's head reared back as he took in the screen. Risking a glance up, I stopped short as Millicent's—or Maggie's—photograph stared back at me from the upper left corner of the screen. Next to it was her rap sheet, a dozen arrests for fraud neatly displayed in chronological order. Jeff seemed equally stunned. We gaped at each other. Then he turned back to the screen.

I propelled the chair back, putting full body weight into driving the hard edge of the keyboard into Jeff's exposed Adam's apple. The force of the blow threw him gagging against the bookcase, where a furious hiss preceded Flash's claws-extended touch-and-go down the exposed length of Jeff's face. Contact was met by a gurgling scream and followed an instant later by an explosion as the gun went off, shattering the computer screen. My ears ringing, I slammed the keyboard against Jeff's head. He slumped, his arms coming up to protect himself. The keyboard came down, again and again, until he lay still, covered in his own blood. I stared down at the keyboard, the broken plastic case cracked and smeared with crimson, the keys mangled from the blows. Bile rose in my throat and I gagged, dropping the keyboard and reaching up to cover my mouth, unable to look away from the devastation.

At my feet, a loud meow brought me back.

Chapter Thirty-nine

I kept my hands wrapped around the Styrofoam cup, trying to force some vestige of warmth into my chilled fingers. The little room was stifling with the summer heat and nonexistent air-conditioning, but shudders racked me. I sat on a hard, straight-backed chair, pulled close enough to a rickety table so I could no longer see the blood splatters on my shorts and legs. Flash had abandoned me, moving to one corner of the room and going to sleep. He lay on his back, his sleek gray-and-white body fully stretched with his paws over his head, their pads tapping against the air as he dreamed. The door swung open and I cringed, hunching my shoulders and pressing my legs together as I stared at the congealed cream on the surface of the coffee.

"Sara?"

"Is he dead?"

"No. How're you doing?" Sergeant Wesley's graveled voice held real concern. I looked up at him, blinking back tears of relief and revulsion as another vision of Jeff flashed through my mind. Wesley had loosened his tie and removed his jacket, revealing a crumpled white short-sleeved shirt with sweat stains under his arms. The gray of his eyes was steady and reflected the same genuine caring I had heard in his voice. I bit hard on my lip to stop it from trembling.

"You're sure he's not dead?"

"I'm positive." He moved to the far side of the table and pulled out the other chair, slumping his heavy frame into the tiny seat. "I just talked to my guy over at the hospital. Randall's gonna be fine. He's got a concussion, couple of broken bones, and some cuts and bruises. No big deal."

"I did it." The cup in my hands began to crumple under the pressure. Quickly Wesley reached over and removed the Styrofoam from my grip, peeling my fingers away and placing the lopsided cup off to one side on the small wooden table. "He was going to kill me. He was going to kill me." I wrapped my arms around myself, my fingers digging into my upper arms.

"Yes, he was." Wesley agreed gently. He leaned forward, resting his arms on the table in front of him. He was being so nice I wanted to cry.

"You know?" Barely a whisper.

"Yeah."

"He killed that private detective. Cort. The one in the alley." My fingers dug deeper into the flesh of my upper arms as I tried to hold the shakes inside.

"You did what you had to do, Sara."

"Can I call my husband?" Suddenly I wanted Connor with an intensity that swamped me. He would come. I knew he would. Even if he was still mad about before, if I called him he'd show up. To help me. To be with me. The shaking intensified. "Please."

"I already called him. I had to leave a message. Is there another number we could try?"

"Why are you being so nice? I'm arrested. I hit him. A lot. And I meant it, too." I blinked, feeling a slow tear roll down my face. I wiped hard at it before deliberately folding my hands and placing them on the table. I sat up straighter, pulling myself together with all my strength. All I wanted was to go home.

"You're not arrested, Sara. You're the victim. We only brought you down here to answer a few questions, maybe tie up a couple of loose ends." He reached for his pocket, pulling out the same tattered notebook he'd been carrying the night I found Cort in the alley. When was that? Tuesday? Wednesday? It felt like a lifetime. Someone else's lifetime.

"Okay."

"Why did you go to the house?"

"It was the picture."

"What picture?"

"Jeff showed it to me the first day. When I went to talk to him about Flash. He had a picture of Millicent— or Margaret, or whoever she was—holding the cat. But when I went through her room, she didn't have any pictures. None at all. Nothing personal, even though the whole room was opulent and, well, not staid. But he had a picture of her. In a frame. She wasn't wearing the ugly suit. The boring stuff was the public Millicent. The other stuff, blond hair and fashionable clothes, that was Margaret. He had a picture of Margaret." I was trying to keep things straight in my mind but it all came out in a tangle.

"Margaret? You mean Margaret Trilling?"

"You know about that?" I shifted in my chair, pulling myself infinitesimally closer to the table.

"Why don't you tell me what you know about Margaret Trilling?" He flipped a page.

"She switched places with the real Millicent. She'd been arrested. Fraud, mostly. And she worked with a partner. She was arrested, then—I think, anyway—turned evidence against her partner. He went to prison. She took her cat and went straight, or tried to. She put the money they'd stolen into a trust for her cat." I reached for the abandoned coffee, taking a gulp of the tepid liquid. I gagged at the taste. I put the coffee cup aside, carefully matching its position to the ring I had already left on the pressed-wood surface.

"And how did you figure out Millicent was Margaret?"

"I didn't. Cort did. We just followed his trail."

"So when you found out, you knew she was running

a game on Masterson?" He looked up, raising one
eyebrow.

"That's what we thought, yeah. It wasn't true. Masterson hired her. Got Jepsen to do it, actually, but Masterson knew about her background all along. It was on
his computer. He was setting up Jepsen to take the fall
when the theft was discovered, but no one would believe
Jepsen had the computer know-how to pull it off alone.
Margaret had the tech background. She'd always worked
with a partner and she had a record. The worst part was
that she was trying to go straight, so she wasn't worried
about how things would look. She wasn't up to anything.
When the theft was discovered, who'd believe her?"

I massaged my temples, my head pounding. I pushed
my hair behind my ears and then pulled it free again. I
was so tired.

"It's a good theory," Wesley said, "but we've got as
much circumstantial evidence against Masterson as we
do against Jepsen."

"I hope she didn't know she was getting played from
the start. Maybe she did take advantage of people in her
past, but I think she did genuinely try to change. She
was there for Emma Burke. And if she used people in
the past, she got used back. Jeff. Masterson."

"A couple of real prizes," Wesley agreed.

"Exactly. The will was just overkill."

"What will?"

"Masterson was getting ready to execute a new will
disinheriting his children and leaving all that remained
of his estate to Henry Jepsen. It was a final screw-you
to all of them. He goes out of his way to tell his offspring
he couldn't care less about them while gifting Jepsen
with a big bag of nothing. All the while, he's sipping
rum drinks on a nonextradition beach somewhere with
millions in the bank. He really was a bastard."

I took a sip of cold coffee. "How did you figure out
the money was missing? Everyone had been sworn to
secrecy."

"The feds served a subpoena on Masterson Enterprises at six this morning."

"The feds work on Sunday?"

He laughed. "Took me by surprise, too. Maybe that's why they do it that way."

I grunted in near amusement, too tired to put any energy into a laugh. "So what went wrong? I mean, if that's Masterson's body in the house, he never made it to the promised land with the cash. Who killed him?"

"Henry Jepsen, if you believe the secretary. They're both playing Let's Make a Deal. She told us that Jepsen confessed to her. He went to the estate . . ." Wesley cleared his throat. "Excuse me, allegedly went to the estate, to have it out with Masterson about the lawsuit. Masterson told him he'd never see a dime, that he— Masterson, that is—would strip the company of every last dollar before Jepsen got near a judge. Jepsen went crazy and shot him. Jepsen's version is that Masterson attacked him and was killed during the struggle. Self-defense."

"I hadn't realized self-defense required burying somebody behind a wall."

He shrugged. "A good point. It does look like Masterson was behind the theft, but it's hard to argue with ballistics. I wouldn't be surprised if the bullet we dig out of that body turns out to match one of the guns we found at Jepsen's house. Seems Henry favored the thirty-eight."

"How does he explain Mitchell Burke?"

"More self-defense. A lot of that going around. Said Burke came to him and tried to blackmail him with information about a pension swindle. When Jepsen said no, Burke attacked and Jepsen defended himself."

"And pushed his car off a cliff?"

"Yeah, the story's got some holes."

"How could he put him behind the wall? I don't think he knew about the room. Or at least how to get in." I was confused.

"Don't quote me, but I think our girl Millicent put him there."

"Why?"

"Randall was already on the scene. Millicent either witnessed the murder or found the body. She did live there. She couldn't go to the police. Like you said—zero credibility. Besides, she had Randall to contend with. If he knew that Masterson was dead and the money was out of reach . . ."

"He would have killed her in a New York minute."

"He's a bad guy."

"How did you get in?"

"It was an electronic opener on her key chain. It opens the garage, too, so no one ever thought about it, and the fob had an M for Millicent. Or Masterson. What's the secretary's version?" I asked. Somehow, I knew she'd have a version.

"She didn't know anything. She picked up her boss and that's it."

"Did you go to the impound lot?"

"Yeah, I took some of our crime scene guys out with me. The locals were not happy. There are some inconsistencies; plus we've got chain-of-custody and evidentiary problems. Anyone"—he leaned closer and stared hard at me—"anyone could have gotten in there and tampered with evidence. It'll be a tough case."

"But it's an open case?" I asked.

"Yeah, it's open."

"What about the official cause of death?"

"We're changing it to suspicious. We'll get them. It'll take some time, but we will put them away."

I believed him. I knew I wouldn't want Sergeant Wesley tracking me.

"Millicent—I mean Margaret—was she involved at all?"

"Everything we found out seems to indicate that she really had tried to turn her life around," Wesley said. "She made up a story to get a job, but she did the work.

Everyone I talked to at Masterson Enterprises liked and respected her."

"She had lousy taste in men, though. What about Flash's trust fund?"

I looked over to where Flash was twitching in his sleep, unconcerned by his financial future.

"Real money. We confirmed with the bank. North of two million."

"That's a lot of catnip," I said.

Chapter Forty

Russ was waiting for me when I finally left the station, holding a cardboard pet carrier. I reached through the cutout on the side and stroked Flash's fur. He didn't stir.

"Are you okay?" Russ asked.

"Yeah." I hugged him, the cat, and the cardboard all at once. "Where's Connor?"

"C'mon. The car's this way. We've got to hurry." Russ started down the street, using his long legs to eat up the blocks.

"Hurry where? Where's Connor?" Maybe he was still mad about before. I wondered if he'd stay mad forever.

"He's on his way to the airport."

I stopped short. "The airport? You mean he's leaving?"

"He had to." Russ pulled at my arm. "He got a call. He had to go. We didn't know where you'd gone or what had happened to you."

"But I called. I left a message."

"I don't know about any message. All I know is, the guy was beside himself with worry. What the hell were you thinking, anyway? Then he got this call and he had to go back right away."

"But he didn't say good-bye." We reached my car and Russ opened the door for me, pushing the carrier into my hands.

"He left you a note."

"Where?"

"At your place."

"What did it say?"

"I don't know. I didn't read it. All I know is that he's on a plane to San Diego in exactly"—he glanced at his watch—"twenty-one minutes."

"Do you have the note?"

"He locked the door."

"What?"

"I saw him write it; then I walked him out. When I got your call, I went back for the note but the door was locked. If you're going to keep doing that, I should have a key."

I fastened my seat belt with numb fingers. Russ's taking the first corner on two wheels brought me back to reality. I turned and looked at Russ, his white-knuckled grip on the steering wheel, his hunched shoulders and maniacal concentration. I'd escaped death, only to get into a car with Russ behind the wheel. The same Russ who had passed the driver's test only on his fifth try and had laughingly described the ashen-faced, middle-aged examiner with twenty years on the job as "the nervous type."

"Hurry, Russ." I was losing my grip. That was what it was. I was racing like a lunatic through the streets of Seattle chasing a husband I hardly knew who left without saying good-bye. And despite the very limited driving abilities of my present chauffeur, I was yelling at him to go faster.

"We'll never make it." I gasped, my hands clenching the sides of my seat as Russ flung the car across three lanes to a chorus of angry horns. Flash howled in protest.

"We'll make it. We'll make it. If these chuckleheads would just get out of the way . . ." The car leaped into a narrow opening behind a fast-moving Mercedes. I gripped harder, staring out the front window, frantically searching for a sign indicating the airport. The hot wind gushed into the car, and my heart beat in response to its roar.

"Why would he just go like that?"

"Work. It was about work."

"Why didn't he wait?"

"I don't think he could. Who knew the cops would keep you that long? Not that we knew that was where you were."

"Did he seem mad?"

"You could have called."

"I know. I know. I screwed up. So did he have to just leave like that?"

"They called. He had to go."

"But he didn't say good-bye."

"Small logistical problem, Sara. You weren't there to say good-bye to." Russ stuck his arm out the window to return a one-finger gesture from the driver he had just cut off.

"He doesn't even know I found Flash." I leaned down, reaching into the carrier and receiving a bite for my trouble. Flash had had a tough day. The car ride wasn't helping as he clawed at his cardboard cage.

"So we'll find him and tell him."

"There's the exit. Look out." The car screeched to a halt abruptly as Russ careened down the exit and very nearly into the back end of a speed-limit-observing shuttle bus. I was flung against the seat belt and then back, my head slamming into the headrest. Flash thumped in his box.

"Go around. Go around," I yelled.

Russ was already moving onto the shoulder and around the blockade. He pulled back onto the road and we peeled down the ramp.

"Which airline?" I asked.

"He's going back to San Diego. Alaska. It's probably Alaska."

"Probably?"

"I don't know. It's a guess. The flight was, like, ten

minutes to six. That I do remember. He said that. So check the board, and if there's no flight scheduled for then, try another airline." Russ whipped into a space outside the terminal.

Suddenly I hesitated, afraid. "What am I supposed to say even if I do find him?"

"You're not going to find him unless you put some hustle in your bustle, kiddo."

"But—"

"No buts. It's five thirty. They'll already be boarding. Run, Sara."

I was paralyzed. I couldn't move. I wanted to see him. To tell him. Something. Anything. Everything. He was leaving. I had to go. I heard the seat belt click as Russ unlatched the clasp. He reached across me to unlock the door, pushing it open. I stared out the windshield.

"You've got to go now, Sara."

I turned to look at him, our faces inches apart. "What do I say?" I whispered.

He placed his hands on my shoulders and gave an encouraging squeeze.

"Try 'hello.' With him, it will be enough."

I could feel tears well in my eyes but I knew that was ridiculous. I didn't cry. I never cried. Russ's chocolate brown eyes shimmered. I reached out and hugged him tight, pressing a kiss to his cheek. He hugged me back hard.

"I'm jealous, you know," Russ whispered into my ear. Then he sat back, using his hands to break the embrace. "Go, Sara."

I jumped from the vehicle, flinging the door closed before hesitating, looking at Russ through the open car window.

"You're the best. Thanks." I turned and started toward the glass doors.

"I love you, too," he yelled, the words catching me between my shoulder blades.

I ran to the nearest Alaska Airlines departures monitor and scanned the listed flights. There it was: five fifty-two to San Diego, gate C1. I spun and sprinted toward the gates. Where were all these people going? And why wouldn't they pay attention? They walked four abreast and stopped to gawk at every sign they saw. They toted too much luggage and let their children run wild. Didn't they realize that some people were in a hurry? I dodged and weaved, barking an, "On your left," to the slow-moving retirees who wouldn't get out of the way. I rudely pushed my way in front of a large group of Japanese tourists waiting at the security checkpoint. A heavy-set guard in a too-small uniform asked to see my boarding pass. A boarding pass I didn't have.

I stepped aside and looked through the security gate. I jumped, trying to catch sight of him moving through the security line. The guard escorted me out of line and back toward the ticketing area as if I were a terrorist. I saw him signal to another security guard, who came over and took me by the arm.

"I missed him."

"Yes, ma'am."

"My husband, I mean. I missed him."

"Yes, ma'am."

I had no idea what I was going to say, and now that I wasn't going to get a chance to say it, I felt bereft. I walked to the huge windows, where the brilliant summer sunshine mocked me. I leaned closer to the glass, close enough for my breath to fog the surface, and whispered one word: "Hello." Then I rested my forehead against the hot pane.

My breath was coming in little gasps, and my chest hurt. Ached. Truth was, I hurt all over. Everywhere you couldn't see. I didn't blame him for going. I was stubborn and defensive. I called too late. If I were him, I wouldn't have stayed either. How many ways did I have to say I was independent before he figured out I meant it? We just weren't compatible. He was sharing and I was solo. Total opposites.

I stepped back from the window and dropped into one of the uncomfortable plastic chairs the airline provided.

I wrapped my arms around myself and shivered with the cold from the air conditioner. I pulled my feet up and rested them on the edge of the chair. I laid my head down on my upraised knees.

"The one thing I've learned from this life is that you have to make your own chances. Missing him here doesn't have to be permanent. Nothing is until you're dead," Russ's soothing tenor said behind me.

I lifted my head to look at him. I knew his history. Despite his outward joie de vivre, Russ hadn't known much real love. His lover had committed suicide without leaving a note, devastating Russ. And yet here he was, advocating emotional risk. I was such a coward.

He sat down beside me, putting his arm around my shoulders. "You've got a real chance here. So you missed the big good-bye scene at the airport. No big deal. Call him. Or better yet, get on a plane and go there."

"I can't just show up like that."

"Sure you can. You're his wife."

I cleared my throat. "It's not that easy."

"It can be. If you let it." He lifted his head and looked straight into my eyes. "Try, Sara. Try hard to be happy. Tell him you want to be married to him. Tell him you wish he were here."

"He left," I whispered.

"He went to work. It's not the same as leaving."

"You're right." I sat up straighter. "I'm going to go home and call him. Tell him I'm sorry he's gone."

"Getting on a plane is more immediate. And 'I love you' is more to the point."

"When it comes to my personal life, I've never been a big proponent of getting to the point."

He laughed, rising to his feet and reaching out for my hand.

"That is as accurate a statement as I've ever heard anywhere." He pulled me to my feet and we began to walk out of the waiting area. We strolled out. Now that I was no longer in a hurry, the crowds had miraculously vanished. And I didn't feel a need to rush. Connor wouldn't be in San Diego for a couple of hours. I didn't want to talk to a machine. I wanted to talk to him. In person. Russ had a point. My situation wasn't like his. I could still make things work. I just had to try. Give a little. I could do that. Connor seemed willing to do his part. We could talk about it tonight. Maybe schedule another visit.

I absently followed Russ to the passenger side of my car, where he produced my keys and opened the door. I put one foot in, then halted, pulling my leg out of the door and turning to face Russ. I held out my hand.

"On second thought, I'll drive."

"I didn't actually hit anything this time."

" 'This time' being the operative phrase."

"A good memory is an unpardonable offense in a true friend." He handed me the keys.

"Thanks," I said as I pulled out of the parking space.

"Sure. Any time. For what?"

"Helping me. Talking me in off the ledge." I slowed at the parking booth and slid the parking ticket Russ handed me into the machine. The electric arm flew upward.

"Jeez," I said.

"Here's your hat. What's your hurry?" Russ added.

We laughed. It felt good. Almost normal. We drove in silence for some time. Even Flash had stopped his crying. It was strange. Russ didn't usually allow for silence. He always seemed to need to fill the empty spaces. Tonight he didn't. I was both grateful and unnerved.

"What are you thinking about?" I asked.

"You. Connor. You and Connor. You and me."

"It has been you and me for a long time. Is that what you meant when you said you were jealous?"

"Partly. I'm not used to having to share. You always tell me about things first. Work. Family. What you're thinking. Or you used to. Now you're racing home to swap stories with someone else. He gets to hear all the good stuff first. Did you realize that we aren't even talking on the phone every day anymore? The guy is here for a week and you're forgetting who your friends are." His voice was soft, stripped of its usual humor, although a quick glance in his direction showed a small smile.

I did understand. Russ hadn't been in a serious relationship in years, since his partner's suicide, but he hadn't lived the life of a cloistered monk either. Every time there was a new man in his life, I held my breath, waiting to be replaced. Expecting to come second.

"You're still my best friend, Russ." I reached over and squeezed the hand resting on the gearshift.

"It's okay." He shifted in his seat, tugging at the shoulder harness. "Besides, we're not supposed to be talking about me. We're fixing you today, remember? You are going to call him, aren't you?"

"Yes, Mother."

"It would be better if you went to see him. We could turn around. You could still catch a plane tonight. It's much more romantic."

"I got the impression preplanning might be required. San Diego is just a convenient spot for a base. I gathered that they didn't necessarily spend much time actually working from there. By the time I got to his place, he could be gone. And he didn't leave any clues about how long 'gone' might be. Hanging around waiting for him to show up isn't my idea of romance. Besides, I'm better from a distance."

"I got the distinct impression he preferred proximity." I glanced at him in time to catch a flash of his wriggling eyebrows.

"You have a one-track mind."

"Since I'm not the one waking up next to Mr. Gorgeous, I've been forced to rely on my one-track mind for entertainment."

"Try getting a hobby." I flicked on the turn signal and passed a slow-moving truck. In the distance, I could see the skyline of the city as we neared our exit.

"I have a hobby. Analyzing you. Can I ask you a question?"

"Can I stop you?"

"Why were you so convinced that Connor wasn't coming back? I mean, I only talked to him a couple of times, but he made it pretty clear he wasn't going anywhere. Not for long, anyway."

I considered the question. I couldn't really explain why I had been so sure that Connor would go and not come back. It wasn't anything he'd said. In fact, he'd been so sure that we could work things out that we'd never really discussed his leaving. I just hadn't expected it to feel like it had. It was so sudden. And extreme. I knew it was ridiculous to miss something you'd had for only a week, but I did miss Connor. Him and the idea of him, too. Not that it made any sense to me. It just was.

"Why, Sara?"

I took the exit. The streets were nearly deserted. I didn't try to answer him until we were parked in the lot, the engine off.

"I'm not sure I can explain it so you can understand."

"You don't really have to explain it to me, Sara. But maybe you ought to spend a little time figuring it out for yourself. So the next time you're not quite so out-there."

I turned and looked at him, peering through the gloom. "How very odd."

"What?"

"You giving me advice on how not to overreact."

He chuckled quietly. "There's a first time for everything," he said.

We got out of the car and walked to the building. I carried Flash in his little cardboard box. He reached out a paw to swat at me. Russ entered the code in the keypad. Smiling, I made a mental note to ask the manager to change the code as soon as possible. We climbed the stairs, stopping outside my door.

I cleared my throat. "Thanks for driving me to the

airport. And helping me." I hugged him around Flash. He hugged me back.

"Any time." His response was quiet, subdued even.

I lifted my head to look at him. He seemed years older, his eyes sad.

"I really need to go." I gestured toward the door.

"Tell him I said hello."

"I will." I stepped into the apartment and closed the door. Flash jumped out of the carrier the second after I opened it, racing into the living room, darting toward the kitchen.

If I closed my eyes, I could see Connor standing at the end of the hall, bathed in golden light, just as he had been a few days ago.

"Meow." Flash came back, rubbing against my legs and head-butting my sneakers before reaching out with a paw for a quick swipe at an offending shoelace. I reached out and flipped on the overhead light.

"Hey, buddy. I bet you're hungry. Let's see what we've got for dinner." I reached down to pet him, his back arching in pleasure. He purred loudly, seemingly none the worse for his recent adventures. I had never had a pet, but Flash's apparent appreciation for my company was pretty nice. I straightened and started down the hall, only to grab the wall for support when my newfound friend decided to try to take me out of the play.

"Look out. You may not realize this, but if I fall on you, you die, cat." Flash, completely unconcerned with the threat to his life, sat down in the center of the narrow hallway and tucked his tail around his hindquarters, nonchalantly cleaning a paw.

"Excuse me." I hesitated, then stepped over him, keeping a close eye on the would-be assassin.

I went to the kitchen and spied the note sitting on the kitchen table. I read it once, then more carefully. He had to go. He wanted to tell me in person but he couldn't find me. A phone number. Three lines. Signed, *Love, Connor. Love.* Smiling, I began rummaging in the cup-

boards, coming up with a can of tuna. I watched while
Flash inhaled the fish; then I headed into the bedroom.

The bedside lamp glowed softly. Connor had made
the bed. Everything in its place. I walked to the closet
and pulled the doors open, stopping at the small gap in
clothes that indicated where his few items had hung. I
reached up to touch the empty hangers before pushing
the doors closed. I walked to the dresser and stopped,
my hands resting on the drawer pulls. I pulled the drawer
open slowly, a surprised laugh escaping from between
clenched lips. One pair of socks, one pair of shorts. I
carefully straightened the articles before pushing the
drawer closed and resting my hands on the dresser top.
I looked up, straight into the mirror. For a second I
really looked at myself, trying to see what he saw. Instead I was confronted with the same wild curls and
pale complexion that had burdened me my whole life. I
reached out and covered my reflection with one hand. I
caught a streak of gray in the reflection as Flash launched
himself onto the bed, immediately rolling around and chasing his tail. Laughing, I turned.

"I never said you could sleep with me, pal. For the
record, a girl likes to be asked." Flash turned and
twisted, reaching out to bat a small object that went
sailing with the force.

"If you aren't going to play nice, I'm going to have
to oust you." I walked around the bed to retrieve the
missile. It was nestled against the leg of the bedside
table, and I reached down to pick it up, hesitating mid-
way as I recognized the jewelry box. It was small, a
square of midnight velvet. I held it in the palm of my
hand as I backed up, sitting abruptly when my legs felt
the bed. Flash immediately reached around me to have
another whack at the box, but my fingers closed protectively around it. I flipped up the lid and stared inside.
A narrow platinum band winked up at me. I reached in
and pulled the ring free from its moorings, placing the
box on the bed, where the cat immediately pounced on
it. I brought the ring to my lips, barely breathing; then

I held it out at arm's length. A glint on the inside of my ring lured me into investigating the delicate inscription. The date we were married and one word: *Instinct.*

For the first time in years, I cried.

Read on for an excerpt from

DOGGONE,

Gabriella Herkert's next novel,
coming in September 2008.

F*orty-seven minutes to naked.*

I looked at the text message again. I'd never been the sort to turn my cell phone on the second an airplane landed, but then again, my messages were getting better. At least my propositions weren't coming from strangers anymore. I caught my seatmate glancing at my screen. She was a grandmother in a housedress who'd spent the journey showing me pictures of gap-toothed adolescents and waxing rhapsodic over their amazing achievements.

"Porn," said grandma, sighing. "I miss it."

I tried to cover my choke with a cough and reached for my carry-on.

Where? I typed, lining up in the airplane aisle behind the harried parents of screaming twin toddlers.

Anywhere?

I shook my head and tapped. *Where r u?*

Security.

Safe sex?

Flirt!

U started.

I shuffled off the airplane and into the terminal. The airport was bright, the tinted windows blocking the brutal glare of the San Diego sun. I walked beside the moving escalator, too impatient to stand and wait to be transported. I saw Connor through the plexiglass at security, the sun streaming behind him giving him a sort of halo. He looked up from his cell phone to watch a twenty-something Lucille Ball in a tight, short dress walk by him. I snapped my phone closed and moved past the checkpoint.

"I can come back if you're having a guy moment," I drawled.

Man, he looked good. Really good. An Adonis with a navy haircut. I tried to smooth my hair. No man should look that good when static electricity was turning me into a jeans-wearing Medusa. He grinned, amused. Fine. I'd just be cool. Oh, what the heck. Amused could be done naked.

Connor pushed a loose curl behind my ear and kissed the skin beneath my lobe. He whispered, "Forty-three." Then he grabbed my hand and steamrolled toward baggage claim.

"That's it?" I asked, half running to keep up. "I don't see you for three weeks, fly for hours behind hyperactive five-year-olds, and I all I get is a peck? I must look really bad."

He stopped. Turned. Let his eyes wander from the top of my head to my toes and back up, stopping at his favorite parts.

"Or not," I said weakly, covering my cheek with my hand.

"Not." He started pulling me again but I balked under the baggage claim sign.

"Um, Connor?"

"Yeah?"

"I didn't actually check any luggage." I half turned, showing the carry-on bag I had draped over one shoulder.

"That's it?"

"Yep."

"One overnight bag for a week?"

"Well, um, yeah," I shrugged.

"You are the weirdest woman. But I like that. One suitcase. Thirty-eight." He took my bag and herded me out the door into the bright sunshine.

"Because I can fit my jammies in one suitcase?"

"You're not going to need pajamas."

An older woman in a gray suit looked over her shoulder at us, silver eyebrows raised. What was this, shock a senior day?

He stopped next to a convertible. Black. I couldn't help smiling. Honestly, sometimes the guy thought he was James Bond. The convertible was at short-term parking, which was half the distance and twice the price. Money well spent. He tossed my bag into the car before backing me up against the hot metal and really kissing me hello. I wrapped my arms around his neck and kissed him back. Connor could kiss.

"Get a room." An old guy muttered as he climbed into a Buick in the next slot.

"Great idea." He whispered, reaching behind me to open the door.

"You are a bad influence." I slid into the passenger seat, fanning my face with one hand. "But we have a great car."

"We?" he asked, getting behind the wheel and reaching across me. I felt the tingle slide all the way down my spine. I swatted at his hand, but he just opened the glove compartment and took out the parking ticket, holding it up for me to see with his most innocent expression. An angel he was not.

"*We.* California is a community-property state. I never thought I'd own even half a BMW." I looked over at him. "Impressive as it is, if you boosted this car I never saw you before."

The engine roared to life and Connor drove toward the exit. He moved his hand to my thigh and I could feel his heat through the denim. I gave him my best what-are-you-up-to look—like I didn't know—but didn't move his hand. This flirting thing was fun.

"What's the new case about?" He yelled over the rush of wind. Once in fifth gear on the freeway, he returned his hand to my thigh, migrating just a little north.

"Fraud. One of those identity theft things." I yelled back, stroking the back of his hand. "Except that my thief is bolder than most."

"Bolder?" He slid his fingers up two inches of denim.

I pushed him back to the relative sanity of my knee. Crashing wouldn't be good here. "Yeah, bolder. My guy isn't just in it for the money. He wants the fame, the attention, the invites to the swankiest parties in town."

"I'd pretend to be somebody else to get out of one of those things."

"I bet you look great in a tux. Sort of James Bond-ish."

"I'd look like a waiter."

"Well, a waiter at a nice restaurant, anyway," I laughed.

Weren't we the normal married couple? Recently married, with the flirting and sexual tension—normal. Half the time it felt like I was pretending to be married and Connor was just a figment of my imagination. A very good, very vibrant imagination, but make-believe nevertheless. It was probably the Las Vegas thing. Knowing him a week and then getting married. The long delay before he showed up in Seattle. His casualness about the whole thing. If this were the real world, there would be a lot more panic. Hyperventilation and hand-wringing followed by drunken excuses and annulment. What the heck? If I was going to hallucinate a hot husband, a hot car, and the promise of hot sex, I might as well enjoy it.

"Or you could wear your uniform," I suggested. "Sort of a blond Tom Cruise. Now, *he's* cute."

He squeezed my leg and I squirmed with a laugh. Now he knew I was ticklish. Another late-to-the-party discovery.

"He's short. Besides, you wouldn't throw me over for a midget actor in an ice-cream suit, would you?"

"I would if he'd give me a deal on chocolate-chocolate chip. Men are great, but they're not dessert."

He lifted my hand and kissed my fingers, and then my palm. "Depends."

I curled my fingers over the spot. "Watch the road."

"Yes, ma'am."

"So, anyway . . . my identity thief gave this interview to some right-wing radio guy, all about how he had amnesia for years and wandered around homeless. Then, one day, he just woke up and remembered who he was."

"Rich and famous. That's handy," he said, pulling onto the San Diego–Coronado Bay Bridge. I grabbed at his arm, craning for a better look at the view.

"Amazing." I leaned back in my seat. "What? Oh, yeah. He remembered he was rich. Not so famous, though. My guy, the real guy, he's practically a hermit. Makes Howard Hughes look like a party animal. Which is why John Doe—that's what I call my mystery man—why John needed to do interviews. He wanted to raise his profile. Become *Time*'s Man of the Year."

"Gutsy," Connor said.

"Maybe, but definitely not genius material."

We were pulling onto Orange Drive, heading toward the Hotel del Coronado. I wanted to go see the old hotel, maybe check out the ghost stories. I looked at Connor. Maybe we'd do that later, but at the moment we were on our way to his place. It was weird. I never thought of myself as half of a couple before. Planning little adventures for the two of us. It was amazing how quickly I was adjusting to this new two-person configuration.

Connor pulled in front of a condo, parking in a red zone. Apparently he was also seeing some advantages in the relationship. I smirked.

"Welcome home, Mrs. McNamara," he said.

I giggled. He yanked my suitcase off the backseat and sprinted around the car. We laughed and chased each other into the building, stopping for a mind-blowing kiss just inside the door. Seven floors in the sluggish elevator and he had my shirt mostly unbuttoned, sending tingles down my back. Ten floors and we could have been arrested.

His apartment was at the end of the hall. We kissed and touched and he fumbled with his keys. I leaned back against the door, pulling him closer to me as the door collapsed behind me. I grabbed for him to keep from falling backward.

"You must be Sara."

Connor pushed me behind him with enough force to make me stumble, and I grabbed for my open shirt. I struggled with the buttons, peering around his shoulder to gape at the intruder.

"Either that or you got some 'splainin' to do, Lucy."

A younger, darker version of Connor waggled his eyebrows at me. I stood horrified as the Norman Rockwell portrait of mother, father, brother, and sister stood framed in the open doorway, all assessing me and my state of undress. Oh my God. They had to be his family.

"You ever think of calling first?" Connor asked harshly, sexual frustration evident in his voice.

Great. Terrific. Now, not only was I seducing their firstborn in a public hallway, but he was openly resenting his own family. Family. As in stuck-for-life relationships. I'd barely considered meeting his family. If I had, I wouldn't in my wildest, darkest dreams have imagined this nightmare.

"I couldn't stop her," Connor's father offered. "You know how your mother is when she gets an idea in her head." He shrugged, turning up his palms and not seeming even a little embarrassed. "Ryan, Siobhan, come into the living room. You, too, Liss. Let's let them have a minute."

His mother looked like a Madonna. All serene and unnerving. His sister seemed to share my mortification. Ryan gave me a leering wink before he turned away.

Grimacing, Connor looked at me. I kept one hand over my mouth to keep from retching. The other hand clutched my blouse closed.

"God, Sara, I'm really sorry. I didn't know they would

be here." He reached for me but I jumped away. His family. Half-naked. Hallway. God.

"It's okay," I choked.

It was so not okay.

"I'm sorry."

"No big deal. I just met my in-laws while stripping their eldest in a public area. At least I assume that's who those people were. I mean, maybe they're just voyeuristic burglars or we interrupted the plumber fixing the sink." I concentrated on buttoning my blouse. Maybe he'd confirm one of my wild suggestions. Even a lie would be good here.

He shook his head.

"I'm sure I'll be able to look them in the face again. In about a hundred years." I put more room between us, rubbing at my arms. When did it get so cold? "Could you fix yourself?"

He looked down. His T-shirt was half-untucked and the top button of his jeans was undone. He looked . . . mauled.

"They know we're married, Sara." He straightened his clothes.

"There's knowing and then there's *knowing,* Connor. This would be an overshare." With a groan, I covered my face with my hands. A phone rang behind me as he tried to pull me into his arms, but no way was I going for that.

"They're grown-ups, babe. I don't think we've shocked them. Endangered, yes. Shocked, no."

"Oh God," I moaned.

"Uh, Sara?" The younger brother was back. "The phone's for you."

Exactly five minutes too late for premortification intervention. Timing was never my strong suit.

"Thank you."

"I'm Ryan, the younger, smarter, better-looking brother." Ryan flashed dimples at me.

"Hi."

"Hi. You're nothing like I was expecting."

"Ryan, shut up." Connor snapped. He moved to steer his younger brother back toward the interior of the apartment, but Ryan didn't budge.

"I'm not sure I want to know," I said.

"No, it's good."

"Why don't you take it in the bedroom, Sara?" Connor suggested as Ryan reached for my hand.

"Particularly since the hall has gotten so crowded," Ryan choked.

Ryan grinned and shifted his weight to avoid being moved. With his green eyes, he could pass for the Cheshire Cat. Well, if the cat had been a surfer dude. Connor was flushed, finally sharing my embarrassment. Served him right.

"I could distract the 'rents for you, but you won't have time to get that shirt off a second time. Which is too bad, because that's a sexy bra," Ryan assured me.

"Uh, thanks."

"Any time."

"Ryan, get the hell out," Connor snapped, closing the door in his brother's face

"Sara, this isn't as bad as it seems."

"Oh, I'm pretty sure it's every bit as bad as it seems."

"I'll get rid of them."

"Permanently?"

Connor looked shocked. I held up a hand. "Kidding."

"I'll send them out to dinner or something. Then, when they come back you can meet them normally."

I stared at him. Yes, please, new in-laws, if you could just give me an hour alone with your sex-starved son and his unbuttoned jeans, I'll be ready to exchange personal chitchat over coffee for the rest of the evening. Honestly, for a smart guy . . . I took a deep breath.

"I'm going to answer the phone. If I'm lucky, it's an emergency that requires my immediate attention. If I'm really lucky, I'll fall and smack my head on a table lamp and wake up having lost my own identity."

"Honey . . ."

"Don't honey me. Just"—I pointed toward the apartment—"deal. I'll be right back."

Connor opened the door and held it. I walked past him and toward the bedroom I could see at the end of the hall. Toward the phone, and if I was really, really, *really* lucky, an unlocked window and a fire escape.

About the Author

Gabriella Herkert currently lives in Seattle, where she works as an attorney. *Catnapped* is her first novel.

The Tooth of Time

A Maxie and Stretch Mystery
by
Sue Henry

Zigzagging around the country in a mini-Winnie
means endless adventure—and Maxie McNabb is
always up for something new. So she and her dog,
Stretch, head for the heat of New Mexico, where
Maxie plans to learn how to weave. But everything
changes for the sleepy town when a local woman
attempts suicide. A casualty of her husband's
mid-life crisis, she was replaced by a newer, sexier
model. And to top it off, a sleazy conman has set
his sights on this woman. Maxie may be on
vacation, but she's determined to help the poor
thing. With her nose for trouble, she'll leave no
mesa unturned until she brings two dogs to
justice—neither of whom is Stretch.

Available wherever books are sold or at
penguin.com

DONNA BALL

RAPID FIRE

A Raine Stockton Dog Mystery

With her kennel business and her part-time job with the forest service, Raine Stockton is having a hectic summer when the FBI drops in to see her about her old flame Andy Fontana. Fontana disappeared from her life when he was connected with an act of sabotage that left several people dead. Now, he's an eco-terrorist on the Ten Most Wanted list, and the feds think Raine can help them bring him to justice.

ALSO AVAILABLE

SMOKY MOUNTAIN TRACKS

GUN SHY

"DONNA BALL...KNOWS HOW TO WRITE A PAGE TURNER."
—BEVERLY CONNOR